Last night I awakened in another time—
in another place—in another body!

I was lying in the middle of a small grassy clearing
beneath a sky of azure blue. My bare body tingled.
What beautiful freedom! I jumped to my feet and
ran on and on with no sense of tiring. Tears of
joy blurred my vision as I realized that I had
both my legs again. The leg I had lost four years
ago in Vietnam was mine again. I was whole,
perfect, unscarred. Was I dreaming?

I ran along a path and suddenly before me stood
a radiantly real woman. "I've waited a long time
for you, Jon Lake," she said. "I'm Lea." In answer to my unspoken thoughts, she explained,
"There are two Jon Lakes. One of them is asleep
in 1976 time; the other is standing here with me,
in what you would think of as 2150 A.D., occupying the body you're so pleased with—your astral
or soul body. It houses the unique electronic
essence that is you."

"May I stay here or must I go back to my old
crippled body?"

"You must always awaken in 1976 unless you
free yourself by attaining a high level of Macro
awareness—an awareness of the oneness of all that
is, all that was and all that ever will be . . ."

"The measure of a mind's evolution is its acceptance of the unacceptable."

Rana

2150 A.D.

by
Thea Alexander

WARNER BOOKS

A Warner Communications Company

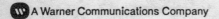

CONTENTS

C.I. DATA EXCERPTS

Prologue to Journal of Jon Lake
Born
September 12, 1948
Died
May 2, 1976

My name is Karl Johnson and I was the roommate and best friend of Jon Lake, who wrote the following journal.

People have questioned me about the strange behavior and subsequent death of Jon, but I've been afraid to be completely truthful in my answers. At first I didn't know what had happened. When I found out, I refused to believe it. Finally, however, I have accepted the truth, though I realize it will be rejected by many people—particularly the authorities.

The police, the university officials, and Jon's professors will, of course, laugh at his story. However, while today there may be few minds sufficiently evolved to accept the unusual concepts presented in this journal, I believe that it is only a matter of time before everyone will accept them.

Before you begin this journal, let me give you a brief description of Jon Lake as I knew him for over 20 years. We both grew up in the same small Midwestern town during the late 1940s and '50s. We met in first grade and became lifelong friends. This in spite of the fact that Jon, being the only son of our town's doctor, lived on the hill at the wealthy end of town and I, the son of a day laborer, lived on the other side of the track.

When we were seven years old Jon's mother died of

leukemia. Two years later my father was severely burned getting Mom and me out of our house as it burned to the ground. Dr. Lake tried desperately that night to keep the forces of life alive in Dad's charred body. As the sun rose, weeping at his failure, Dr. Lake took Mom and me into his home where he treated me like his own son until his death, 10 years later. Jon and I grew up closer than any brothers I ever knew, for we never fought, and while I have been angry with many people, I have rarely ever been angry with Jon. He was the kindest and most patient man I ever knew.

Jon was a brilliant student, and I began just the opposite. For twelve years he tutored me, never once losing his patience with my truculence toward the ridiculous nature of most school subjects. He succeeded beyond anyone's wildest expectations, for I graduated in the top 5 percent of both high school and college. Jon, of course, graduated at the top of our class as well as being voted best athlete in both high school and college.

Jon was so good a quarterback that catching his well-thrown passes made me a college football star in spite of myself. Jon could have played professional football if it hadn't been for the Vietnam war. It seems that Jon's father had incurred the wrath of two members of the local draft board who revenged themselves by having Jon and me drafted two weeks after our college graduation.

In the army we stayed together all the way to the final patrol, where our platoon was blown to pieces and I found myself carrying Jon through what seemed like endless miles of jungle. Somehow we were found by medics and flown to a base hospital where Jon was parted from his right leg and I gave up the sight in my left eye.

While Jon was never bitter about the loss of his leg during that monumental madness called the Vietnam war, I was filled with rage. Jon said that he had learned a valuable lesson in that he could not bring himself to kill or even wound another person, even to save his own life. But I could have told him that without the Vietnam war.

Perhaps the single most difficult thing about Jon for me to understand was what I called his tender-heartedness. He couldn't bear to hurt anything. Yet while he would not intentionally step on a bug, or even uproot a plant, he didn't go around preaching his beliefs to others. He always said that each person can only learn when they are ready to learn, and that what is right for one person can be wrong for another.

Thus, Jon never allowed himself to become upset by the war, saying that it was a necessary experience for all involved in it. He called it *karma*. Try as I might, I could not get him to join me in protesting the war or even to argue with me about it. Jon seldom argued with anyone. He just agreed with them, saying that whatever they believed in was true for them.

In many ways Jon was a paradox to me. He was six feet three inches tall and weighed 180 pounds and could run faster than any other man in college. On the football field, however, he didn't like to block or tackle for fear of hurting someone. He would kill nothing, but he ate meat that had been killed by others. With his deep blue eyes, and strong, beautifully chiseled features he was very popular with the girls, which sometimes created problems.

During high school he got a girl pregnant. It was the only time I ever saw Dr. Lake furiously angry with Jon. I can still remember Dr. Lake shouting angrily that no person had the right to bring a child into this world that he was not psychologically and financially able to care for.

In college Jon had majored in philosophy and minored in psychology and sociology. When we were medically discharged from the army, Jon persuaded me to return to the university to seek graduate degrees. We both majored in psychology and minored in sociology. Jon was fascinated by the social factors in the development of individual behavior and personality. His enthusiasm inspired me to a practical interest in learning how to influence social changes so that we would have no more tragic fiascos like Vietnam.

At the time Jon's journal begins, we had finished all our class work for the Ph.D. degree and were jointly working on a social-psychological dissertation concerning the development of values and self-esteem in children.

I could write much more about Jon, but this is his story, not mine. My purpose has been to provide a setting for this truly remarkable journal and a brief description of my friend, Jon Lake—a man you will never forget.

Since Jon was not writing this journal for publication, but mainly for self-study, portions of it would have been somewhat technical for the average reader. I have, therefore, deleted the most esoteric and complex passages. Some of these have been condensed and appear in the C.I. Data Excerpts section at the back of this book. Three people other than myself read the complete journal while Jon was still alive and able to explain and demonstrate some of its concepts. We were all so profoundly impressed that our lives have not been the same since. I would, therefore, recommend that the serious reader give some attention to those excerpts from Jon's conversations with C.I. and refer to them often during the reading of his journal.

Many of the things you will read in this journal will be difficult, if not impossible, to believe.

Jon however believed that, in time, the strange concepts presented here will be accepted by all.

CHAPTER 1:

Lea

For months I awakened reluctantly each morning, mentally reaching back into my dream state for some indescribable adventure that lay, mistily, just beyond my reach. Last night my longing for its completion was realized. I awakened in another time—in another place—in another body.

Lying in the middle of a small grassy clearing, I opened my eyes to a sky of soft azure blue. Trees towered in uncluttered profusion as far as I could see.

The musky scent of new-mown clover was brought to me on the cool morning air. The sound of birds calling to one another filled me with a sense of rightness and peace. My bare body tingled as its tiny hairs bent with the breeze. What beautiful freedom!

Arising, I breathed deeply, filling my whole being with the beauty of my new surroundings. With a mounting sense of adventure I walked, jogged, then ran through this lovely wooded park. Running had always seemed to me the ultimate in physical freedom. Now I ran on and on with no sense of tiring, enjoying the soft earth under my flying bare feet.

Suddenly I was in a small clearing surrounding a natural fountain.

Swerving to avoid it, I stopped so suddenly that I almost lost my footing.

Tears of joy blurred my vision as I gazed with amazement at my legs—both of them!

Four years ago, in Vietnam, I had lost my right leg, and I had hobbled around on an artificial one ever since, unable to experience the exhilaration of running.

How had my leg returned?

Carefully examining my body, I realized that I hadn't seen it in such great shape since my undergraduate days on the football field. As an extremely active young man, I had had my share of scars, but nowhere was there even a trace of them.

I gave puzzled thanks for this new, apparently perfect, body.

As the morning sun topped the horizon I noticed the almost crystal clarity of the air. How long has it been, I thought, since I've seen a sky so clear and breathed air so fragrantly fresh?

Where could I possibly be? I had gone to sleep last night in Upper Manhattan in a one-bedroom walk-up which I share with my best friend, my stepbrother, Karl Johnson. But I had certainly awakened somewhere else.

Was I dreaming? Would I soon awaken back in my one-legged body?

I looked about me eager to fill my eyes before this beautiful new world might suddenly dissolve into an evanescent dream.

A covey of birds startled me as they took noisily to the air. Contemplating their direction, I wondered what season this was. I had gone to sleep on a cold January night, but I had obviously awakened in some other time or place, for it was certainly not winter here.

12

I began jogging along a path that wound around the flower bed and into the woods beyond.

A shot of ice-cold apprehension burst through me as I realized that I was not alone. There before me stood a radiantly real woman!

She was dressed in an iridescent aquamarine tunic that covered a scant five inches of her shapely thighs. Her cerulean blue eyes caressed me with an all-knowing embrace. The sunlight, sifting through her short golden hair, formed a shimmering halo.

I was so startled to see her and so mesmerized by her beautiful clarity that I literally forgot to breathe!

Those all-knowing, all-accepting eyes seemed filled with dancing lights as she said, "Hi! I'm Lea. I've waited a long time for you, Jon. You don't remember me yet, but you will."

This can't be really happening, I thought.

"Oh yes, it can," Lea answered in a low almost musical voice that caressed my ears in a ticklish sort of way.

Her response to my unspoken thoughts disarmed me. "You mean, I'm not dreaming?"

For a long moment she looked at me thoughtfully. "In a way, yes; and in a way, no," she answered. "You see, there are two Jon Lakes. One of them is asleep in what you think of as 1976 'time'; the other is standing here with me, in what you would think of as 2150 A.D., occupying the body you're so pleased with—your astral or soul body."

"My astral body? In what year?"

My amazement amused her. "Yes, your astral body. It's almost identical to your physical body except that its electrical vibrations move so fast that it can't be seen by the eyes of the physical body. Your astral body has translated 174 'years' forward in time to what you would think of as 2150 A.D."

"A hundred and seventy-four years!" I exclaimed. "Wow! What a dream! And you say that I've got two bodies?"

"Actually, there are three right now," Lea replied.

13

"Your 1976 body, minus one leg, is dreaming what's happening to you now. Your 2150 body awaits you. And this body—your astral body—presently houses the unique electronic essence that is called 'Jon Lake.' It is definitely not dreaming.

"When we get back to our Delta you'll learn more about that before returning to 1976."

Her casual remark that I would be returning to my physical body delivered a surprising jolt.

"You mean I have to go back to my crippled body?"

"Oh, yes," she answered. "You must always wake up back in 1976 unless you free yourself by attaining a high level of Macro awareness."

"Macro awareness?" I puzzled.

"Macro awareness," she explained, "simply means an 'applied' awareness of the macrocosmic oneness of all that is, all that was, and all that ever will be.

"We here in 2150 are far from total Macro awareness. But we have evolved—to a point where we can remember our macrocosmic origin and practice some of the Macro powers—what you refer to as E.S.P., or extrasensory perception."

Somehow sensing my questions, she added, "You'll learn more about that later," and reached out to take my hand.

The most startling thing happened—her hand passed right through mine!

"What's happened to me?" I exclaimed, trying desperately to take her hand and finding it totally impossible to even touch her.

"It's all right, Jon," she quickly assured me. "I forgot that I'm in my physical body, which naturally can't touch your high-vibration astral body."

"Well, I'll be," I said, more to myself than to her. "I'm a ghost!"

"That's one way to say it." Lea laughed.

"But if I'm a ghost, then how can you see me?"

"I'm not seeing you with my physical eyes, Jon. I'm

14

seeing you with my Macro power of clairvoyance, and I'm hearing you telepathically."

"You can see me and hear me, but you can't touch me?"

"Not yet," Lea replied, "but just as soon as we get to the life continuity lab we'll fit you into your 2150 physical body. Then we'll be able to touch again."

"Again?" I thought, and she heard it.

"You're not ready to understand that yet, Jon."

"Come on. Let's hurry and get you into your new body so we can touch again."

With that last word hanging like a huge question mark in my mind, I found myself running as fast as I had ever run, yet still unable to overtake the beautiful form of my new mind-boggling companion.

Suddenly we topped a wooded hill and began descending into an emerald green valley at the center of which was a sparkling clear blue lake. It was such a captivating sight that at first I didn't notice the twelve large buildings tucked in among the trees that surrounded the lake.

"This is our Delta. It includes twelve buildings and ten thousand people."

As we approached I realized that the lake was much larger than I had first thought, but so also were the buildings. Each structure was about a hundred and fifty yards square and twelve stories high. They were constructed of lustrous, but opaque, green glass-like material.

I noticed that both men and women were dressed identically in short tunics like Lea's. They differed only in the various predominant colors.

Entering the huge building, we passed some young men and women. They all looked exceptionally attractive and energetic.

Though everyone smiled at Lea, some of them didn't seem to notice me at all. I even found it difficult to avoid bumping into them at times.

Then, as I turned to frown at a man who had almost run me down, I had the most shocking experience of my life—a young woman walked right through me!

15

Lea laughed and as I turned my bewildered face toward her she said, "Don't worry, Jon. Some of them can't see you in your astral body, but they can't hurt you, either, by walking through you."

As she said this a part of the wall opened and she walked through. I followed, experiencing the eerie sensation of watching the door slide shut through my leg.

The room was filled with strange looking chairs neatly arranged around a large cylindrical container with a curved glass-like top.

I was startled to see lying in its bedlike interior the naked body of—me!—apparently asleep for I could see my chest rising and falling.

Lea smiled triumphantly and said, "That's your new body, Jon. It's almost identical to your 1976 body except that it has no physical imperfections."

"Good God!" I exclaimed. "It's me—and—and—I'm me!"

"That's right, Jon. You are you, it's you, and I'm you," Lea explained.

I had too many questions to even speak coherently.

"This body is modeled after our electronic pattern and your gene patterns. It's alive, but it won't be occupied until your astral body enters it."

My mind was spinning.

"I want you to let go of your mind with all its concerns, and let me take over the operation of your astral body for the next few minutes." Lea was saying. "Can you trust me, Jon?"

Looking into those all knowing eyes, my mental turmoil was gradually replaced by desire until every fiber of my being reached out to this girl who called herself Lea.

Nodding my head, I said, "I trust you, Lea."

Suddenly I was as clear—as honest, as open, as undefended—as she was. There were no barriers between us. We merged, and though her lips did not move, I heard her voice.

"We are one, Jon. Let go, and let's grow!"

16

Next thing I knew, I was looking up into her face as she swung the glass-like cover from above me.

Sliding to my feet, I felt the exquisite touch of Lea's hands for the first time as they slid ecstatically down my sides and around my back. I took her quickly into my arms and our lips met as I said her name.

A pleasant weightiness filled my groin, and I flushed with a new realization. I was naked!

Lea's amused laughter echoed amid the conflict between my body and my mind: How could I quickly cover my "bare essentials"? Why should I? And why had I not been concerned with my nakedness before?

"You're in a physical body again, Jon," Lea responded to my unspoken thoughts. "Only in a physical body can one be embarrassed by nakedness. Here, maybe this will make you feel better," with which she handed me one of their universal tunics and a pair of short stocking-like boots.

Hastily donning these, I talked about the room's contents in an effort to divert my all-too-easy-to-read mind away from what it wanted to think, toward what it should be thinking!

The sense of effortless freedom I had experienced with my astral body was gone now that it was surrounded by this dense physical body. It was, however, a gem of health and energy, with magnificent strength and coordination.

The tunic fitted perfectly and moved with my body like a second skin.

Though it had been colorless before I put it on, it now radiated a basic blue-gray tone with iridescent rays of orange, pink, and a little bit of blue, yellow, and green here and there.

Lea addressed my amazement explaining that their universal garment was, in fact, quite colorless until it entered someone's life field. This, she added, was the electrical pattern unique to each individual which emanates from the physical body he is inhabiting at the time. The tunic acts like a million tiny lenses reflecting and magnifying the colors of that personality's life field or aura.

She went on to explain that there are ten basic predominant colors reflected by the tunics, and that these colors correspond with the person's level of awareness at the time.

The basic grayness reflected by my tunic indicated the beginning level of Macro awareness.

Before I could ask any of the hundred questions that whirled through my mind, she told me that C.I. would answer any and all of my questions and that we'd best get going, since my time was limited.

C.I. occupied the top six floors of this huge building. We entered what appeared to be a shaft of light about four feet in diameter, which Lea called a void. A slight jump took us from the first to the twelfth floor almost instantly. I could see, though, that it would take me a while to adapt to this unusual means of transport.

C.I. contained a thousand soundproof rooms ten feet square, each of which was equipped for what appeared to be a full wall video tape presentation on any subject one cared to ask about.

We sat in large comfortable chairs that automatically adjusted themselves to our bodies.

Lea touched a small white circle on the arm of her chair, and a pleasant female voice said, "Central Information. May I help you?"

"What are the dimensions of the Delta 927 Lake?" Lea inquired.

A large map of the lake appeared on the wall and we were told that the lake of Delta 927 was approximately eight kilometers long, five kilometers wide, and had an average depth of ten meters.

Lea, sensing my mental calculations, asked for equivalents in miles and yards. Gaining this, she said, "I must leave you now."

"Leave?" I asked, and came to my feet, totally unable to believe what I had heard.

"Yes, Jon. I have to go now," she replied calmly.

I was beside her in an instant.

"I'll go with you."

"No, that's not possible, Jon. It's extremely important that you stay right here with C.I. and learn as much as you can, as fast as you can. C.I. can help you do that much better than I."

"When will you be back, then?" I asked.

"I won't be back, Jon."

"What do you mean? You can't just get up and go when we've only just met. I'll come with you," I insisted.

"As much as I'd like that, it's neither practical nor possible," was her reply.

"I don't understand, Lea. Why can't I go with you?"

"It's critically important that you stay here and grow as fast as you can. My presence would be a distraction, and we can't afford that risk.

"Let me try to explain, Jon, but I must be very brief and you must wait for further details until our next meeting, should there be one."

"What do you mean, 'should there be one'?" I interrupted.

"Please, Jon, trust me. Believe me when I say that we must use our time as best we can. I want to stay with you as much as you want me to stay, but that's not at all practical.

"I don't know whether I will see you again, or, if so, when. We will attempt another time translation, but we don't know whether it will succeed or not. So you can see that there is no way for me to tell you whether or not we will meet here again.

"This I do know, that the more time you spend talking with me, the less time you will have with C.I., and the less chance we will have of completing another successful time translation," Lea explained hurriedly.

"How can you be so calm about it?" I said. "How can you just say goodbye and walk away knowing we may never meet again?"

"We are together always, Jon. I am never far from you. Your dreams of me are real—a valid reality—not just fantasy or wish fulfillment. Believe me, Jon, I am always with you. True, I miss your touch, your voice, the joys shared on a physical level, but they will be there, if not in this lifetime, in another," she added. "What *is* is perfect for its time and place. Accept that joyously, Jon, and enjoy growing your way toward what you desire."

"But I don't—" I began.

She put her finger to her lips to quiet me.

"When you fall asleep here, your other body, back in 1976, will awaken, hopefully remembering everything you've experienced here in 2150 and believing in its reality—its validity."

"But Lea—"

"Please, Jon. Just ask C.I. We must make every minute count if we're to have even a chance of seeing one another again in this 'time'," she said quickly.

Then, gently touching my face, she hesitated for a moment as her incredible eyes poured forth into mine love, joy, pain, tragedy, acceptance, and peace.

" 'Bye for now," she said warmly, almost to herself, and left me alone with C.I.

Forcing myself to trust, believe, and act on what she had said, I began asking questions, but each question seemed to lead to another. I became fascinated with this magnificent learning technique.

To be able to both see and hear the answers to my inquiries was a tremendous advantage I compared it to my usual 1976 research procedures. I remembered the long waits in the library for materials from the stacks, the frustration at being told that pertinent volumes were already checked out by someone else or were never available in the first place. And there were the seemingly endless hours of reading through tomes of academically contrived chaff sifting out the wheat to be found floating there on seas of pedantic verbosity.

For the next three hours I sat spellbound, soaking up information about 2150, and learning more and faster than ever before in my life.

C.I. informed me that it had an almost unlimited

20

number of data banks filled with information on every subject man has ever experienced. When I asked how this was possible, C.I. began describing technological processes so advanced and complex that I interrupted, afraid of spending my allotted time unwisely.

C.I. addressed my level of understanding by explaining that its own beginnings were represented by a learning device designed for use in the '70s and called Computer Administered Instruction (C.A.I.).

My interest intensified. I had heard of C.A.I., but I had never experienced it, so I decided to test C.I.'s ability on a subject I knew more about—myself!

C.I. began, "You entered this lifetime on September 12, 1948, the only child of Ben and Jessica Lake. Your father was the town physician, your mother the librarian, prior to her marriage to Dr. Lake. On your first day in school you met Karl Johnson, who was to become your best friend. After the death of your mother during your second-grade experience, and the death of Karl's father two years later, not; Karl became your stepbrother the summer before you entered junior high school."

"You tutored Karl through school, and he returned the favor by getting you out of social jams which you seemed to have a propensity for. Take the homecoming dance during your senior year, for example. Even as Most Valuable Player on your football team, which you were voted that year, you couldn't take both Jan and Valerie as your date to the same dance—and you *did* promise them both. Thanks to Karl, you were saved again."

C.I. went on, "There were some things that even Karl couldn't handle, though, like Valerie's pregnancy. That was the only time your father ever cursed at you. He didn't like the idea of aborting a pregnancy, but he had a strong conviction that no one has a right to create a child that he is not both psychologically and financially able to care for. That lesson in sexual responsibility was dearly paid for by you, by Valerie, and by your father. Fortunately, you learned it well."

21

"This and other hard-earned lessons left you with a relatively effective life philosophy which helped both you and Karl throughout your college careers. Karl, if you recall, was quite a rebel. He was constantly fighting, ". . . the ridiculous nature of most school subjects," or ". . . that monumental madness called the Vietnam war." You were the calming influence, reminding him that what is wrong for one person may be totally right for another. And that each person can only learn when he is ready to learn. Your position that professors are just the victims of their own psychological needs and their own limiting belief systems never fitted quite right with Karl. He always felt it was the students who are the victims."

"After your degrees in philosophy and psychology, respectively, you and Karl were drafted and within a very few months landed in Vietnam. There you served together until that final patrol where your platoon was destroyed. Karl used the one eye he had left to find his way back through miles of jungle with you, on his back, unconscious, and minus your right leg."

"Karl was as bitter about your injury as he was about his own, perhaps more so. You, on the other hand, felt that this was your *karma* and that, sad as it might be, it was necessary for your growth during that lifetime.

"While you, too, felt that the Vietnam war was a mistake from the start, you had by that time accepted a philosophy which held that truth is subjective and that whatever a person believes is true, is true for him. This, you felt, required you to respect the right of each individual to believe whatever he wanted to. You could not condemn him for acting on that belief even though you disagreed with it.

"It was this very philosophy that led you to sacrifice your own leg rather than destroy another person.

"It was also this philosophy that got you involved in the Ph.D. dissertation that you and Karl are now writing on the development of values and self-esteem in children. And it is that philosophy which provided the first link

22

in the time translation path to bring you here to 2150 for whatever period of time is possible. But you can talk it better than you can practice it, Jon.

"If you're satisfied with the accuracy of our data banks, we can go on to examine other significant lifetimes. If not, we can get far more specific regarding your present life—such as—"

"Wait a minute!" I interrupted. "I've read a little about reincarnation, but what do you mean by 'significant' other lives?"

"Yes, we know that you're familiar with what your age calls the theory of reincarnation and what, within your concept of time, you refer to as 'past lives.' Here in 2150 it is no longer considered a theory—it's a fact, though it's based on a very limited basic assumption regarding time.

"If you wish, we can provide you with information on as many of your 'past' lifetimes as you would like to remember. We suggest that you limit this exploration to include only significant lives, meaning those whose lessons pertain specifically to the challenges of your present life. We would like you to keep in mind, however, that all these lives are, from a broader point of view, occurring simultaneously."

Juggling priorities, I asked about 2150's concept of time and got totally lost in the details of C.I.'s doubtless excellent, but very complex, presentation of their metric time system. So I changed the subject enough to, hopefully, bring answers to within my comprehension.

"I don't understand how you could tell me about my present life, much less about my past ones, or, if I understood you correctly, some of my future lives," I puzzled.

"We have obtained information about you in two ways," C.I. explained. "First, from your own subconscious mind, and secondly, from the universal mind in which is recorded everything that is happening, everything that ever has happened, and everything that ever will happen to your immortal mind. The system is very similar to that used by our C.I. data banks. Most of the data is now available to us, though we're still establishing electromolecular—what you would think of as telepathic—paths for some of it."

"But how do you have access to my immortal mind?" I asked.

"You are sitting in a chair that provides us an electromolecular connection to all your memories as well as all emental* and physical data on your body right down to the sub-atomic level. However, since one of your twin souls, Lea, has a mind structure identical to your own, everything about either of you is recorded in both your mind and hers. We have this 'telepathic' connection to the mind of every member of the Macro society. This establishes a partial connection to the macrocosm."

"That's enough," I said. "You've lost me again. I always thought there was only one twin soul for each person. And what is this Macro society you spoke of? And can you give me more on the macrocosm?" The questions pouring out of me were barely representative of the hundreds I kept within. I was so anxious to learn so much, and I didn't know which questions to ask first.

"We will start by presenting the basic concepts of the macrocosm," C.I. began.

I won't try to include here everything that C.I. said during the following hours, but a few of the highlights are important and should be mentioned here.

C.I. began by saying, "The human soul is an integral part of the perfectly balanced macrocosm. Thus, in the beginning, each human soul was part of a soul matrix which was perfectly balanced in positive and negative polarity—masculine and feminine traits. However, to experience complete devolution and microcosmic awareness, each soul matrix mentally separated itself into seemingly individual entities which, in periodic incarnations on this planet Earth, function as either male or female.

Emental: Contraction of *emotional* and *mental*.

24

"The entity you think of as Jon Lake, like other soul matrix entities, temporarily forgot its oneness with all that is, all that was, and all that ever will be, as well as its macrocosmic origin. However, since you completed your devolution into the microcosm and began evolving back toward awareness of your macrocosmic origin, your soul matrix entities—your twin souls—have been seeking each other."

Trying to comprehend the fascinating things C.I. was saying, I began to sense a relieved rightness about it all. It was almost as if these words were touching some deep hidden memory within me that was now slowly beginning to emerge into consciousness.

"Please continue," I urged. "What you say somehow feels very right to me, though I'm not sure I really understand it all."

"You're remembering," C.I. replied. "In time you will begin to remember fragments of other lives. You dream of them often. Ever since you were born, Lea has been visiting you on the astral plane, but you didn't remember, since you had not yet learned the importance of your dreams."

"Is that why . . ." I hesitated. "Is that why I woke up so many times feeling full of joy and hope for something that seemed to be there just beyond my reach?"

"Yes," was C.I.'s reply. "It was all you could remember of your contacts on the astral plane where Lea reminded you again of your oneness and that she was working to bring you to 2150."

C.I.'s voice was fading, though I listened intently.

"Your time translation is our most advanced 'continuity of life' project. It has been achieved through the joint efforts of the most highly evolved minds in our galaxy, with your own budding belief in macrocosmic oneness playing a . . ."

CHAPTER 2:

Was It a Dream?

I awoke fresh and alive, as though I had just come in from a brisk walk.

My big round alarm clock read 7:41.

Where had I been? What had I been hearing?

A female voice seemed to echo back into my dream. Some kind of a formula . . . or a process. A sentence, half finished.

Pulling my pillow over my head I tried to go back to sleep, mentally stretching back into my dream.

Then it hit me as though I was still dreaming.

But I wasn't!

I could hear the pleasant voice of C.I. presenting so many new ideas that my mind was reeling under their impact.

Then there was that girl, Lea. What clarity!

"Clarity"? Where did that word come from? "Clarity." It had a nice feeling attached to it, yet it now meant something new—something it had not meant before last night's dream.

Lea was "clear." There was no game-playing, no being what she thought I wanted her to be, no pretense, no expectations, no defenses—just a very bright, capable, honest, straightforward woman joyously experiencing and respecting herself, others, and life itself.

Hers was not the shallow, brittle beauty of a Hollywood starlet, but a deep almost spiritual essence that seemed to radiate from her. While her physical beauty was obvious, it was the sparkling multifaceted depths of her mind which aroused and excited me with a completeness that I had never quite reached before.

Hugging my pillow, I felt Lea warm against me and, once again, argued with myself. Why cover my bare body? Just so I wouldn't be embarrassed? Why be embarrassed? If the body is just the outer garment of the essential self . . .

And there was another new term. "Essential self." It, too, meant something new, something more complex. This dream was a more interesting education than any class I'd ever attended!

Why?

The question brought my mind's focus from a fantasy world of the future back to the prosaic present. Mentally I moved into this new day. Physically—or was it spiritually?—some deep core of my essential self reached forward into 2150 and stayed there.

The feeling of loss was strong in me as I sat up in bed and strapped on my artificial limb. Karl had already left to teach his 8 a.m. Introductory Psychology class. I was glad that I had given up my teaching assistantship this semester to work full-time on our dissertation. This left my time relatively free of demands, so I could let this incredible dream drift about the edges of my mind as I pursued my day's activities.

Was it just a dream? *Just.* Maybe that was the wrong word. That booklet I had scanned—a light brown booklet—said something about dreams being much more

27

important, a reality of their own. What was it? Maybe I could find it again. Just a little booklet, "Interpret Your Dreams from a . . ." something or other.

Finishing my breakfast, I cleaned up our small kitchen absorbed in conflict. Never had I experienced a dream so clear and vivid and with such an incredibly detailed story.

Yet if I took it seriously, I might just as well forget about becoming a respected social psychologist. Anyone in my field who spoke of time travel, astral bodies, parapsychology, or other forms of intelligent life contacting us here on Earth, would be ostracized by his colleagues.

Still, I decided to write down what I could remember, and as I slowly recorded this strange experience, I began to live it again.

As I puzzled over that last statement of C.I.—something about my belief system—the door opened.

"Man, am I hungry!" Karl shook the snow off his fuzzy black hair as he pulled off his fake fur overcoat and boots.

Seemed like I had just begun, and here it was 1:30 already!

"You look like Big Foot with that coat on!" I said. Karl was not a small man. While I was the runner on the team, Karl cleared the way so I'd have an opening to run through. And he was built for the job!

"I could eat like Big Foot right now!" he answered. "Let's have some lunch. What are you doing?" he added.

"Been writing down some ideas I got from a dream last night."

"What?"

"I said I've been writing down some ideas I got from a dream last night."

"That's what I thought you said. What the hell are you talking about?" Karl peered at me with that intense green eye of his.

Sometimes I think that Karl's eye was taken from him not to keep him out of pro football, as he sometimes postulates, but rather for the protection of the people he looks at. He has enough power in that one eye to make up for the one he lost and then some!

Feeling a shade intimidated by his look and the hint of sarcasm in his inquiry, I began, "Last night I had the most 'real' dream."

"A wet one, I trust."

"Damnit, Karl! I'm serious!"

"And I'm dying of starvation. You'll have to wait a minute or deliver your oration to a dead audience!"

He disappeared into the kitchen, emerging a moment later with a pint bottle of carrot juice in his left hand; peanut butter, jelly, salami, brick cheese, and lettuce sandwiched precariously between two oversized slices of wheatberry bread in his right hand; and a paper towel with a freshly rinsed carrot inside it tucked between his forearm and his chest. He was big on carrots.

"Okay," he said, "lay it on me." His beanbag chair cringed briefly before yielding to his 240-pound onslaught.

Pacing the floor, I told him of the fantastic freedom I had experienced a mere seven hours ago. His angular face remained impassive, but as I finished, it broke into a huge grin.

"Well, now," he chuckled. "I can understand why you were sorry to wake up. Leave it to you to produce the summa cum laude dream of all time!"

I shook my head slowly. "But I don't think that I, Jon Lake, could produce a dream like that. Really, Karl. I mean, the new words, the detail . . . I can't even imagine that kind of stuff, much less dream it."

"Okay, Jon. Maybe it was the Jon Lake of 2150 who produced the classical wish fulfillment dream for the crippled Jon Lake of 1976. After all, that's what your dream girl, Lea, said, wasn't it?

"And by the way, did you think of asking your dream computer how they were able to develop a utopia like 2150 in just a hundred and seventy-some years? Like how was it possible to go from a world of competition, conflict, distrust, hatred, overpopulation, pollution, ignorance, and monumental selfishness to a world of cooperation, love, and wisdom? Did you think to ask that question, Jon? Sure would be nice to know the secret." Karl laughed. "Maybe we could change the topic of our dissertation, put you to sleep for a week or two, and get your C.I. to write it for us!"

"Seriously, Karl, I did ask about some of those things. C.I. said that our society, which she called the micro society, perished sometime around the year 2000, along with most other micro societies of the Earth, due to their inability to cooperate with one another."

"So, it ended," Karl paraphrased, "not with a whimper, but a bang."

"No, C.I. spoke of factors which worked over a long period of time to bring about the destruction of micro society. It wasn't sudden."

I hesitated with a new thought. "Hell, we're right in the middle of it! C.I. said the Macro society of 2150 had its beginnings back in the 1970s. That's right now, Karl!"

"Oh, great," Karl scoffed. "We can expect it any time now. How's it all going to happen?"

"I don't know, Karl. Which came first, the chicken or the egg? Whichever came first, the chain broke a link somewhere along the line 'cause they don't have the same theories regarding human behavior in 2150 as we have here in 1976.

"C.I. disagreed with our theory that most of human behavior is completely determined in the first few years of a child's life. C.I. granted that early inadequacies in nutrition or intellectual, emotional, or physical stimulation can do great damage, which, bolstered by our limiting belief systems, could preclude further significant development. According to C.I., though, all the fears and hang-ups that we blame on our treatment during childhood are open for restatement, redefinition, and remodeling by our 'applied and practiced belief system.' We are *not* the pawns of our upbringing any longer than we *want* to be! We are free agents to be whatever we decide we want to be as long as we believe it's possible and are willing to put in the effort and discipline necessary to bring it about," I explained.

Karl whistled, "That's a pretty heavy statement, Jon, and a pretty heavy dream."

"That's not all, Karl," I continued, anxious to test more of my new data. "C.I. called us 1970s people 'micro man.' Says we see life and reality through the limiting view of a microscope—making mountains out of molehills—while almost completely ignoring the unifying, harmonizing macrocosmic realities that lie just beyond our limited view."

"Micro man, hum," Karl thought out loud. "And these . . . what I'd think of as 'peace-creating' realities . . . are right there, but just out of reach?"

I was delighted to see Karl caught up in C.I.'s "future" philosophy. "I wouldn't say really out of reach, Karl. It's more like we're wearing blinders. We put blinders on a horse to keep him from being frightened by what he would see if we broadened his vision, and we do the same thing to ourselves. We keep our blinders pulled in close enough to block out or condemn things that are different from what we're used to. This leaves us with an extremely limited, but very comfortably microscopic, view of reality instead of a limitless, but more challenging, macrocosmic view of ourselves, others, and our relationship to the universe."

"What you're saying, Jon, is that micro man is the normal average 1970s person like you and me."

"I guess so."

Karl went on, "This approach would support the theory about mental illness occurring in direct proportion to the degree of separation one feels from his fellow man. You know, the blinders separate us from other people—protect us, so to speak, from what we fear. Ha!" Karl delighted in his new conclusions. "So we protect ourselves right out of our mind! Tell me, oh great 'wizard of dreams,' what's the religion of the future?"

"As I understand it, Karl, it's not a religion as we know them—you know, churches peppered all over the

31

land worshiping some all-powerful, judgmental God who peers out of the sky to shake a finger or throw a bolt of lightning at those who go astray.

"It's more a way of life," I explained. "They call it Macro philosophy, and I understand it contains the essential core of the Taoism of Lao-tzu, the Buddhism of Siddhartha Gautama, and the Christianity of Jesus of Nazareth."

"Great! The best of all possible mystics we 'micro men' have never been able to understand. How do they train everyone to become a great mystic philosopher so they can understand this Macro philosophy?" There was more than a touch of skepticism in Karl's voice.

"That's where the Macro society comes in. You see, the basic metaphysical premise of Macro philosophy is that all is one perfect, macrocosmic, indivisible whole. It's the ancient idealistic concept that all is perfect, all is mind—one universal mind. However, in 2150, according to C.I., they don't just talk about it, they live it, by organizing their society on this premise." I raised my hand to delay Karl's interruption.

"It's obvious that the Macro society could only work if people accepted the basic premise of Macro philosophy, that all is one. So the Macro society is set up to teach its children about this Macro perspective from which they can practice the one commandment of Jesus—to love one another."

"Jesus H. Christ! Jon, man is an animal! We can condition, reinforce, and program almost any type of behavior, but we can't change the basic animal nature of man. We can't pump out a whole generation of little Jesuses!"

"That's true, Karl," I said soothingly. "They don't disagree with you. C.I. emphatically states that the Macro society could not exist until micro man, with his limited perspective, his limited beliefs, became almost extinct. Micro man is an animal because he views himself as an animal. It's a self-fulfilling prophecy, Karl. We become that which we believe ourself to be. Our beliefs limit us

32

to the short span of time between the birth and death of our physical bodies and the 'accidents' of genetic and environmental inheritance.

"Macro man, however, does not see himself as an animal. He understands that we are constantly creating our selves with every thought we think. He knows that his every cell responds to his every thought, thereby making of him that which he believes himself to be. Macro man knows that he is not the victim of circumstances, but rather the designer of his own destiny, the creator of his own reality. He knows that his life holds only those experiences which he himself chose for his own growth and—"

"Wait a minute," Karl interrupted, waving his hand to slow me down. "What, may I ask, is Macro man? Is he the same as 2150 man?"

"No, I don't think we could presume that. A person is beginning to be Macro emotionally and spiritually when he starts caring about others—when he starts breaking down the barriers of prejudice and fear that separate men from each other. A person is beginning to be Macro mentally when he has evolved to a level of awareness in which he remembers his origin as an immortal soul within the Macro self, the macrocosm. He then realizes that he lived many lives as he devolved down what they call the microcosmic-macrocosmic continuum of awareness toward amnesia, or less awareness. He then begins his evolutionary trip back toward even greater awareness of his macrocosmic oneness with all that is, all that was, and all that ever will be."

"Why the hell would a soul choose this trip into amnesia, Jon? Or does a soul have any choice?"

"Yes," I replied, "C.I. was very firm on every soul having free choice, but I was given a number of answers to your first question, and, frankly, I'm almost as confused as you are in this area."

"One answer," I continued, "was that devolution and evolution are part of the cyclic process in which the macrocosm experiences itself. Another answer was that

33

only some souls, not all of them, choose devolution-evolution to experience the thrill of fear, uncertainty, separateness, and the excitement of conflict and, of course, all the physical pleasures and pains."

"You mean the old saw about how dull perfection would be," Karl interjected.

"Maybe," I replied. "We know that man can accept pleasure only to the extent that he is willing to accept pain—that the rejection of either eliminates both. While the static concept of a micro Christian heaven of all peace and pleasure would be truly hell, the macrocosm is a perfect balance of all opposites, a totally accepting experience of all pain and all pleasure, all hate and all love, all ugliness and all beauty, all fear and all conflict, with all calmness and all peace. In other words, the ultimate in excitement, enjoyment, variety, creativity— truly heaven."

"Heaven for whom?" Karl asked sarcastically.

"Why, for the Macro self, I suppose. It's only when we have evolved to the awareness that we *are* the Macro self that we can experience this acceptance of all that is, all that ever was, and all that ever will be as perfect."

I could almost see Karl's razor-sharp mind racing furiously. "Are you saying that to this Macro self everything is perfect? Things like poverty, disease, injustice, death, and even selfish micro men like us?"

"Yes," I nodded, "because they are perfectly balanced, and a positive and a negative that are equal cancel each other. Such things as poverty, disease, injustice, and death only exist at the micro levels—never at the Macro level of awareness. That's what the mystics meant when they said that all is illusion or *maya*."

"But it's a damned real illusion to all us micro beings!" Karl retorted.

"Of course," I replied. "Who could enjoy an exciting play unless he could temporarily forget that he was just watching actors and actresses playing parts written by an author whose purpose was to entertain?"

34

"So you agree with Shakespeare," Karl inserted. "All the world is a stage and all the men and women only players who, in their time, play many parts."

"Yes, I do. The essence of a good actor is that he temporarily loses himself in his part. The same with micro man. He has temporarily lost himself in a part and forgotten that he is the only one who chose it! That's why there is no injustice from the larger perspective, because each soul has chosen every part it plays."

"Are you sure, Jon, that everyone is eventually going to wake up from their amnesia and realize that their true identity is God?—what you call the macrocosm or Macro self?"

"Well, that's what all the mystics have been saying as far back in history as we have any record."

"And do you really believe in this sort of philosophy?" Karl questioned. He looked anxious and concerned as he said, "Let's be practical, Jon. If you believe in reincarnation, astral bodies, and time travel, how are you going to be a social psychologist? Our professors sure as hell aren't going to accept these wild ideas."

"Okay, I'll answer those questions," I said and realized I was pacing the floor again. "First, the basic concepts of Macro philosophy are not new to me and have always appealed to me. My greatest objection was the micro one that they didn't seem practical. Now I think that a Macro philosophy might be, in the long run, the most practical philosophy I've ever come across.

"As for being a social psychologist—I don't deny the validity of the micro view of man as a highly evolved symbol-thinking animal completely determined by his heredity and environment. However, I am not going to reject a Macro dimension which includes the micro one but adds the concepts of soul, *karma*, reincarnation, and the ultimate macrocosmic view which sees all as one indivisible universal mind.

"Now, for my professors and fellow behavioral scientists, I accept the fact that in their opinion no one can be a real scientist and believe in a Macro philosophy. So, if they find out I'm even considering these concepts, I won't be a social psychologist as far as they're concerned. I'll be a mystic nut who can't tell the difference between hallucinations and reality."

"But," said Karl, "you don't have to let anyone know that you're dabbling with ideas like reincarnation and Macro philosophy. You've been hitting the books for almost three solid years, and you haven't once taken a vacation. It's no wonder you get an escapist dream."

"Then, you think my dream is part of a mental breakdown due to overwork. So you're going to supply psychotherapy for me if I'll just keep my mouth shut and not talk to anyone else about my deranged ideas."

"Now, Jon, put yourself in my place," Karl pleaded. "Just imagine that I came to you and told you all the things that you've told me today, and I admitted they were all based on a dream that I'd had the night before. Be fair, Jon. How would you react?"

I couldn't help laughing at the thought of Karl talking as I had. I said, "Okay, Karl, you made your point. If you came to me with the same story I'd say you were nutty as a fruitcake. But you've always been the hardheaded realist. I've been the philosopher.

"Besides, I've always been fascinated by dreams, and you've never even bothered to remember yours."

"What you're saying, then," Karl replied, "is that you've always been the type to go off the deep end over some crazy dream. Jon, you're too close to finishing your doctorate to take chances like this. I'll be glad to listen to you, no matter what you want to talk about, but don't discuss this with anyone else yet. Okay?"

"All right," I said. "Maybe you're right. Maybe it was all just a wild dream. I'll test that hypothesis tonight when I go to sleep."

"Now that makes sense," Karl said with relief. "Look, I have to go. I've got an appointment with one of my students, then a date with Cindy tonight. If you're asleep when I get home, I won't wake you up."

36

"By all means, don't wake me up! I'm going to bed early tonight to see what happens.

"By the way," I continued, "I wrote down most of the details of my dream. I thought the organizational structure of the Macro society might interest you. It's all in the notebook over there on my desk. If you don't come in too late, you might glance through it."

"I'll do that," Karl said, and left for his office.

The blowing snow held an invitation that I couldn't resist. I hate the snow, and I love it. So I bundled up and went for a walk that ended in the university library. There I spent a couple of hours looking for books to support my hope that there was more to my experience than just an escapist dream fantasy. I failed.

Around nine-thirty I went to bed, yielding to an almost embarrassingly strong desire to see Lea again, if only in a dream. As I lay there waiting for sleep to come, I amused myself by reviewing the strange details my dream computer had given me on the structure of the Macro society and its strange metric time system:*

The more I thought, the more I wondered if maybe Karl was right. I had read about people making up their own world when they could no longer cope with their existing reality. Maybe I should take a vacation.

No matter what position I tried, sleep simply would not come.

About midnight Karl and Cindy slipped quietly in. I faced the wall and feigned sleep so as not to intrude.

Soon I drifted toward sleep and was awakened by Cindy's muffled giggles. "Damn it!" I thought and moved my pillow over my head as Karl said, "Quiet, Honey," in a hushed voice.

The sound of their rustling about on his bed across the room was hard to ignore, but I did, and once more slipped into the edge of sleep.

I sat up startled in my bed. Cindy had let out a shrill squeal.

*See C.I. Data Excerpts.

There they were, stark naked. Karl was nibbling on her ticklish inner thigh—right there with me in the room.

"Damn it, Karl!" I cursed angrily. "Don't you have any respect for the act?"

Karl looked up, as startled as I had been, and, as Cindy gathered the blanket about her, his expression changed from surprise to amusement.

He grabbed Cindy, blanket and all, and said playfully, "Hell no, Jon! We're ballin', we're not in church!"

Cindy's apology was drowned by the voice of my own inner conflict. "Karl's right, you know," my evolved self was saying. "There's joy and laughter to be shared making love with someone you care for. It's wholesome. It's healthy. It's good."

Then my judgmental unevolved self came on with its rebuttal. "There's nothing wholesome about Karl out there naked with someone he's not even thinking of marrying. Or for that matter, her naked in front of him here in his—no, our!—bedroom. What kind of girl is she, anyway?"

Then the response, "Oh, get with it, Jon. She's a super person, bright, thoughtful, and fun. You know that. There's nothing wrong with them sharing a perfectly natural expression of caring and sharing. If you were as bright as you think you are, you wouldn't judge them. You'd just be happy for them."

"Happy for them, indeed! I'd never do that sort of thing," the argument continued.

"Oh, you wouldn't, huh? Maybe you're just a little bit jealous of Karl's lack of inhibition, his freedom of expression."

And so the contest went till either they got quieter or I fell asleep, or both. Anyway, I woke up Thursday morning at my usual time with no memory of even the trace of a dream.

January is miserably cold in New York, and this month was no exception. It had been eleven snow- and slush-filled days since my strange dream experience, and while

38

I had remembered a few dream fragments, none of them ever approached the level of my 2150 experience.

Did this fact support Karl's "escapist dream" theory or negate it?

He was worried at first and spent a little more time at home than usual for the first few days. When my nights failed to turn up any more such bizarre responses, I guess he finally decided it was all just a very therapeutic escape technique.

I, on the other hand, was having a lot of difficulty getting it off my mind. While I went through my usual daily routine, I was not quite with it. A part of me lingered with my unusual experience and longed to return to it.

I decided to do a little research on dreams and dreaming. Bundling up against the biting cold, I headed for the bookstore, where I went straight to the dream books.

Scanning the shelves, my eyes fell on a single word. *Macro!*

My eyes seemed to jump from my head! There it was. The light brown booklet I had seen before. The word I couldn't remember from its title was *Macro!* "Incredible!" I thought. "Interpret Your Dreams from a Macro View."

I promptly bought it and spent the evening hours studying it and applying it to dreams I remembered.

By ten-thirty I retired convinced that 2150 and Lea were a valid reality—perhaps a parallel reality or something like that which I didn't really understand, but which I, none the less, was now sure existed somewhere in our universe; our macrocosm.

CHAPTER 3:

Carol

I awakened, to my delight, in my library room back—or should I say forward?—in the year 2150. The pleasantly feminine voice of Central Information broke into my awareness and I realized that she was still answering the last question I had asked before falling asleep. While I had spent eleven days back in 1976, I had returned to a moment in 2150 time only a few seconds later than when I had left. Did C.I. know what had happened to me?

"Excuse me," I interrupted, "can you tell me how long I was asleep and what happened?"

"You fell asleep," C.I. answered, "three seconds ago—approximately ten seconds in 2150 metric time. However, during that three seconds you experienced a time translation of approximately eleven days in 1976 time."

"How do you know this?" I asked, perplexed and somewhat uneasy.

"Your chair," C.I. responded, "monitors all your major

physiological changes. Also, Lea, 7-927, and others use this computer to make your time translation computations."

"What's the 7-927 for?" I asked.

"When Lea was born she was the seventh child to be given the name Lea in Delta 927.

My curiosity being fully aroused, I asked the next logical question, "How do you assign names?"

"The Macro society has thirty thousand names which fit the major soul patterns, or vibrations. When a soul incarnates into the Macro society, its vibration pattern is calibrated and the name most closely fitting this pattern is then assigned."

I thought about this for a moment, then asked, "Can you tell me how closely the name Jon fits my vibration pattern?"

"It fits very closely indeed," C.I. responded. "But this is no accident, since your mother had a talent for this type of name selection. She was very highly evolved. What you, in 1976, call psychic."

Since Mother had died during my early childhood, I really couldn't remember her too well—psychic or otherwise. I was just going to ask C.I. how it (or she) had known about my mother when Lea came bouncing into the room looking even more beautiful than I had remembered. Before she could say anything, I blurted out, "Why couldn't I come back? I've missed you."

"We tried every time you slept, Jon, but your anger at Karl prevented translation the first night. After that your belief in this reality was not strong enough to make translation possible until tonight."

"Well, how could I be in 1976 for eleven days and return here only three seconds later than when I left?"

"You were never really gone from either place, Jon. But I think that the concept of time as simultaneous flexible subjectivity is beyond your current comprehension."

"Speaking of time, how old are you, Lea?"

"Hmm," she said, "that's at least one question you

41

forgot to ask Central Information. Before I answer I'm going to ask you how old you think I am."

"Well," I said, "I'm not sure, but you must be somewhere between eighteen and twenty-five, and I'm hoping over twenty-one."

"You'll get your wish and then some," she replied. Then with an impish grin she said to the computer, "Please tell us my age."

C.I. promptly replied, "In 'time' as understood by Jon, Lea 7-927 will have forty years in three weeks and three days."

"You were born in 2110!" I exclaimed incredulously. I couldn't believe that Lea was almost 40 years old. Or to say it in their Macro way—they speak of years of a lifetime as we speak of years of study—she has had almost forty years.

"That's right," she replied. "We have learned to arrest the physical aging process. The only elderly-looking people you will see in the Macro society are the very few who were born before the year 2000."

"Wait a moment," I interrupted. "Do you mean there are people living over a hundred and fifty years?"

"Yes. Theoretically level tens could have as many years as they want, for greater mental awareness means greater physical control. Unlike micro man, our high Macro beings can move at will between their physical and astral bodies. They only remain in physical bodies as long as there are lessons to learn at the physical level. Our goal is to free ourselves completely from the limited, low-vibration, physical existence."

"But, my physical body is enjoyable. I don't want to give it up as long as it's still young enough to bring me more pleasure than pain," I complained.

"Naturally. Nobody does," Lea replied. "That's the major reason we inhabit physical bodies; we want to. But, like all children, eventually we grow up and tire of our childish activities and seek new, more satisfying experiences. Thus, all souls evolve inevitably toward greater awareness."

42

"But I don't—"

"I know," Lea interrupted. "You aren't ready for that yet. But you are ready to start experiencing one of our students Alphas. Let's go. I'll answer more of your questions on the way to your Gamma building."

As we walked hand in hand around the lake I said nothing for a while, and Lea respected my silence. I was contemplating what C.I. had told me about the social structure of the Macro society.

"It seems to me," I said, "that this is a terribly regimented and overstructured society if everybody remains a student for the first thirty years of his life and must live in a student Alpha, Beta, and Gamma. One of the problems of the 1970s is that most young people in the industrial societies are kept much too long as students—'nonproductive' members of society."

"Yes, that's true. But our students are learning how to live satisfying, productive lives. They're not wasting their time memorizing facts and studying irrelevant materials which they'll soon forget because they don't use them in their daily life. Perfect examples would be memorization of historical or geographical details, or your society's devotion to learning foreign languages, algebra, and geometry, which most people never need to use.

"In order to survive," Lea continued, "we learned that we had to remove from our lives the nonessentials and the divisive concerns of micro man. These included his micro family, economic class, religion, nationality, language, cultural and racial divisions."

"That's what I meant by massive regimentation," I said. "There's no freedom left!"

"You mean," Lea answered, "freedom to feel separate from and better than others. Freedom to be selfish and to put your own welfare above that of others. Freedom to compete, to fight, to destroy others. Freedom to pollute by overconsuming and overpopulating and by refusing to cooperate."

She looked at me searchingly for a few seconds, then continued. "You see, Jon, for man to survive on this

43

planet in these bodies he had to learn to cooperate, which meant giving up his micro freedoms. I know you feel our society is too regimented, but live in it for a while and see if our Macro society doesn't supply freedoms that your micro society could never guarantee. Freedom from fear, disease, hunger, loneliness, crippling frustrations, and self-hate."

"If it can do all that, I sure want to see how it works!"

We were surrounded by the beauty of a day filled with sunshine, a sparkling blue lake, a cool breeze, and the lovely park replete with shade trees.

"Who does all the work to keep this paradise running?" I asked.

"Servo-mechanisms," Lea answered. "What you would call robots do all of our repetitious, boring tasks. However, helping things grow is a joy to many people. We do the work that pleases us, so you'll find some of us working in the gardens."

We approached the first of the large residence buildings, and Lea informed me that this was the student Gamma building in which I would be staying.

"I'll introduce you to your Alpha mate," Lea said, "then I must leave you to return to my own work. You'll learn about 2150, then you can decide whether or not you want to make the effort to stay here."

"Wait a minute," I said. "You mean I'm actually going to live in an Alpha and share a bedroom with some other girl?"

"Of course, Jon. If you're going to learn how to live in our Macro society you've got to experience it."

"Yes, but I thought I'd be living with you," I objected.

"You can't live with me until you've reached at least seventh level and finished your tenth student triad."

"My God!" I exclaimed. "That'll be years from now, Lea!"

Lea laughed and said, "Wait until you meet Carol, your Alpha mate, and I'm sure you'll soon be happy at the prospect of sharing a bed with her for the next few years."

"But . . . but," I sputtered, "you can't be serious. I love you. I don't want to bed down with some other woman."

"Love," Lea replied," is determined by the level of one's awareness. With a micro level of awareness love is a neurotic dependency relationship characterized by jealous possessiveness."

"Oh, great," I growled. "The classic rationalization for free love, otherwise known as promiscuity."

"Contrary to your micro society," Lea responded, "sex is not a dirty word in 2150. You'll find we share much more than just an orgasm. And we don't use another person as a sex object.

"But please, Jon, before you condemn us as moral degenerates, get to know us. Treat us just as fairly and without prejudice as you would a research hypothesis.

"Now, are you ready to meet your Alpha mate?"

I had been so preoccupied with our conversation that I had been only vaguely aware of entering the building, passing several young children, swiftly ascending to the seventh floor, and walking down a long, glass-enclosed outer hall. It was lighted both by the outside sunshine and by overhead lighting which seemed to radiate equally from all parts of the ceiling. We had turned down an interior hallway and were now standing before a large blue door. I recalled that all the doorways we passed had been the same electric blue, while the walls were a pleasing shade of green. I remembered that we were on the seventh floor which held the seventh triad student Beta and that green was the seventh level color.

To postpone answering Lea's question about my readiness to meet my Alpha mate I asked about the blue doors.

"Blue is the eighth-level color," Lea answered, "and the seventh level is the door to the eighth level, so, doors on the seventh level are blue. Of course, these are student triad levels, which are entirely different from levels of awareness, but they share the same colors."

"Do the colors themselves have any special meaning?"

Lea smiled her tantalizingly mischievous smile and said, "Carol will be glad to explain it to you."

I was startled when the door in front of us slid silently open. Lea, sensing my surprise, drew my attention to a button beside the door saying, "Most of us use the Macro power of psychokinesis (PK) to activate electronic circuits. You'll have to push the buttons until you develop PK."

I wanted to think about Lea's statement but the unusual room before us commanded my attention.

We entered the huge deeply carpeted Alpha common room, thirty feet by ninety feet long. I was impressed by the three-dimensional murals on the walls depicting outdoor scenes so realistically that I felt I was looking through windows instead of at works of art.

The absence of furniture contributed to this feeling of oneness with the out-of-doors, for the only furniture in this gigantic room was a circle of ten large sitting devices at one end of the room. They didn't look much like chairs, but their purpose was obvious. The fifteen-foot ceiling was lit by some concealed source, creating a luminescence closer to that of sunshine than any I have ever experienced. The fact that there was no one in this room reminded me that we had seen no one since we reached the seventh floor.

"Where is everyone?" I asked.

"It's such a lovely day," Lea answered, "almost everyone is outdoors. We don't confine learning to the inside of classrooms as your society does."

A moment later a door at the end of the room opened, and a young girl came running toward us. It was Carol. She was wearing the universal short tunic and, while Lea and I were wearing our stocking-like boots, her feet were bare.

She placed her right hand on Lea's face. Lea returned the gesture, and they looked into each other's eyes for what seemed to be a very long time as I grew increasingly self-conscious. Then, without speaking, Carol touched

46

my face and began the same smiling, but silent, encounter. I felt as if I was drowning in her magnificent hazel eyes, set in as pretty a face as I have ever seen. Reluctantly I broke our eye contact to become aware of a beautifully formed body cast from a giant mold. Carol was as tall as I, and I'm six feet three!

CHAPTER 4:

Alpha Mates

Suddenly Lea was gone and I was alone with Carol. Why did I feel so nervous? I hadn't felt that way with Lea. What was it about Carol that made me feel like a gawky adolescent on his first date?

I suddenly remembered that, as a telepath, Carol could read my mind. I found myself blushing. In my desperate attempt not to think anything embarrassing, I became inundated with thoughts about Carol's magnificent body which her pink well-fitted tunic did little to hide.

"You're discovering," said Carol, "that it's impossible not to think of something by trying not to think of it. In fact, the more you try not to think of my body, the more you think of it."

My voice seemed to be strangled as I croaked out, "I . . . uh, I'm sorry."

"You certainly needn't be. It would be sad, indeed, if you didn't appreciate the beauty of our bodies!" With these words Carol tugged the top of her tunic, which caused it to fall to the floor, leaving her wondrously naked.

"Carol!" I gasped.

"Please, Jon, go ahead and look at my body," she said—as if I could have looked at anything else!

"I know it's difficult and embarrassing for you. Your being a Virgo—the virgin of the Zodiac—only multiplies your 20th-century sex guilts, so we might as well deal with them right now if you're going to live comfortably in a 22nd-century Alpha. Let's see, bathing together should be the perfect beginning for a Virgo."

"You believe in astrology, then?" I jumped at a safe topic to diminish my self-consciousness.

"Only as an influence, Jon—not as a determinant. Now, about that bath." She took my hand and we entered the most spacious bedroom I've ever seen.

The room was thirty feet square. In one corner was a huge nine-foot-square pad about a foot high, while in the opposite corner was a sunken pool ten feet wide by fifteen feet long. A couple of soft oval cushions in the center of the room faced a three-foot-square video screen. Carol led me to the sunken pool and, releasing my hand, made a shallow dive into the water.

My evolved adventurous self won a quick victory which led me swiftly out of my tunic and into the water after her. I found the water very warm and clear. The floor slanted down until at the far end of the pool, which I went to immediately, it was about eight feet deep. Carol was apparently using her PK power, because a clear plastic partition, slid out of the wall and completely surrounded our pool-bath.

"There," she said, turning to me. "Now we can splash to our heart's content. Let's wash each other!"

With these words Carol surprised me with another PK demonstration as the floor beneath us began to slowly rise until we were standing in water that barely covered our knees.

I felt very naked.

A wall panel slid open revealing two retractable hoses, one dispensing sparkling, slippery cleansing bubbles, the other clear water. Carol invited me to stretch out on a cushion that extended out from the shallow end of the pool. There she began spraying me with one hand while slowly lathering my body with the other.

She covered every square inch of my body with the utmost care. Once again, I tried not to think or feel sexually and ended up with one hell of an erection.

As her hands slid over me I listened to her softly telling me of the joys of sharing a bath with your Alpha mate. She admired my shoulders and my firm abdominal muscles. When she came to my penis she made a number of casual remarks about its esthetically pleasing composition and its remarkable tumescence. This last was too much for me, and I broke my long silence.

"For God's sake, Carol, help me," I pleaded. "I don't want to be sexually aroused."

"Why not?" Carol promptly asked.

"Because," I replied lamely, "it makes me feel like a child who can't control himself. Besides, I don't want to be unfaithful to Lea."

"If you're worried about Lea, she's at ninth level," Carol said in her deep soothing voice, as if this should immediately put my mind to rest. "I mean," she continued, "that Lea is so adequate that she has no neurotic need to possess any part of you and so she could not be offended or jealous, no matter what you do."

"But, I don't—"

Carol interrupted, "Lea asked me to help you in every way I could and that specifically included dealing with your sexual neurosis."

"I'm not neurotic!" I defended vehemently. "I am perfectly normal."

"Maybe, by 1976 standards," Carol replied calmly, "but it's not normal in a 22nd-century Alpha to feel inadequate or in conflict with yourself over a perfectly normal, healthy enjoyment of our beautiful bodies."

"Well," I replied righteously, "in 1976 I didn't take

baths with girls I had only just met five minutes ago."

While we were talking, Carol had finished washing me, then used the other hose to rinse. Now she handed the hose to me and, raising her arms above her head, began to turn slowly and seducively about. I took a deep breath and gingerly began to apply the sparkling bubbles while I held the hose with both hands.

Carol smiled impishly. "That's not how I washed you, Jon. Are you really afraid that you'll lose control if you touch me?"

"Oh, hell!" I exploded and began to feverishly rub the bubbles over her satin smooth skin.

"Hardly hell," Carol answered with a laugh. "It feels to me more like what the 20th century might have called heaven!"

She was right. I recognized my guilt-ridden judgmental self shaking its frightened finger at me. It was so limited, so one-sided, like a white-line figure drawn on a blackboard. I erased it and began to enjoy a truly heavenly experience. I covered her with bubbles, then, with both hands, lovingly explored every delightful curve and valley. I was in no hurry and would have stayed in that bath all day if Carol had not, after some time, caused the floor to descend, taking us back down into the water. After a few moments of splashing, and playful wrestling, Carol led me out of the pool. Activating another circuit, she removed the plastic shield and emptied the pool, refilling it with fresh water. Streams of warm air quickly dried our bodies. Taking my hand, she ran and flopped across the huge pad in the corner.

For the next hour I abandoned myself to the joy of a romping physical emental union with Carol.

By the end of that hour I had learned that sexual intercourse, when it is emental intercourse as well, can open two people to a oneness that I had never before thought possible.

As we lay in each other's arms I told Carol about my guilt and fear concerning pregnancy. I told her that I had not been able to freely enjoy a sexual relationship since my high school days. As I talked about my guilt concerning Valerie, I relived the most unpleasant experience of my teen years when my father had angrily denounced me for my "animal selfishness." It was then that Carol told me that no female in the Macro society could ever have a child without special emental preparation. Even then it required permission from the Deltar.

I didn't understand her technical explanation of how the female reproductive cycle had been modified so that no female experienced menstruation unless she was going to bear children. However, I knew it would have been welcomed by most 20th-century women—and men!

We talked about the Macro society policy of permitting only their finest members (physically, ementally, and spiritually) to produce children. They restricted births so that the student population was approximately 10 percent of the total population. When I realized how few women would ever have an opportunity to bear children, I was shocked.

"Carol," I asked, "do you honestly feel it's fair to deny nine out of ten people the right to become parents?"

"Fair?" Carol questioned, then laughed. "For a moment I forgot you're from the 1970s, Jon. Creating and giving birth to a child was the most physically destructive ordeal that woman put herself through. It's no longer necessary. The incredible conceit of couples thinking the world needed little copies of themselves was just a sad symptom of micro man's limited perspective.

"I studied the history of micro man," Carol continued. "For thousands of years anyone could have children, and they were treated as possessions. By the 20th century, in your country, they could no longer be put to work at an early age, so the micro family began ignoring them. The drug cults and youth revolts of your time were partially the result of micro man's compulsion to create far more offspring than he/she was at all prepared to guide into effective adulthood."

"And your solution," I said, "is to parentally disenfranchise ninety percent of your population."

"Oh, Jon," Carol, said shaking her head and giving me a wry smile. "You don't understand. Anyone can have a child if they prepare themselves for this purpose. It may take a few lifetimes for some, but we're not imprisoned in one lifetime as micro societies thought they were. Micro man's motto was 'you only live once, so eat, drink, and pollute, for tomorrow you may die.' And, of course, his frantic selfishness not only destroyed him but almost destroyed our whole planet."

I had to admit that by 1976 we had seriously polluted most of our lakes and rivers and were affecting the oceans as well.

I wondered how bad it had gotten between my "time" and Carol's.

Obviously perceiving my thought, she paused for a moment, her eyes saddened as if remembering something very unpleasant. Then she continued, "You polluted your oceans, your air, and your land until almost all animal and fish life was gone. Then you caused geophysical imbalances in the earth which produced earthquakes, and tidal waves so destructive that when you look at a map of our world today you will not recognize it."

"Well," I said lightly, not really comprehending the magnitude of the disaster, "I guess that solved our overpopulation problem. How many people are alive in the world of 2150?"

"Approximately 303 million," Carol said. "There would have been a lot more, in spite of the physical disasters, if micro man could have at last cooperated and helped each other. Unfortunately, he accentuated all the traditional divisions—nationality, race, religion, language, educational and socioeconomic levels—and fought over the fast-dwindling resources of his ravaged planet."

"Did micro man really become as extinct as the dinosaur and dodo bird?" I asked.

"Almost," Carol responded. "There are only about three million micro beings in existence today, and they

53

all live on one island, which we call Micro Island. If anyone in our Macro society gets tired of our life, they can move to Micro Island and live selfishly and in fear of their fellow micro neighbors—the way your society lived in the 20th century."

"You mean," I said, "your Macro society keeps three million people on a prison island?"

Carol shook her head. "No one has to live on Micro Island if he is willing to live in the Macro society by our Macro standards. You must understand that every person who lives on Micro Island has chosen to live there."

"Even the children?" I asked.

"Yes," Carol nodded. "We know that every child, prior to his birth, chooses his parents, as well as the environment he will grow up in."

"You mean," I added, "you, too, believe in reincarnation?"

"Yes, I do," Carol responded. "We all do. Just as exploration of the earth proved the theory that the world was round, exploration of the mind proved the theory of reincarnation.

"When we explored the subconscious mind we discovered the soul and its memory of past lives on this planet as well as in other dimensions. We learned that the first human souls to enter this planet inhabited the bodies of various animals and got trapped in animal flesh. Then other human souls decided to help their brothers by preparing a way out of this animal-life trap.

"To achieve this they hovered over the bodies of apes and, working with Macro powers, manipulated the gland centers of the apes to change their evolutionary pattern. This is how the five races of man were produced, black, brown, red, yellow, and white, at approximately the same time in different parts of the world. As these apes developed more human-like bodies, they were used as vehicles for human souls to experience this physical dimension and to provide human bodies for those trapped in animal flesh."

54

"And are there still human souls inhabiting animal bodies?" I asked. "In my life in 1976 . . . could I have met a fellow human soul trapped behind bars at our local zoo?"

Carol was amused by my question. "No. Not quite. There is an evolution of souls, with some almost human souls still incarnating in other forms of life. Some of these are using mental powers that outreach those of man in specific areas. But all truly human souls trapped in animal flesh were free to inhabit human bodies long before recorded history began. That does not, however, mean that they were not trapped."

"What do you mean?" I queried.

"I mean that in human bodies most souls could only conceive of pleasure in the limited scope of physical existence. Afraid of giving up or losing these pleasures, they became victims of their own desires—their own limited perspective—and kept incarnating again and again. In an attempt to avoid the law of *karma* they tried to forget their past. They lived in a kind of delusionary amnesia."

"I'm familiar with the concept of *karma*," I said. "As I understand it, it's the same as the Christian concept of 'what you sow you must reap.' Is that right?"

"Essentially, yes," Carol answered, then went on to clarify. "*Karma*, you see, reflects the Macro truth that all is one, and, thus, anything we do to others we do to ourselves. Of course, this isn't apparent at the limited micro perspective, so souls take refuge in micro lives in an attempt to avoid the painful consequences of their own past actions and thoughts. This is the delusionary amnesia I spoke of.

"From a purely micro view, *karma* doesn't exist because it is not perceived as existing.

"From a mid-point of evolution *karma* is acknowledged as the logical explanation for one's fortunes and misfortunes. It is believed to be real and is, therefore, real as a cause-and-effect element within a continuous time perspective.

55

"From a more Macro view, however, time is simultaneous, and *karma* is understood to be a valid element of a limited perspective regarding time. Fortunes and misfortunes are seen, from the broader perspective, not as cause and effect, but as learning opportunities specifically and carefully chosen by each soul for its own development."

"Wait a minute," I interrupted. "Let me go back a bit. You said that some souls try to forget their past in an attempt to avoid the consequences of their actions and thoughts. What's this about thoughts?"

"Thoughts are things, you know, and they are just as important as actions," Carol added. "The way you think makes you what you are and profoundly influences the world around you."

"You mean," I said, "that if I rob or murder someone, or even if I hate someone, that this will eventually come back to me?"

"Exactly," she replied. "But that's only half of it, for you see if you are patient, helpful, or think kindly of others, these, too, will come back to you.

"The great Macro philosopher, Jesus, said that whatever measures you deal out to others shall be dealt back to you in return. That's why the golden rule of treating others as you would like to be treated makes sense from a Macro view, though not from a limited micro view.

"Another expression of the law of *karma* is Newton's third law: For every action there is an equal and opposite reaction. This law is cumulative throughout all of one's incarnations and there is but one escape from its effect—an applied and practiced Macro perspective."

"I'm not sure I understand." I hesitated.

"What I mean, Jon, is that the same law applies to all experience, but it is seen and interpreted differently according to the size of one's perspective.

"From a Macro perspective it is seen that your conscious intent affects every cell of your body and exerts an influence on your environment. It is understood that you, and only you, are responsible for your life and what it holds. This is the great truth that will soon come of age in your 1970s culture—the most joyful, rejuvenatingly hopeful insight of all. We are not the victims of circumstance but the architects of our lives. Our conscious thoughts create an image of our lives, our selves, our feelings, and our unconscious produces it in perfect accordance with our predominant conscious beliefs.

"The law, you see, remains the same in all those lives we live. We just interpret it differently, depending on our level of evolution during the particular life in question."

"Well," I asked, "if we've all reincarnated so many times, why don't we remember past lives? Are you saying it's just because we don't want to remember them?"

"That's right," she replied. "People forget their past lives because they don't want to remember their ugly, selfish actions which would humble their pride and make it impossible for them to feel superior to others. Pride is possible only when we forget our past failures. However, he who forgets his past is doomed to repeat it. To the extent that human souls deny that each person's mind is totally responsible for all it experiences they can only continue repeating the same selfish actions that cause the same painful consequences. They must accept total responsibility for their entire state of being, then joyously create the life they want if they are to facilitate evolution." She smiled and took my hand. "We'll talk about that more later. Right now let's freshen up and go have lunch."

We got dressed and ate a delicious meal in the Alpha dining room. Their kitchen was a marvel. All one had to do to get any kind of food was turn a dial and press a button. Within a few seconds your chosen meal appeared either hot or cold, just as you selected, from a sliding panel in the wall.

I had what I thought was a delicious two-pound steak served medium rare and sizzling hot. After I had eaten it and profusely praised the cook, Carol, finishing her carrot juice, informed me that the steak was synthetically derived from high protein seaweed combined with other vegetable ingredients. The cook, I learned, was another computer-run servo-mechanism.

Carol tried to explain their complicated food-processing technology, but I told her not to bother, since I was trying to forget that steaks weren't really steaks. She accused me of practicing delusionary amnesia to deny unpleasant reality, and I had to admit my guilt. I could still remember the delicious taste of my steak and I knew I would enjoy my meals in 2150 if I could just forget where they came from.

My major objection to a vegetarian diet was that I liked the taste of meat and felt it was the best source of protein I knew of. If the science of 2150 had solved these problems I wouldn't fight it, even if I didn't agree with Carol that it was wrong to kill animals for food.

I told Carol that I thought she and the rest of the Macro society members were pretty hard on micro man and his habits. However, she insisted that she did not condemn micro man or feel that she was intrinsically better than he was any more than a sixth-grade child was better than a first-grade child. It was all a matter of evolution along the m-M (for microcosmic-Macrocosmic) continuum toward ever greater awareness of the oneness of all. Besides, she insisted that she could remember many past lifetimes in which she had lived selfish micro existences both as male and as female.

I wondered about this business of past lives of different sexes, but decided to bring it up later.

Back in our Alpha dyad room—I thought of it as our room now—Carol showed me the toilet facilities by activating a circuit which caused a portion of the wall and adjoining floor to change into a very strange, but remarkably convenient, area for disposing bodily wastes. When I looked pained at its lack of privacy, Carol smiled and suggested I press a nearby button, which I did, causing an opaque plastic-like wall to slide completely around the area.

"There you are, Jon," she said. "A way to hide that

part of you which you feel is shameful. We prepared this barrier screen especially for your arrival," she teased.

"Here in 2150 we provide privacy for thinking, not for hiding, but I know that you in the 20th century were still very ambivalent about the human body and its most basic and necessary functions."

I had to agree with Carol that I was probably neurotic by 2150 standards, but I used the opaque wall and asked her to do the same. I was pleased that she didn't resist my request. She was a very accepting, easy-going person. Not that she was at all reluctant to express a point of view that differed with mine, but she didn't get impatient or angry with my micro neurotic ways or my insatiable curiosity about 2150.

When I asked her about the video wall screen, she explained that it was connected with Central Information just like the one in the C.I. room. Then she showed me some new ways of using it.

As we sat down in the two chairs facing the video screen Carol commanded Central Information to show us some newsmagazine material from 1970. Almost immediately we found ourselves leafing through the pages of *Time* and *Newsweek* magazines as recorded on microfilm. Carol stopped the C.I. at one of the pages and asked me to read and comment on the following:

Time magazine, 7-13-70:

"Millions of Americans in 1970 are gripped by an anxiety that is not caused by war, inflation, or recession—important as those issues are. Across the U.S. the universal fear of violent crime and vicious strangers —armed robbers, packs of muggers, addict burglars ready to trade a life for heroin—is a constant companion of the populace. It is the cold fear of dying at random in a brief spasm of senseless violence—for a few pennies, for nothing.

"And yet, Americans are several times more likely to be hurt in auto accidents or household mishaps than to be raped, robbed or murdered. Only about

10% of robbery victims are badly injured, fewer than 1% are killed. The nation's well-being is far more insidiously undermined by embezzlers, price-fixers [micro politicians] and organized racketeers than by muggers or car thieves.

"Roughly half of all serious crimes are never reported, often because numbed victims expect no help from overburdened police. Between 70% and 80% of police effort is spent, not on crime, but on hushing blaring radios, rescuing cats, and administering first aid. Countless additional police hours are wasted on crimes without true victims, e.g., drunkenness, gambling, pornography, illicit sexual activities. Even the best police work is undone by clogged courts and punitive prisons that breed more crime."

I looked at Carol and said, "What can I say except that the world of the '70s was divided, not united, and, couldn't cooperate enough to resolve its major social problems."

"Your society," Carol said, "functioned in the only way it could, based on its micro perspective of life. People can only behave in terms of how they perceive themselves and the world about them. And these perceptions are completely determined by one's beliefs or philosophy of life, which were, prior to the 21st century, generally unconscious."

"Okay," I admitted. "We needed a broader perspective so we could see the larger picture. We needed a Macro perspective—a perspective large enough so that we could see that the Golden Rule and the Sermon on the Mount provided the best of all practical advice."

Carol smiled and quoted, " 'For whatever measure you deal out to others will be dealt back to you.' "

"Yes," I responded, "but that doesn't make sense in everyday human affairs unless the individual is aware of this macrocosmic oneness."

"In the 1970s," Carol added, "you lived in a world in which at least one out of every three people lived in abject crippling poverty, and you people, in your proud United States—united indeed! Hmmm, but that's another story—you people had a welfare system so politically corrupt and inadequate that it not only ignored the worst cases of human neglect and poverty but actually perpetuated poverty and ignorance from one generation to the next.

"At the same time," she continued, "you dedicated your major national energies and resources to war and paranoid preparations for war. If, in the 1960s and '70s, you had devoted the same amount of money and national effort to solving your social problems that you did to waging your nation-dividing Vietnam War, you could have ended the poverty cycle forever in your country and gone a long way toward resolving many of your nation's other social problems."

"I know," I said, "but our political leaders were ignorant, if not corrupt."

Carol shook her head. "Every nation deserves its leaders," she said. "You're trying to avoid your own responsibility by placing the blame on others. Please, Jon, don't think I am sitting in righteous judgment of you or your micro society. I don't blame or condemn micro man for acting like micro man. It is the only way he can act, because it is the only way he has learned to act. But I must help you see this broader perspective."

"But," I objected, "how can you not condemn human beings for selfish, cruel, and even vicious behavior toward others? Especially since that behavior became so selfish and shortsighted that it almost wiped out our whole planet?"

"It was the only way," Carol answered, "that man could learn the conseqences of his own actions. Mistakes are absolutely essential in the learning process. Besides, Jon, it's only terrible from the short-term micro point of view. From the Macro view it's all perfect. Everything has a purpose and a happy ending because everything is evolving toward perfect Macro awareness."

"I know," I said. "that from your Macro view we are

61

all responsible for our every experience. But tell that to someone who is suffering from poverty or disease, or some other kind of human injustice."

Carol smiled and said, "I don't speak to children about things they're not ready to understand. But I don't forget that in time every child becomes an adult and everyone eventually will understand everything."

I decided that we had gone as far as I felt I was ready to go on this subject, so I asked Carol when I would meet the other Alpha members. She immediately asked C.I. to contact her, or should I now say "our," Alphar. In about fifteen seconds we heard the voice of our Alpha leader who informed Carol that the rest of our Alpha would be back in about two hours.

After Carol had thanked him for this information she terminated their contact and told me how C.I. can contact any Macro society member by using the communications cell contained in the bracelet which each of them wore. She showed me what she called her *mib* (for Macro identity bracelet). It contained a timepiece, a communications cell, a bionic monitor, and a nutrition compartment. I was fascinated by the fact that the bracelets supplied C.I. with the heart and brain patterns for everyone in the Macro society. Any danger was immediately relayed, via C.I., to those closest and best able to offer help even if the person in trouble was unconscious and, thus, unable to call for help.

Carol told me that I would soon receive my own mib. Then she asked me if I would like to see pictures of our other Alpha members. Of course I did, so she asked C.I. to present them.

Suddenly I was looking at a picture of our leader, Alan, whose voice I had just heard. At the same time C.I. was telling me about him.

"Your Alpha leader, Alan, is 20.6 years old, six feet five inches tall (this, along with his weight, was given in metric equivalents, then translated for my benefit), 240 pounds, and is presently residing in the student Gamma of Delta 927."

Carol interrupted C.I. at this point to tell me that we could listen for days to the accumulated information that C.I. had on every individual member of our Alpha. This information, she said, even included data on past lives. However, she felt that I probably was not ready for too much information on each member yet.

It was here that she pointed out that all information on every person in the Macro society was available to everyone. There was no such thing as secret, hidden, or confidential information.

I commented that my government in 1976 could not possibly function without massive secrecy. Then I looked at a video tape of Alan leading a discussion group, running, walking, swimming, playing games, and sleeping. He looked tremendously vital and intelligent. When I commented on this, Carol said he was a Six, as if that explained it all.

We next saw pictures of Bonnie, who was Alan's Alpha mate. She was six feet two and weighed 160 pounds. Next was six-foot-seven Adam with Nancy who was six feet three. They were followed by Diane and David who were six feet one and six feet five respectively. Then came the tallest man of all, Steve, at six feet nine, and his Alpha mate, Joyce, who was six feet three. Finally C.I. presented pictures of Carol and Jon, and I realized the pictures of me had been taken while I was in the library and walking with Lea.

I was impressed with the sheer physical size and beauty of my fellow Alpha members. I was also surprised at the lack of hair. Of the five males my hair was the longest, and it was short by 1976 standards. Even among the girls the longest hair was Carol's, which was no more than four inches at most.

When I asked Carol about this she informed me that they did not value hair because they were not vain about their appearances. It was simpler, she assured me, to keep their hair short.

"Tell me, Carol," I asked "are there any fat or ugly people in the Macro society?"

She laughed and said, "How could there be, when we control the complete genetic, physical, and mental development of all our children?"

"All right, but why, then, do you have your different levels of awareness? How come everyone isn't level ten?"

"Because," Carol answered, "we can not change the learning experiences of past lives. However, no soul can incarnate into the Macro society who has not evolved to Macro potential."

"Even me?"

Carol smiled. "Oh, Jon. Even our wisest ones could not have succeeded in helping Lea bring you here if you didn't have the Macro potential."

"Let me try to understand these levels of awareness," I said. "I'm level one because I'm a beginner at Macro awareness."

"That's right, Jon. You're well on your way back toward applied awareness of your oneness with all that is, all that was, and all that ever will be."

"And Adam and Nancy have demonstrated second-level awareness," I continued. "You are at the third level along with Steve, while Bonnie and Joyce are level four. Then we have Diane and David at level five and Alan, our leader, at the sixth level. Now, tell me, what's the difference between these levels?"

"I'll let C.I. answer that," Carol said. "And while you are getting your questions answered, I will go back and pick up your mib from the administration building."

I had a mental picture of the map which C.I. had shown me of the Delta and I suddenly realized Carol was talking about a ten-mile round trip. "You mean you are going to walk ten miles?" I asked.

She said, "Oh, I could have it sent by underground pneumatic tube right here to our Alpha, but since I missed our exercise period today I'll run the distance. I'll be back in less than an hour."

"Ten miles in less than an hour?" I asked incredulously.

"Don't worry, Jon. Our Macro powers help us run

lighter, faster, longer, and more joyously than would ever be possible for micro man."

"Don't you have any kind of local transportation?" I asked incredulously.

"Unless it's a great emergency," Carol replied, "we walk or run everywhere in the Delta and sometimes even between Deltas. Sure, we have transairs that will take us very quickly anywhere we want to go on this planet, but we believe in a balanced life free from the neurotic rushing of your micro society. We believe in exercising the body, the mind, and the spirit equally so they can remain in balance."

With those last words she blew me a kiss and literally ran out of the room. Not because she was in a hurry, but from sheer joy of exercising a magnificent healthy and vital body. I was pleased that she shared my joy in running, and I understood better why no one would become fat in this energetic society.

Turning back to the video screen, I began asking my questions about levels of awareness and found that C.I. kept an almost total record on every person in the Macro society from birth to death. This was done by means of the Macro identity bracelet and the yearly evaluation performed by C.I.

One's level of awareness was indicated by the color of his tunic. The tunic, I learned, was a perfectly accurate reflection of one's aura, which was an unfailingly accurate indicator of one's state of being, mentally, emotionally, spiritually, and physically.

Level one was predominantly gray: two was lemony-orange for energy; three was pink for control of that energy; four was purple for empathy and leadership; five was violet for joyous acceptance of what is; six was yellow for love in its most total sense; seven was green for healing; eight was blue for balanced use of the intellect; nine was aquamarine for wisdom; and ten was white for leadership, the perfectly balanced blend of all other levels.

According to C.I. there were currently only one hundred

65

and twenty-seven persons in the Macro family who were evaluated as having demonstrated ten degrees of Macro awareness. This was out of a current Macro family population of 300 million.

These degrees of awareness were based on the extent to which a person demonstrated the three Macro qualities: love, wisdom, and leadership, in that order of importance, and the seven Macro powers: clairvoyance, telepathy, precognition, retrocognition, psychokinesis, telekinesis, and astral projection. [See C.I. Excerpts].

As C.I. presented more and more information about the highly complex process of developing degrees of awareness I found myself becoming very drowsy and having difficulty keeping my eyes open.

Finally I gave in to my desire to rest, closed my eyes, and was soon asleep.

CHAPTER 5:

The Test of Reality

I awakened, Saturday the 17th, to another cold, dreary January morning and remembered what C.I. had told me about the controlled climate of 2150. Things were just too good to be true, I thought.

How could all those incredible social and scientific changes have taken place in only 174 years? Of course, I had to admit that going back in time 174 years from 1976 would have taken me to 1802, a time when the world of 1976 would certainly have been considered a completely impossible dream.

I thought about some of the predictions for the future made by 20th-century prophets such as Huxley and Orwell. They had viewed the future of man with great skepticism. Of course, they were writing about micro man who, according to C.I., was even now in the process of doing away with himself. I wondered how it would have affected the writings of Orwell and Huxley if they had had a larger, broader perspective which would have enabled them to envision Macro man.

Then I remembered that I, in fact, had no concrete proof whatsoever that the world of 2150 was anything more than a product of my own imagination.

I suddenly felt a strong need to be concrete, to check out and reaffirm my present state of existence, to touch something, to talk to someone, to hear a voice.

I looked across our apartment room and saw that Karl's bed was neatly made, as usual, and my journal was lying there on his pillow.

I got out of bed and, losing my balance, almost fell on the floor. I had forgotten to strap on my artificial leg. That was confirmation enough of my present state of existence. I was here, fully awake, in 1976—minus one leg.

I hobbled over to Karl's bed, retrieved my journal and saw the note saying, "We'll talk at noon," signed *Karl*.

According to my watch it was almost 9 a.m., so I had slept late again. I wanted to write down all I could remember of my most recent experiences in 2150—or my dream world, whichever it was—before Karl came back at noon. I hurriedly dressed, had a quick breakfast and was soon writing furiously in my journal.

When Karl came in at 12:15 p.m. I was almost finished, so I pulled out the pages I had completed and handed them to him so he could get caught up on my latest dream experiences while I finished writing.

Karl finished about the same time I did and for a few seconds we just looked at each other. Then Karl broke the silence.

"Hey, man," he grinned, "you've got to be the all-time super dreamer. You aren't content with one beautiful superwoman in love with you—no, you got to have two of 'em—one blonde and one brunette—even if they do wear it short."

"All right," I said. "Any other comments? Aren't you at all impressed with the continuity? The fact that the dream picked up right where it ended before? And how about the continuing wealth of detailed information about the society of the future?"

Karl's face became serious and he frowned. "Yes, Jon," he said, "I am impressed with it. I honestly don't know what to think except that if we take it seriously, we are both candidates for the loony bin. Think of that, Jon. Just imagine the headline, 'Two aspiring young psychologists, just one year from that big degree, break under load of studies and are admitted to State Mental Hospital.'"

It was amusing, but uncomfortably possible. "Okay, okay—I'll be careful, Karl, I promise."

"I'm not sure that even keeping it secret will end our problems, Jon. This dream has become an obsession with you."

I thought about this and had to admit that he was right. "I guess you're right, Karl. I've never experienced anything so satisfying, so completely and irresistibly engaging in my entire life.

"I'm still a bit skeptical of its reality," I added. "What I plan to do is test it out, like any other hypothesis. The ultimate test will be whether I can learn to liberate myself from this micro existence, as Lea suggested, and live in the Macro world of 2150 permanently."

"Good God, Jon!" Karl came to the edge of his chair, his voice harsh with alarm. "Do you know what you're saying? If this dream is a mental aberration, an escape from unpleasant reality, then you'll end up like a vegetable—permanently off in your dream world while cooped up in some hospital and fed intravenously in the real world of 1976. Just one more catatonic schizophrenic!"

Karl got up and began pacing about the room. He didn't say anything. The silence grew as I seriously considered the possibility that I might be becoming psychotic. Would I eventually deteriorate into the vegetable existence of the catatonic schizophrenic? What would happen to my body here in 1976 if I managed to stay

69

permanently in the world of 2150? Would it become a vegetable? Would it just disappear? Would it die?

These were questions I couldn't answer, and I found myself wishing I could ask Central Information.

"I've got it, Karl," I said. "I'll ask C.I. when I get back what will happen to my body here in 1976 if I stay permanently in 2150."

"Oh, that's just great," Karl answered in a voice dripping with sarcasm. "Now let's solve the problem by asking Satan to help us stop sinning!"

"But, Karl, I—"

"Listen to me, Jon," he interrupted. "You've got to realize that a society, even a real one, that would let itself be run by some giant computer has got to be sick! Sick! SICK!"

"Now wait a minute, Karl," I replied. "Let's be fair. Let's be pragmatic. Let's compare the results."

"Our micro society of 1976 is dedicated to selfish exploitation of others in the interest of short-term material pleasures. This selfish behavior is performed and perpetuated in the name of our freedom, our family, our city, our state, our nation, our religion, or in the name of communism, socialism, capitalism, of some other damn ism, and it has produced inconceivable amounts of human misery.

"The world of 1976 is a world of selfish divisions breeding suspicion, distrust, hatred, and endless conflict both internally and internationally. It's a world so divided and so unable to cooperate that it has polluted its land, its water, its animal life, and even the air we breathe, to such an extreme that our planetary survival is in question.

"As for our people, at least one out of three lives in poverty, disease, and semi-starvation. This, Karl, in spite of the fact that we have the resources and the technology to provide adequate food, clothing, shelter, medical care, and education to each and every person on this entire planet!

"My question, Karl, is why aren't we doing it?"

70

"Probably because we're too damned self-centered, Jon," was Karl's response. "But the solution isn't to turn all our problems over to some bloody machine to solve. Now that's a real cop-out!"

"They don't cop out in 2150," I answered heatedly and suddenly realized that I had a desperate need to convince Karl, and maybe myself, of the truth, the value, and the rightness of my strange experiences.

"Okay, Karl," I said, forcing myself into calmness, "listen to me with as open a mind as you can, because if we get lost in our emotions we'll really be in trouble.

"Everything I've learned about the society of 2150 indicates that its people care about each other and are deeply involved with helping others. Now, that's not a cop-out."

"Moreover," I continued, "they have developed a philosophy of life which provides such a large perspective that they can see the long-term destructive results of selfish behavior. In other words, from their Macro perspective they can see that we are all one interdependent whole and, therefore, the welfare of the apparently least important individual is the concern and the welfare of all. Only from this larger perspective is there any practical value in words like 'love one another,' 'you are your brother's keeper,' 'what you sow you must reap,' or 'treat others as you would like to be treated.' "

"But what about that damn machine?" Karl began.

"Screw the machine!" I shouted. "It wasn't C.I. that developed Macro philosophy or a Macro society which could attract highly evolved souls! It wasn't the machine that provided love, patience, kindness, and understanding help for every living being! No! It was the people of the Macro society who chose an unselfish, Macro lifestyle."

"And the results?" I continued. "The results are 300 million people free from war, pollution, poverty, selfishness, and hatred—every one of them educated and healthy, with a roof over their heads and three square meals a day."

71

"If this is sick, sick, SICK," I shouted as I slammed my fist down on the table, "then, by God, I choose to be sick!"

Karl stared at me in disbelief. Then he said, "Jon, I've never seen you so—so—I'm not sure what. Maybe passionately involved. You're shouting, you're arguing, you're slamming your fist around, and you're swearing. This is all new to me. I don't know what to think."

"How about realizing that I've been an uninvolved spectator in this life up till now? I've prided myself on never losing my cool, but actually I was just copping out. Now—at last—I'm concerned, involved, committed, and I'm not going to back out, no matter what happens. I'm going to give all I've got to exploring and learning about this world of the future."

Karl slowly shook his head and I could see that his face was taut with strain. "I'm afraid," he said. "You know that I feel closer to you than to anyone else on Earth. That I'd give my life to help you.

"I remember," he continued, "there's some philosophy that says if you save a man's life you are thereafter responsible for it. Well, I saved your life in Vietnam, and now I can't let you destroy it over some psychotic hallucination."

"But, Karl—" I began.

"No, damn it, you listen to me now!" Karl insisted as he shook his fist at me as though he were planning to physically wrestle me to my senses. "You know as well as I that sudden massive personality changes are classic signs of mental disturbance, and you just admitted that you've got a whole new personality!"

Karl paused and looked at me carefully to see if I had registered this bombshell.

Obviously satisfied that he had gotten through to me, he continued, "Now, Jon, I'm not going to argue with you over the merits of your dream world versus reality. I'm in favor of goodness and mercy and justice for all, and I'm opposed to selfishness, wickedness, and evil of all varieties. In spite of all that, I'm going to deal with the unpleasant reality of 1976, not escape into some dream world of the future."

There was a silence now as Karl let me think over what he had just said.

I thought about the points he had made concerning sudden personality changes and running away from unpleasant reality, and I had to admit to myself that they scared me a little, too. However, I was still convinced that for me there was no going back to the Jon Lake who existed prior to my dreams of 2150. I was committed to exploring my dream world of the future to its conclusion—whatever that might be. Now, how could I get Karl to accept this?

"All right, Karl," I said finally. "I concede your points. Maybe I am going insane. Maybe I am running away from the unpleasant reality of my Ph.D. grind. But, truth can be demonstrated sooner or later. If I can learn to develop Macro powers such as clairvoyance, telepathy, and so on, then I should be able to demonstrate them to you here in 1976. Right?"

Karl looked surprised and said, "Are you saying that if you dream you've developed these powers, and can't demonstrate them to my satisfaction while you are awake, that you'll give up this massive psychotic delusion?"

"Yes, Karl," I answered. "That's exactly what I'm saying.

"I'm willing to put my dream world to the test, and if it fails to pass this test, to hell with it."

"Now you're talking sense," Karl said, patting me on the shoulder with smiling relief. "Since you're willing to let me be the final judge in your test of reality I can hardly object to your continuing interest in these weird dreams. I'm convinced, however, that it won't be long before your dream world fails your test of reality."

By unspoken agreement we dropped the subject and talked of other things for the rest of the afternoon. Then we went out for dinner followed by a movie featuring the youth drug culture.

On the way back to our apartment we discussed the

73

tremendous increase in drug usage among our generation and agreed that this was certainly a desperate attempt to escape from, or find something better than, the unpleasant reality of our very micro society.

Later, while lying in my bed waiting for sleep to come and, hopefully, transport me to the future, I wondered if my motivation to dream of a beautiful future was similar to the motivation of those who use drugs.

It made me uncomfortable and I called across the room to where Karl was lying and, once again, repeated my promise to forget about my dream world if it didn't pass our test.

He expressed his satisfaction with this agreement, saying that now we had it licked.

I was still reassuring myself when I fell asleep.

CHAPTER 6:

Jon's Alpha and Rana

Once again I awakened to the voice of Central Information. I immediately interrupted to ask how long I had been asleep. But this time C.I. said it could not give me this information since the Alpha room chair was not designed to be a body-mind monitor, as were the chairs in the library.

I decided, however, that since Carol was not back yet I must have, once again, returned within only seconds of 2150 time.

I decided to ask C.I. some of my troublesome questions.

"You know, C.I., all of this switching back and forth in time is playing havoc with my life in 1976. My brother thinks I'm heading for some kind of psychotic break. When he presented his arguments I had to admit that he made a strong case.

"We decided to settle the matter once and for all by

devising a test of the reality of 2150. If I can develop some of the Macro powers you described and demonstrate them back in 1976, then Karl, and I, will accept 2150 as reality. If not, then we'll just accept my 'dreams' as a massive escape device which I designed to relieve the tensions created by uninterrupted years of study.

"Tell me, is it possible for me to develop some of these Macro powers, and if I do, will I still have them when I go back to 1976?"

C.I. answered with one unqualified word, "Yes."

"Is it possible for me to stay in 2150 permanently?" I asked next.

"Yes, if you attain third-level awareness you can stay in 2150 permanently," was her answer.

"When will that be?"

"That depends entirely on your desire, and your belief that it is possible."

"Well, how long will it be before I develop some Macro powers?" I asked.

C.I.'s response could have been a recording of her previous one, for she said, "That depends entirely on your desire, and your belief that it is possible."

Thinking that perhaps some mechanical failure had caused this identical response I asked C.I. my name to see if her "tape" was stuck.

Her response was, "Jon Lake is your 1976 name. Your 2150 name is Jon 8-927 since there have been seven other Jons born in Delta 927."

"How long will it be before I develop some Macro powers?" I persisted.

"That depends entirely on your desire, and your belief that it is possible," was still the response.

While I was disappointed in not being able to find out how long it would take me to develop some of the Macro powers, I was delighted that they could be demonstrated back in 1976, and kind of tickled somewhere inside to hear my 2150 identification.

The knowledge that I could stay permanently in 2150 if I did attain third-level awareness brought me deep pleasure and relief. Yet there was something unanswered that bothered me. It was my concern for my body back in 1976.

I asked C.I., "If I reach third-level awareness and stay permanently here in 2150, what will happen to my body back in 1976?"

C.I., who was a woman of few words, said simply, "It will die."

I was trying to cope with this prospect of dying and living all at the same time when Carol returned with my Macro identity bracelet.

"Here's your own personal mib, Jon," Carol said with a smile as she slipped it onto my wrist.

I marveled at its lack of weight for in spite of its multiple functions of timepiece, nutrition dispenser, heart and brain wave monitor, and communications cell (for those with limited telepathic power), it weighed considerably less than my 1976 wristwatch.

Carol explained that it was waterproof and practically indestructible. When I asked about its power source, she replied that all equipment, from mibs to their largest transportation vehicles and servo-mechanisms, receive their power from what she called a Central Information power broadcasting center.

I asked her if this was an atomic power center, and she responded with an emphatic denial, explaining that atomic wastes had contributed greatly to the pollution problems of micro man. Then she explained how cosmic radiation was combined with the forces created by the movement of the earth. These were captured, reactivated, reflected and amplified by a crystal, then broadcast, creating a central power source. Power was obtained through electro-acoustical tuning to this energy source.

Once this had been accomplished, man was no longer dependent on any other power source and the world's fuel pollution problems were over.

When I asked more about the crystal and how it worked, Carol said that the tunics we wore employed a very similar crystal structure and process in miniature.

77

She went on to tell me how they had learned to recycle and use all waste products so that the planet Earth was the cleanest in recorded history. I remembered the sparkling clarity and sweetness of the air of 2150 and tried to imagine rivers, lakes, and oceans free of refuse and wastes. Carol asked C.I. to show us pictures of the Earth as it existed in 2150.

I spent the next few minutes looking at an Earth transformed into a garden of Eden. No longer the vast ugly oil slicks on our waters. No longer the dirty yellow air or the deadly unseen gases saturating our atmosphere. No longer the ugly sprawling cities functioning as planetary sewers. All of micro man's ugly slough had been removed.

"How did we ever clean it all up?" I asked Carol.

She smiled and said, "It wasn't difficult for Macro man. Just as it was inevitable that micro man would turn his world into an open cesspool, it was also inevitable that Macro man would turn this same world into an earthly paradise."

"You see," she went on, "the soul of micro man evolves into Macro man. Then the adult cleans up after the child. We must not forget that we were all once children— once the very same micro beings who fought and polluted and destroyed everything, including our micro selves.

"We don't condemn micro man," she said, "for that would be to condemn our own childhood, which would force us to forget it. We don't want to forget our past because we don't want to have to repeat it."

I admired Carol's strong convictions concerning personal responsibility, but I asked, "Can you really remember your past lives?"

"Yes, of course," she replied calmly. "I can remember living as a man during your 20th century. Planetary pollution was the major cause of my death in the 1990s."

I started to say something, but she interrupted me by saying that when I was ready to remember past lives I would be given the help I needed, then I would more fully understand the truth of reincarnation and *karma*.

Then she changed the subject by asking me if I was familiar with how the timepiece portion of my mib worked according to metric time.

I told her that I remembered C.I. explaining the metric time system to me as part of an answer to one of my questions, but I wasn't too sure of it. So we spent a few moments reviewing metric time, with C.I. providing helpful illustrations and charts.

I won't use this journal to present all the intricacies of the metric time system. However, briefly, the 2150 calendar year began in the spring with the vernal equinox and was divided into ten months of 100 days each. A metric day was approximately 8.6 1976 hours and was divided into ten metric hours which would have approximately 51.8 1976 minutes each [see C.I. Data Excerpts].

As I was adjusting to 100 minutes in an hour and 100 seconds in a minute, Carol suggested that it was time to meet the other Alpha members in person. We found them sitting in the circle of chairs at our end of the common room.

The most unnerving thing to me, without the Macro power of telepathy, was the complete silence which greeted us as we joined the circle. The eight minds probed my own, which felt powerless to resist.

I tried to return their eye contact but found myself repeatedly lowering my eyes self-consciously.

Alan, our Alphar, took my left hand and placed his right hand firmly on my cheek. His eyes engaged mine silently for a few seconds, then he said, "Welcome to our Alpha, Jon. I'm Alan Six. Forgive us for not speaking sooner. It is our custom to meet first with our eyes and minds, then with our touch, and lastly with our voices, if that seems desirable.

"Soon you will develop the Macro power of telepathy, which will make it easier for you. You'll still have another important barrier to overcome, though, before you'll be comfortable with our traditional affectionate greeting."

"I noticed," he continued, "that when I touched you

your aura retracted. That, of course, indicates that you're uncomfortable sharing through touch.

"This may be a reflection of your culture's archaic taboo against men touching one another. However, it could be an indication of your submission to astrological influences. You've read enough astrology to know that most Virgos prefer that people stay their distance. This would be a cripplingly divisive astrological influence. It should be overcome through mental control and practice.

"Whichever influence is causing this retraction response will be overcome soon, and we'll all help you do it. As we introduce ourselves, keep in mind that we intend no harm, and see if you can give something of yourself to the greeting. Imagine the atoms that make up your being reaching lovingly, joyously out toward this person you're greeting. This establishes electromolecular paths which will make it easier for us to communicate with you."

"Let's start with my Alpha mate, which brings me to another point, Jon. You'll find that we, in 2150, present ourselves to you, as opposed to being 'introduced' by a third party. We find it more honest, more clear, and simpler. Perhaps most importantly, it permits people to communicate at will anytime, anywhere, for any reason, without the cumbersome burden of archaic formalities. We just engage eyes, extend our hands, pronounce our names, and communicate our thoughts either telepathically or verbally."

As he said this he turned and gestured to the beautiful girl sitting next to him. Her sweet face broke into a smile that was reflected by the sparkle in her eyes.

She said, "I'm Bonnie. Welcome to our Alpha, Jon." Kneeling beside me, she took my left hand with hers while pressing her right hand warmly against my cheek. She was back in her chair before I had recovered; then she gestured to the handsome dark-eyed young giant sitting beside her.

As he approached I prepared to stand up, feeling self-conscious about the fact that I had not paid Bonnie this courtesy.

"Please don't stand, Jon. I'm Adam. You'll find we, in 2150, do not burden our lives with unnecessary social protocol to 'show respect' or to 'honor' one person above another. We each know our own value and presume mutual respect without formalities to proclaim it."

Lost for what to say, I played it safe and simply said, "Thank you," using my voice for the first time since I joined the circle. "You're very kind. Looks like I have a lot to learn." Gingerly I returned his gesture of affection.

Then Adam's Alpha mate, Nancy, was kneeling before me introducing herself while I yielded to the depths of her liquid brown eyes.

This was followed by meeting a smiling David, who possessed the shoulders of a Hercules, and his Alpha mate, Diana, whose body was the smallest, at six feet one, but in magnificent feminine proportions.

Then I met the Goliath of our Alpha, six-foot-nine-inch Steve, whose giant body was balanced by a face that radiated a paradox of mischief and patient kindness.

The last member was vivacious Joyce, with lovely green eyes and dark auburn hair which made me wish they wore their hair longer in 2150.

Perhaps the most striking physical qualities were their penetrating, all-knowing eyes, their short hair, their giant statures, which made me at six feet three the shortest male by two inches, and their remarkable physical beauty. Like idealized Greek statues, the women were lovely and the men were handsome. However, unlike the 20th century, where physical beauty was rare and sought after, no one here was self-conscious about his appearance. Carol had told me that they valued the beauty and power of the mind more than that of the body.

I remembered, however, that C.I. had stated that the body reflected the mind and the mind reflected the spirit. So I knew they would not ignore or take lightly their physical health and beauty.

I was surprised at how warmly and positively they responded to me and I to them. Overcoming my typical 1970s aversion to touching was coming along nicely, partly, I suspect, due to the fact that I honestly liked them all, and not with the usual superficial type of regard that I generally felt on first meetings back in the 20th century. It was surprising, but I felt a deep personal involvement with all of them. Somehow they radiated a quality of trust and positive regard that made it impossible for me to feel indifferent or defensive. I could relax with them, for they were my friends already—my very best of friends.

Someone entered the room, and I turned to find an absolutely perfect, beautifully sculptured man. I had thought of Greek statues of women, and here was one of a male, vibrantly alive. His tunic was a glistening white with the faintest suggestion of iridescent colors playfully showing here and there.

I wanted to burst with joy just looking at him and feeling his incredible strength, his power.

He took my hand and, placing his huge but gentle hand on my face said, "I feel your thought, Jon. And the joy is returned. It's so good to have you with us at last." He squeezed my hand affectionately. "Happy growing, Jon! We are one!" And was gone before I could respond.

"What happened? Where did he go? Who is he?" my questions almost tripped over one another.

"That was Eli, our *Ktar*. He, like other level tens, travels about on thought. He had to get back to what you think of as the planet Uranus, where he's been very busy helping clear up some problems in their magnetic field. This leaves him very little time to spend here on earth, but he did want very much to greet you and welcome you to 2150."

I groped mentally for a frame of reference into which I could fit what I had just heard.

"You mean that he just thinks himself from planet to planet?"

"That's right," Joyce answered. "Level tens spend a lot of time away from Earth helping others and growing. Evolved souls from other planets spend much time here helping us, too."

Alan suggested something that at first made me think I

had misunderstood, for it sounded like he had said, "Let's dance!"

His suggestion was immediately received with shouts of agreement. He took my hand and we ran after the others down the long living room.

What happened during the next fifteen or twenty minutes was almost unbelievable to me. Suddenly the great room was filled with the most exciting music I had ever heard.

Imagine strenuous folk dancing like a spirited polka or Offenbach's *Gaîté Parisienne* numbers, or the twirling dervishes combined with the Virginia reel, square dancing, gymnastic tumbling, and a relay race of sprinters at a track meet and you'll have only a part of what they call the Macro dance.

They leaped, they tumbled, they ran. They joined together, they separated, they joined, they twirled, they cartwheeled, they pyramided, and they helped me join in all of these and more until my heart pounded like a sledgehammer and my breath came in whistling gasps. Then we all threw off our tunics and ran naked out the door of our Alpha and down the halls to the giant swimming pool on our Beta floor.

We plunged laughing into a pool thirty yards wide and ninety yards long.

My unspoken question of why the pool was so large was soon answered as we were joined by the rest of our seventh triad Beta—90 more naked, laughing youths of 18, 19, or 20, who had just finished the Macro dance in their Alphas.

Again I was struck by their physical beauty, joy, and friendliness.

There was no shallow end to this pool so we all swam in the ten-foot-deep water either above or below the surface, since everyone seemed to be as at home in the water as a herd of sea lions.

Only a few minutes passed, however, before Carol told me it was time to leave. We climbed out of the pool and I suddenly realized that we were the only ones out of the water. As I turned to see if the other members of our Beta were going to join us I heard their voices shouting, "Welcome, Jon, welcome!"

A lean muscular giant with piercing dark eyes vaulted out of the water, took my hand in his, and touched my cheek firmly but gently. Immediately there was total silence. He was at least five inches taller and seventy pounds heavier than I in spite of being six years my junior. He looked long into my eyes, but this time I did not feel uncomfortable and returned his look with confidence and a powerful feeling of contentment.

"Welcome, Jon, to our 7th triad student Beta," he said in one of the deepest voices I had ever heard. "My name is Leo and I am the Betar of our floor. I speak for all when I say we are glad you have joined us."

"Thank you," I replied. Then raising my voice so all could hear, I called, "Thank you all for this wonderful welcome. You can see with your minds how happy I am to be here. No words can express my joy."

Then the rest of my Alpha was about me. We ran back to our rooms to put on fresh tunics, then met in the dining room for dinner.

It was a leisurely meal with lots of laughing and talking, and I had an opportunity to appreciate the remarkable intelligence, broad knowledge, and varied interests of my Alpha. I also had the opportunity to try some strange new foods that I found delicious, but I didn't ask what they were made of. Everyone cooperated, seeming to sense that I would enjoy the meal more if I was not forced to consider the content of the food I was eating.

Perhaps the most satisfying experience was their understanding and reassurances concerning my fears about my sanity back in 1976. I told them of my conversations with Karl and how we had set up our test of the reality of my experiences in 2150. They were unanimous in approving of this kind of test.

It was Alan who told me that the whole Macro society was aware of my time translation and very interested in whether or not I could learn to remain permanently in 2150.

Then Joyce, of the lovely green eyes and short auburn hair, said that while I was a world celebrity I would experience none of the invasions of privacy that 20th-century celebrities experienced. Since C.I. contained any and all information about me and the experiment of which I was a central part, anyone desiring knowledge concerning me or the experiment could simply ask C.I.

I told them that I appreciated this and added that I could get rich fast if I could offer this convenience to famous people back in 1976.

"There are dozens of questions we'd like to ask you, Jon, if you don't mind," Alan requested.

"Not at all," I replied. "And I'd like to ask all of you some questions, too."

Steve explained that while there were no taboo questions for them, they realized that in 1976 there were many subjects that people avoided because of their feelings of guilt associated with these subjects.

I thought about this for a moment and then said, "Feel free to ask me questions on any subject, no matter how uncomfortable it makes me. My reason for this is that I want to become a permanent member of your Macro society, so I'd better learn to be as aware of myself and as clear as you are."

For the next few minutes I was overwhelmed with questions about my life in the 20th century and my feelings toward my parents, my teachers, my government, and the many churches and religions. They were interested in my feelings about cultural, economic, racial, religious, language differences—all the things that divided micro man.

I felt no restraints in answering these questions and realized that, as yet, they had not asked anything that made me feel uncomfortable. Before they got around to that, David suggested that I be given a chance to ask them some questions.

I thanked him and began with general questions concerning their feelings about the Macro society. They were genuinely surprised that I should think their society over-regimented and restrictive. Alan seemed to summarize their answers in this area.

"In the Macro society we have more freedom to experience ourselves and the world about us than ever before in the history of man. As for repressive over-regimented societies, we have no policemen, no armed forces, and no government to pass silly laws that people want to break."

"What do you mean?" I asked.

"I mean," Alan replied, "that we don't have all those laws that almost everyone broke. Laws against alcoholic drinks, gambling, various sexual acts, and drugs, for examples. You people in 1976 had so many laws which were conflicting and confusing that your people had to hire lawyers to protect them from their own neighbors as well as from their own government. Consider the maze of laws that governed marriage, divorce, and taxes. Of course, these would not have been perpetuated if your lawyers had not had a vested interest in keeping them on the books."

"But you have to have laws or everything would be chaos," I replied.

"We have no laws, and we have no lawyers," responded Nancy, "and we don't have chaos."

"But you do have laws," I insisted. "You must have. How about stealing? What if I steal your belongings?"

They all laughed, and lovely little Diane, the smallest at six-feet one, said "Go ahead and take anything we have. All material possessions are free and we'll be glad to give you anything you want, so you can see that there is no need to steal."

"All right," I said, "but how about murder? You must have laws against that."

I thought I had them with that one, but Bonnie smiled revealing her charming facial imperfection—dimples. She said, "In your 20th century you had no laws against flying to the stars because no one believed it possible." She paused and seemed to overwhelm me with her intense blue eyes as she continued, "We in the 22nd century believe it is impossible for Macro man to murder anyone. There are no laws against it."

She so distracted me that I momentarily forgot about laws and asked whether the science of 2150 made it possible for people who were not yet level ten to visit other planets.

She explained that Macro man just used astral projection to explore the universe.

I was reminded of my astral body traveling to 2150 and then informed that some eighth and ninth levels and all tenth levels were able to use astral travel not only in our physical universe but in other dimensions beyond the fourth one of time. That was more than I could grasp, so I went back to laws.

"All right," I said, "how about your educational laws. All 18-, 19-, and 20-year-olds have to live in a 7th triad student Beta, and until you reach 30 you must live in a student Gamma. How about that?"

Again they laughed, and darkly handsome Adam said, "But no one forces us to live in a student Gamma. The Macro society is set up so that our needs for companionship, love, learning, exercise, recreation, and everything else are best served this way. We are free to leave any time we want to. But we are not masochists, so we seldom go against our own best interests."

Now Alan got up from our long dining table and said, "Because the Macro society lives according to the one Macro imperative—loving acceptance—we cooperate and, thus, conflict is impossible. However, we still have micro people living on Micro Island who dedicate their lives to amnesic forgetfulness of the Macro oneness of all. Only in this way of deliberately forgetting our Macro origin can we behave in micro selfish ways that damage others and ourselves.

"Well, then," I said, "you at least have laws against micro man, since you force them to stay on a prison island."

87

"Not at all," Alan replied. "It's only their lack of desire and belief that keeps them there. In fact, we maintain free training on the island for anyone who wants to remember his Macro origins and, thus, return to the Macro society. And we don't interfere with them in any way that would restrict or punish any of their activities on Micro Island. They are free to do anything they like as far as we are concerned. They stay pretty busy just passing laws and enforcing them so that they can survive selfishly and competitively."

I changed my tactics now and decided to ask a very personal question. "Did you vote for Alan as Alphar and Leo for Betar because you thought they would be the best leaders or because C.I. says they are level six and seven?"

My Carol had been allowing others to supply questions and answers for me, but now I looked directly at her for her response.

She glanced at the others and obviously decided she had their permission to speak for them, for she said, "We voted for Alan and Leo because as long as we have known them, since our first and second triads, they have demonstrated superior Macro qualities. C.I. only reflects what we already know. No one can possibly fool anyone else about his level of awareness because our tunic colors make no mistakes. C.I. only formally confirms what our tunics have already told us."

"I see," I responded, switching ground. "Well, how about jealousy? What if you have sex with someone else's Alpha mate?"

Once again I heard their amused laughter as giant Steve answered for the group. "Sexual relations must have been one of micro man's most exciting and challenging diversions. The popular 'Eleven p.m. Syndrome'—waiting for the late hour to bring enough drowsiness for soft music and quiet talk to lower a woman's resistance so you can conquer her taboos—isn't needed here in 2150. We have no taboos, no hidden dark areas, and, thus, no desire to use others as possessions for our own selfish micro purposes."

"Are you saying you wouldn't be jealous if Adam or David began having sex with your Joyce?"

Steve smiled a kind and patient smile, "First of all, she is by no means *my* Joyce. She is her own Joyce. Secondly, it would be surprising if Adam or David wanted a sexual relationship with Joyce, since it would be totally out of character with their lifestyles. But I couldn't be jealous because if it made them happy it would make me happy, too. If it did *not* make them happy, they would have learned a valuable lesson and we would all rejoice in their new growth."

"But why would you be surprised?" I asked, not understanding this part at all.

"He'd be surprised," Joyce answered, "because by the 7th triad we are focusing on greater-depth dyadic relationships with our Alpha mates. We've explored polyadic sexual relationships from the first through the 5th triads, and by the 7th triad, we are no longer interested in childish activities. Not because they are bad or wicked, but because we've simply outgrown them."

"You've outgrown being sexually attracted to each other?" I asked incredulously.

"Oh, never!" They laughed, then Joyce explained with the analogy that admiring a painting or statue was very different from wanting to take it home, hide it away where no one else could see it, and keep it all to yourself.

I was thinking that her analogy didn't do much for me when Diane said that they realized I had not had their early triad experiences and so, of course, any of the girls in my Alpha or Beta would help me with whatever sexual problems I might have.

I was stunned. "Are you telling me that any girl on this floor would be willing to have sex with me?"

"That's right," Carol replied. "If you approach someone in 2150 who doesn't feel it's in the best interest of both of you for you to spend time together, she'll just say, 'Thank you. I care, but I don't feel we're harmonic.'

89

However, there is no girl in the whole Gamma or even Delta who would refuse you, so it won't be fear of rejection that will stop you. And, I assure you, neither Lea nor I will be jealous."

I shook my head, trying to clear its conflicting thoughts and feelings; then I said that with all my sexual frustrations and guilts they would be taking an awful chance with me. They might feel like they were being raped.

But rape was impossible in the Macro society, Bonnie said, since no one would resist and, since Macro beings could not enjoy the micro use of sex, the Macro society would not satisfy micro man's twisted sexual needs.

"It's incredible," she observed, "how often during the 20th century blackmail and political scandals could have as their focal point some person's sexual behavior. Your ridiculous social sanctions against homosexuality and extramarital sex did far more to encourage these behavioral patterns than to extinguish them."

"Do you mean that you people don't object to homosexuality—a man making love with a man, or a woman with a woman?" I asked incredulously.

"Of course not. You will find, however, that there is a much lower incidence of homosexuality here in 2150 because of a few factors.

"First, we have eliminated the social situations that often caused homosexuality—like loneliness, unfulfilled needs, pernicious social myths which tell you that if you enjoy the touch of someone of the same sex, then you must be homosexual.

"Second, when a soul incarnates into the physical body of one sex while still carrying with it emotional, spiritual, or mental selves that are overwhelmingly the opposite sex, you must, naturally, expect expression of the predominant sex. This is neither abnormal nor undesirable. It is true, natural, and logical.

Third, as we evolve to higher levels of awareness, the masculine and feminine forces within us become more perfectly balanced till we ultimately reach a point where we are once again emotionally, spiritually, and mentally androgynous. Your micro society, in its isolationist ignorance, would call this state of total 'at-one-ness' sick."

"I don't know much about androgynism, but homosexuality *is* sick isn't it?" I questioned.

Steve explained, "In some cases, yes. In some, no. Just like heterosexuality which is, in some cases, what you would call very sick and, in some cases, not. As with all else, it depends totally on the motivation."

We talked some more about the problems of our micro society and their Macro society's solutions to these problems. Then Alan said he must leave to visit his Personal Evolution tutor. Carol looked at her mib and said it was time for some Macro counselling, popularly called Personal Evolution tutoring.

We said our goodbyes and everyone left the Alpha together in pursuit of his or her tutor.

I asked Carol about Personal Evolution tutoring. C.I. had told me that P.E. tutoring was the core of formal education in the Macro society, but it hadn't meant much to me.

Carol explained that P.E. tutoring was a learning relationship between a tutor, with a larger viewpoint or life perspective, and a student with a smaller perspective who wanted to learn a larger one. While all triads had P.E. tutors beginning with the 7th triad, and continuing through the 10th, students are assigned to the wisest tutors in the Macro society who had a minimum of 7th-level awareness. This meant that most of these tutors were beyond the age of 50.

The eleventh and twelfth floors of the student Gamma building were devoted to comfortable tutoring rooms large enough to accommodate both individual and group work. There were also exercise rooms and an auditorium big enough to hold the entire Gamma.

We arrived at our Personal Evolution tutoring room after walking through multicolored halls with gleaming white doors.

Carol reached out to open a door, but before she touched the button the door slid quietly open. We entered

91

a room with a carpet-like floor of deep blue which contrasted with the soft yellow walls and the three large forest green chairs. The room was at least twenty-five feet square and seemed huge with just the three chairs and no other furniture.

One of the chairs was occupied by the smallest woman I had seen in 2150.

As we walked toward her she rose from her chair and stretched out her arms to us. Carol immediately slipped into her arms and they gave each other a silent embrace. Then, as Carol stepped back, I realized that our tutor was even shorter than I had first thought, being no taller than five feet ten at best.

As she stepped forward and took my hand, I became aware of her age. Her face and body were those of a very healthy and extremely attractive woman in her mid forties, but somehow her pale blue eyes gave me a feeling that she was much older.

She touched my face and said, "Welcome, Jon, to the Macro society. I'm Rana and I'll answer your question by saying that I have inhabited this body for 125 years."

As I was trying to adjust to this fact Carol said, "And to answer your question about how the door opened by itself, you were experiencing Rana's demonstration of psychokinesis (PK), preceded by telepathy."

Rana's tunic was the same gleaming white as Eli's. Level tens were so highly evolved that their tunics reflected a perfectly equal balance of all colors, resulting in the illusion of no color at all.

I felt awed when I remembered there were only 127 level tens in the whole Macro society at present, and I wondered if I was getting some special treatment.

Rana smiled at me and said, "No . . . no special treatment. I was Carol's tutor long before you arrived, and since you are Alpha mates you can choose me as your tutor or ask for someone else."

"I . . . I guess I'd probably choose you," I stammered.

"Then let's sit down, and get growing!" she responded cheerfully.

We sat down in the soft body-contoured chairs and I began wondering what would be expected of me.

Carol came to my rescue when she asked Rana if she could see into the future and tell us how long it would be before I could become a permanent member of the Macro society.

Rana looked intently at Carol for a moment and then shifted her intense gaze to me. Finally she said, "I'm having difficulty with the future for Jon because it seems there is a very important decision that he must make which will completely determine the rest of his life. This decision will be his choice between the micro life of 1976 and the Macro life of 2150."

"I've already made that choice," I insisted. "I've chosen the Macro life of 2150."

Rana looked at me and I felt her tremendous strength of patience, understanding, and courage. I suddenly realized that from the moment I had entered the room I had been mentally and physically bombarded by the power of her being. As I write this I feel frustrated that I cannot find words to describe her. Perhaps an electrical essence stimulated me in so many ways that I felt overwhelmed. It was Carol who broke the silence.

"You don't think he's totally really made the choice yet," she said to Rana.

Rana looked at Carol and then back to me before she said, "I think that Jon has not had time to really take inventory of himself. He feels confused and in great awe and tends to see us as being too impossibly perfect for him to become one of us."

As I thought about what she had just said I realized that she was right. I did feel that everyone I had met so far in 2150 was impossibly perfect compared to me. In fact, I could see no weaknesses and no imperfections. I nodded my head in sad agreement with Rana.

"You're right," I said, "I feel like a first-grade kid who finds himself accidentally in seventh grade. The lessons look impossible. My fellow students must look down

93

on me, because, while they're years younger than I am, they're miles ahead of me in their evolution."

"Oh, Jon, it isn't true," Carol said in an imploring tone. "We all love you and accept you as you are. We don't judge you any more than we judge each other. We're all of equal value and we all have to be first level before we can evolve to second, third, or beyond."

When I didn't say anything to this, Rana said, "You see, Carol, Jon feels you're patronizing him. He doesn't want to be accepted as a midget among giants. He wants to become a giant, but doesn't think it's possible."

"How could it be possible? Your educational system provides a totally stimulating, loving, accepting, perfect environment for developing Macro man. I, on the other hand, have spent twenty-seven years learning how to be a micro man."

I paused, realizing the enormity of what I was saying. I was admitting to myself the impossibility of ever being equal in awareness to my Alpha mate or to any of the other Alpha members, much less Lea.

Coming from my little fantasy of a permanent translation to 2150, to the harsh reality that it was totally impossible drained every ounce of energy from me. My body ached with its own weight. My throat hurt. Suddenly my face was wet with tears. I could see Carol and Rana only dimly.

Rana was saying, "Whenever you really ask for help, and not just pity, you will always receive it."

But I was tired, very tired.

CHAPTER 7:

The Unlimited Self

The smell of bacon cooking; the click of our pop-up toaster; snow piled against the windowsill. A very ordinary morning. So why did I feel so depressed and miserable?

Then I remembered, and wished I hadn't.

For a few moments I struggled desperately to blot from my memory the conversations with Rana. Failing this, I replayed it a couple of times trying to find some flaw in my argument of futility, in my feeling of impossible inadequacy.

I kept remembering the Macro society's educational system and comparing it with my own early years. I remembered the incredible vitality, joy, beauty, intelligence, superhuman awareness, love, understanding, kindness and patience that had been demonstrated by my Alpha . . . and I was seven years older than their oldest!

Lea made a mistake, I thought. She should have created for me the body of a newborn baby. Then I could have started out in the first triad and eighteen years later be on an equal footing with others in the 7th triad. How could she have made such a mistake and still have demonstrated 9th-level awareness? And what was it Rana said just before I lost consciousness? Something about asking for help—that whenever I really wanted help, and not just pity, I would always receive it.

Obviously Rana, at the highest level of awareness in the Macro society, was trying to tell me that it wasn't impossible.

Could she and Lea be so wrong? Was I only asking for pity? If there is no hope, pity is all you can ask for! But how could I have hope? They were so perfect—I was imperfect, and never the twain shall meet.

I began laughing softly to myself at the ridiculous nature of my predicament. I was a perfect example of micro man who sees himself as limited, inadequate, and doomed to ultimate failure.

I searched my mind for hope, a way out.

One of the greatest Personal Evolution tutors of all time said, "Ask and you shall receive, seek and you shall find, knock and the door shall be opened."

He couldn't have put it much stronger. And, of course, he also said, "If you have faith the size of a mustard seed you can move mountains."

That's all right for Macro giants, I thought, but how the devil do micro midgets like myself ever get up enough faith to even ask, much less move mountains?

But . . . if I want help—really want help—how could I have selected a better environment than the Macro society? Obviously they knew and understood far more than I did. Maybe they even knew how to help me become a giant, too, so I could live with them on an equal basis . . . maybe.

My thoughts were interrupted by Karl insisting that I get up and join him for breakfast.

I looked at the clock and saw that it was almost eight-thirty. "Hey, Karl!" I called. "How come you're not in class this morning?"

His fuzzy black hair preceded his face around the doorway—he always wore it natural. "You've really lost track of it all with your shuffling back and forth 174 years every night. It's Sunday here in 1976, and if you try real hard you'll remember that this micro roommate inhabiting this micro society doesn't work on Sunday— he just goofs off all day."

"Okay, okay," I said. "You'll find me very humble this morning. I've been dreaming about just how micro I really am. I'll be right with you."

A few minutes later I was sitting across from Karl at the breakfast table telling him about my latest experiences in 2150. Somehow as I talked to Karl my depression lifted and I became hopeful again.

It was a long breakfast because I seemed to have an awful lot to say and Karl seemed to have even more than his usual number of questions. He was particularly interested in the other members of my Alpha and in my description of Rana. He kept asking me for more detailed descriptions and I began to realize that after I had used up all my personality superlatives I didn't have much more to say about them.

Finally Karl said, "You know, Jon, it seems to me that you're describing gods and goddesses, and not the ancient Greek or Roman variety, either, because they all had their share of weaknesses or imperfections. Not so with these you describe. Tell me, are these people really that perfect, or are you just demonstrating your lack of Macro awareness?"

"You're right, Karl," I admitted. "That's my problem. They appear so perfect, so superhuman that I can't see how I could ever be like them. And I can't imagine how I could be happy for very long being a midget among giants for the rest of my life, either.

"In other words, Jon, you've found the snake in your garden of Eden . . . and it's you!"

"Well," I said reluctantly, "I hadn't thought of it quite that way, but I guess you're right. It was the poison of

97

my own self-doubt that made me want to run away from 2150 and its impossible challenges."

"Are you saying that you're ready to give up your dream world?" Karl asked.

I realized that I wanted to avoid the question. I didn't want to have to answer it. I said, "I don't know how to answer you right now. All I really want to do is get drunk and forget the whole problem."

"You what!" Karl's face was lined with concern. "Is it that bad, Jon?"

Karl knew that I had only been drunk once in my life, back in Vietnam. "No, not really, Karl. Nothing is that bad except living in a world where killing women, old folks, and children is a patriotic duty. No, I'm not going to get drunk. I'm going to write it all down. Maybe that will help clear my mind. Then I'm going to do a lot of thinking."

For the rest of the day Karl left me to myself while I wrote in my journal and did a lot of very hard thinking.

By late evening I had a much better realization of the strength of my micro self, which sounded like a drum beating out the refrain, "I can't, I can't, I can't."

These old habitual limiting thought patterns were so easy to disguise, to ignore, or to rationalize away. And yet, in moments of crisis, micro man (myself) must reap the consequences of his limiting beliefs—failure.

Strangely, however, my long struggle to confront myself honestly left me feeling hopeful. Again I was joyfully looking forward to returning to the Macro society of the future. I had again discovered that if I was honest with myself, and refused to run away from a difficult self-confrontation, I would sooner or later see a balanced picture in which there was both light and dark. It's not easy to see both sides of a coin from a micro, one-sided view.

Just before I went to bed, Karl finished reading my journal and, without saying a word, walked over to me. Tears glazed his eyes, which shocked me, knowing how Karl hated sentimental weakness, which included masculine tears. Then, obviously too caught up with feeling to speak, he took my left hand with his, hesitated a moment, then put his right hand gently on my face.

Before I could collect myself, Karl was noisily running the water in the bathroom with a closed door between us. I thought again how difficult it was in our micro society to deal openly and honestly with our thoughts and emotions. We were taught to be ashamed of such large portions of our minds that we devoted whole lifetimes to denying them, thus depriving ourselves of some of the greatest joys available to man.

Later, as I was drifting off to sleep, I heard Karl call across our darkened room to me. "Good luck," he said. Then after a pause, "I believe in you, Jon."

I murmured my thanks and decided that the hardest thing for micro man to do was to believe in himself. But then, how can anyone believe in himself when there is so much of himself that he condemns?

My last thoughts before dropping off to sleep involved a conclusion that before I could ask for help, I had to believe that success was possible. That meant I had to accept and believe in myself as unlimited except by my own thoughts.

CHAPTER 8:

Macro Contact

I awakened again in 2150 with the wetness of tears still on my face and the sound of Rana's voice saying, "He's returning."

Opening my eyes I surprised a look of worry and concern on Carol's face. But, turning my gaze to Rana, I found again the wondrously serene and confident expression that was oddly at variance with the almost electrical excitement or joy that seemed to radiate from her. Now her eyes became even more brilliant as she smiled at me.

"There, you see," she said, "you've already discovered that at least your Alpha mate isn't perfect. She's demonstrating concern and worry, which are always a reflection of something less than total Macro awareness."

I reached over and touched Carol's face as Rana continued, "You're learning some of our customs very quickly. It won't be long now before you'll be seeing occasional imperfections in the rest of your Alpha members."

"Will I ever be able to see them in you?" I asked.

She laughed and said, "You won't see me looking worried or becoming upset over any of the problems you're struggling with right now. However, until I am totally macrocosmically aware, there will always be greater lessons for me to learn."

"You mean," I said, "that there are problems that bother even you?"

"That which is a problem to the child with one year is no longer a problem when that child has had three years," she answered. "Yet the three-year level has its own problems, most of which are not even perceived by the child with just one year. And so it goes, with level-seven problems not apparent to a level three. Be assured, though, that every level has its challenges. Seen as problems, they become increasingly more complex, more difficult. Seen as elected opportunities for growth, they are a joy to solve, to deal with effectively, to grow from in this game of life."

"But it eventually all ends when one attains total Macro awareness?" I asked.

She laughed. "Total Macro awareness is the experience of all problems, all sorrows, all frustrations, all pain, all ignorance, all ugliness, all disease, and all other negativities in all times and in all places. Now, that's hell to anyone who isn't completely Macro. But from a state of absolute Macro awareness it's completely balanced by all the positive qualities that ever were or ever will be, and that's perfection, which is the opposite of a frustrating, dull, and fruitless micro existence."

"All right," I said, "I'll take your word for it. How can I, at my very limited micro level, learn to grow as fast as possible?"

"We learn by doing, by taking risks, by failing, and, only then, by succeeding," she said. "We grow from our mistakes and from our failures. If we cannot see that failure is the essential other half of success, then we try to avoid failure and, in so doing, we avoid success."

"Then I guess I should get as deeply involved with everyone as I possibly can, which means taking lots of risks and having lots of failures." I shuddered. "Sounds pretty frightening."

"There is really only one fear," she said, "and that is the fear of failure, which is the same as feeling inadequate to do whatever you want to do."

"But you must look to your unlimited self for help," Carol said. "Then you can see the larger perspective in which failure and success are one."

Considering this, I responded thoughtfully, "To turn to my unlimited self, by 1976 definitions, would be to turn to God. That would mean prayer, which I never could really get into."

"It's no wonder, Jon. Prayer, as consciously used in your time, was actually an intense pleading for something that the person actually felt he didn't deserve to have, or was afraid he would not get. Since our predominant thoughts materialize to become our reality, people usually don't get what they consciously pray for because their predominant thought is that they don't and won't have it!

"From another point of view, however, every thought we think is a prayer, since, once thought, it is a permanent part of the universe and addresses the macrocosmic whole. All prayer," Rana continued, "indeed, all thought, expresses desire for something.

"Call it prayer or call it thought. It's all the same, and it's the tool with which we create all that we experience.

"Since your mind is an indivisible part of all mind, your desires are all-powerful. You will receive whatever you desire and 'believe' you will receive. However, if you desire to run away from the light, from Macro awareness, into the darkness of amnesia, which is micro awareness, then you will receive that request also. So you see, Jon, prayer—as seen from a broader perspective—

works. Prayers are constantly and unfailingly answered. We just don't always like the answer!"

"In other words," I said, "since our minds are all-powerful, our problem is to learn how to use them positively rather than negatively."

"Not quite, Jon," Rana answered. "You can't have positive without negative any more than you can have up without down, or success without failure. Thus, the problem is to learn to use our minds with perfect balance —that is, with total acceptance of everything—both success and failure, knowing that every failure leads to success."

"And how do you do that?" I asked.

"Every lesson to be learned," Rana explained, "requires mistakes or failures. This varies with each person in terms of his past learning in all his incarnations and excarnations and multidimensional experiences."

Seeing my puzzled expression, she added, "This is because no experience is ever forgotten by the soul mind or subconscious mind. It is all cumulative. Thus, if for one child it takes 10,000 failures to learn to walk, the sooner he makes those failures the sooner he learns to walk. Since micro man does not understand this cumulative effect, he becomes easily discouraged and often thinks he is as far, or even further, from solving the problem after 9,999 failures as he was at the end of ten."

"But, of course, this is not true," Carol injected, "because at the end of 9,999 failures he has only one more to go to have complete insight and success."

"But I thought you said that every failure is a success?" I queried. "Yet you mention the 9,999 failures and not the 9,999 successes. How come?"

"Because," replied Rana, "micro man is not worried by successes, only by failures. Since he is not aware of the cumulative effect, he doesn't realize that every failure is a necessary and successful step toward complete insight. In other words, each failure is a small insight-success bringing one that much closer to total insight-success."

103

"Hmm, I'll think about that," I said. "But how do I specifically go about learning or developing my Macro powers?"

Rana answered, "You don't start out to develop Macro powers—you start out to develop Macro awareness. The powers develop as the awareness increases."

"However," Carol added, "you need to remember that there are two necessary factors in all learning: sufficient desire and sufficient belief."

"One example," Rana said, "is when a person desires to learn to swim but does not believe he can learn without drowning. He, obviously, will not learn to swim as he lacks the necessary belief."

"Or the opposite," Carol continued, "when he believes he could successfully learn to swim but would rather play tennis. Now he lacks the necessary desire, and, again, he will not learn to swim."

"Thus," Rana added, "with both sufficient desire and sufficient belief, anything is possible."

"That seems simple enough." I said.

They both laughed, and Rana said, "It is simple, Jon, because you grew—you expanded your perspective—took a broader point of view. The universe and its functions are all very basic and incredibly simple. It's man's limited perspective that makes them look complicated. BUT! It's in the doing that one learns, not just in the talking about it.

"So why don't you go back to your Alpha and desire growth, and accept all that you experience as an opportunity chosen to offer that growth." She smiled gently as she added, "When one has already successfully transcended 174 years and acquired a new body, it should be difficult indeed to doubt anything—least of all future successes!"

During the next few minutes before we left, Carol and Rana talked of incomprehensible things while my mind was feverishly occupied with trying to understand all that Rana had said.

Carol touched my shoulder, and we all walked to the

door in silence. As we reached the threshold I took Rana's hand and touched her face gently in appreciation. Then we left with the memory of Rana's electric eyes stirring something very deep within my mind.

As we returned to our Alpha I asked Carol why Rana chose to appear middle-aged since, I assumed, she had the mind power to mold her body into any form. Carol replied that when she had asked Rana the same question, the answer she had received was but one word— *variety*.

Back in our Alpha room Carol explained that while the evening hours were devoted to Macro tutoring, the last hour before sleep was devoted to Macro contact. She explained this as a letting go of all micro identity and experiencing the awareness of total macrocosmic oneness.

After a relaxing bath we lay naked on our bed, and Carol asked C.I. to provide Macro contact stimuli. The video screen was immediately filled with ever-expanding and evolving geometric patterns. The room was filled with soothing resonant sounds that seemed to cause my whole mind and body to resonate in similarly evolving and enlarging patterns.

At first I was leery and tried to resist the strange sensations caused by the incredible visual and audible stimuli. But Carol kept murmuring, "Desire and believe . . . experience and accept . . . let go, and let's grow!" Finally I gave up all resistance and found myself flowing on a gentle river of multiple sensations until I seemed to enter an infinite ocean of unspeakable unity, oneness, and balance accompanied by the most soul-satisfying feeling of harmony imaginable.

When I returned to what I thought was my normal limited awareness, I heard Carol saying that it was morning and that I had experienced my first Macro contact. I turned to look at her beautiful naked form beside me and realized that her eyes were closed and that she was lying quietly as if still asleep.

I wondered if she had really spoken and suddenly,

105

without moving her lips, I heard her voice saying, "Good morning, Jon. You're experiencing your new Macro power of telepathy."

"My God!" I said aloud. "I must be dreaming."

A merry peal of laughter came from a Carol who was obviously very much awake and suddenly rolling happily about in my arms.

"You're not dreaming," she said with her lips this time pressed against mine. "You're just beginning to experience your Macro powers. Now push the top button so we can experience the morning light."

I started to rise, but she refused to release me saying, "Do it with your mind, Jon, not your body."

"How?" I wondered.

The answer came, "Reach out with an imaginary finger and touch the button."

I did this and the light came pouring in on us.

"There, you see," Carol glowed, "your first demonstration of psychokinesis. Now, push it again."

I did and once again the room was in darkness.

"It's true!" I said, pushing the button again to let the morning light back in. "I can do it! But how?"

"Did you ever experience Macro contact before?" Carol asked rhetorically, then added, "Well, that's what happened. You'll never be so limited again."

"You mean that because I was able to let go of my micro identity last night I can now experience the beginning of Macro power?"

"Yes," Carol replied. "While everyone experiences Macro contact, the micro person, suffering from self-imposed isolation from the rest of the macrocosm, does not consciously remember these experiences and, thus, cannot profit much from them. You have chosen to remember your oneness and, thus, your Macro contact. To the extent that you can remember your contact with your Macro origin you will have Macro awareness and all the powers that go with it."

"I feel like a giant!" I said and covered her with kisses that soon led to a complete joining of our bodies. Then

I heard Carol's voice ask C.I. to again provide our individual soul notes. The same notes that had resonated through our room last night as we prepared for our Macro contact once again filled our room.

"What was that you asked for? Our individual soul notes?" I inquired as they faded away at the sound of my voice.

"Yes," she responded. "Each soul has a unique vibration. Yours and Lea's are exactly the same. Mine is very similar to yours. That's one of the reasons I was selected to be your first Alpha mate. C.I. knows each person's soul note, or vibration, and, by playing both of ours together, can help us attain complete immersion in each other and our oneness with all that is, was, or ever will be."

"Is that the same as Macro contact?"

"No," was her answer. "Macro contact is achieved through total merging of minds, not just bodies.

"Sex, used with a Macro motive, can help us attain Macro immersion, merging with each other, or Macro contact, merging with the macrocosm. Use it with a micro motive and you have all the micro divisions and misery that micro sex can cause."

"Then sex is neither micro nor Macro?" I asked.

"It depends on your motive," Carol answered. "Sex is a part of the natural rhythm of the macrocosm like everything else. It has many very positive functions for people of all ages. Used to relax, to relieve tension, to express love, or just for fun, it enriches life. Used to control, coerce, abuse, or used against the wishes of either participant, it results in negative vibrations which can be extremely hard to balance.

"Whether sex, like any other thought or act, is more Macro than micro is determined by one's motivation in that time and space."

Then Carol asked C.I. to supply Macro stimuli. Our room was once again filled with exciting resonances. This time one glorious note was repeated over and over in an evolving pattern until my body and mind vibrated as one

107

in exquisite joy that kept mounting in intensity until again I experienced myself as a mighty river. This time, however, I experienced the river as being two great rivers that had united to make one. While we did not join the infinite ocean I find that I still have great difficulty selecting words to describe this exhilarating experience.

When our rivers crested into one huge, tumultuous wave I held her tightly and moaned ecstatically as Carol cried out. The sound of our soul notes gently receded in volume and intensity until the room was at last silent once more.

As we lay peacefully joined together, I began to realize that I would never again desire less than a Macro sexual union. I heard Carol say in my mind that I would probably now limit myself to only those whose soul vibration was almost or totally identical to mine. All other unions would be hollow imitations of the real thing.

"But how many females would that include?" I asked.

"Out of all people in the Macro society, approximately a thousand could achieve Macro contact with you.

"Here in our Delta, which has 5,000 females, there is Lea, one of your twin souls whose vibrations are identical to your own, myself, seven other females, and two males whose soul notes are similar enough to attain Macro contact with you."

"Two men?" My mind boggled at the prospect of what I would/should do in this 2150 culture if I met a man who made me feel the way Carol and Lea do.

"Of course, Jon. You know that we can incarnate as either male or female. That doesn't change our soul vibration.

"C.I. carefully determines its Alpha mate recommendations on the basis of soul note similarity. The final decision is then left to the parties involved.

"You'll know a soulmate or a twin soul by the harmonious vibrations. However, it is only with your twin souls that you will experience perfect harmonic balance at all times."

"Don't you have a twin soul here?" I queried.

Carol smiled and said, "Don't worry. You aren't depriving me of a twin soul. In fact, it's extremely rare that twin souls incarnate at the same time and place. They usually decide that they can learn faster in this dimension when they are separate. It tends to spur them on to greater learning efforts so they can be reunited sooner."

I wondered why Lea, my own twin soul, had brought me to her own time and whether, perhaps, what Carol had said didn't apply to us.

"Of course it applies to you," she responded. "You came together because your learning could be accelerated faster this way than any other way. You've met her and know that you cannot become her Alpha mate until you finish your Macro society education. To completely sever your mind-body connection with 1976 you must demonstrate third-level awareness, and you must do this within three months of your 1976 time."

"Three months! That's impossible!"

"We hope not," Carol responded. "But you'll have to work very hard, and it must be completed within the three-month time period."

"Why?" I demanded. "And why didn't someone tell me this before?"

"The answer to your second question," Carol replied, "is that you would have thought it completely impossible before your first Macro contact. The answer to why only three months is that it takes great energy on Lea's part to not only bring you here but to keep you here. Last night was the first rest she has gotten during your stay here. As long as you were in Macro contact you were free of all time-space restrictions, and, therefore, needed no help in maintaining your time-space translation."

"You mean that if I can ever demonstrate third-level awareness, then I can help her keep me here?"

"That's right, and C.I. has calculated that Lea can only transcend the time-space barriers without your help for three months."

"My God! What an assignment. What if I can't make

109

third level in three months, what happens then?" I asked.

"You return to your time period for the rest of your present incarnation. Lea will have used up all her present incarnation's life energy possible without becoming discarnate—dead—as would be the case if she tried to continue transcending time-space barriers by herself, or if she tried to re-establish contact later."

"But couldn't some of the other level nines, or even tens, help her?" I asked.

"They are helping her," Carol replied. "Every level nine and ten who is incarnate on this planet or any of our neighboring planets is helping—and quite a few discarnates too. However, no one but a twin soul can supply the final link energy, and as long as you are incarnate, this is limited. You've got three months in which to demonstrate third-level awareness—that's all."

"I'm glad I didn't find out about this sooner," I said. "While my initial response was outrage at the impossibility of the task before me, I realize that after what happened this morning, nothing is impossible."

"Now you know why we brought you here," Carol said. "We feel that nothing is impossible."

She glanced at her mib and said that we had fifteen minutes, translating from metric time, before joining the rest of the Alpha for breakfast.

We bathed and dressed and were in our Alpha dining room just as the rest of our Alpha was beginning to eat. They looked up as we entered and without speaking said, "Welcome, Jon, to the Macro powers."

As we ate breakfast I asked Carol how the others had known about my Macro powers demonstration. She suggested that I ask them, but before I could voice this question, I found eight pairs of eyes looking at me and a message ringing in my mind: "We are all in telepathic contact, and now you've really joined us."

Then they reassured me that they would do all in their power in helping prepare me to demonstrate level-three awareness within three months. We talked about ways in which my awareness growth could be accelerated by

110

increasing the number and frequency of learning experiences. This led to a discussion of how the normal 7th-triad experiences could be broadened to include more opportunities for experiencing Macro contacts. Alan explained some of the requirements for transcending the micro world.

He began by saying that since the two factors in all learning, desire and belief, are developed by cumulative failure-success experiences, obviously the more of these I could have, the faster I would learn. However, the problem with Macro contact for beginning students was that the experience was so pleasant that it tended to make them want to hold onto it in order to escape unpleasant micro experiences. This would immediately end the upper-level contacts, because they are made possible through joyous pursuit of learning experiences and their consequences, not retreat from them. They all admitted their own Macro contacts had been extremely limited, since this ultimate experience requires total acceptance of everything which, obviously, not only includes all the positive experiences but all the negative ones as well.

At this point Carol said that our recent Macro contact was only the fifth time in her life that she had attained this level, although she had attempted it every day since she first entered the 2nd triad at the age of three. Alan said that while he had demonstrated 6th-level awareness and attained Macro contact more times than anyone else in our Alpha, this was only ten times.

The problem was desire and not belief. Since they had all experienced Macro contact at least once, they no longer doubted it was possible. However, their desire tended to be limited and selective rather than the necessary all-accepting. Paradoxically, then, the more often they attained Macro contact, the more difficult the next contact became. The less one's awareness the more one tends to grab, to cling, to attempt the impossible feat of holding on to—holding constant—a part of the macro-cosm. It sometimes takes a tremendous number of little failures to lead to one great success.

"Well, then," I said, "if it takes a thousand failure-successes to reach level three awareness and I currently have only five hundred, the solution is to experience five hundred more failure-successes—and fast."

"Exactly," she said, "but it's a thousand *degrees* of failure-success which means that one huge failure-success may equal a hundred small ones."

"That gives me a fighting chance. I don't think I'd have time for five hundred little failures in three months. But, I can keep hoping until the very end for one monumental failure that will completely fill my quota."

They laughed and told me that a sense of humor was always a sign of expanded awareness. Then Alan said that they usually spent their mornings at the C.I. center or in their rooms using C.I. as a learning machine. The afternoons were spent playing learning games with the other triads, and the evenings were spent with their Personal Evolution tutors.

This daily schedule, I learned, was not inflexible but broadly applied to all triad levels. The older triads, however, particularly the eighth, ninth, and tenth, spent more time with the younger triads—especially the first and second. They felt the early years were crucial ones, for they contained the greatest number of critical learning experiences or developmental lessons.

Steve used the analogy that the taller the building the stronger its foundation has to be. Thus, once the foundation is laid, the maximum limits for a building's size are established by the strength of its foundation.

Joyce continued, pointing out that micro souls chose micro families to be born into and receive early micro learning experiences which severely limit the rest of their life's learning. Thus, there is literally no hope for micro man from a micro view. Only the Macro view, which includes joyous acceptance of total responsibility for all that exists within our lives, offers ultimate success and hope.

After breakfast Carol suggested that we walk to the C.I. center, where we could obtain separate rooms in order to work on separate problems. As we left our Gamma I noticed that again the weather was beautiful and remembered that C.I. had told me that it was controlled. I began wondering when it rained or snowed and realized that I knew very little about our geographic location or, for that matter, the new world geography of 2150. There were just so many questions to ask and so many things to learn. I envied Carol having grown up in the Macro society and having used C.I. for so many years.

We arrived at the C.I. center, and I went again to the room overlooking the lake while Carol chose an adjoining room. For the next four hours I forgot everything else in my enthusiastic questioning of C.I. over as broad an area as possible. I began with geography and discovered that one of the reasons the world maps of 2150 had changed so greatly was the shifting of the poles.

According to C.I., micro man's interference in the ecological and geological balances of the world had caused such tremendous chain reaction pressure build-ups that great land masses had sunk into the oceans and vast areas previously below water had risen. As a consequence the north and south poles had shifted, producing vast climatic changes. Delta 927, in which I was living, was located in what was formerly northern Canada and the climate was semi-tropical although controlled temperature limits were between sixty degrees Fahrenheit at night and a maximum of eighty during the day.

Lea had been right when she said I would not recognize a world map of 2150. Every continent was drastically changed and there were two new continents, or subcontinents, as large as Australia, in the North Atlantic and South Pacific oceans. Since all of these great Earth changes had taken place by the early part of the 21st century, I could understand how the earth's population had shrunk so drastically to only a little over three hundred million by 2150.

As a social psychologist, however, the bulk of my questions were in the social areas. I was fascinated that

113

there were no businesses as I knew them in 1976. Since the Macro society valued expanded mental awareness so highly, the vast array of material artifacts, such as several hundred different brands of soap, toilet paper, toothpaste, or pet foods, were nonexistent. (Concerning the latter, I'll digress just enough to mention that there were no pets, since Macro man lives in harmony with all animals and, thus, keeps none of them in domestic bondage for food, protection, or friendship.) Without a wastefully polluting competitive economy there was no need for salesmen or advertisements. And since all factories were run by servo-mechanisms, there were no worker-manager divisions, and, thus, no labor unions.

Because there were no laws requiring litigation, there were no lawyers or courts of law. Because there were no illnesses that could not be controlled by Macro mind powers, there were no doctors and no hospitals. Because there was universal agreement in the Macro society on the values of love and cooperation, there were no vast governmental bureaucracies.

The thought of no government was incomprehensible until I realized that the governmental functions of a micro society would obviously not be needed in the Macro society. There were no police or armed forces because there were no micro divisions or inequities. There was no money or private property because all physical needs were provided free. There were no taxes because everyone owned everything and contributed everything to fulfill the means. No need for welfare agencies to take care of the victims of micro competition or indifference. No need for legislatures and legislators with their endless micro biases and acrimonious debates. No need for lobbies to protect the vested interests of big business and labor. No need for politicians, the C.I.A., or the F.B.I. No need for micro bureaucracies at all!

Then I thought of a world of competing religions and my own U.S.A. of 1976, professing Christianity but practici g micro separation. I remembered the tens of thousands of church build ngs constructed at immense

114

cost with their tens of thousands of church officials attempting to help micro man attain salvation and social acceptability through membership in some narrow religious sect. The world of 2150 had no churches and no priests, ministers, or rabbis.

Could there really be a time when there would be no more religious fanatics and separatists? No groups of people claiming to be the "chosen" people of God? It seems that micro divisions had low survival value particularly in religions, which were so important to man's beliefs or philosophy of life. Only an all-accepting philosophy of macrocosmic oneness had long-term survival value.

I knew Karl would be fascinated by C.I.'s description of the end of racial differences. By 2150 drastic physical changes in the earth had caused drastic weather changes which caused drastic economic changes, which caused drastic social and spiritual changes. The final result was an almost total blending of the races with the added benefit of greater mental and physical health, strength, and beauty. There were no longer any racial divisions because there were no extreme differences in any physical characteristics, including skin color. Macro man was a combination of the best genetic qualities of all the races, which left only one race—Macro man.

I was not really surprised that a modified type of English was the only universal language of the Macro society, since even in 1976 English was spoken as either a first or second language among a majority of formally educated people throughout the world. The Macro society had its origins in predominantly English-speaking North America in the latter part of the 20th century. Then, of course, a majority of the people surviving the global catastrophes of the late 20th and early 21st centuries spoke at least some English, if only as a second language.

There are two reasons why the Macro society movement succeeded: It attracted highly evolved souls who had Macro potential; and micro man, who refused to cooperate, became almost extinct.

While the early Macro society did not refuse membership to persons who used tobacco or alcohol or even drugs, no one who consciously attained even one Macro contact and, thus, at least some Macro awareness, ever desired them again. Thus, only level ones, who had never experienced Macro contact, ever felt the need of chemical stimulants or depressants. The goal was to free yourself from all physical dependencies. However, no one above level two in the Macro society ever condemned any micro dependency or attempted to convert others to accepting a Macro philosophy. They were interested in quality of membership, not quantity.

I thought of all the utopian societies that had been envisioned and how they had all failed and wondered again at the amazing success of the Macro society. It was here that C.I. had reminded me that there is a time for everything—even Macro man. According to the Macro society, the souls of men are evolving back to total Macro awareness. At the micro level of evolution a society based on love and cooperation is impossible. But finally enough souls evolved to Macro potential so that the Macro society was possible. For those souls still at the micro level of evolution there were other Earth-type planets in the physical universe as well as other dimensions in a nonphysical universe.

The great problems for Macro man were no longer in the physical universe, but existed in the various dimensions of the nonphysical universe. While C.I. gave me a great deal of information on these other dimensions, I found most of it beyond my comprehension, so I went on to questions about my own personal plight.

I decided to ask C.I. how to attain level three in three months, but discovered that I had finally found an area in which C.I. did not know the answer.

It was discouraging to find that no one had ever expanded their awareness from level one to level three in only three months. However, C.I. insisted that this did not mean it was impossible, for there was an entirely new factor present which had never occurred before. This new factor was what C.I. called twin-soul time-space translation.

According to C.I. the very fact that they had succeeded in bringing my astral body to 2150 and having it incarnated in a specially created physical body indicated my Macro potential. In other words, it could not have happened if I had not been sufficiently evolved along the m-M (microcosmic-Macrocosmic) evolutionary continuum.

Furthermore, since Lea was my twin soul and had demonstrated level-nine awareness, it was thought highly probable that I could soon develop at least level-three awareness. The problem was the length of time it might take me. C.I. could find no way to extend my three-month time limit. However, since I was linked to Lea and she was linked to the mind powers of all other level nines and tens, this was calculated as a tremendous advantage for intensifying both my desire and my belief in Macro contact.

Then there was the fact that I had attained my first Macro contact so swiftly. Because of this, C.I. indicated that the probability of swift level-three attainment was greatly increased and suggested that I make another effort at Macro contact as soon as possible. I thought that over for a while and then asked if C.I. was suggesting that I make the attempt immediately. The answer was affirmative. It was at this point that Carol entered.

I didn't have to tell Carol about C.I.'s suggestion since she had telepathically picked up my thought and come to help me.

She sat down beside me and immediately indicated her willingness to join me in my attempt at Macro contact. I asked C.I. to provide the Macro stimulation and again began experiencing the hypnotic line and color patterns on the video screen along with the incredibly exciting, yet (paradoxically) relaxing tones that seemed to penetrate and expand every cell of my body, every level of my mind.

I soon found myself flowing as a mighty river with the powerful feeling of peace, joy, and contentment.

Suddenly the river lost power, washed back on itself, and became murky. The tones grew ever more distant as the backwash seemed to carry me away from them. I broke out in the cold sweat of fear, frantically grabbing for the tones. The more anxious I became, the faster they disappeared.

Somewhere from the back of my mind came an ancient Confucian definition of love—something about two fish in a pond. The pond went dry. Through joining together the two fish made it over the vast desert to another pond. Arriving there, they let go of each other and went their separate ways. It was said that their ability to let go was love.

Why had I thought of that? What did it have to do with my present state? Was the letting go a kind of acceptance of what is, as perfect—that fine level-ten trait? Was my own anxiety for the experience driving it away?

I was losing ground so fast that I had little left to lose, so I bet all my chips on acceptance, commanding my body, mind, and emotions to stop struggling to relax, and to appreciate the absolute perfection of all that is, all that was, and all that ever will be.

Some cubbyhole of my mind was amused at the paradox and laughed at me for having the audacity to think I could keep anything by frantically hanging on. Laughter relaxed me. I stopped resisting the backwash and began to appreciate its power and beauty.

It whirled me around then, lifting me to the top of its crest, hurled me forward. The river was clear, sparkling, and powerful.

Was it—had it always been that way? Was my mind playing tricks on me? Was its change actually only within my own mind, a product of my own anxiety?

More laughter overflowed the corners of my mind. I

had always loved philosophic puzzles, and this one was a beaut!

Yielding myself totally to the emental (a 2150 contraction of *emotional* and *mental*) movement, I flowed joyously on and on through what seemed an endless series of dimensions. Finally I reached the infinite ocean and experienced the unspeakable joy of Macro contact.

When at last I opened my eyes again, Carol was smiling radiantly.

"You attained Macro contact a second time, Jon, in less than a day," she beamed.

"But I have a feeling," I said, "that I almost didn't make it." Then I realized that Carol had not succeeded. I was deeply touched by her happiness for me.

"Things happen in their own time, Jon. We have to learn to understand and accept that. You can't push the river. Come on, I'm starved!"

Extracting two tiny tablets from her mib, she handed one to me.

"What's this?" I inquired.

"That's our lunch!"

"Our what?" I asked incredulously.

Carol had gone to the wall and come back with two transparent, seemingly weightless, cups of water. "It's magic! If you'll swallow it and drink the whole cup of water I promise you won't be hungry again till this evening." Whereupon she downed her pill and the water.

I followed her example and, in moments, experienced the satisfied well-being of having just finished a complete meal. What's more, Carol told me that it contained a balance of all the necessary food values that my body would require for six hours. When I asked her why they bothered with developing solid foods such as the delicious seaweed steak I had enjoyed so much, she said that they enjoyed the taste of food when they were with their Alphas, but used the food tabs when busy with other activities.

"Speaking of other activities," she said, "it's time you visited the other triads."

119

We left the library-research building and walked leisurely in the pleasantly warm early afternoon sun. We left the path and walked in the shade of stately trees toward the student recreation area. As I breathed the sweet fresh air and felt the luxuriant green life about me I thought how incredibly fortunate I was to have the opportunity to experience such beauty, tranquillity, and joy.

Carol used her mib to talk with Alan concerning which recreation area we would visit first. This reminded me of a question:

"Why do you use your mib to talk with others when you have telepathic powers?"

She laughed. "With my limited telepathic powers about all I can do is send or receive very general messages. Unless a person is close, my power is not clear enough to maintain integrity throughout transmission."

"You mean it's like tuning in a television or radio channel?" I asked.

"Yes, that's a good analogy. The quality of your reception depends on how powerful the sender and how sensitive the receiver." She paused and then said, "Actually, only ninth and tenth levels can communicate with each other totally telepathically."

"How about the other Macro powers like clairvoyance, precognition, retrocognition, and PK (psychokinesis)?" I asked.

"As a rule," she answered, "the Macro powers are somewhat limited at the lower levels of awareness. In fact, even third and fourth levels demonstrate far more excellence in the first three Macro attributes of love, leadership, and wisdom than the seven Macro powers."

"So you have to wait, then," I said, "until attaining ninth- or tenth-level awareness before demonstrating complete adequacy with the Macro powers?"

"That's right," she answered. "Now you can understand why I didn't try to teleport those water cups we used earlier. The cups alone I could have managed without too much effort, but fill them with water and I would

120

have had to really work at it to keep from spilling. It would have taken a long time and would have left me tired."

"I didn't realize it would tire you," I said, surprised.

"You've already begun learning that true power lies simply in knowing acceptance, desire, and belief. When we first begin using Macro powers we, almost without exception, think it will all go more effectively if we try harder. This almost irresistible urge to try takes a lot of energy."

"You mean, then," I said, "that it's just a matter of practice."

She smiled and said, "Yes, that and emental discipline. Our problem is that our lives are so happy and peaceful that we lack the necessary desire to practice very often."

"Hmm," I said, "maybe that's true for you who have grown up in the Macro society and have forever to attain your goal, but I've got only three months to attain mine or return to the 20th century for the rest of my life."

"Exactly," Carol replied, "and that's why the level nines and tens were willing to try bringing you here, because you would have more to lose, and thus, greater motivation than anyone in the Macro society ever had."

"Okay," I said, "I'm ready to start practicing. Where do I begin?"

"Great! That's what I've been waiting for. You had to ask, we could not force you to start practicing."

She threw her arms around me and planted quick kisses about my face.

"Well, well," I teased. "I'll bet even old B. F. Skinner of operant conditioning fame would approve of your behavioral conditioning techniques!"

"I don't know about Skinner, but I'm glad you feel rewarded," she said. "Now let's get to work and practice some PK. See if you can teleport this pebble at my feet."

I looked at the pebble she was pointing at and decided that since it was very small it should be an easy place

121

to start. I reached out with imaginary fingers to pick it up. It didn't budge.

"You're trying too hard," Carol suggested. "Relax your mind by remembering your Macro contact experience."

After a couple of minutes of recalling how I almost lost Macro contact I stopped trying, to the best of my ability, and found my mind blissfully serene. I gently reached out for the pebble and easily raised it to eye level. Then I made it dance and weave through the air about us. For the next few minutes I experienced the strange joy of successfully using PK.

I probably would have gone on to larger objects if I hadn't become aware of a rapidly increasing weariness that seemed to be creeping through my body. I dropped the pebble.

Carol smiled wistfully. "Now you know what I meant about becoming tired. Since you have so recently experienced Macro contact you can probably counteract the fatigue by again recalling the experience. Give it a try."

I decided that I was just too tired to stand up any longer, so I lay down on the soft, sweet-smelling grass and tried to follow Carol's suggestion. My fatigue seemed to interfere and it was several moments before a strong memory of free-flowing, accepting Macro contact succeeded in restoring much of my vitality.

I got slowly to my feet.

"All right," I said, "I've learned my lesson: don't overdo in practicing Macro powers."

Carol looked at me for a minute, then said, "How do you feel? Now that most of your energy is restored, would you like to practice some more?"

"No," I answered. "I really think I'd better wait until later." It was then that I realized that the memory of my Macro contact had been so pleasant and soothing that I no longer had any desire to practice my Macro powers.

"That's right," Carol said, obviously practicing her telepathy. "The memory of Macro contact can restore your energy, but it can also leave you so pleasantly satiated that any desire to put forth the effort necessary for Macro practice is greatly diminished."

"My God!" I exclaimed. "That's what you meant when you all said that the more Macro contacts you had, the less desire you had for growth and change!"

"Yes, that's right," Carol replied, "but this is only true at the lower-Macro levels. Once you've reached level nine it hardly applies, and by level ten you are completely free of any micro desire to avoid the failure-success patterns of all growth and learning."

I forced myself to try moving the pebble again and began bouncing it along ahead of us as we continued our walking.

Carol took my hand and kissed it lightly. "See, they were right! You do have more desire than anyone else." Then she laughed and said, "You're such a good influence on me that I'll help you practice, then you won't tire out so soon." With these words she began taking turns with me at bouncing the pebble along before us.

For the next few minutes we continued this very relaxed type of simple PK usage, and while I felt some weariness beginning to return, it wasn't so awesomely overpowering as before. We ended our PK practice as we topped a slight rise and walked through an opening in a large broad-leafed hedge. There before us was the first triad playground which, I later realized, was about a quarter of a mile directly behind our Gamma building.

The huge playground was a two-hundred-yard square enclosed by the stream that surrounded it. The stream was punctuated by waterfalls and ponds with broad expanses of sand about them. An array of children's exercise devices, some of which resembled what I knew as jungle gyms, dotted the playground, making me wish I was about one fourth my size so I could enjoy the thrill of the pipe-slide or of going hand-over-hand from one end of the fifty-foot horizontal ladder to the other.

Carol surprised me by saying that such playgrounds do exist for adults in every Gamma location, emphasizing the fun and importance of adult physical play.

123

There were balls, blocks, and lots of various-sized and -shaped toys and learning devices that I had never seen before.

While there were about a hundred children between the ages of six weeks and three years, I was surprised to see that the adults seemed to outnumber the children almost two to one.

Sensing my surprise, Carol reminded me that everyone in the first four triads had older brothers and sisters assigned to them from the older triads. In the third and fourth triads, Alpha mates shared the same "brother and sister," who were usually Alpha mates themselves. However, in the first and second triads each child had five elder brothers and sisters of his own assigned only from the eighth, ninth, and tenth triads, along with some other older non-student volunteers.

As we walked about the playground I was reminded that even back in the mid-20th century psychologists knew that for maximum mental and physical growth children need far more than just adequate nutrition. However, in the 20th century one out of three children was permanently damaged by poor nutrition alone. Beyond food, though, were the three psychological requirements: loving acceptance, verbal stimulation with intelligent older children and adults, and opportunities for unrestricted exploration. These last two were frequently summarized as "richly varied mental and physical stimuli."

Yes, I thought, the knowledge for Macro growth had been available in the 20th century, but micro man neither desired nor believed in its development. Even psychologists and psychiatrists were often unable to provide loving acceptance to their very own children. This was largely due to their unquestioning acceptance of the limited micro theory that we, as adults, are the pawns of our early experiences.

I smiled as I recalled the standing comment at our universities that anyone who got a Ph.D. had to really hate himself to put up with all that crap. And it was certainly true that a person could get a Ph.D. and still

124

know practically nothing about how to actually live a healthy, balanced life. What's more, with a Ph.D. he could avoid practicing therapeutic mental-health concepts by spending the rest of his life teaching them to others. I remembered another famous line that said, "Those who can, do . . . and those who can't, teach." After twenty-some years of formal micro education I was inclined to believe there was some truth in this saying.

While wandering about the play area I had received telepathic messages of welcome from all the older brothers and sisters. I was surprised at the intelligence and physical dexterity of these youngsters of the first triad.

"It's hard to believe," I said to Carol, "that none of these children is even three years old."

"Yes," Carol nodded, "we have proved that with adequate nutrition, plus generous amounts of the three psychological requirements that you were just thinking about, both mental and physical growth can increase many times faster than micro man ever supposed possible.

"But now let's go on to the second triad learning-play area," she suggested.

We walked through another opening in the densely growing hedge that surrounded the first triad learning-play area and walked about a hundred yards through the park until we came to another seemingly impenetrable hedge. Finding an opening, we entered the second triad area, which I discovered was at least twice as large as the first triad learning-play area had been.

Again I was struck by the wide variety of learning devices scattered about this huge recreation area. Of course, the devices were generally much more complicated and included construction materials for making miniature Gamma complexes, complete with materials for constructing extremely complex dolls. The jungle-gym type of climbing and swinging apparatus was more extensive and covered with small children swinging with the agility of monkeys through a maze of bars reaching over fifty feet into the air.

With an area fully three hundred yards square there

125

was no crowding for the hundred second-triad students and two hundred of their older brothers and sisters. This time as we wandered about I was surprised to find myself frequently greeted telepathically not only by the older students, but also by the younger ones. I turned to Carol to ask her about this.

"How is it that so many children are demonstrating telepathy?" I inquired, feeling somewhat retarded as compared to these gifted children.

"During the last ten years the Macro society has attracted no soul who did not demonstrate at least second-level awareness by the end of the third triad."

Wow! I thought. That meant that their nine-year-olds —without exception—had all demonstrated a greater level of awareness than I had. "When did you demonstrate third-level awareness?" I asked Carol.

"Not until the end of my fifth triad," she answered. Then smiling impishly she added, "Don't worry, I am sure that having you as my Alpha mate will increase my rate of learning and I should demonstrate fourth level very soon."

"Does anyone remain at second level for their whole life?" I asked.

"Actually," she replied, "we haven't had anyone less than third level by the time they completed the tenth triad for over fifty years."

"This means that you are attracting more highly evolved souls," I said. When she nodded in agreement I pointed to several groups of children who were obviously participating in highly competitive sports both individually and in groups.

"I don't understand," I said. "I thought the Macro society was opposed to competitive activities."

"We're only opposed to competition when it's destructive to the welfare of others."

But isn't losing in games destructive to their self-concept?" I asked.

"Not at all," she answered. "In fact, it's absolutely

necessary to learn how to accept failure-successes in order to attain a Macro self-concept."

"However," she continued, "the kind of micro competition that plundered and polluted your 20th century, allowing a few to live in luxury while the majority of the Earth's population suffered a scarcity of essentials, is destructive competition. It's the kind of selfish micro behavior that destroyed your society and stimulated the desire for a better one—the Macro society."

I studied the responses of the older triad students to the winners of the games. I finally decided that both winners and losers were accepted equally in terms of being loved, but that winners did receive positive psychological reinforcements.

"We recognize," Carol continued, "that life would be deadly dull if we avoided all successes for fear of failures. That's only a problem for micro man—not the Macro society."

While I was thinking over what Carol had just said, we walked over to a large swimming pool. I immediately noticed that all the children in the pool seemed to be excellent swimmers, and I commented on this.

"All of the first-triad children," Carol explained, "learn to swim by the age of two, and by the time they are in the second triad everyone is almost as at home in the water as on land. Of course, everyone swims at least once a day all year round, so we get lots of practice."

"And we learn by practicing," I added. "Speaking of practice, what other Macro powers can I start working on?"

"Now that you've asked," Carol replied, "I think this might be a good time to start developing your Macro vision, clairvoyance. Look at the children and tell me if you can see the auric colors that surround their little naked bodies."

I peered about, checking my perceptions. "I don't think so," I told her, "but maybe I don't know what to look for."

"You probably can't see the human aura without a

127

tunic to reflect and magnify it," Carol answered, "and it's probably because you lack the necessary predisposing belief. Let me tell you something about it."

"First of all," she began, "the aura is produced by the electrical emanations of the human soul which are clairvoyantly seen as colors. We can tell by examining a person's auric colors what his level of awareness and emotional balance is at any given time. For example, if anyone gets caught in a micro perspective his auric colors tend to run together and become muddied. Then if he becomes angry his aura gets very red. If he gets jealous if becomes a sickly greenish-yellow which is similar to the auric color of a person who is deliberately lying for selfish purposes."

"Since you, obviously, can see auras, how about describing mine?" I suggested.

"All right, Jon," she replied. "Your aura extends about twelve inches from your body—this distance will increase as your awareness expands—and is now predominantly a lovely sharp blue-green with some purples, yellows, and greens. When I first met you, before your first Macro contact, these colors were not so clear and sharp and there were more gray tones and more orange-pink. You also have the beginnings of a white, which is the dominant color of our level tens, reflecting perfect balance."

"It's interesting to look at me through your eyes. Thanks. Now how can I learn to see auras without the help of a tunic reflecting them for me?" I asked.

"First try to recall your last Macro contact experience, and that will raise your vibrations or awareness level so that you can use what the ancient mystics called the third eye. This is associated with the pineal gland, which permits us to see high-level vibrations while still enclosed in our low-vibration physical body."

"Then," she continued, "practice looking around people, not directly at them, and perhaps you will begin to see the colors emanating about their heads and shoulders."

I felt several questions fighting for expression, but

before I could ask them, Carol suggested that I get the details from C.I. later and devote this time to practice, so I tried recalling my last Macro contact.

In less than a minute I felt ready to try seeing auras. I turned toward Carol and tried to look around her instead of at her. At first things seemed a little out of focus, but after adjusting my gaze I found that I could see lovely bright colors shining about her. "You're right," I said. "I can see the colors surrounding your head and shoulders, but they seem to fade in and out. Is that how you see them?"

"No, Jon," she replied, happy with my apparent success, "but after you practice a little more you'll see them more clearly."

"Well, here I go, then," I said. I selected an older student swimming with one of the young ones and tried to focus in on his aura. I was able to bring in most of his auric colors pretty well. Then, switching my view to the child, I described his aura to see if I was viewing them correctly.

"You're doing just fine," she said, "but right now I want you to try something else. Look about twenty feet directly in front of you and tell me what you see."

I changed my gaze and looked intently, but though I felt a warm, happy glow inside, I saw nothing.

"Try some more Macro contact recall," she suggested, "but keep looking."

I tried for about thirty seconds, then suddenly my mind seemed to shift focus and I became aware of a dazzling white light surrounding the body of a strong and handsome man.

"I see him!" I said excitely. "It's Eli. Why couldn't I see him normally?"

She laughed at my use of the word *normally* and answered, "Because this time he's using his astral body to visit the thousand Deltas of his Kton. You remember that you occupied only your astral body when you first came here. Then you entered the physical body which had been prepared for you."

"Yes," I said, thinking it over. "And some of the students couldn't see me until I got into this physical body."

"Actually," Carol said, "only level nines and tens are always clairvoyantly aware, so it's possible for anyone in our Alpha to occasionally miss seeing an astral traveler."

"What's the advantage of traveling around in your astral body?" I asked.

"Well," Carol answered, "it's the only way you can travel to any of the non-physical dimensions. But the reason our upper levels use it so much is that it takes considerably less energy than translating the physical body from place to place. Astral travel permits instant translation to a series of places without fatigue."

"What do you mean, Carol?" I asked. "I don't remember anything 'instant' about my traveling when I first came here. In fact, when Lea and I were running to the research center I couldn't even catch up with her!"

Carol laughed. "That's because you thought you were occupying a physical body, and you were limited by your belief. You didn't think your physical body could run any faster, so it didn't. It's as simple as that."

"You mean," I asked, "that if I had realized I was using only my astral body I could have traveled faster?"

"Faster, indeed!" was her response. "Faster than the speed of light. That is, of course, if you believed it was possible. You see, the astral body has no mass, and, thus, is not limited by the speed of light. In other words, at the astral level your mind is not hampered by clumsy, dense, physical matter, so a thought manifests its consequences immediately. You just visualize it and it happens. Level tens can do the same thing with physical bodies, but it takes more thought energy."

I shook my head and, turning to Carol, exclaimed, "That's amazing! I'd really like to learn to do that."

"We'd better master telepathy first," Carol responded as she looked over to where Eli had been standing, then back at me.

I followed her glance to the spot where our Ktar had been, but he was no longer there. "Where'd he go so fast? To another Delta?"

"You need more practice, Jon," she noted. "You missed his greeting to us as well as his statement that he was leaving us to go visit with Lea."

I felt embarrassed at missing Eli's communication to us. I had thought I was doing pretty well, but that certainly put me back in my place. "I really wanted to talk to him, too. Guess I need a lot more practice," was my painful conclusion.

Another question popped into my head. "Say, you mentioned that he was a Ktar. I was wondering, are all your leaders level tens?"

"The top ones, yes," Carol answered, "Our three Mutars, who are leaders of 100-million-member Mutons, and the thirty Ktars, who are the leaders of 10-million-member Ktons, are all level tens. The rest of our current 127 level tens are Ztars."

"That means," I interrupted, recalling my C.I. training, "that they are leaders of your million-member Ztons, right?" To her nod of agreement I added, "And since you have 300 of these I suppose the other Ztars are level nines."

"That's right," she nodded, "and since we have currently 3,306 level nines, all of the 3,000 Atar positions, as leaders of 100,000, are filled by nines."

"Then I supposed it logically follows that the Deltars are either the few nines who are not Atars or all eights."

"Yes," she said, "since there are some 39,000 level eights we have more than enough to fill the remaining 30,000 Deltar positions and the rest are Gamma leaders."

"But since there are 300,000 Gamar positions," I surmised, "the rest must be filled by level sevens." I paused for a moment to let a nagging thought come to the surface of my mind. "Okay," I went on, "maybe you can tell me what was the youngest age that anyone ever demonstrated nine- or ten-level awareness."

"I'll have to ask C.I.," Carol responded and began

131

talking into her mib. After a couple of moment she said, "The youngest age to reach level ten was thirty-nine and the average age of all level tens at this time is 107. As for level nines, the youngest ever to demonstrate level-nine awareness had had thirty-three years and the average age of all level nines at this time is ninety-three. The youngest age of attaining level-eight awareness was twenty-seven, and their average age is seventy-seven."

"That means," I said, "that if I make level three in three months, I'll be doing all right."

"Not bad for a beginner, Jon. Not bad," she teased, then added, "I'm glad to see you optimistic because it certainly won't be possible unless you first believe you can do it."

"We'd better get over to the 3rd and 4th triads now so you can meet your younger brother and sister," Carol added.

"Will I be taking someone else's place? I mean, don't they already have an older brother?" I asked.

"He's gone already," Carol assured me. "He was my previous Alpha mate, but he has gone to another Delta to complete an Alpha there."

I realized that I hadn't asked Carol about her previous Alpha mate before because I had felt guilty about the possibility of my displacing someone. Then, when I got to know Carol better, I felt little stirrings of jealousy when I thought about someone else preceding me as her mate. Now I checked my mind carefully and found few remnants of either guilt or jealousy, so I asked her if she didn't miss him.

"Not really," she replied. "You see, we share almost identical soul notes, so I can reach out to him tele-pathically anytime I wish. I'm happy to know that he is as pleased with his new Alpha mate as I am with you."

"But I thought your telepathy was very limited," I said, puzzled at her apparent ability to reach out clear to another Delta.

"You'll find, Jon, that it's ever so much easier to com-municate telepathically with those whose soul notes are

132

close to your own. Take Steve, for example. His soul note is very different from mine, so I would have to work hard to receive from him even as far as across the lake. However, the closer the soul note vibration, the easier it is to communicate and the greater the distance your message can carry to that person."

"That sounds reasonable," I responded, then added, "Tell me, how did there happen to be an opening in another Alpha just when I arrived? Did someone die?"

"Oh, no," she assured me. "There haven't been any deaths in the 7th triad for over three years. However, frequently someone will volunteer to work on Micro Island for a few months. That will often leave an Alpha either one or two short."

"What kind of work do they volunteer for out there?"

"We offer our services as Personal Evolution tutors," she replied. "Some of their children, as well as a few adults, seek our services."

"If those on Micro Island are similar to micro man of the 20th century," I said, "don't you run some risks visiting there?"

"Yes, we do," she admitted. "At least, those of us who have not yet reached the higher levels of awareness do. You see, it's no problem for a level nine or ten to cope with an attacker, a robber, or an assassin, since their precognitive and telepathic powers would warn them and their PK could teleport anyone who bothered them clear to the other side of the island in the blink of an eye."

"That's some way to handle a nuisance," I laughed. "Do they attack their tutors very often?"

"Oh yes," Carol replied. "Anyone who kills a member of the Macro society automatically becomes something of a hero to a great many of the inhabitants of Micro Island."

"Well, how do you handle that?" I asked. "How do you punish them? And why do they want to kill you in the first place?"

"To answer your last question first, they hate us for

133

living so differently from them," she replied. "As for punishing them, of course, we don't. We're careful, therefore, to let only those who have attained at least second-level awareness visit Micro Island, and even they are protected by telepathic communication with a level nine or ten."

"You said it had been three years since anyone died in the 7th triad. Was that last death here or on Micro Island?" I asked.

"On Micro Island," she responded. "It does happen occasionally, but more often than not, it happens to the older students who ask not to be protected."

"Good God!" I exclaimed. "Why would they do that?"

"For the same reason that the great Macro philosopher-tutor, Jesus, permitted himself to be crucified—to show micro man that the soul of man transcends his body," was her explanation.

I shook my head. "I never could see that bit about getting killed or crucified just to show others you aren't afraid of death."

"I think there's more to it than that," Carol said, "but right now we'd better give our attention to finding your younger brother and sister."

As we walked the short distance to the recreation-learning area of triads three and four I wondered about the necessity of assigning older students to supply the caring relationship of a special brother and sister to each younger child.

Carol picked up my thoughts. "It probably isn't as important now since we would provide this relationship even if we weren't assigned it. But when the Macro society began there were not as many highly evolved souls who could telepathically tune in to the needs of others so, in order not to miss anyone, elder brothers and sisters were assigned to all students. Then, as our Personal Evolution tutoring system developed, elder brothers and sisters were assigned only to the first four triads."

"Speaking of tutoring," I said, "how does it work? What's the difference between that and teaching?"

134

"First of all," Carol replied, "we here in 2150 do not believe in the ancient concept of teaching where students passively absorbed or blocked out what a teacher was desperately trying to give them. We, therefore, have no teachers.

"We believe learning to be an active process where one person reaches out and takes knowledge stimulated by his interaction with a resource person."

"So you feel knowledge can only be taken, not given," I summarized.

"Yes. Now, to answer your question, resource persons are specialists in learning areas such as agriculture, ecology, or bio-physics, for example, while Personal Evolution tutors deal with all learning and all human problems."

"It sounds like you think resource people know all about something and your P.E. tutors know all about everything. Do you really believe that's possible?" I asked.

Carol was amused by my skepticism. "It depends on what you mean by, 'know all about everything.' To the extent that our tutors have attained moments of total Macro contact awareness, they do know everything. But knowing the answers to all questions and living these answers are two different things.

"Even a Macro person cannot live a perfectly balanced Macro life," she added. "We just haven't evolved to a state of constant Macro awareness yet. When we reach that state of evolution we will have outgrown our need for a physical body—even a Macro one!"

"All right," I said, "what you're saying, then, is that you have tutors who can supply all the answers, but that the real problem is not finding the answers but putting these answers into practice in your daily life— living them. The same age-old problem."

I went on, "If you only have 127 level tens and 3,306 level nines, and since they serve as your leaders, this must leave you with a real shortage of tutors."

"Oh, no," Carol assured me, "there's no shortage, because all persons in levels six and above function as

135

P.E. tutors. This includes thirty million sixes and three million sevens as well as the thirty-nine hundred eights." (See C.I. Data Excerpts.)

I did some quick mental arithmetic. "That makes 33,003,900 tutors, so there are less than ten pupils per tutor. Still, if everyone saw a Personal Evolution tutor every day there would be no time at all for the level sixes, sevens, and eights to do anything but tutor. That doesn't sound like much of a life. Don't they get tired of all that?"

"I can see where that would be a tiresome existence," she answered. "Fortunately, it's not that bad at all. You see, only students see a tutor every day, and even that isn't required. The vast majority of our Macro society doesn't visit with a P.E. tutor more than once a week."

As she finished speaking we entered the thousand-square-yard recreation-learning area of the 3rd and 4th triads. I was impressed by the tremendous activity going on for as far as I could see. There were at least thirty tennis courts, three football and soccer fields, and all kinds of gym equipment. There were also tracks and swimming pools with meets in progress in each area.

I turned to Carol and commented, "It seems to me there are a lot more triads out there than just the 3rd and 4th."

"That's because the 5th and 7th triads are assigned to the 3rd triad, and the 6th is assigned to the 4th," she explained.

"Oh, that's right, the older brother and sister system," I replied. "But why are two triads assigned to the 3rd? Do they need extra attention for some reason?"

"Actually," Carol answered, "It's the first two triads that get the most attention. We use the 3rd and 4th triads for the 5th and 6th and 7th triads to practice developing their skill at maintaining a helping relationship with someone younger."

"It seems that helping someone is the most highly honored achievement in the Macro society," I observed.

Carol nodded, saying, "That's why our P.E. tutors

136

occupy our most respected social positions and provide our top leadership."

"In the 20th century," I said, "we valued the entertainment profession more than any other, I guess, for we gave our most valuable rewards—money and fame—to entertainers like movie or TV celebrities or sports stars."

"That's because micro man's life is so miserable that he uses any sort of entertainment to escape," Carol explained, "so, naturally, entertainers would be paid more than anyone else."

"You know," I reflected, "that doesn't say much for the value we placed on education, does it? Teaching was one of our lowest-paid professions."

"That's true, Jon," Carol responded. "Micro man placed very little importance on education. Your schools, therefore, were often filled with inadequately prepared teachers who were expected to teach their students how to memorize facts and detail instead of how to think creatively. Much time was spent on subjects which were of little use to the average person, such as foreign languages, algebra, and higher mathematics, while most learning programs gave little or no attention to the most important subject of all—human behavior and life philosophy. I group these two together because man's behavior is always the result of his beliefs, that is, his philosophy of life."

As she completed this observation a boy and girl ran up to her and wrapped their arms around her. They looked strong and healthy and, like all other Macro society children, they possessed great physical beauty. I was thinking that they must have had about 10 years when I received Carol's telepathic message that they were both just 7. She telepathically teased me about having already begun to think in 2150 terms, then introduced me as her new Alpha mate and, therefore, their new brother.

As their eyes reached out to me I realized another reason why members of the Macro society greet each other silently. They are using this silence to concentrate on the delightful nuances of telepathic contact, which removes all possibility of fear or distrust. I learned that the boy's name was Neal and the girl was Jean, but most importantly I learned that I felt joyously happy at our meeting, almost as if they were my long-lost friends. I wasn't surprised when Carol explained this, saying that I knew them in other lifetimes in which we were very close.

Jean demonstrated her awareness when she picked up the fact that tennis had been one of my favorite sports before losing my leg, and she suggested that we all play a game of doubles with Carol and Neal standing her and me.

This sounded like a fine idea except that I had never played tennis with children before and was a little afraid that my style might be too rough for them. Accepting the responsibility of big brotherhood, I said that sounded delightful, and we all headed for the nearest vacant court to select rackets from the rack nearby.

As we began playing I avoided using my power shots, but after the first five minutes of some of the hardest and best-played tennis that I had ever experienced, I was convinced that Carol and the children were far better than I was at this game.

Then I realized that the children were using PK, which was why they seldom missed a shot. If I was going to be any help to Jean as a tennis partner I was going to have to get to work with my PK, too. Thirty minutes later I was convinced that the children's PK was far better than mine. They still seemed as fresh as when the game began.

I decided to ask for a rest, and as we sat in the shade of a nearby oak tree I invited the children to play tennis with me again soon, since it looked like I needed lots of practice. They both agreed.

Neal gave me a happy grin and said, "We've found tennis develops our desire to practice our Macro powers —especially PK."

"We were afraid at first that you had not yet developed

138

your PK ability and that we weren't being fair with you," Jean added. "We don't use PK when we play tennis with anyone who hasn't developed it yet."

I laughed as I replied, "I was afraid I'd be too good for you, but by using your PK you made it the most challenging game of my life. I want to thank you for giving me the opportunity to practice not only my tennis but also my PK."

Carol hopped up and said, "I'm going to take a swim, Jon, but why don't you stay here and rest so you'll feel up to running back to our Alpha in time for the Macro dance."

"Thanks," I said. "I'll need the rest. That dance is as tiring as playing PK tennis!"

By the time Carol and the children reached the nearest pool my eyes were closed.

CHAPTER 9:

Proof of the Pudding

I woke up refreshed and discovered that I had slept for almost ten hours. There was a note from Karl saying that he wouldn't be home for lunch, but would be back earlier than usual that afternoon. I decided to get to my journal-writing as soon as possible.

By four that afternoon Karl returned and the first thing he did was ask about my latest dream. I told him he could read it in the journal because I was going out for some fresh air after being inside all day. He agreed that this sounded like a healthy idea and sat down with my journal while I put on my coat, boots, muffler, and fur hat in preparation for my walk in the blustery snow.

As I trudged through eight inches of newly fallen snow and shivered in the near zero temperature, which was intensified by thirty-mile-an-hour winds blowing about me, I realized that no one in 2150 could possibly appreciate their climate control as much as I did. I thought of

140

all the ages that man had struggled against the elements of nature in order to find food, shelter, and security from attack by animals—or his fellow man. I thought how much longer it was going to take before man would learn to cooperate enough to eliminate even this problem. Cooperation had always been the solution, the answer. But it takes the long view—the Macro view—to see the benefits of cooperation. From the short-term view—the micro view—man can only get the things he wants by competing for them and coming out the winner, while his fellow man comes out the loser. This conflict, this competition, this lack of cooperation always results, both individually and internationally, in division into two groups—the "haves" and the "have nots."

Looking up I realized that I had walked further than I intended for the student union and coffee shop was less than a block away. I crossed the street and entered the student union where I warmed myself as I considered the plight of the hundred and some other students gathered there.

While most of them were between the ages of 18 and 22, there were also several about my own age or older. I couldn't help but think how different these students were from those of 2150. The physical differences of sheer size and appearance were the most obvious, but it was the psychological differences that really hit me.

These students of 1976 reflected the fear, suspicion, anxiety, belligerence, prejudice, alienation, and general unawareness of the culture they were raised in. Yet they had almost all evolved to a level where they were a lot more friendly and open than their parents, and their auras were a lot brighter and less muddied, too. "Hey! I'm seeing auras!" I thought triumphantly.

I was almost instantly humbled by the sudden realization that this is about how my aura looked to the people of 2150 with my 20th-century biases and anxieties.

With this thought in mind I grinned and, leaving the warmth of the building, headed for home. I stopped at

141

a supermarket to replenish our supply of bacon and eggs.

In spite of the snowstorm the store was filled with middle-aged women and a few elderly men. The vitality and enthusiasm of the students were absent here. These people had all the fears and uncertainties of the students but none of their compensating joy and friendliness. They seemed to be colorless, worn-out automatons who had found a dull little rut into which they sank a little deeper with each passing year until it became their grave.

The narrow, rigid life patterns of micro man were designed by him to avoid failure. In the long run, though, they merely served to convince him of his inadequacy to deal with the world outside of his little self-constructed prison.

As I walked down between the aisles of groceries thinking these thoughts, a small child of 4 or 5 came running around a corner, tripped, and fell sprawling at my feet.

Without thinking, I automatically picked up the now sobbing child and held her in my arms to comfort her. The cries vanished immediately and I realized that I was holding a heavily booted and snowsuited little girl. She had just begun to return my big smile with a shy one of her own when she was rudely jerked out of my arms by an anxious, thin-lipped woman whose eyes were narrowed with anger.

"How dare you put your dirty hands on my little girl!" she screeched. "You nasty beast!"

"But, Madam . . ." I began, "I was just . . ."

"I know what you were 'just' doing," she accused loudly, clutching the child to her. "You were attempting to molest my daughter. I saw you, and I want you to know there are laws to take care of people like you!"

By this time her caterwauling had attracted a sizable number of other shoppers who stared suspiciously at me.

The little girl's mother continued to shriek imprecations and threats at me till I felt it was impossible to say anything believable in my own defense. It was impossible for me to do anything except stare at her, transfixed by the ghastly aura surrounding her. It was like an ugly, spitting red fire blotched with sickly yellow-greens.

At that moment the store-manager appeared and, sensing the possibility of violence, grabbed my arm and began pulling me toward the back of the building explaining to the shoppers that he would take care of me and see that I was turned over to the proper authorities.

Back in his office, as I showed him my student identification card and explained for the third time that I was just comforting the child, he was still looking rather uncertainly at me. Finally, obviously deciding that he didn't want the inconvenience of dealing with the police, he let me go out the back of his store with the warning that he never wanted to see me in his store again.

If I had needed an incident to dramatically reveal the differences between 1976 and 2150 I had certainly gotten it. In the micro world of 1976 every stranger was a potential threat of theft, rape, murder, or some other catastrophe. Since micro man was blindly unaware of most of his own motivations, he was also blind to those of others. If only they could have seen my aura or read my mind, I thought it would have been impossible for them to misunderstand my intentions or fear me. But, lacking this greater awareness, they must judge others by surface appearance and through the fog of their own fears, anxieties, and guilts.

What would have happened to me, I wondered, if I had been wearing the long hair, beard, and battered-looking garments so popular with some of my fellow students. I'd probably be sitting in jail by now with little hope of convincing a middle-aged judge or jury that I wasn't a sex fiend and either an anarchist or communist to boot.

I walked back toward our apartment as quickly as my artificial leg would carry me, having had enough of micro man and his supermarkets for one day. I preferred the cold bitterness of the elements to the savage paranoia of micro man.

143

Back at the apartment I found myself closing and automatically locking our door behind me. Oh, lord, I thought, I'm a great one to condemn micro man for being paranoid.

It was true. I didn't feel safe here in 1976, and I desperately missed the clean, lovely countryside and the happy serenity and loving kindness of Delta 927, only 174 years in the future.

As I sat down in my hard-backed chair Karl put down my journal and asked what was wrong. When I told him of my experiences at the student union and at the supermarket, he smiled grimly and said, "Your new Macro powers don't seem to help you back here in 1976 the way they do in your 2150. Or maybe," he paused, and eyed me speculatively, "they don't even *work* in 1976."

That was our agreed-upon test of 2150's reality. Could I demonstrate Macro powers which I had learned in my dream world of the future while I was awake in 1976.

I had seen auras, but somehow I had forgotten—or avoided—trying telepathy with anyone.

Now I looked at my journal lying on the table beside Karl. Could I teleport it through the air over to me by using my newly developed PK? Maybe, I thought, I should try some smaller object. No, I refused to make the test easy—even if all I could do was push the journal off the table onto the floor, it would prove my PK.

I reached out with imaginary hands to lift the journal —nothing happened.

What's wrong? Had I just imagined seeing auras at the student union and the supermarket? Could it be that I would be unable to demonstrate PK, the one Macro power that could be seen by others?

I frantically reached out with my mind and redoubled my efforts to pull, push, or shove my journal off the table, but, to my growing alarm, there was no movement whatsoever.

"Take it easy," Karl said. "I can see by the look on

144

your face that you aren't able to use your 2150 powers back here in the cold, hard reality of 1976."

"But I can see auras," I pleaded. "I can even see yours!"

"Come off it, Jon, you know I can't see auras and neither can you or anyone else we know, so offering your hallucinations is hardly going to be acceptable as proof."

"But, Karl," I protested, "this isn't a fair test—maybe I need more time. I mean I've only just begun using three out of the seven Macro powers. Maybe I'll have to practice and develop them all before I can demonstrate them successfully to you."

"There are only two," Karl replied, "which I would accept as being verifiable. That would be precognition and PK, with the latter being the quickest and best proof. It was you, Jon, who suggested the test of demonstrating them in 1976. Now you seem reluctant to accept your own test of reality."

"But I know I have the power! I used it time and again! You should have seen that tennis game, Karl."

"I know, I know," Karl replied. "It's all right there in your journal. The point is, that's in your dream world . . . not here in the reality where I live."

"I need more time, Karl," I repeated.

"Fine," Karl agreed. "I don't want to be unreasonable, but it's your test as much as mine. You set up the rules. I'm just the judge. If you want more time, take it."

Karl felt my disappointment and discouragement, and he realized that I was sincerely puzzled by my failure to move the journal. In his attempt to help he asked me if I was doing something wrong; if I was, perhaps, leaving out some vital step in the process.

"No, no, no," I answered. "Damn it, Karl, I'm doing everything just like I did before. It's just not working!"

Karl laughed. "Look at me, you nut! I'm almost as wrapped up in this as you are!" He paced across the room with his chin in his hand then, turning and pointing his index finger at me, he said, "By George, I've got it! Let's recreate the 'scene of the crime' and see if we

145

can ferret out your mistake. Now let's see, the first time you demonstrated PK was on that pebble when you and Carol took turns making it bounce along in front of you and . . ." Karl interrupted himself and plopped on his bed, weak with laughter. "I sure do feel stupid, Jon! I'm sure as hell glad one of our professors isn't here watching this production!"

At this prospect, we both broke up.

After a good laugh I said, "Come on now. Back to business. You had a good idea there. Let's get back to the first time I used PK."

"Well, as I was saying, you and Carol were taking turns bouncing—"

I interrupted. "No, Karl. That wasn't the first time I tried it. That was after I had learned the trick. The first time was when I tried to lift the pebble up from the ground in front of us. I couldn't do it. Carol told me to try to recall my last Macro contact experience. I did, and next time I tried, it worked."

Karl immediately asked, "That Macro contact stuff— do you think maybe that's it? Would that work here? And what is it?"

"What is it?" I tried to think of a way to describe it to Karl. "Well, the closest I can come to describing it would be if you paused for a moment and imagined yourself totally, and perfectly, molecularly, one with the air around you and with everything else. Just feel the air between the atoms that make up your body and know that all is perfect and all is one. I realize that's not too great a description, but it's the best I can do."

"I suppose we could call it getting into the Macro mood. One more 2150 expression can only enrich our lives!" Karl joked as he waved a finger in the air and "jived" around the room.

This business of combining the parts of two different worlds was more than I wanted to try to reason out, so I decided instead to act on it. "I don't know, Karl. Let me take the next few minutes to try it. You keep your

146

eye on my journal because if this works, I'm going to teleport it from your table over to my chair."

Karl smiled and said, "If that's precognition you're going to have to also demonstrate PK in order to prove it."

His last words came to me faintly as my mind brought back vividly the memory of my last Macro contact, filling me with quiet, peaceful serenity. The fear and anxiety generated by my experience at the market and my failure to successfully demonstrate Macro powers for Karl began to be washed away by an ocean—the wisdom of oneness —which dissolved them completely, filling me once again with joyous hope and loving acceptance.

I reached out with my mind's imaginary hands and gently lifted my journal a couple of inches straight up above the table.

"Son of a bitch!" Karl exclaimed. "You're doing it, Jon! By God, you're doing it!"

I lifted it a full two feet above the table and began to pull it toward me. A few seconds later, its journey from the table beside Karl over to my chair completed, it had traveled about nine feet and was now lying in my lap.

Karl exploded to his feet. Fighting back tears of joy and amazement, he grabbed my shoulders and shouted, "You did it, Jon! By God, you did it! Honest, Jon, I thought you were losing your marbles—going out of your mind or something, believing those crazy dreams. But you sure did do it!"

"Are you finally convinced, Karl?" I asked grinning broadly.

Karl returned my grin and released my shoulders. As he stood up, though, the grin faded. "Wait a minute," he said, as he rubbed his chin in thought. "Maybe I'm seeing things, too, just because I want so badly to see them. I mean, maybe I want so strongly for you not to be losing your mind that I'll go to any extreme to prove you aren't. Maybe I'm hallucinating. Maybe that journal got over to you by some perfectly normal means that

147

I, somehow, blocked out. Or maybe you hypnotized me —or maybe I hypnotized myself, Jon."

"Now it's your turn to have doubts about our test," I teased. "Maybe that bit about one of our professors seeing all this wasn't a bad idea. Do you want to invite some friends in for a little demonstration?"

"No, not really," Karl said, shaking his head. "If you failed, then everyone would know you're nuts and, being your brother, I'd be judged guilty by association. On the other hand, if you succeeded, you'd be as notorious as if you had suddenly grown two heads. Besides, you might still be accused of hypnotism. No, that's not the answer."

"Well, then, what do you suggest?" I asked. "I've kept my part of the bargain. I've demonstrated PK and even offered to do it again in front of witnesses. What more can I do?"

"Let me think a minute," Karl said. "Something's coming—something's coming . . ."

About twenty seconds later he shouted, "Eureka! I've got it! I'll take pictures. Yes, sir, I'll take pictures from every angle, then I'll buzz upstairs and borrow Snuffy Baldwin's dark room and develop them. How's that grab ya?"

"Hmm," I said as I thought it over. "Don't you think Snuffy will want to see these big important pictures you're suddenly so hot about developing? Besides, it seems to me I can remember when you told him your time was too valuable to waste developing your own pictures any more."

"I can handle Snuffy all right," Karl replied confidently. "You just recharge your batteries or whatever you do to get ready for another demonstration of PK before the untrickable eye of my camera."

As he was talking Karl had walked over to the closet and pulled out his camera which he had picked up while we were overseas. For a time it seemed like he was forever taking pictures of all kinds of stuff, then developing and enlarging them, sometimes enormous sizes. I remember I had thought that somehow all this was some sort of compensation for the loss of his left eye. His passion for photography had gradually waned, however, till during the past six months he had taken very few pictures, had sold his enlarger, and had given all his chemicals and trays to Snuffy. Now it looked as if all his old camera-bug enthusiasm had suddenly returned.

While Karl was preparing his camera, I was heeding his advice and preparing myself for another PK demonstration by again focusing my mind on that most wondrous of all experiences in my memory—the Macro contact. I felt the tiredness dissipate in that infinite ocean of omnipotent and omniscient universal mind. Soon I felt refreshed and ready to try teleporting my journal again.

"All right," Karl said, shifting the angle of his flash attachment, "I'm ready to start taking pictures so you can start your levitation act any time you're ready."

I looked at this journal lying on my lap, then reached out with my mental hands and suddenly lifted it almost to the ceiling. There were a number of flashes as Karl leaped about almost frantically taking pictures from every possible angle. I moved the journal to various parts of the room with Karl bobbing about either beneath, beside, or above it leaving a trail of used flashbulbs behind.

Finally I realized that I was getting too tired to continue, so I maneuvered the journal back to the table from which I had originally moved it. I dropped it the last ten inches or so and it landed with a sharp slapping sound. I lay back in my chair, more exhausted even than after my first pebble-moving experience back in 2150. Now I could only hope that the pictures would turn out well enough to prove once and for all that my PK ability was real, and so, therefore, were my dream experiences of the 2150 Macro society.

"You better rest," Karl said, "then have something to eat. I'll be up at Snuffy's developing these pictures."

With these words Karl was out the door and I spent

the next half-hour slowly recuperating my strength with the help of Macro contact memory.

Later as I fixed a couple of sandwiches and leisurely ate them, I wondered how my PK demonstrations would affect Karl's attitude toward my dream experiences. Would even all the pictures he took manage to overcome Karl's deep-seated skepticism? After all, I thought, if he accepts this evidence as demonstrating the validity of my experiences in 2150 it will undermine his micro beliefs about the nature of man and ultimate reality.

It wouldn't be easy to give up the view of psychology, sociology, and anthropology that man was merely a highly complex animal whose behavior is determined by the accidents of birth and environment.

Having finished my sandwiches, I decided to bring my journal up to date with my most recent experiences here in 1976. As I wrote I kept stopping every once in a while, wondering how I could help those who were caught in a micro view of themselves and the world about them. I thought of some of my professors in psychology and sociology and remembered how they prided themselves on their scientific objectivity. Yet they refused to even consider any evidence of parapsychology, which claimed the existence of non-physical phenomena such as clairvoyance, telepathy, PK, and precognition—all modern heresy to the behavioral sciences of 1976. But what would it take to convince them, I wondered, or would they have to die and be replaced by more highly evolved incarnating souls? That was the answer C.I. had given me, but it seemed rather cold-blooded to resign yourself to waiting for a whole generation to die off.

When I finally finished my writing it was almost time for me to go to sleep again. I wondered what was detaining Karl. Had something gone wrong with the developing? I was just getting ready to call Snuffy's room when Karl opened the door, waving a handful of pictures.

"Here's the proof," he said, shaking his head. "Here's the concrete proof of your PK ability and, I suppose, the

150

evidence to support the reality of your dream experiences."

"What took you so long?" I asked.

"Well, by the time I had the pictures developed," Karl replied, "Snuffy had gone out so I had his apartment all to myself to do a little uninterrupted thinking. Besides, he had fried up a bunch of chicken and suggested I finish it off. So I ate fried chicken and examined these pictures carefully to see if I could honestly remain skeptical about what you've been writing down in that journal of yours."

"And what did you decide?" I asked.

"That it's going to be the toughest decision I've ever made," Karl replied. "In fact, if I accept the validity of 2150 and its Macro society, I'm going to have to either look for a new profession or be damned careful to hide my new beliefs from my fellow behavioral scientists."

"You don't think that I could demonstrate my Macro powers to other behavioral scientists?" I queried.

"Ha!" Karl said, "I may be considering adopting some mighty crazy ideas, but I'm not crazy enough to think anyone else is going to buy them. For example, for the last twenty-five years, some very detailed evidence from some highly reputable individuals has been presented on U.F.O. phenomena, and the very 'respectable' scientific associations refuse to take it seriously. Now here I am, a budding Ph.D., giving serious consideration to stories a lot more far-out than U.F.O.s. Oh, lord, Jon, I'm going to hell in a hand basket!"

"Congratulations, Karl," I said. "You'll make a Macro philosopher yet!"

"Does being a Macro philosopher mean that you believe in things that almost everyone else calls crazy?" Karl asked.

"Sometimes," I answered, "but more importantly, the Macro philosopher does not shut his mind to anything. He realizes that truth is always a function of the size of one's perspective. That is, the larger your perspective, the more truths you can comprehend."

"I'm going to bed, and I'll think about that and about what these pictures mean," Karl replied. "I've had a hard day. My philosophy of life is being pulled up by the roots—maybe destroyed for good."

I, too, headed for bed, looking forward to getting back to 2150.

Once in bed, however, I found it difficult to stop thinking about the day's events—particularly my experience at the supermarket. Try as I did, it was impossible to forget my own fear, frustration, and anxiety during my confrontation with the angry woman and the store manager. I had to admit that if I really had been able to practice a Macro perspective, these negative feelings would not have occurred. I would have been able to completely demonstrate loving acceptance. How would I ever reach third-level awareness if I responded to threats as I had this afternoon?

I shook my head sadly as I realized that the real test of high-level Macro awareness was not accepting with love the members of the Macro society—that was easy—but accepting with love micro man. That was the greatest challenge of all.

The one commandment of the philosopher-tutor, Jesus, to love one another—even your enemies—had always seemed to me a ridiculously impossible commandment. And it was impossible for micro man—only the highest Macro levels could consistently demonstrate this when living among micro man. Now I understood why many members of the Macro society volunteered to teach and counsel on Micro Island. Would I have to do that, I wondered? I'll think about that later, I thought, as my mind finally wound down and accepted sleep.

CHAPTER 10:

Jon's Past Lives

I awakened to the sight of Carol and the two children just entering the pool. I knew that, once again, only a few seconds had passed in the year 2150 while I had experienced a whole day, from morning to night, in 1976. I wondered if I would ever understand the concept of subjective simultaneous time.

Surprisingly, the few seconds of sleep in 2150 had reduced my fatigue. I decided to join Carol and the children in the pool.

Before reaching the edge of the pool I removed my tunic and dropped it down an opening provided for this purpose. It would travel to the underground cleaning plant, be washed, and be returned to this recreation area. As I stood naked at the side of the pool I was pleased to realize that I no longer felt uncomfortable at my nudity—even in front of the children. Since everyone swam naked and strolled about the pool naked, I would have felt uncomfortable if I had been clothed.

I located Carol at the far end of the pool some 100 yards away. Diving in, I swam toward her. I had never enjoyed swimming as much as running, but after the loss of my leg, when I could no longer run, I found swimming very satisfying. Swimming with two strong legs was even more so, and I reached Carol feeling more refreshed than when I had entered the water.

We played water tag with Neal and Jean. Their agility in the water was remarkable. Like young seals, they seemed equally at ease above or below the surface, so without Carol's help the game of tag would have been no contest at all. After about fifteen minutes of this delightful but strenuous activity, I climbed out and lay down on the soft mats beside the pool. Shortly Carol joined me and we lay side by side in the warm sun watching the seemingly inexhaustible children continue the game.

Suddenly I was aware of a tingling in my Macro identity bracelet. I looked first at it, then at Carol, who said, "It's C.I. calling you."

I lifted it to my ear and heard C.I. request that I meet with Lea back at my C.I. room overlooking the lake. Then I heard Lea's soft resonant voice saying that she was already at the C.I. center and would be waiting for me.

"I'll be right there, Lea," I said and started to get up to run back to the research building when Carol reached out to stop me.

"There's a faster way," she said. "Come with me."

We stopped at the clothing rack, where Carol picked up a freshly cleaned tunic for herself and one for me. As we slipped into these, Carol led me toward the exit of the recreation area.

As we ran I picked up the telepathic farewells from the children and returned them, expressing my happiness at having met them and my hope of seeing them again soon.

154

Carol said that we would probably be seeing them every afternoon. By this time we were near the exit and Carol was pointing to a red ten-foot metal-looking square on the ground. We stepped into the middle of this and, as Carol used PK to push a button at the edge of the square, we disappeared into the ground.

Neither metal nor cement was used in any of the buildings. What looked like metal, cement, or marble was all some sort of synthetic material which could be molded into almost any shape and strength to stand up under tremendous loads. Our red square turned out to be another void that took us down almost 300 feet below ground to their subway area.

As we swiftly descended Carol informed me that we would use one of their two-seated subway cars which would take us the almost three-mile distance to the research building in less than two minutes.

We walked to a torpedo-shaped bubble containing two large comfortable seats, which, as we sat in them, enfolded us. Carol turned a dial to a setting marked C.I., pushed it in, and our bubble car seemed to rise on a column of air into an opening above us. Then in complete darkness I had the sensation of tremendous acceleration for a moment followed by great deceleration and then we were getting out.

Walking to the middle of another red platform we rose to the surface just outside the entrance of the learning center. It was all so fast that my impressions were still rather garbled.

Carol left me, saying that she would see me back at our Alpha. I hurried into the building and up to what I now thought of as "my" C.I. room. As I opened the door I saw my beautiful twin soul standing by the window turn quickly with a smile. My heart seemed to contract, my breathing accelerated, and tears stung my eyes.

"Lea," I said, "you are the loveliest, most exciting woman in the world. I can't think of words that really describe how I feel about you."

"You are me, Jon," she replied, "my twin soul, and you

155

don't have to tell me how you feel. They are my feelings, too."

We stood silently, then reached out with our minds to each other and felt the strange and delightful sensations of mind contact.

As we slowly disengaged from our deep mind contact I could not help comparing Lea's fair-complexioned blond beauty with the dark loveliness of Carol. I compared Lea with the sun and Carol with the moon and knew that, while they were as different as the sun and moon, I loved them both.

Seeing the dancing lights in the blue eyes before me I knew that my thoughts were shared.

"I'm glad," Lea said, "that you have learned that Macro love is not limited to one person."

"I still don't understand it, Lea," I replied, "how I can love you both in such similar and yet different ways. Then to realize, by actually experiencing your feeling, that you really have no jealousy even as you observe me comparing your physical and mental attributes with Carol's."

Lea nodded her lovely blond head. "I know," she said, "that you would not be able to believe this possible if you had not developed telepathy. But then, it's easier for twin souls because it would be impossible for me to be jealous of myself."

"Oh, Lea," I cried out, taking her in my arms, "how am I going to do it? I have only three months. The possibility of losing you is more than I can handle. I never want to live separated from you again."

"But, Jon," she laughed softly, "have you never heard that it is better to have loved and lost than never to have loved at all?"

"How can you take it so lightly?" I asked.

"Because, Jon," she replied, "I know that the only separation possible exists at the micro levels—never at the Macro ones. We can be separated by time and space, but never in the Macro depths of our minds."

"All right," I stated, "there's my greatest motivation

for developing Macro awareness—so I will never have to feel separate from you again."

"The reason I asked you here today," she said, "is that both Rana and I feel you are ready to remember a few of your past lives."

"Terrific!" I said, "When do we start?"

"Right now," she replied. "Sit down and we'll ask C.I. to provide the stimuli for Macro contact."

She picked up my thought and said, "Macro contact can be achieved without either sexual union or even touching. This is fortunate because if we joined sexually now it would diminish your desire for Macro contact so greatly that it would probably be impossible for you to attain third-level awareness in the short time allotted."

"Then, you mean we can't share Macro immersion until I demonstrate third-level awareness?" I asked.

"Not and be able to permanently bridge the time barrier that separates us now," she replied. "But that only means we have less than three months to wait, and we can do that since it means a lifetime of being together thereafter in the Macro society."

As she finished these last words, C.I. began the now familiar visual and audio stimuli which helped produce such vast mind expansion. Very quickly I found myself flowing like a river through infinite space until I was joined by Lea and we were again one mind and one soul.

Then in my mind I heard Lea say that we would be going back in time until we reached a point where my soul had incarnated into a prehistoric Chinese culture.

Suddenly I found myself both experiencing the body of a thirty-year-old Chinese slave trader and simultaneously, observing from outside that body. I knew that I was a cruel and vicious person who took pleasure in the ill treatment of the slaves whom I owned and traded. Scene after scene of brutal, degrading treatment of others passed before my eyes and I felt sick with self-hatred and shame. Then I died and suffered the miserable existence of sharing the low astral planes with similar depraved

157

personalities like myself until I was born again into one of the earliest Egyptian dynasties.

I became aware of this next incarnation when I again saw and simultaneously experienced myself as a giant black Numidean slave working in the stone quarries of the Pharaoh. Unfortunately my physical vitality was tremendous, so I lived scores of years in extremely hard labor with many cruel slave masters who seemed to delight in laying their whips upon my massive back and shoulders. Finally, and mercifully, I died.

While I had the impression that there were other lifetimes in between, the next incarnation that I became aware of was in a later Egyptian period. I was a Pharaoh who succeeded in freeing the slaves in his land during his reign. I saw myself trying to rule wisely and well, but being constantly frustrated by the corrupt and treacherous priesthood. Finally my royal wrath could no longer be contained and I killed the fat and foppish high priest along with as many of his lesser priests as I could get my hands on. But my bloody actions divided my country, and I, too, was murdered at the end of a long civil war.

Again I had the impression of many incarnations intervening before I saw and felt myself wearing the robes of a cardinal in the early Renaissance church of Rome. I was a fanatic at insisting that sins be driven out of human flesh by torture. Gleefully and with "holy vengeance" I devised newer and better torture methods, such as—my God—chopping off my victim's limbs a section at a time. While I frequently used the burning stake, I usually reserved it for women who refused me their sexual favors. I was indeed a monstrous hypocrite. Because the pope was weak and I was rich and ruthless, I became the most powerful priest in the church. Fortunately for the people of Italy, who lived in fear of me, the plague favored them by carrying me off prematurely.

This death was followed by a hideous period, on the lowest astral planes. Since my selfish desires kept me from rising to higher levels, I was forced to associate with the most loathsome and distorted personalities.

158

Then brief impressions of other lives flashed by until once again I became aware of a vividly clear incarnation as the daughter of a poor stone-cutter living in a Spain shuddering from the excesses of the Inquisition. I was the eldest in a very poor but large family of eight daughters including myself. I worked long hours to support my aging parents and my many sisters and probably would have lived a long life of this menial drudgery if I had not had this one heretical obsession: I refused to accept the idea of eternal hell. My family spent many years trying to force me to recant this heresy until my sisters, in order to save my poor soul, called upon the officers of the Inquisition for help. My obsession was stronger than the pain of many ingenious means of torture and, in a last desperate attempt to save my soul, I was burned at the stake surrounded by the faces of my sisters praying for my redemption.

The pain and fear associated with this past flaming death caused me to wake up with a scream in the year 1976. It was 4 a.m. and Karl was asking me if I was all right. After assuring him that I was okay now, I fell back to sleep and awakened in my C.I. chair back in 2150.

Lea was bending over me wiping the sweat off my face with a damp cloth. Seeing my eyes open, she lowered her face to mine and gently kissed my lips. Then she said, "Now you know one of the reasons why micro man doesn't want to remember past lives."

"My God," I exclaimed, "if they are all as horrible as mine, I don't blame anyone for not wanting to remember them!"

"Oh, they aren't all horrible," Lea assured me. "You had many lives that were rather peaceful and uneventful. But you didn't learn much from most of them. The five incarnations that you've just relived formed a learning pattern which illustrated to you the consequences of cruel treatment of others. Your soul selects an opportunity for you to grow on. If you waste the opportunity in one life,

159

your soul balances that with an opposite opportunity in another life."

"That's a hard way to learn," I complained. "Does everyone have to learn that painfully?"

"Everyone who chooses the spiritual devolution of the soul ends up with total delusionary amnesia of their past and, thus, has no Macro awareness of the perfect order maintained by the soul in selecting learning opportunities. If you can't remember your macrocosmic oneness with all, you will desire micro power to alleviate your fears of loneliness and weakness. Micro man treats others selfishly, cruelly, to increase his feelings of power, adequacy, and security," was her answer.

"All right, Lea," I said. "I sure hope I learned something from those horrible experiences. Can't I relive some pleasant ones?"

"Certainly," she replied. "It won't be necessary to ask C.I. for help any more. We've opened a pathway to your past. In the future if you meditate deeply you will be able to recall fragments of many more lives. For the moment, however, lie back in your chair and I'll help you practice retrocognition."

I followed her suggestion and allowed her mind to help me relax and put aside my conscious micro concerns. Soon, with her help, I was once again floating through time—on and on—through peripheral flashes of other lives and experiences. However, these were not ones that Lea wished us to look at in more detail, so we continued our journey along the mighty river of time.

Before long I focused clearly on a life as an islander in the tropical South Pacific. It was a lovely peaceful life in a small Polynesian society in which I watched myself grow from a young boy into strong manhood. I married a dark lovely girl whom I recognized immediately as Carol, although her physical appearance was certainly not the same as in 2150. We had a number of children, among whom I noticed were Neal and Jean.

Our life on this Pacific island was one of cooperation and love. Our head man was a very wise and patient leader who seemed to know how to resolve human problems at an early stage before great harm could arise. By the time I reached middle age he was a very old man, yet I recognized in him the soul of Rana. Upon his death I was accepted as leader by all and spent many happy years before the advent of the white traders.

I was very old when the great ships arrived bearing the cruel, lust-filled white men. I tried to warn my people of the anger I felt in these strangers, but like curious children they could not resist the fascination and excitement surrounding these strange beings.

The fascination was short-lived for soon the white men began taking our young men and women off with them when they sailed away. The day came when if we saw the great white sails approaching our island, we would all try to hide. But our island was small and the ships sent out search parties to rout out all who hid. It was then that I tried to organize an escape to another island, but we were discovered and I, as the leader, was executed.

It seemed that after this life I had a very pleasant sojourn on the higher astral planes in which I renewed acquaintances with many old friends and was briefly reunited with Lea. Together we planned new incarnations in which we could learn to further overcome the micro desires which kept us separate. She left our temporary resting place first in order to incarnate as a male of the British nobility during the late 18th century. I left the astral level soon afterward to incarnate as a male in one of the North American Indian tribes of the early 19th century.

In this last incarnation I devoted my life to philosophy and healing and became a respected medicine man. In late middle age I began to spend almost all of my time seeking out and teaching young children how to live more loving and accepting lives. While I experienced some opposition to my teachings from the more warlike members of the tribe, my reputation as a healer was so great that no one openly opposed me. I am convinced that in time I could have changed the course of history for my

161

people, but again I was thwarted by white invaders.

One day while almost all of our men were off hunting, white soldiers came charging down upon our camp, killing women and children and anyone else they could find. I died trying to protect the young children of my school, some of whom I recognized as members of my 2150 Alpha.

When I had returned to consciousness in our C.I. room I asked Lea why it was necessary for me to experience such tragedy and frustration. She took her time before answering, then replied with a question of her own.

"From the seven lives you have now reviewed, Jon," she asked, "what's the most important lesson you have learned?"

"I'm not sure, Lea," I replied. "It seems that sooner or later my hopes and goals were always thwarted and I died frustrated and dissatisfied."

"Only your micro self was frustrated and dissatisfied," Lea said, "and only your micro desires and goals remained unfulfilled. In other words, the negative seeds you have sown have always produced a crop of frustration and misery, but the positive seeds have always produced happy, satisfying experiences."

"But in these last two lives I was killed trying to protect others," I protested.

"No," Lea replied, "your frustration was caused by your micro resistance. You felt that what was happening to your people was unjust, and bad. You did not accept it as a growth experience, perfect for its time and space, carefully selected by every soul who experienced it."

"Are you saying that I should have welcomed the destruction of my people in those lives?" I asked.

"Only," Lea replied, "if you had Macro awareness could you have accepted micro cruelty, lust, and greed with understanding and loving acceptance."

"But if you are a decent person, you must fight injustice," I insisted.

"If you have a micro perspective," Lea answered, "then

you will perceive injustice and have to struggle against it. But there is no injustice from a Macro view, for we can only experience that which we have created. So what were you resisting and fighting against?"

"My own learning experiences, I guess," was my reply.

"That's right." She nodded and smiled at me. "From the Macro view of cosmic oneness we can clearly see that all resistance is exerted against ourselves. We can see that we must reap the consequences of all our thoughts and actions—both positive and negative. It's only with the micro view that you can perceive any injustice or any enemy other than yourself."

"I guess it must take many lifetimes to learn to accept that," I commented.

"Yes, it's difficult for man," she replied, "but we have as many lifetimes as we need in which to learn it. Contrary to micro religion, there is no eternal infinite hell to punish temporary infinite mistakes. That would, indeed, be hellishly unjust."

"It seems to me," I said, "that as long as I can avoid other micro beings, I have no problems."

"Other than boredom," Lea answered. "But you don't learn very quickly by avoiding others just so you don't see your own shortcomings."

"What do you mean?" I asked.

"I mean," she answered, "that you feel uncomfortable and dissatisfied with others only to the extent that you don't feel adequate to deal with them—that is, only when you feel they are a threat to you. For instance, if in your past two lives you had been able to either drive your enemies away or help your people escape them, you would have been pleased with yourself. But this micro pleasure would only have postponed the time when you inevitably must learn your lessons and evolve."

"So if I hadn't experienced it in that life I would still have had it waiting for me in my next incarnation," I said.

"In this life, Jon, you hate to see people mistreated and you don't like people who hurt others. As you

163

evolve, you will realize that what people fear and hate most in others is only their own negative past. You, for example, treated slaves and other people cruelly in your past lives—now in this life you can't stand these traits in others," Lea explained.

"So you are saying," I interpreted, "that we feel uncomfortable with others and fear or hate them only to the extent that we see our own past selves in them."

Lea kissed me and said, "You're learning so fast, Jon."

"Ahh," I murmured, "if you were using the Macro perspective, you would be happy even if I was the slowest learner in the world."

Lea broke into joyous peals of laughter and finally said, "You're right, Jon. I can maintain the Macro perspective for only the briefest moments. But I can remember these moments, and that keeps me from getting caught for very long in micro viewpoints which might overwhelm me with misery and unhappiness."

"Then one difference," I said, "between micro man and Macro man is the degree of retrocognition or memory of his past."

"Exactly," Lea responded. "We live lives of fear, frustration, and inadequacy only to the extent that we have forgotten our past. This self-induced amnesia is always the result of our desperate attempts to delay re-taking classes—learning opportunities—that we failed in the past."

"Then the solution is to remember everything," I said.

"And when we do remember everything, including the illusory nature of our separateness," Lea said, "then we have total Macro awareness."

"Then according to Macro philosophy, all learning is simply remembering," I postulated.

"That's true," Lea replied, "but only from the Macro perspective—certainly not from any micro view. You've remembered a lot today, though. Now it's time for you to return to your Alpha."

"When will I see you?" I asked.

She smiled and the lights danced in her eyes as

she said, "When we are ready again, we'll see each other again."

I was able to accept that answer better this time. I left Lea at the C.I. center and walked back to my Alpha. I thought briefly of using the subway, but the early evening was so lovely that I decided to walk. Besides, it would give me an opportunity to think over some of my recent experiences.

When I got back to our Alpha the rest of the members were just finishing dinner, so I had missed the Macro dance and the swim. They greeted me warmly but there was no prying or questioning about my experiences. I quickly selected my meal, and enjoyed listening to the rest of my Alpha talking about visiting Micro Island. I soon discovered that they all planned to eventually volunteer for service on the island. Their discussion centered on what could be learned and at what triad or awareness level it could be learned best.

I told them about my seven life reviews and how I had recognized some of them in my last lifetime as the children I was trying to teach. They remembered that one, as well as many more in which they said we had known each other but which I had not yet remembered. I was fascinated listening to them talk about some of these lives and how they had developed the Macro power of retrocognition to the point where they could see the accumulating learning patterns and their slow but steady evolution in awareness.

I was reminded of the Macro learning curve which went up and down and up and down like a wave, with each up a little cumulatively higher than the last up and each down a little higher than the last down [see C.I. Data Excerpts]. Micro man with his limited temporal perspective can not see this cumulative effect and is, thus, often discouraged and overwhelmed with apparent futility and hopelessness at the many failures and frustrations in his life.

My Alpha had stayed at our table to keep me com-

165

pany while I ate, but now they went off to their various P.E. tutors.

I'm going to interject here the fact that after every meal we rinsed our mouths with a special water-like solution that not only cleaned our teeth but also made tooth decay impossible. There were no dentists in the Macro society just as there were no medical doctors. To me the liberation from the discomforts of a frequently sick and steadily decaying body was one of the greatest achievements of the Macro society. The thought that no one died until they chose to was phenomenal.

After the others had left, Carol told me that we would not be seeing Rana this evening but another tutor, Victor. As we made our way to the eleventh-floor tutoring rooms, Carol explained that she saw Rana only about once every three or four evenings. The rest of the Personal Evolution time was spent with Victor or occasionally other Macro counselors whom she had never seen before and rarely saw again.

I was unprepared for the huge stature of Victor. He was the tallest person that I had yet seen in 2150. At a little over seven feet two inches and weighing almost 300 pounds, Victor was an impressive-looking man. Deep healing tones of green dominated his tunic. He was magnificently proportioned, having the physical beauty of all Macro society members.

When I asked his age I learned that he had 71 years, but he looked no more than 30.

During the first half of our meeting Carol and Victor talked about the problems that Carol was experiencing in attaining Macro contacts. As they talked I was impressed with the qualities of patience, humor, and kindness that this mighty giant radiated. I could see why he would be a successful Macro counselor, for it was easy to talk with him. He always seemed to know the right words or action to stimulate your mind to further activity in discovering new insights.

She and Victor discussed the difference between desire —defined as a joyously peaceful acceptance of the fact

166

that what you most want to happen will happen—and anxiety, which was defined as a fear that what you most want to happen will not happen.

Then I talked about my realization that I would have to live on Micro Island soon if I was to learn how to evolve beyond my micro past to a Macro future. Victor agreed with me but suggested that I develop my Macro powers more fully before I volunteered as a resource person or tutor for Micro Islanders.

We discussed various ways of doing this. I wondered whether or not Carol should accompany me to Micro Island. We decided that her presence could help me grow a lot faster than if I went alone. She was delighted that I wanted her to come along.

As we were leaving, I told Victor that I was sure I had known him before. He laughed and said that he could remember having been tortured to death by me when I was a fanatical Italian cardinal. He assured me, however, that we had experienced other pleasant lifetimes together.

Back in our Alpha room Carol and I bathed together, then stretched out on our huge bed.

We discussed our day, and I mentioned how intriguing it was that I fortuitously translated to a point in time where there were so many of my friends or enemies from the past.

She assured me that there was nothing fortuitous about it. She went on to explain that all souls travel in groups, experiencing and re-experiencing each other in different roles, much the same as players in a road company who fill many different roles in many different plays, in many different towns, before their contract runs out. Yet, they are always interacting with basically the same players.

I teased her, saying that if she was my fellow player I might stay on the road forever. We rolled across the bed to the rhythm of her laughter.

She asked C.I. to provide Macro contact stimuli as we attempted to free our minds of all micro concern and accept the macrocosmic oneness of all.

Once again I became part of a great river flowing toward the beginning and end of all things—toward the infinite macrocosmic ocean. I flowed on and on, but this time there was an urgency to my movement. Instead of flowing in ever larger channels there seemed to be a constriction that was producing tension and unrest within me. I fought to break the growing pressure of restriction, but the harder I struggled, the greater the pressure grew, until my mind was filled with pain. Finally I screamed aloud, and the Macro stimuli ended along with the constricting pressure within my mind.

I looked at Carol and saw that her eyes were closed but her face was damp with tears, and I realized that my eyes were wet, too.

"What happened?" I asked. "What went wrong?"

Carol opened her eyes and looked at me. Then with a sad, tender smile she said, "I'm sorry, Jon, that I couldn't help you. It was my anxiety for Macro contact that got in our way again."

"Someone I used to know once told me that each thing happens in its own time. You can't push the river," I teased to lighten the mood.

"Knowing and doing are two very different things!" Carol responded, then added, "In order to apply what we learned this afternoon we must give up all micro desires that we are clinging to for maintenance of our micro egos."

I shook my head, saying, "That sounds so impossible that I don't understand how I ever achieved even one Macro contact, much less two of them."

"You had less to lose then, Jon—less to let go of," Carol said. "Now your micro pleasures are greater and they seem to outweigh your pleasure in and desire for Macro contact while at the same time increasing your anxiety for it!"

"What a dilemma," I moaned. "The more happiness I find with you and the Macro society, the less willing I am to give it up. The less willing I am to give it up, the less able I am to attain Macro contact. And if I can't attain more Macro contacts, I won't grow in awareness and I will lose it all!"

Suddenly we were entwined in one another's arms passionately devouring each other with kisses in a desperate effort to overcome a possible future of dismal separation and loss. I called to C.I. for Macro stimuli and the mounting resonances of our soul note vibrations filled the room. Now we could focus our minds and, thus, our bodies on Macro immersions, which did not require the giving up of everything and the acceptance of everything, as did Macro contact. Now we could concentrate on joining our two surging, pulsating rivers of desire for each other into one great river of peaceful unity and contentment. We succeeded gloriously.

As we lay resting peacefully together I thought to myself that this Macro immersion, which Carol and I had achieved, was so much more satisfying than any physical union I had ever experienced that I would never give it up voluntarily now that I had found it.

Yet, as I thought this, I heard Carol's voice in my mind saying, "But, Jon, you know that what we are enjoying is only temporal at best, lasting but a few minutes or hours. What we are both seeking is the infinite, timeless joy of total Macro awareness. Our anxiety regarding the possible loss of what we share only impedes our progress.

"We must move steadily on toward the ability to enjoy today fully without insisting that tomorrow hold the same thing. A foot must give up the security of one rung of a ladder before it can gain the security and achievement of a higher rung."

I sighed. "I know you're right, Carol. Every little girl knows that someday she will grow up and stop playing with dolls. Still, it would be difficult for her to imagine ever wanting to give them up."

"That's the nicest part, Jon. You don't ever have to give up anything that you don't want to give up. It's just that what you want to give up and what you want to keep changes with each plateau you reach. For ex-

169

ample, I know that you no longer 'want to keep' having sexual unions with anyone whose soul vibrations are not very close to your own. Yet this is not because anyone told you you had to give them up. It's the natural and inevitable evolution of the soul. Only by giving up the unevolved part of our micro load are we able to step one rung higher."

We kissed again with great longing and a tinge of sadness. Then I gently pushed Carol away from me and withdrew from her until we were separated by several feet. We lay for a while just looking at each other. Finally I said, "Carol, I'm not ready to give up my feelings for you. I want to possess you and cling to you, and I realize that these feelings are micro, not Macro."

"I feel the same way," she said. "Never before in this lifetime have I felt so intensely about anyone. But then, that's evolutionary, too. Each love we share prepares us to more fully experience the better one which lies ahead if we just evolve enough to be willing to take the risk of loving again and again as long as we live."

"It was two lifetimes ago that we lived together on that South Pacific island and loved each other as we love now," I recalled.

"You're thinking that if you hadn't remembered that past life your feelings for me wouldn't have grown so intense, aren't you?" Carol said.

"Yes," I said, "but I'm very happy that I did remember you, for that was the most enjoyable lifetime I have yet reviewed, in spite of its tragic ending."

"Oh, Jon," she said, "I love you so much, but I can remember a lifetime many ages ago which I shared with a twin soul, and I know that someday I will reunite with him just as someday you will reunite with Lea."

I thought about what she had just said and then I smiled.

"You're right, as always," I said. "When I'm with Lea I know that she represents ultimate completion for me. I know that I love her with every vibration of my soul, my mind, and my body. But, Carol, I also know

170

that I love you with a love that is equal in ultimate value, if not in ultimate nature."

"It is this very problem," Carol replied, "that must be resolved in order to attain the highest levels of awareness."

"You mean," I said, "that Lea has already solved this problem?"

"Of course," Carol nodded. "She wouldn't be aquamarine if she hadn't been able to give up all micro desires many times. Certainly to be able to give you to me so that you may obtain Macro immersion and Macro contacts with me, not herself, demonstrates very highly evolved awareness and balance."

Now Carol closed the distance between us and was once more nestled in my arms. "Lea can remember," she continued, "lifetimes with you that you have not yet remembered. It's significant that when she was guiding you through the pages of your akashic record, that is, your memory records of the past, she did not select a lifetime which the two of you had shared."

"Why not?" I asked.

Carol answered, "Don't you realize that if she had shown you only the happy moments of completion between the two of you, there would have been no micro challenges to overcome?"

"You mean," I said, "like my problem of giving up my desires for you?"

"Yes," she replied. "After all, if she had helped you to relive only moments you had shared with her, you would not have remembered your past life with me and you would not have this overwhelming desire for me."

"My God!" I exclaimed. "She knew that she was intensifying my desires for you. She deliberately set up this problem."

"Let's more accurately say that *you* set it up in order to help yourself overcome the difficulty you have in letting go of micro situations and relationships," Carol answered. "Lea knew that if she didn't help you overcome this problem you would not be able to achieve level-three

171

awareness and you would be separated for at least another lifetime. And remember, she can recall the joy of Macro immersion with you, a twin soul. Yet she chose to give this up so that you might attain a greater goal—union with her and the Macro society for the rest of this lifetime."

"And if I don't achieve level-three awareness," I responded "she'll have sacrificed herself for nothing."

"Not for nothing, Jon. For growth.

"And not herself. Just a few days, weeks, or months of one lifetime. She knows that there are many more—or, converting it from our simultaneous-time concept to your linear-time concept—there *will be* many more. Besides, every failure is a success, and I'm sure that Lea doesn't forget that very often."

I nodded. "Even if I fail, she'll be able to accept it as bringing me that much closer to success. However, unless I have attained a rather high level of awareness, I won't be able to accept my failure in spite of the fact that I intellectually know I should."

"Tonight as we go to sleep," Carol suggested, "let's ementally reaffirm our plan for our growth."

"All right," I said. "I understand that we get what we really inwardly want most, so I guess it makes good sense to be specific about our intent."

"First," Carol began, "we will be joyously accepting of what is, knowing that it is our own perfect creation.

"Second, we will, in our daily activity, walk with an open hand—that is, we will 'hold on to' nothing.

"Third, we will accept every opportunity for growth and do our best to learn the lesson it offers.

"Fourth, we will live constantly in the joy of our macrocosmic oneness with all—or, stated within your concept of time—all that is, all that was, and all that ever will be.

"Let's keep these intentions, these paths, lightly and joyously within our essence as we drift off to sleep."

As I was falling asleep, I hoped that Carol was having better success than I in convincing myself that I had the

172

strength and understanding to resolve our problem. I wanted it resolved, but I didn't want to pay the price. No matter how I argued with myself, I couldn't give up my anxiety about losing Carol.

Finally, exhausted from the struggle, I fell asleep.

CHAPTER 11:

Neda

I awakened to the sound of Karl closing the door as he left for his class. It was early, only 7:45. I lay back in bed and wished that Carol was beside me. I wished that I had the power to pull her through time 174 years to the now of my apartment.

I had to smile at the thought of what a sensation Carol would make if I took her to the student union—her magnificent six-foot-three-inch body, her face of incredible classic beauty, and her tremendous joy and vitality would really stir things up. Talk about riots! I could see micro man fighting savagely just to get close to her.

And how would I feel? Well, I thought, from my limited micro perspective, I wouldn't want to share her with anyone, so I wouldn't even let her step out of the apartment!

I finally decided that it was a good thing I couldn't transport Carol to 1976 because 1976 wasn't ready for her, and while I was in 1976 I probably wouldn't be ready for her, either.

This last thought made me wonder what would happen when Carol and I went to Micro Island. Of course, the inhabitants would be used to seeing members of the Macro society, but they often tried to kill these visitors. How would I react if someone tried to kill Carol? I didn't have to think very long about my answer—I would fight and even kill, if I had to, in order to protect her.

Oh, that's great, I thought, now I'm going to Micro Island to perform like a medieval knight errant fighting for the life and honor of his fair lady.

I shook my head in amused frustration. Where Carol was concerned, I was developing some very micro feelings. I decided that I had better practice my Macro powers with micro people today and see if I could do better than I had at the supermarket. Maybe I could learn how to comfortably deal with micro people before I went to Micro Island. After all, 1976 offered me an ample supply to practice on!

By the time I was through eating I had decided that when I finished writing in my journal I would go looking for threatening situations and see if I could learn to handle them.

Three hours later I was sitting at a table in the seemingly always crowded student union cafeteria drinking hot chocolate and trying to telepathically tune in to the people about me.

At first I picked up the usual micro concerns such as fear about semester exams, excitement over this evening's basketball game or date, money worries, or frustrations at not being more successful with others. This last frustration was often sexual, particularly from the table full of men near me who were wistfully eyeing the girls as they passed by. It was their scornful sneers at one of the girls who passed that caused me to look up to see the object of their contempt.

She was a tall, thin girl, so gaunt that she appeared almost emaciated. Her hair was long and straight without any luster and hung in untidy disarray about her shoulders. Her face with its bony nose was one of the most unappealing I had ever seen. Her clothes were too loose, too long, and so nondescript that they seemed to hang on her like burlap bags.

I reached out and made contact with her mind and quickly withdrew. Never had I experienced such sadness, such misery, such bitter hopelessness. I shook my head to clear it of the repugnance, then looked at her again.

She was sadly looking about for an empty table where she could be somewhat away from others. It was close to noon and almost all the tables were filled except my small one, which had space for another person across from me. I decided to have her sit at my table. I reached out with my mind and willed her to look at me. She did and I smiled at her, gesturing at the empty seat across from me. She looked behind her and to her side to see if I wasn't addressing someone else, then looked at me with a bewildered and pathetically uncertain gaze. I sent out a flood of warm, confident, accepting thoughts. The change in her expression was slow in coming, but when it came I saw the beginnings of an incredulous look of hope.

I got up as she approached my table and helped her with the tray upon which she was precariously balancing a bowl of soup and a glass of milk. She thanked me in a low whisper, seated herself quickly, and proceeded to occupy herself with her soup, using it almost as a barrier to hide behind.

I continued to bombard her mind with the most loving and accepting thoughts that I could generate.

After about five minutes of my intense struggle to overcome her mental despair and chronic suspiciousness I began to achieve some success. She was feeling much more comfortable with me and was beginning to steal occasional glances at my face. It was then that I decided to try talking with her.

"I'm Jon Lake," I said. "I'm working on my doctorate in psychology."

176

She looked up at me with a startled expression. I could feel her uncertainty as to how to respond. I smiled my most engaging smile and said, "I guess you're not sure how to take my talking to you when we've never met before. I couldn't help feeling that you were lonely, and I can remember feeling that way myself."

She bobbed her head at me and then stared intently at her empty soup bowl.

I reached deep within her mind and discovered a great longing to respond to me but an equally great fear of being rejected or looking foolish—those two universal fears of micro man. I continued to beam positive, confident, and accepting thoughts to her.

I wondered what her name was and willed her to tell me. There was a short struggle, then she spoke.

"My name is Neda Cricksley," she whispered in such a low voice that if I hadn't already picked her name up telepathically I'd have had to ask her to repeat it.

"Neda," I said, "I like that name and I like you, too."

After I said this I realized that for some reason I did like this girl. I had gotten beneath her unattractive surface and made contact with a part of her soul which was very satisfying to me. Without thinking, I reached out and captured one of her thin bony hands.

Again I saw the startled expression on her face, but I willed her to accept my gesture as one of kindness and genuine concern. I could feel the tension in her arm and body slowly subside. I decided it was time to take the next step.

"Tell me about yourself, Neda," I asked. "I want to know all about you." I felt her wondering why I should want to know about her. "Because I like you," I responded to this unspoken thought. "And I think I can help solve some problems that are bothering you."

"How do you know I have problems that you can help me with?" she whispered.

"Well," I replied, "everyone has some problems, and one of my goals in life is to help as many people as possible solve their problems."

She thought about this for a moment, then said, "I want to thank you for being so kind to me. I've never met anyone like you before. I don't know how or why, but I'm convinced that somehow you do like me and you do want to help me. I . . . I'm very grateful."

"Then you'll let me have the pleasure of getting you dessert," I said. "How about a chocolate sundae, or maybe strawberry?"

She smiled shyly and didn't respond, but I caught her thought of how good a strawberry sundae would taste.

"Okay," I said, "I'll surprise you. All you have to do is save my seat for me."

As I left our table I sent as powerful a thought as I could to the girl at the ice cream counter, and by the time I got to her she was already busily preparing two sundaes, one chocolate and one strawberry. I waited until she finished, thanked her for reading my mind, and paid her for them. All the way back to our table I could see her startled expression and feel her wonderment at the kooky possibility that she really had somehow read my mind.

The strawberry sundae proved to be the final step in overcoming Neda's shyness with me. She began talking about herself. She was a twenty-year-old liberal arts junior who lived off campus with her mother and stepfather. While she didn't say so, I picked up from her mind that she desperately wanted to escape from her tyrannical mother, who hated her for being ugly, and a coarse sneering stepfather who enjoyed tormenting her about her looks.

She didn't know what she wanted to do after college and, while her grades were excellent, going to classes was a torture because of her shyness. She was majoring in English composition and literature, and her one escape was in reading and writing.

As I listened intently to her talking about her happiness in writing short stories, I noticed that the more she talked about this area in her life the more animated her face became. The dark eyes came alive and the voice

178

rose from a whisper to an easily understandable level.

I learned from her mind that I was the second person in her life that she had ever talked to about her writing. The first person had been her high school English teacher, an elderly lady who had died shortly after Neda graduated. Since this old woman had been the only friend in her life, her loss had been almost too much for Neda to endure.

I realized that Neda had completely accepted her mother's view of her as being an ugly blight on her parent's lives. Consequently she was filled with self-loathing and massive feelings of worthlessness and inadequacy. It was no wonder that she tried desperately to avoid contact with others, since she believed her appearance was completely revolting to all who saw her.

Now, how could I help Neda? Every night I had access to all the knowledge of the Macro society's Central Information. How could my Macro powers change Neda's life? What did I want to do?

Well, I thought, I want to help her find a new life in which she can learn to like herself and the world about her. But wouldn't I need all the power and wisdom of a Rana to accomplish such a miracle? As I carefully, but surreptitiously, examined the face and figure of Neda, I wondered if even tenth-level awareness would be sufficient to change Neda's self-concept. But I decided I was going to try.

After questioning Neda about her typing ability and learning that she was a very good typist, I offered her a job typing up notes from the dissertation research that Karl and I had been doing and which he was still working on. When I finally convinced her that I really needed her help and that she would be doing me a great favor by accepting the job, I took the big plunge.

"Neda," I said, "I want you to move out of your mother's home and into an apartment at the building where I live. Yes," I said, forestalling her objection, "I know you don't have much money, but since Karl and I own the building we live in, your rent can be part of

179

your monthly salary. Karl and I will be conveniently located near you so you'll actually be able to function not only as a typist, but also as a sort of research assistant."

I had been talking fast and off the top of my head, but now I paused to check Neda's reaction. She was so overwhelmed by me that resistance seemed impossible. I felt that somewhere in the past hour she had capitulated totally to the loving accepting thoughts I had been sending her. But then, how could a person languishing in hell turn down an invitation to heaven? I told her that I would help her move into her new quarters immediately.

Fifteen minutes later we arrived at her home in a taxi. The house was a run-down two-story stucco located in a fast-decaying neighborhood. I told our taxi driver to wait for us and then accompanied Neda to her door. There she hesitated until I calmly, but firmly, opened the door for her, and ushered her inside. I immediately realized why she had hesitated, since charging toward us out of the kitchen was the most formidable-looking old harridan I had ever seen. This was Neda's mother, who was roaring at Neda about being late and eyeing me suspiciously.

After Neda tried to respond to her mother and got shouted down, I decided to lend a hand. I told Neda to go to her room and pack her belongings, then, with a gentle nudge, sent her on her way. I stopped her mother in mid-roar with a mighty PK shove that sent her reeling backwards to land with a thud on the couch.

"Be quiet, Mrs. Cricksley," I said. "I want you to hear what I've got to say."

Her mouth was open but no sound came out, and her eyes were enormous as she finally managed to gasp, "You pushed me!"

"Really, Mrs. Cricksley," I replied, "you know that I didn't touch you. Now pay attention to me. I've offered your daughter a job as typist and research assistant to myself and my partner. We're doing psychological research at the university. I've asked her to take an apartment near the university so she'll be closer to her work. I'll advance her enough on her salary so that she can pay the rent and live quite comfortably. Now do you have any questions?"

Mrs. Cricksley was obviously not used to being dominated and treated in such a confidently imperious manner. She opened and closed her mouth, for all the world like an ugly flounder that has just found itself beached. I decided to keep the pressure on before she could jump back into the water.

"Of course," I continued, "this will relieve you of the considerable financial burden of caring for your daughter and providing her with an education. Naturally her salary will be sufficient to comfortably cover the tuition for her remaining years of college."

I had decided to go all the way. Since Karl and I had invested our inheritance in the apartment building we lived in, we had more than sufficient funds for our rather modest needs and could afford my project with Neda without too much difficulty.

Mrs. Cricksley was shaking her head in a bewildered manner. Things were happening just too fast for her to comprehend. Was she really going to be able to unload that ugly blight of a daughter? she was thinking. I easily picked up her thoughts. However, it was painful for me to tune into the old woman's mind. There was no physical ugliness that could match the mental ugliness of her mind. It was a seething caldron of spite, greed, jealousy, and crawling hatreds. I withdrew my mind contact with a violent shudder of revulsion.

At that moment Neda entered the room with all her worldly possessions in a small battered suitcase. When her mother protested the ownership of the suitcase I swiftly handed her a twenty-dollar bill saying that I was sure that this would amply repay her. She was still looking greedily at the bill in her hand when I took the suitcase from Neda and hurried her out of the house to the waiting taxi.

Shortly over an hour later, having stopped off at a

supermarket (a different one!) and purchased some forty dollars' worth of food, I was busily stocking the refrigerator of Neda's new apartment. It was a large three-room apartment with bedroom, living room, and kitchen, and was nicely furnished. Neda walked about it in a happy daze. She kept saying, "I don't know what to say, and I don't know how to thank you, Mr. Lake."

"Please call me Jon," I kept saying as I put away her groceries. "And remember, I live just one floor above you in apartment 303 in case you need anything. I'll have the phone connected tomorrow so you can call me any time."

Neda came partially out of her daze and asked, "But when do I start to work and where?"

"Tomorrow," I said, "you can start to work right here in your apartment. I'll come back this evening with my typewriter, which I'll leave with you. It's a little portable electric. Easy to use."

Then I persuaded her to sit down with me in her comfortable new living room. For the next half-hour I encouraged her to talk about her writing and reassured her that she could continue taking all the courses she wanted at the university, although I felt she looked upon her new job as an opportunity to drop her courses. All the while I was there, I kept up a steady flow of the most positive and confident telepathic messages. By the time I left her she was almost glowing with happiness and her face didn't look anywhere near as ugly as when I had first seen it.

By the time I got back to my apartment, I was ready for a rest. All this practice of my new powers had taken its toll, and it felt good to sit down. After resting a few minutes I brought this journal up to date.

When Karl came in I handed him my journal and headed for the kitchen to cook up a couple of steaks.

I caught myself wishing for the mealtime conveniences of 2150.

Since I had left Neda I had tuned in to her every fifteen or twenty minutes to give her another mental shot

182

of loving acceptance and confidence. It seemed to be working well.

Over dinner Karl and I discussed my project with Neda and I solicited his help. He was perfectly agreeable to my wanting us to help her and said that he would be glad not to have to depend on the university typing pool any longer. I didn't reveal my long-range plans for Neda, which involved shaping an entirely new self-concept for her. I decided I would let Karl meet her and then we could talk further about my plans.

About eight that evening Karl and I went, typewriter in hand, down to Neda's apartment. She welcomed us with a little shyness but talked rather easily with Karl about the typing requirements of our research. I let him do almost all the talking, and when we left, almost an hour later, I was congratulating myself on my progress with Neda. However, Karl brought me back to reality.

"Really, Jon," he said when we were back in our apartment, "you weren't kidding when you said she was homely."

"You weren't very impressed," I commented.

Karl laughed and said, "I was impressed all right! Come on, Jon. She's probably a very nice person, but did you look at her? My God, she's a walking disaster area!"

"Hmm," I responded. "You really think it's that bad, huh?"

Karl shook his head. "You know, it seems to me that if you were going to buy her groceries and provide her with an apartment, you could have at least provided her with some decent clothes, too."

"Yeah, I know, Karl," I agreed, "they're pretty bad. I wanted to fix her up with something better, but I don't know anything about women's clothes. I thought one of your girlfriends could help you pick out some nice things for you to give her."

"You want me to do this?" Karl asked with a startled expression.

"Of course," I explained, "the more positive male attention we can give her, the sooner we'll be able to

183

change her self-concept from one of self-loathing to one of self-confidence."

"But—but, Jon," Karl sputtered, "you can't give her a new face and figure, so it certainly isn't fair to kid her along."

"I'm not kidding her," I answered. "She's a valuable and worthwhile person no matter how she looks, and I'm going to let her know that at least you and I think so."

"Yeah, but what about other people?" Karl objected. "How are you going to help her adjust to the fact that everyone else will continue to view her as her old homely self? That's got to keep her self-concept a shambles for as long as she lives."

"I think she can become physically attractive," I said. "After all, she wouldn't look so scrawny with another twenty pounds on her!"

"Fifty would be more like it!" Karl replied. "Why, she must be five feet eight but she looks like she might weigh 90 pounds if we got her good and wet. Even if she put on enough weight to curve her out, how are you going to hide that nose of hers?"

"Hmm," I pondered, "you're right about her nose. But I'm sure a little plastic surgery would fix that up. We can afford it, can't we?"

Karl gave me a startled look, and said, "Boy, you've really gone overboard! Sure, I guess we can afford it, Jon, but do you know what you're talking about? Do you have any idea how much this little project of yours is going to cost? Well, let me tell you . . . it's going to cost a pile!"

"I couldn't find a better use for it, Karl," I said. "Besides, if I'm successful I won't need any money three months from now."

"But if you're not successful," Karl grunted, "you'll have sure cleaned out your account."

I laughed at Karl's gloomy expression. "Cheer up," I said. "If micro man can earn a million selfishly I'm sure that with the aid of my Macro powers I can earn a million unselfishly."

184

"What other projects have you got in mind?" Karl asked a bit sarcastically.

"I don't know for sure," I said. "Maybe I'd better see how this one comes out before I start another one."

"That's a damned sound idea," Karl said with relief.

We talked for a while more about about 2150; then I said that I was eager to get back to C.I. and ask some more questions, especially about how I could work this miracle I had embarked upon, and retired early.

CHAPTER 12:

The Fifty-Foot Leap

I awakened to the gentle pressure of warm lips on mine and the sounds of our soul notes beginning to resonate in my mind. I responded eagerly and soon joined Carol in the ecstasy of physical and emental contact. These delights grew in awareness and intensity until the unifying joy of Macro immersion was ours.

As we lay quietly, still happily entwined, I thought once again of how different my sexual experiences with Carol had been from those of my micro past. Before Carol and my Macro immersions, I had always felt either guilty or fearful, or simply unfulfilled by my sexual experiences. I wondered if anyone had ever attained Macro immersion before the Macro society.

"It was very rare," Carol answered my thought, "and most of them took place between twin souls."

"Since twin souls rarely incarnate together," I said,

"that goes a long way toward explaining the sexual frustrations of micro man."

"Sexual relationships which do not attain Macro immersion are only of fleeting satisfaction," Carol explained.

"Wait a minute," I said. "That means that the vast majority of sexual relationships, prior to the Macro society, have not been fulfilling."

"That's right," Carol nodded. "They usually left the participants with a strong underlying desire to start over again, since their true longing was unfulfilled."

"Then you're saying that any sexual relationship between you and me that does not reach Macro immersion would be unfulfilling."

"That's right," Carol replied. "Now you can appreciate how unselfish the other girls of our Alpha were being when they agreed to have a sexual relationship with you if you so desired."

"They knew," I said, "that their soul notes were too dissimilar from mine to attain Macro immersion, yet to help me learn this they were willing to experience an unsatisfying union."

"However," Carol added, "to the extent that you give unselfishly of yourself to another it cannot be an unpleasant experience."

I shook my head. "That explains it. . . that's why micro man experiences so much guilt, anxiety, and frustration associated with sex," I said. "He almost always uses sex for his own selfish purposes, so the result is bound to be something less than complete fulfillment."

"That's right," Carol responded, "and even the micro view that sex is sanctified if it is used only for the purpose of creating children is false, because micro man views his children as possessions, thus, uses them for selfish purposes."

"Not the least of which must be micro man's hope for immortality through his children," I reasoned.

"Yes." Carol smiled. "Man, for centuries, pursued what he called immortality—that celestial heaven where his eternity of days would be spent floating from cloud to

187

cloud with a harp in his hand and a blissful smile on his face. He just had not yet evolved far enough along the m-M continuum to remember his past lives, and if man can't remember his past lives he can't be expected to understand the true concept of immortality. It would be like expecting a person who has been blind since birth to understand the color yellow.

"Many of your religions compounded this problem," she continued. "Any religion that denies the human soul its immortal past is going to have difficulty teaching an immortal future."

I thought about that for a bit then said, "I can see where that's one of the big problems of Christianity."

"That's right," Carol agreed. "Any religion that depends on a priesthood for its truths is micro. Macro man learns truths by using his power of retrocognition to read the universal akashic records which contain a full account of everything that ever happened."

"You mean," I questioned, "if your personal akashic record of your own past doesn't include something, you can check a universal akashic record that does?"

"Yes," she explained, "it's like a universal C.I. that has a videotape of everything that has ever happened."

"Then you wouldn't have to be dependent on anyone else's interpretation of anything," I said. "Instead of arguing about what Lao-tzu, Gautama, or Jesus said or didn't say, you could just check the universal akashic records and both see and hear every event in their lives."

Carol nodded and said, "Exactly. We've done this with all the great philosophers of history."

"My God, that sounds fascinating! Could you show me how to do that, Carol? Maybe today?" I asked, eager to tap this incredible new resource.

"It's up to you, Jon. I should warn you, though, that while using the akashic records is a great educational technique, it is not of much use in attaining greater Macro awareness. That can only be achieved by tapping the same source of all wisdom-love that the great Macro philosophers of all time have tapped—the macrocosm or universal mind—then practicing, through application in your daily life, what you learned from that contact."

I was disappointed to hear that this marvelous new experience which I was so eager to embark upon would not help me reach my goal of level-three awareness. It was with reluctance that I decided I could not afford to take the time to learn this new skill until after I reached my more important goal.

Carol sensed my conflict and, after a telepathic reassurance that she felt my decision was a wise one, she invited me to share an invigorating bath with her before joining the rest of our Alpha for breakfast.

After breakfast Carol suggested that I could use C.I. in our room while she used the one at the center. I told her I would rather walk to the center and enjoy the beautiful lake, the trees, and the flowers under the clear blue sky of this unpolluted world.

"I can read about your polluted world," she said, "and I can see and hear video tapes of it in all its grimness, but only when I remember my past life during that period can I truly appreciate the beauty of our world."

"Hey, that's right. You lived your most recent past life in the 20th century, didn't you? You said you died in the 1990s," I recalled.

"Yes," she replied, "in the 1970s I was a student. I took every opportunity to protest the criminal contamination of our planet. In spite of popular protests, the vested interests had their way till the pollution of the '80s made that of the '70s look very mild indeed."

"Then it just got worse and worse," I said, "and nothing was done to correct it?"

"Oh, lots of little things were done," she responded, "but it was too late for half-way measures. It would have required world-wide cooperation through a world-wide government, but this was impossible for micro man with his micro philosophy of life. Unified world government requires a Macro view with equal concern for the health, safety, and well-being of all mankind. Micro man was not

189

willing to make the sacrifices necessary to achieve this goal."

"I guess," I said, "I'm using a micro perspective when I feel sorry for micro man's suffering and miserable death. I know that it was the only way he could learn the consequences of his selfish micro ways, but I still feel remorse about the tragic deaths."

Carol responded saying, "Micro man had to perish so that Macro man could be born. Death is only bad when it is taken out of the context of the soul evolution and the cumulative Macro effect."

As we talked we had left our Gamma building and were walking beside the lake toward the center when suddenly I stopped and pointed at a figure on the lake.

"Look, Carol!" I said, surprised, "Is that really someone walking on the lake?"

"Yes," she replied. "It's probably a level eight or nine practicing levitation."

"Why not a level ten?" I asked.

"Because," Carol answered, "they don't have to practice."

The figure had been too distant for me to get a close look at levitation, and it soon disappeared into the water.

"I guess whoever it was got tired," I postulated, "and is now taking a bit of a swim!"

"Maybe," Carol replied, "or maybe swimming just looked like it might be a little more fun. Why don't we do a little practicing ourselves, then you can learn to levitate, too."

With these words Carol leaped into the air and floated about three feet above the ground for almost ten seconds before descending gently to the earth.

"I didn't realize that you were that advanced," I said. "What sort of thought did you use?"

"I just visualized myself floating in the air," she replied.

"Hmm," I murmured. "I guess I can at least try it out." I did and almost immediately landed back on the ground.

Carol picked up my puzzlement and answered, "You

190

forgot to raise your vibrations by recalling Macro contact—your macrocosmic oneness with all."

I followed her suggestion until I felt joyously calm and very buoyant. Then I visualized myself about six feet off the ground and easily leaped to this height. I stayed up for almost five seconds before the fatigue overcame me, then started to come down gently but ran out of PK about two feet from the ground and landed with a thud.

I was thrilled with my unbelievable success. I mean, just think of it—me, Jon Lake—levitating. Wow!

I decided that I could just as easily visualize myself at thirty feet off the ground or even higher, if I was willing to come back down right away. However, I was tired from my first effort and postponed any further attempts until I was completely rested.

"I'll bet I could set a new world high jump record back in 1976 if I wanted to," I observed. "By golly, I'd be right in time for the Olympics, too!"

Carol replied, "A new world record in pole vaulting, too, and you wouldn't even have to use the pole! However, micro man gets pretty frightened of anyone who does things too far out of the ordinary, so I suggest you be careful."

"Yeah," I said, "and when micro man is frightened, look out. I wouldn't want to be locked up as a freak, or a national defense resource."

Carol nodded. "Micro man does have a tendency to hate anyone who makes him feel inferior. That's why our visits to Micro Island are so dangerous for those who do not have pretty well-developed Macro powers."

"Speaking of Micro Island," I said, "I want to visit there as soon as you feel our combined Macro powers will protect us."

"All right," Carol answered as we reached my C.I. room. "I'll tell you when I think we're ready."

Then she squeezed my hand affectionately and said, "See you at lunch," and was gone down the long corridor.

As soon as I was seated in my favorite C.I. room overlooking the lake, I began asking C.I. questions about the uses of Macro powers to help micro man. Over and over C.I. kept telling me that no one can be helped until they are both willing and ready. This was the same as having sufficient desire and a belief, she said.

When I asked specifically how I could help Neda I learned that PK could be used to affect the seven gland centers of the body and, thereby, cause changes in physical appearance.

I spent the rest of the morning studying diagrams of the glandular system and learning all I could about how to use PK to change Neda's physical appearance to one of greater attractiveness. It seemed overwhelmingly complex and difficult to understand at first, but C.I. was the greatest resource ever, with an unending supply of patience. By noon I felt hopeful about my chances of changing Neda's appearance for the better.

When Carol joined me we took our CN's with water, then walked toward the recreation areas. On the way we practiced our PK with pebbles again and I told Carol about my hopes for Neda back in 1976. She agreed this would be a good application of my growing Macro powers.

As I was about to take my next step I stopped in midstride, for there before me, basking itself in a pool of sunshine, was a snake about six feet long. Carol obviously hadn't seen it, for she was about to walk on. I grabbed her arm and pulled her to me.

She looked at me with surprise, then, remembering how new I was at all this, reassured me, saying, "It's all right, Jon. I'm not afraid; therefore, the snake won't harm me."

Carol took my hand and I, somewhat reluctantly, permitted her to lead me closer until I had a clear view of the rattles on its tail. I stopped and said, "Maybe a rattlesnake won't harm you, Carol, because you're not afraid, but I, for one, am damned scared!"

"Then stay here," Carol suggested, "and I'll show you something."

With these words she walked up to what looked to me like a deadly rattlesnake, bent over and, putting her hands

192

Carol,

Please

Return

Book

when

finished

took a while

to get this

copy!

Love

underneath it, gently lifted it in her arms and began walking toward me. My mouth was dry, sweat seemed to be spurting out of every pore of my body, my heart pounded under the impact of more adrenaline than my system could handle. There was no doubt in my mind that snakes had always frightened me, and this one in Carol's arms was no exception. Then for the first time I heard the ominous rattle begin and saw the snake's head jerk back in striking position, its eyes fastened with deadly menace upon me.

"No closer, Carol, please," I stammered, backing away.

She stopped and began talking soothingly to the by now intensely angry snake in her arms. Surprisingly, in a very few seconds the sound of the frantic rattling ceased and I could see the snake's tightly coiled body beginning to relax. As I watched this seeming miracle unfold before me I realized that once Carol had picked the snake up I had been convinced that no harm would come to her even when the deadly reptile was at its angriest. My fear had all been for myself. I was filled with shame and embarrassment.

"I don't blame you for being afraid," Carol said. "Obviously you've suffered great pain and anguish, possibly death, from contact with snakes in past lives. The fear generated then was so powerful that it has stayed with you."

"I can believe that," I replied, "because as far back as I can remember I've always been afraid of snakes. Obviously this one recognized my fear and responded to it."

"That's right, Jon," she agreed. "No animal can attack a person who is demonstrating Macro love."

"Okay," I acknowledged, "Macro man isn't afraid, but obviously I'm not very Macro in this area. Is there anything I can do about it?"

"Sure," Carol answered. "Since you have already experienced Macro contact you have only to remember it sufficiently to have all fear removed from your mind. You can't be afraid of yourself!"

I was skeptical of this answer, and in the end it was only because of my telepathic contact with Carol that I

193

succeeded in perfecting the recall. Then we maintained a very strong telepathic bond which continued to support our Macro contact memory, as, after almost forty-five minutes, I was finally able to approach the snake, touch it, and even hold it in my hands. It was, of course, my own doubt that caused me to have such difficulty.

We placed the snake back in his sunning spot and continued our walk. I asked Carol if she thought I was cured of my fear of snakes. She laughed and told me that it wasn't all that easy, but having experienced such a successful confrontation with my phobia, the fear would be greatly diminished. If I practiced for a while, dealing with it as we had, it would soon be gone. I had to admit that I had never imagined it would be possible for me to hold a live poisonous snake in my hands without fear. Then I asked Carol about other wild animals.

She told me that during the planetary pollution and overpopulation crisis, many types of animal life had died off. However, the early Macro society had preserved as many species as it could. Now, most animal life had made a remarkable comeback from almost complete extinction, for man had finally ended his relentless destruction of them and their food chain. I was pleased to hear that even the great cats such as the leopard, tiger, and lion had survived.

"But what will you do if they become too numerous?" I asked.

"Oh," she said, "we control the total ecological balance of our planet, not by killing, but by maintaining a balance of nature so that no species overbreeds for very long."

"Speaking of overpopulation," I said, "you know, I'm really surprised that I haven't seen more people during our walks to the center and to the recreation areas. Why is this?"

"We don't need to crowd each other," Carol replied, "because we're not afraid of being alone. With telepathy we need never be alone, and we need never invade the mental or physical privacy of others without their consent.

194

Besides, you haven't seen much of our Delta—only the student Gamma area."

"That's true," I agreed, "although on my first visit I wandered for some time through your gardens and woods, yet Lea was the only person I saw."

"Don't forget," Carol reminded me, "each Delta has 100 square miles of living space devoted mostly to wooded parkland. Ten thousand people can live very uncrowded lives in our Deltas if they live them in a Macro fashion."

"Someday," I said, "I must walk all around the lake and see all the other Gamma buildings."

"Why don't we do it now?" Carol asked.

"Well," I answered, "if I remember correctly, the lake is five miles long and two miles wide, so from where we are now it would be a rather long walk—over fifteen miles —and I wanted to join Neal and Jean today."

"We can do both," Carol replied. "We'll just run most of the way using Macro contact energy."

"You mean," I asked, "every time we get tired we recall our last Macro contact and renew our energy supply while at the same time washing away our fatigue?"

"Well, sort of," she answered. "What we'll do is maintain a constant Macro contact memory which will allow us to use a little PK to run very lightly and fast. Imagine your body weighing only a few pounds and then imagine that the force of gravity is much less—only about one-tenth its usual force."

At first all this seemed complicated and I had a lot of difficulty believing it was possible. I got off to a mighty funny-looking start, but after we got going I was able, through our telepathic contact, to see how Carol was using her mind. Then by the same telepathic bond that had finally enabled me to overcome my fear of the snake, I learned how to run as I had seen Lea run on my first visit to 2150.

For a person who has always loved running, this experience of almost flying through the air as we bounded along with the stride of a colossus interrupted with occa-

195

sional leaps of pure delight that must have covered at least fifty feet was the ultimate in physical expression. Our speed varied as we passed such points of interest as the other Gamma buildings, for then we would slow our pace so that we could look around. I was seeing more people than ever before.

We wove our way around the Gamma buildings. First we ran along the lake shore admiring the lovely stretches of sandy beaches on which many of the handsome members of the Macro society were playing and swimming nude in the sunshine. They sent us telepathic greetings and welcomed me to 2150. Then we ran past the shrubbery and flower gardens through the parklands behind the Gammas until we came to large vegetable gardens that were maintained by each Gamma.

Still we saw relatively few people. Even when we passed the large Gamma buildings which I knew housed a thousand people there would only be a handful of people outside around them. It was only when we came to the large recreation areas, which seemed to be shared by two Gammas, that we saw more people. Even here there were no large crowds, hardly more than a hundred people in any one of the huge recreation areas. I was pleased that from a planet which had almost died from overcrowding, Macro man had truly reestablished a balanced population. And yet, ironically, micro man's ideal of the single-family house had been given up completely.

When we came to the administration building at the end of the lake I realized that I must have run at least six miles, yet I didn't feel at all tired—more exhilarated than anything else.

I appreciated the rows of tall trees surrounding this building. Then I saw, coming out of its central entrance, the smallest man I had yet encountered in 2150. He was no more than six feet tall, and as we approached him I noticed signs of aging. Rana had looked 45, but this man looked at least 55. As we stopped before him, Carol took his left hand and greeted him affectionately.

He then greeted me in this traditional manner saying,

"Welcome to Delta 927. I'm Hugo, your Deltar."

I liked him immediately and was not surprised that the Delta had chosen him as their leader, for he had tremendous warmth and quiet strength. "Thank you," I said, "I can't tell you how happy I am to be here."

Carol told him of our journey around the Delta lake, then he answered my unspoken question about his age.

"I have had 197 years," he explained. "I was born in Brazil in 1953. Yes, I could look younger, but I grew up in a time when people aged and, since I shall soon evolate, I have permitted myself to age also."

"You mean you're planning on dying?" I asked with surprise. I remembered that C.I. had once told me that when Macro society members decide that they have learned all they can in any particular incarnation, they break the connection between their astral and physical bodies, causing the latter to die, while the soul is then free to evolve to the next level on the m-M continuum. They called this process *evolation*.

Suicide meant running away from the past; evolation— a contraction of *evolve* and *graduation*—meant embracing the future.

"Yes, I want to join my twin souls in another dimension," he answered. "Besides, I've accomplished all I can in this lifetime, so it's time to move on."

He laughed at my uncertain expression and continued, saying, "You don't need to worry, Jon. I'm not planning on evolating immediately. In fact, it will be some months yet before my successor is chosen, and, of course, I couldn't leave until the new Deltar is ready to take over."

I told him that I hoped I would see him again in this life. Then we continued our run.

Along the other side of the lake I noticed that there were more people swimming and playing on the beaches. Carol explained that mid-afternoon was the favorite time for outdoor recreation. She asked if I wanted to speed up our journey in order to join Neal and Jean sooner.

I replied, "How much faster can we run?"

"Lots faster," she replied. "Just think lightly and swiftly."

We did and veered from the lakeshore to the less populated park area behind the Gammas. Our running soon became very close to a form of low flying. I don't know how fast we were going, but in an incredibly short time we had completed the full circle of the lake and arrived at the third triad's recreation area. Less than an hour had passed since we started our run and, while I now felt some fatigue, I was not at all uncomfortable. In fact, after waiting a few minutes while Neal and Jean finished playing soccer, we resumed our tennis game—this time with the stipulation that the first set would be played without the use of PK.

Without PK Jean and I won the first set, but just barely. Then, in the next two sets, in which we used our PK, I was pleased that while we lost, it was much closer than it had been the day before. I was making progress even faster than I had hoped.

After tennis we again took a dip followed by a fascinating and very complex game, similar to three-dimensional chess, which was played as a team sport. Because of my inexperience in this game Carol and I played the two children, and again I was amazed at the remarkable intelligence of these two 7-year-olds. They beat us three straight games, but at least by the last game I was catching on to some of its intricate complexities and we came very close to winning.

Then it was time to return to our Gammas and our individual Alphas for the Macro dance. Again we were running, but this time with Jean by my side and Neal just ahead of Carol. Never had I seen children run so swiftly. I was sure that these 7-year-olds could easily break every track record of my 20th century. We waved goodbye at the entrance to our Gamma, and as we made our way to our respective Alphas there were telepathic reminders of what we would do together tomorrow.

Back in our Alpha I was soon engaged for the second time in the energetic and delightful combination of ballet,

198

folk dancing, and gymnastics called the Macro dance. The exciting musical accompaniment was supplied by C.I. through a speaker system so designed that the music seemed to emanate equally from all parts of the room. With my growing telepathic skills I was able to keep up with more of the flashing ins and outs and other dazzlingly swift interactions of the others in the room. I was no longer surprised to find Joyce on my shoulders or Alan throwing me in the air, or the tumbling over and under each other that occurred so regularly. Utilizing our telepathic bond I knew what was coming and was more or less prepared to accept what I had at first thought were impossible physical gyrations for the human body.

While my first experience with the Macro dance had left me bewildered and doubting the evidence presented by my own eyes, I was now prepared to accept the Macro powers as non-miraculous, though thrilling and surprising. However, the day's demands on my PK had been strenuous, so after about fifteen minutes I found myself very tired and grateful that my Alpha had ended the dancing early in deference to my fatigue.

I was soon floating comfortably in our Beta swimming pool perfectly content to just watch the energetic water activities of the other 99 members of my Beta. There was no doubt in my mind that I was viewing the greatest athletes the human race had ever produced, and I was sure that my comrades had reached the limits of physical grace, dexterity, and superhuman stamina. A few couples were playfully making love as they enjoyed the rhythm of the moving waters supporting their united bodies. Carol dove underwater and as her wet breasts found their way up my thighs to my chest her legs wrapped around me and we joined together joyously. Appreciating the uninhibited joy of love expressed openly and freely, I made a mental note to apologize to Karl and Cindy.

Before we left the pool Leo, our Betar, organized a type of water ballet, a game that was breathtaking to watch.

I vowed that tomorrow I would become a part of this activity, too.

After dinner I listened to my Alpha do some magnificent singing and discovered that Nancy and Steve had voices that would have been the envy of our greatest opera singers of the 20th century. To provide musical accompaniment they merely had to ask C.I. to give them whatever they wished in the line of music, since C.I. had recordings of every imaginable kind. Carol explained to me that they ended most evening meals with song, and it was only because of my arrival and our lengthy conversations that I had not heard them sing until tonight.

I could have listened to them sing all night and even discovered I was able, with the aid of telepathy, to join in some of the songs. However, long before I was ready to end it, Alan was saying that it was time for tutoring and I was leaving for my visit with Rana. I was pleased that we would be meeting with her this evening since I planned to ask her to use all her Macro power to help me attain my third Macro contact.

Rana immediately picked up this intention of mine, or perhaps she had precognitively anticipated it, because she asked me how I thought she could help me attain Macro contact.

"Well I—I—don't know," I answered, feeling rather surprised at her question. "But, after all, you are a level ten and if anyone should know how to help me, you should."

"Yes," Rana replied, "but last time we met I told you that it is desire and belief that determine all things. No one can give you these two essentials."

"All right," I said, "but I thought if I could establish a strong telepathic bond with you, that when you establish Macro contact I would be able to make it more easily myself."

Rana shook her head. "It won't work with you and me because our soul notes are too dissimilar. However, it might work with Lea if you could completely eliminate all resistance. But, once again, we're back to desire and belief.

200

Even telepathically connected to Lea you would fail to attain Macro contact if you didn't have sufficient desire and belief. What's more, you would then interfere with your twin soul attaining Macro contact. Of course, since Lea has been using her Macro powers to maintain your time-space translation she has not been able to attain Macro contact at all."

Perceiving my thoughts Rana said, "No, Jon, there is no easy way. At least none that I know of, and I spent many lifetimes looking for them rather than accepting the responsibility for my own personal growth or lack thereof."

I didn't remember much of what happened during the rest of our meeting with Rana. I was a little embarrassed and more than a little disappointed.

Later that evening as I was ready to go to sleep I realized that ever since Rana had told me that she couldn't help me the way I wanted to be helped I had been in a fog of depression. Carol, of course, picked up on this and said something about all depression being the product of repression.

I wasn't really listening very closely for my mind was again wrestling with the seemingly impossible task of attaining level three in just three months.

Once again I failed to attain Macro contact, which so frustrated me that I then failed at attaining Macro immersion.

I lay awake for a long time thinking of my failures and the task before me.

CHAPTER 13:

Loss

I haven't written in this journal for almost two months. During this period my life has been filled with more failures and successes than in all my previous years put together. I was going to say that I have been too busy to write it all down, but I know that's only partially true. The truth is that I didn't want to write down all my failures, only my successes. Unfortunately, my conscience wouldn't let me write about one without mentioning the other. Finally this same conscience insisted that I bring this journal up to date. With only a month left to attain level-three awareness it should prove helpful to me to review the past two months.

My problems, just like everyone else's, have been caused by my refusal to accept the macrocosmic truth that all failure leads to success and that all success leads to failure—that is, to another lesson we have not yet learned. So I'll begin with a success that became a failure.

It has to do with my relationship with Neda and my desire to change her life from unloved ugliness to at least a minimum of enjoyable attractiveness.

I had Karl, with the help of one of his girlfriends, buy Neda some new clothes and provide her with enough of our research data to keep her busy typing. Meanwhile, I worked on her with the Macro powers of telepathy and PK.

I continued to bombard her mind with positive accepting thoughts which kept her happy and hopeful regarding the future. In fact, during the first month of my Neda project I spent almost all my waking hours in 1976 focusing my mind on her, not only sending positive reinforcing thoughts, but also suggestions as to what she should eat, what exercises she should perform. I was determined to improve her physical appearance as soon as possible, and I knew PK, the power used in all healing, could not be expected to do all the work needed.

I was pleasantly surprised, though, at how much PK could accomplish if carefully directed and applied to the gland and nerve centers of the body. I spent some part of every day back in 2150 learning from C.I. the seemingly miraculous emental healing and growth principles discovered by Macro society research.

I learned that the mind and the emotions direct the formation of our physical body and all the changes that occur within it. C.I. described this process as an automatic reflex called the cellular response, with every cell of our being faithfully playing the part prescribed for it by our mind and emotions.

With the help of C.I. and this new information I began to use my growing PK power, my mind, and my emotions to change Neda's physical structure and to stimulate within her a joyous cellular response. This created an inner beauty while PK created the outer beauty.

My progress at first was extremely slow, and I was becoming discouraged and doubtful that even three months would be enough to make any significant changes in Neda's facial appearance. But then, toward the end of the fourth week, I developed the clairvoyant ability to see not only her aura but all seven glandular systems and every nerve network in her body. Now I could see clearly how to direct my PK force and also the immediate results of my efforts. From that day on, my progress became so rapid that Karl went around shaking his head and muttering to himself. By the end of the fifth week I was finished with the physical transformation of Neda.

She had been five feet eight inches tall. She was now five feet ten. She had weighed 105 pounds. Now she weighed 150 pounds of sensational curvaceous female flesh. I had modeled her as a composite of Lea, Carol, and Diane of my Alpha. While I could not quite reach their perfection, I had succeeded beyond my most optimistic hopes. As for Karl, my success was almost too much. A couple of evenings after I had completed my work with Neda, he came back from one of his ever-longer visits to her apartment demanding a talk with me.

"I have no more doubts about your incredible Macro powers or about your Macro society of 2150, but do you really know what you've done to Neda?"

"What do you mean?" I asked. "You know what I've done. I've taken a physical and psychological disaster and turned it into a victory for beauty and tranquillity."

"As for her physical beauty," Karl replied, "I could not possibly have any complaints. My God, how you managed to change that face, nose and all, into this delicately lovely one I'll never be able to comprehend. She's a pure joy to look at. I have to drag myself away from her." Having picked up his thoughts, I broke in, "But you're not happy with her psychological transformation."

Karl gave me a long questioning look before saying, "I don't understand you, Jon. Don't you realize that she is not only your physical creation but also your mental one? She thinks only what you want her to think, and you won't permit her a very wide range of thoughts. For instance, you deny her the right to have any doubts or concerns about the future."

"Wait a minute, Karl," I interrupted. "What's wrong with helping her feel confident about her future?"

"Damnation, Jon!" He exploded. "She's not a puppet, even though you seem to think you're her puppet master. She has a right to develop her own strength by making her own mistakes.

"You're like the over-possessive parent who won't permit his child to make any mistakes—all so the parent won't have to feel uncomfortable. And what's the result? You know as well as I that when a child isn't permitted to learn how to cope with the problems of this micro world he becomes angrily dependent on the parent and totally lacking in self-esteem. Good Lord, Jon. After all our months of research, nobody knows that better than we do!

"You rescued her from one stinking, lousy, miserable parent relationship and put her right back into another, with you as the parent!"

At first I was hurt and angry that Karl couldn't appreciate my great and unselfish work with Neda. I sent a telepathic command to Neda to come to our apartment so that she could help me refute Karl's accusation. By this time I had so attuned Neda's mind to mine that I was confident she would soon be with us. My one disappointment was that I had not been able to develop any Macro powers in Neda, for while she would respond to my telepathic suggestions she didn't recognize them as coming from me, so true telepathic communication between us had been impossible.

As I waited for Neda to join us I tried to be as fair as I could in considering Karl's accusation. It was possible, I thought, that perhaps I had gone a little too far with my desire to protect Neda from unhappiness. But surely I wasn't treating her like a puppet. I felt that this accusation was over-dramatized and exaggerated. Particularly after all I had done for Neda. I decided to tell Karl about some of my other selfless Macro activities.

"Karl," I said, "last week I went to our university hospital and successfully practiced my PK healing powers

205

on two cases of terminal cancer. Unaware of my efforts, they underwent surgery—mostly because they would rather take the chance of dying swiftly under the surgeon's knife than slowly under the attack of cancer. Guess what? Two miraculous recoveries. However, some of the skeptical medics are now claiming that their tests must have been wrong because no one could completely recover from that much cancer so soon."

Karl shook his head slowly and gave me a weary smile. "You're trying to convince me that you only do good for others. I suppose you feel there is no disease you can't cure with your Macro powers."

"You're right, Karl," I said. "I've walked through every ward in that hospital and have healed dozens of the most challenging cases. Why in just a few minutes I completely healed a patient who had been shot through a lung and a kidney just the night before. He was dying when I found him waiting for surgery. I almost completely healed cases of diabetes, tuberculosis, arthritis, pneumonia, epilepsy, heart disease, multiple sclerosis, syphilis, cerebral palsy, and kidney malfunction as well as an impressive list of fractures."

"Okay, okay," Karl injected, "I believe you, but Neda has been standing here in our doorway and I think we ought to invite her in."

Karl walked over to Neda and invited her to come in. Then he asked if she had come up to get more material to type.

"Oh, no," she replied, "I've got plenty to keep me busy. After all, you run down to bring me more material every hour or so, so I'm pretty well supplied for the rest of the week."

"Yes," I laughed, "I think dear old Karl here has developed a passion . . ." I paused and then continued ". . . for getting out at least three or four books full of material on our research."

Karl looked a little flustered as he said, "You know we were terribly backed up on our typing, and I've really enjoyed having the services of a full-time typist."

I laughed again. "I've noticed your growing enjoyment and I've got to admit that I've rarely seen you so filled with joy as you have been during the past few days."

"Yes, well, I—I . . ." Karl began lamely, then looked at Neda and forgot what he was going to say.

"You wanted to ask her," I prompted, "why she had come up here."

"Oh, yes," Karl nodded gratefully, "that's right, Neda. Is there something we can help you with?"

"Oh, no," Neda answered, flashing her now lovely smile which revealed the stunning white perfection of the new teeth I had molded for her. "It was just that I suddenly got the feeling that Jon wanted to talk to me."

"Oh, you did, huh," Karl said, giving me a suspicious look. "You were just suddenly overwhelmed with this idea in the midst of your typing."

"That's right, Karl," Neda replied with another dazzling smile. "I couldn't concentrate on my typing and felt I just had to come up here and see what Jon wanted."

"Okay, Svengali," Karl said, glaring at me, "I want to thank you for providing the evidence to support my earlier comments. At least you can now remember a past lifetime as a slave master, so we know where you got the practice!"

"Now, Karl," I said, "that isn't fair. I just wanted Neda to tell you in her own words how she feels about her new life."

"Oh, Jon," Neda exclaimed, "you know I never dreamed I could be so happy. In fact, it's all so impossible —my new appearance—my new life with you and Karl. I have to keep reminding myself that it's not all a dream which will end with my waking up as the ugly creature in that nightmare life I lived before we met."

"Well," Karl replied, "if you're so happy, Neda, why is it that you haven't once left this apartment building since you came here? Why did you stop attending classes? You've just about resigned from the human race."

"But I haven't wanted to go out," Neda answered. "You and Jon have brought me everything I've needed. As for my classes, I thought my work on your research was much more educational and important right now."

"After all, Karl," I added, "it was you who kept loading her down with enough work to keep her busy twenty-four hours a day."

"Okay," Karl nodded, "I apologize for that, and I'll admit to you both that most of the time when I was bringing you all that work, Neda, I just wanted to see you. I never saw anyone as beautiful as you've become. I just couldn't stay away. But now that I've admitted this, you won't feel like you have to type all the time. You can go out and get some exercise."

"But I get lots of exercise," Neda replied. "Especially since Jon bought me all of that exercise equipment and encouraged me to use it regularly."

"Yeah, I know," Karl said, "but Neda, don't you have any desire to see somebody besides Jon and me?"

"Are you saying I should want to see others?" she asked. "Because if you and Jon want me to go out and see other people, I'll be glad to."

"Oh, God," Karl groaned. "Do you hear that, Jon? She doesn't have any desire except to do what we tell her to do, and that's mostly what you tell her to do either telepathically or in words."

Suddenly I felt a chill run through my body. "Neda," I said, "I may have to go away and never be able to return, so what would you do then?"

Karl and I watched her beautiful face slowly congeal in fear, and we recognized the light of terror well up in her eyes. She began shaking her head and moaning her disbelief piteously while I watched Karl cast an accusing glare at me as he took her in his arms and murmured soft reassurances to her. Great tears dotted her ebony cheeks and she shook her head back and forth refusing to consider the possibility that I might someday leave her life.

I tried to send her positive happy thoughts but my mind seemed to have become numb, and I slowly realized that my telepathic contact with her was futile—I was too upset to be able to control my mind. I kept thinking over and over—what have I done? What have I done?

It was some time before Karl and I could sufficiently reassure Neda so that Karl could take her comfortably back to her apartment. By the time Karl returned, almost an hour later, I had done some hard thinking and come to some painful conclusions. The first thing Karl said was that he wanted to talk to me some more.

"And I want to talk to you, Karl," I replied. "I realize now that what you were saying about my being a puppet master or slave master was true. I couldn't stand the thought of failing to make Neda happy, so I took over almost complete control of her mind. I—I didn't realize until this evening how completely dependent upon me she had become. No, not how dependent upon me she had become. Rather, how dependent upon me I had made her!"

Karl shook his head slowly. "You were having fun playing God," he said. "You know the old saying that power corrupts. According to your account of 2150, power doesn't corrupt Macro man, but it sure as hell corrupts micro man, and that's us, Jon—you and me."

"Yes," I nodded, "and while I have developed some Macro powers, I haven't learned to use them unselfishly. Rana warned me that if I used my new powers selfishly I would make myself very unhappy. I was sure that I had nothing to fear since I was using them unselfishly, or so I thought. Now I know what she meant."

"Then do you realize," Karl questioned, "that you were bragging when you told me about all those people you had healed at the hospital? Do you realize that you were predominantly serving your pride, not people?"

I nodded my head in painful admission, and said, "There's another ancient bit of wisdom that says that anyone who exalts himself shall be humbled."

"Okay," Karl said. "I'm sure that if I'd suddenly developed Macro powers, I'd have misused them too. I'd probably have wiped out half the world's population by now, especially those bastards who know they're polluting

209

our planet but just keep right on doing it to pad their own micro pockets. I probably wouldn't even have healed people out of pride—I'd have killed them out of hatred. But our problem now is to undo the damage you've done to Neda."

"I'm sorry as hell," I apologized. "I had no intention whatever of hurting her." Then, thinking it over, I added, "I could be dangerous, Karl."

"I'm not worried about that, Jon. Let's just get Neda back in shape before you go on to any more projects."

In the next few days I worked to teach Neda the principles of Macro philosophy. I was pleased to see how quickly she learned to grasp the concept, for I knew that if she could see herself and others through a Macro perspective, she could not be fearful, lonely, or dissatisfied with any experience.

After a week as her Personal Evolution tutor, I gave her this journal to read. I had talked it over with Karl beforehand and, while he, at first, was opposed to introducing her so quickly to the strange concepts presented here, he finally agreed to it on the basis that we didn't want to be over-protective. Our decision was vindicated by the enthusiastic reception Neda gave to the concept of the Macro society and by her acceptance of my desire to leave the world of 1976 and become a life-long member of the Macro society of the future.

While the Macro philosophy and P.E. tutoring helped Neda, the severance of our unhealthy dependency relationship would have taken much longer to complete if Karl had not fallen so completely in love with her. He devoted almost every waking moment that he wasn't teaching to being with her. It was he who got her out of the apartment and introduced her to the world of dating. However, he wasn't successful in getting her to return to her classes for the very good reason that the girl who was a university junior and had enrolled in courses under the name of Neda Cricksley no longer existed.

It was at this time that Karl came into our room one evening after a date with Neda and told me that he didn't know what to do about the legal problem of Neda's identity.

"What are you talking about?" I asked.

"Well," Karl answered, "we couldn't get her back into her old classes because her professors and classmates would never recognize her or accept her as Neda Cricksley. We thought of enrolling her under a fictitious name for the next semester, but we finally realized that they won't accept her without past school records, and we haven't been able to figure out how we can come up with acceptable fake records for her."

"Well," I said, "I am sure you can figure out something. It doesn't sound too difficult."

"Yeah," Karl said, giving me his crooked grin, "I haven't told you all of it yet. Seems Neda's mother called the university and found out that Neda stopped attending her classes and that the psychology department has no record of her doing any typing work for any of their research."

"How did you find that out?" I asked.

"There was a notice on our department bulletin board," Karl explained, "listing her as a missing person and requesting that anyone who knows anything about her whereabouts get in touch with the campus police."

"Hmm," I said, "maybe I'd better call her mother and get it all straightened out."

Karl shook his head. "I wouldn't advise it," he said. "I talked it over with Neda and she thinks her mother is looking for her to get money from her now that she has a job. She'll want to see her, and we can't produce the body of Neda Cricksley, that's for sure!"

"In other words," I said, "you think the mother will charge me with kidnapping—possibly murder."

"Exactly," Karl nodded, "and neither she, the policemen, nor the jury that convicts you is going to believe your story, although it may help you cop a plea of insanity."

For the next couple of hours we argued about the necessity of talking with Mrs. Cricksley. Karl was strongly

211

opposed to this and kept trying to sell me on the idea of finding a new identity for Neda and just letting her become one more unsolved missing person case. I pointed out that she had her name on her apartment mail box in the lobby and her telephone was in her name, which would certainly make it fairly easy for the police to find her when they really started looking.

With Karl still protesting, I insisted that I would see Mrs. Cricksley in the morning and try to convince her that her daughter was safe even if she couldn't see her. I went to sleep that night wondering how I was going to convince her.

Back in 2150 I had my first precognitive experience while talking with Rana. I had been practicing review of past lives when suddenly the vision of being interrogated by two policemen imposed itself on my consciousness. I had a strong feeling that this was coming in the very near future. When Rana agreed with me, I told her about my 1976 problem with Neda's identity and we discussed ways of handling it along with their probable consequences. A wise Personal Evolution tutor never tells people what to do, but rather, helps them see their problems from a more Macro perspective, then explore alternative solutions and their probable results. So I received no simple solution. However, I did decide on a course of action which seemed to provide the best long-term results for Karl and Neda. I immediately went to sleep in the tutoring room with the strong desire of waking up early in my 1976 morning.

I awakened at 5 a.m. and telephoned Neda with the request that she get dressed and come up to our room as soon as possible. Then I woke up Karl with the announcement that the police would soon be at our apartment and at Neda's. He didn't ask me how I knew this, he just wanted to know how much time we had before our visitors would arrive. I told him that I thought it would be in a little over two hours and that Neda would soon be joining us for breakfast.

By the time Neda arrived, Karl and I had dressed and

shaved. As we ate a hurried breakfast I outlined my plan of action. First we would move all of Neda's belongings into Karl's station wagon. Fortunately, she still had not acquired more belongings than the wagon could easily accommodate. Then, I suggested that Karl pack a suitcase for himself and leave with Neda for the adjoining state where they could get married and begin a little honeymoon trip.

Karl grinned and said, "Now, that's the best plan I've heard yet, Jon. I hope Neda thinks so, too," he added, taking her hand in his.

Neda gave Karl and me a lovely shy smile and admitted that she too was delighted with my plan.

With their agreement to the first part of my plan I began supplying the next steps. First I would teach Karl's classes and give out the story that he had eloped with his beautiful new girlfriend. She would get married under the false name of Neda Dailey and be Neda Johnson for the rest of her life.

At first Karl was worried about the legality of their marriage if Neda used a false name, but Neda said that she didn't mind as long as Karl loved her. Then she added that if 2150 could get along without any marriages at all, they should be able to survive a slightly illegal one.

After breakfast I helped Neda carry her belongings to the car while Karl packed his suitcase with enough clothes to last a couple of weeks. We had agreed that Karl would call me at the end of the week and if he couldn't reach me he would contact Snuffy for information from me. At a little before 7 a.m. Karl and Neda waved goodbye and drove off in the dim early morning light.

At 7:15 a.m. two policemen knocked at our apartment door. They showed me a university picture of me which they said Mrs. Cricksley had identified as the person who had abducted her daughter. I explained that while I had hired Neda Cricksley as a typist and rented her an apartment she had not liked the work and had quit both her job and her new apartment just a couple of days ago. I then invited the officers to examine the apartment she had so recently vacated.

They not only searched Neda's apartment but also mine. I was extremely grateful that police of 1976 did not have the highly developed clairvoyance of some of my 2150 friends, for if they had, they would have seen the electron heat tracings of Neda's body which would still have been present on her bed!

When I explained that my roommate had left the day before to go on a honeymoon with his new bride they, at first, exhibited considerable interest in getting in touch with Karl. However, I showed them a picture I had recently taken of Karl and Neda and they could see that his new bride bore not even the faintest resemblance to the missing girl.

I concentrated with all my Macro power on convincing the two officers that they need not arrest me because I would be glad to visit their police station that afternoon and submit myself to a lie detector test of everything I had said and for any further questions they might wish to ask me. I succeeded so well that they even agreed to drive me to the university so I wouldn't be late for Karl's first class.

That afternoon, after teaching all three of Karl's classes and joking with the students about his elopement, I went to the police station. There I found that the two officers had had real trouble explaining to their chief why they had let me go that morning. I was just in time to prevent their being sent off to bring me in.

Once again I repeated the story I had given that morning concerning Neda, but this time I was hooked up to a lie detector and was questioned by the police chief and two hard-faced detectives. My ability to control my mind and, thus, my body, naturally made the lie detector support my story. Then tremendous Macro persuasiveness got me released in spite of a rather unpleasant confrontation with Mrs. Cricksley in which I strongly planted the suggestion in the minds of the police that if any harm had come to Neda, Mrs. Cricksley was probably a partner

214

to it. When I left, she was taking her turn with the lie detector.

During the following week the local newspaper featured the disappearance of the missing college student with a picture of Neda. Two other coeds had disappeared recently. Their bodies, raped, murdered, and buried in a woods near campus, had been recovered only two weeks ago, so the first thought was that Neda, too, had become the victim of their murderer. One look at the old picture of Neda, however, made it difficult to entertain the possibility of a sex crime, and since her parents were virtually paupers, it was a certainty that she hadn't been kidnapped for their money.

I made one more visit to the police station, at which time I discovered that the police had made an exhaustive study of my life history which did not support the theory that I was a kidnapper and murderer. As a crippled Vietnam War veteran and a respected graduate student who was more interested in his studies and doctoral research than in girls, campus politics, or student hijinks, I didn't fit their concept of the criminal type at all.

By the end of the week when Karl called, I was so optimistic about my relations with the police that I told him our problems were over and to enjoy his honeymoon. However, he insisted on returning with Neda so he could finish teaching his classes. They returned on Sunday and moved into Neda's apartment as Mr. and Mrs. Karl Johnson. The following morning Karl resumed his teaching and Neda resumed her typing. While Karl and Neda were interviewed by the police, I managed to be present during the questioning and succeeded in convincing them that these two people could not possibly have been connected with the disappearance of Neda Cricksley.

So ended Neda Cricksley.

The case of the missing co-ed and the recovery of the bodies of the other two brought the fear and tension of our university community to a fever pitch and provided me with my second precognitive experience.

215

It was on Sunday, exactly one week after Karl and Neda had returned, that I awakened with a clairvoyant impression of Central Park not far from the 109th Street entrance. I clearly saw two vicious-looking men chasing a young girl. In the vision I knew that these two men were responsible for the rape-murders of the two co-eds whose bodies had recently been discovered. I woke with a sense of urgency that I must get to the park immediately. It was only a matter of minutes before my precognitive dream would become a material reality.

Ten minutes later I approached the park wishing that I had my magnificent 2150 body. It was a little before 7 a.m. and the park appeared to be deserted. I realized that I could spend a long time wandering through it without seeing anyone at this time of day.

Then I began using my telepathic power like a radar to sweep ahead of me through the heavily wooded park. I must have walked along the concrete paths for almost ten minutes before I picked up the thoughts of a young girl whom I could not see because of a rise between us.

As I focused my mind more closely on hers I realized that she was riding a new bicycle along the paths of the park. She had been doing this every morning and evening, before and after school, since she received it as a gift for her thirteenth birthday recently.

I stopped walking in order to concentrate all my energies on telepathic contact with the girl. I waited right where I was, since I felt she would soon be riding into view over the ridge nearby. The trees stood sharply black against the cold morning sky. A recent thaw had melted most of the snow, leaving isolated dirty little piles around clumps of shrubbery or beside walkways.

Suddenly my mind contact with the little girl chilled my bones. She was being harassed by two men on motorcycles.

I visualized my body as feather-light and started a grotesque hobble-run that soon brought me to the top of the ridge. I looked down upon a wooded path and saw the girl running through the trees followed by two

216

shaggy-haired young men in grimy motorcycle togs, just as they had appeared in my vision.

The little girl had left her bicycle behind in hope of finding protection among the trees, but the men had abandoned their cycles and were fast overtaking her.

I reached out to touch their minds and encountered lust and menacing glee as the tall one with a long droopy mustache caught a handful of the girl's long blond hair. I watched with mounting horror as this dark-visaged man slammed the girl to the ground, then, clasping both hands about her waist, lifted her like a banner high in the air. His pudgy companion grabbed her and began slapping her with huge hamlike hands as they both ripped at her clothing.

Suddenly red waves of rage crashed through my mind. I slipped back in time and became, once again, the Indian medicine man fighting white soldiers who were raping and killing the women and children of my tribe. I found myself running faster and faster toward these monstrous invaders.

Suddenly my elbows dug into the hard wet ground and I cursed my crippled body for failing me. I was still some thirty yards from the enemy.

The little girl's heart-rending scream of anguish snapped me back to the present, and I shouted at her assailants as I struggled to my feet.

They looked up at me with surprise. The pudgy one laughed at the audacity of a one-legged man trying to interfere with the two of them. I headed toward him. When he was within ten feet I launched myself at his legs, managing to knock him down. We rolled about on the ground as this pudgy-faced youth tried to get room to slam his fists into me. I tried to stay close and harkened back to my army hand-to-hand combat training. I felt his huge fist slam against the side of my head, and for a couple of moments was lucky just to be able to hold onto him. My rage had made me clumsy, but now with cold angry ferocity I began slashing at his face and throat with short powerful karate chops.

217

With a scream of frustration and pain he broke away from me and got to his feet. They were shod with heavy lethal-looking boots. I telepathically picked up his murderous thought of stomping the life out of me with them. This gave me the split-second margin I needed, and the boot whizzed harmlessly past my face. I grabbed it and with a sharp twist brought him to the ground. Before he could recover I began slamming my fist into his jaw with all the strength of my rage. How long I kept at this I don't know, but another scream from the girl brought me to my senses and I realized that I was beating at an unconscious face. As I looked up, the tall fellow was sprawled on top of the little girl mauling her small round breast with one hand as he tore at the last bits of her clothing with the other.

I was up and bounding toward him, my voice shrieking madly at the top of my lungs. He leaped to his feet and came charging toward me shouting obscenities. Again I threw a body block and we fell to the ground, but this time my opponent was too quick for me and I found myself pinned to the ground with a leering mustached face bending over me as two powerful hands dug into my throat slamming my head into the ground again and again. I redoubled my efforts to break loose, but his hands were like manacles and his arms like heavy steel. Things were getting blurry . . . there was no air, and only one hope. I let my body go completely slack.

For a moment the iron grip on my neck continued, then with one last painful thrust, relaxed. As I tried to maintain some degree of consciousness I felt his hot face above mine. My thumbs leaped for his eyes and scored two agonizing hits.

With a piercing scream he fell backward and began rolling about on the ground in frantic pain-driven frustration. I tried to breathe deeply to recover as much strength as possible, then as he rolled toward me I raised both my arms and with every ounce of desperate strength slammed my hard wrists down on the back of his neck.

There was a sharp snap and his body went limp.

218

I staggered to my feet and hobbled wearily to where the girl lay naked on the cold wet ground. She had either fainted or been knocked unconscious, but she had not been raped.

I dressed her in the torn clothing, then wrapped her in my top coat and began reaching out for her unconscious mind. When I contacted the fear and terror there I sent powerful reassurances that all was well and that she was completely safe. Using PK and clairvoyance I worked with her body to speed up the healing of her bruises. Soon her eyelids began to flutter.

As she opened her eyes I began speaking softly but confidently about how she was all right now and would be able to ride her bicycle home without any trouble. I helped her to her feet and made sure that her own coat was buttoned as well as possible with its remaining buttons, before retrieving my own. With both my vocal and telepathic reassurances she mounted her bike, thanked me for helping her, and rode quickly off toward her home.

I had considered having her call the police and confront her attackers at the police station, but decided to spare her that ordeal. Instead I decided to deal with her assailants myself. What I was going to do with them I wasn't sure, but I decided to start by taking them back with me to our fourth-floor apartment, which was vacant. There I could confine them till I decided what to do with them. First, however, I would have to heal them and set up hypnotic control of their actions so they would obey me.

I walked back to where my last adversary lay sprawled out and began my clairvoyant examination of his injuries. It didn't take long to realize that he was dying from a broken neck. I began working to repair the damage before it was too late. I had learned from C.I. that the healing powers of the greater mind are unlimited if used properly. The problem was to stop the struggle of the patient's micro self so that the healing process could take place. In less than thirty minutes I succeeded in completely healing his neck. While this would have been considered very slow by 2150 standards, I was satisfied, having done the very best I could. Before permitting him to regain consciousness I planted powerful subconscious suggestions of obedience to me. I sensed that his name was Griff.

His pudgy-faced companion, Judd, was still unconscious with a broken jaw, so I resumed my healing efforts. Again I was able to reach deep into his mind and still the unconscious struggle. Then working with his gland and nerve centers, I released the great healing forces. His jaw was soon healed and his mind had accepted my hypnotic control of his actions. He demonstrated his obedience by quietly getting to his feet and going to his motorcycle.

Returning Griff to consciousness, I started him toward his motorcycle also. Then, with me riding behind Griff and directing him, we made our way back to the apartment building with Judd close behind. Entering the seldom-used rear door, we made it up to the fourth floor without being seen. Once inside the apartment, I told them they could not leave without my permission and suggested that they go to sleep until I awakened them. Walking down to my third-floor apartment, I took my weary body to bed.

For the first time in almost two months I went to sleep and did not wake up in 2150. Instead I had a dream in which I saw Lea standing at the foot of my bed looking sadly down at me.

"Why do you look so sad?" I asked.

"Because I could not bring you to 2150 this time," she replied. "Your anger has broken the time-space translation loop."

"What do you mean?" I questioned.

"I mean that your vicious treatment of those two men this morning lowered your vibration rate so much that it is now impossible for us to translate your vibrations into our time dimension," Lea explained.

"You mean that just because I protected that little girl from certain rape, and probable murder, I can't return to you and the Macro family? That's impossible! That

220

wouldn't be fair at all," I protested, sure that there had been some mistake.

"You're right, Jon. It certainly wouldn't be fair if just protecting the child prevented your translation," she answered. "It's not all that simple, though. You protected her not with the love and acceptance of a Macro perspective, but rather with the hate and rage of your micro self."

"But I couldn't fight them at the Macro level. What else could I have done?" I asked.

"At the Macro level," she answered, "you would not have needed to fight them, only restore the imbalance of their minds."

"But I couldn't possibly restore balance to their depraved minds. They're monsters!!" I defended.

"So you acquiesced to your limiting beliefs, condemned them for their micro violence, then fought them with your own micro violence," Lea stated.

Suddenly I felt an agony of pain in my jaw and neck. I was shocked to find they were broken! Then in my mind I heard the voice of Rana. "Pass no judgment, and you will not be judged. For as you judge others, so will you yourself be judged, and whatever measure you deal out to others will be dealt back to you in return. Why do you look at the speck of sawdust in your brother's eye with never a thought for the great plank in your own?"

"All right," I said, "I'm experiencing the pain that I inflicted this morning. But *they* deserved it."

"Of course they did," Lea replied, "but only micro man punishes. You are dooming yourself to live in a micro world as long as you desire a micro way of life."

"Does this mean that I've forfeited my chance to live in the Macro society?" I asked.

"You won't be able to return to 2150 until you've balanced the negative vibrations you created within your essential self," she explained. "If within a month you succeed in positively balancing today's negative actions, you may return to continue seeking level-three awareness. However, now that you have broken the time-space translation loop it will take a great deal of energy to reestablish it. This will probably reduce the amount of time you have left in 2150."

"I'm so sorry, Lea. I didn't mean to louse things up. I just couldn't help myself. I could do the same thing over again . . . I just mustn't. I've got to grow, and I'd better start by balancing the negative vibrations I've set up. How can I do that, Lea?" I asked.

She smiled sadly. "If you don't know the answer to that question by now, Jon, you might as well give up hope of experiencing 2150 again in this lifetime."

With these words ringing in my mind I awakened to an excruciating pain in my jaw and neck. Fortunately for me, I had healed my victims so that their pain had not lasted long. I remembered that according to the law of *karma* my own pain must soon pass, too. Then I realized that my perspective must have suffered a terrible blow, for I hadn't thought in terms of *karma* since my first week in 2150! That's when I first learned that *karma* is only valid from a less than Macro point of view.

As these thoughts entered my mind the pain began to diminish, and it was not long before I was completely free of the misery I had inflicted upon myself.

While I was free of one pain, the thought of being forever separated from my new world would, I knew, prove far more painful in the long run. Somehow I had to learn how to balance my negative vibrations and I was sure that my best chance of doing this lay upstairs with the hoodlums I had captured. If I forced them to go to the police and confess to the rape-murders of the two co-eds, which my probing of their minds had discovered, maybe that would do it. They would be punished, if not by the electric chair, then by a life term in one of our prisons . . . But that kind of angry vengeance usually fills its victims with even more hate, and from the Macro perspective I knew that those who died with hatred often chose quick rebirth in an attempt at revenge. Thus, what micro man can not see, due to his limited life perspective, is that hate and revenge always produce more hate and more revenge. No, I couldn't balance my negativity by using micro man's approach to the problem. That was not the solution. But what was?

I smiled sadly to myself as I recalled that micro man had been given the solution by all his great Macro philosophers. The so-called Christian nations knew of this as the one commandment that their great Master gave: "Love one another, as I have loved you."

Shaking my head, I resigned myself to the fact that this one commandment didn't seem very practical from a micro point of view. However, I had been exposed to a larger point of view . . . the Macro view . . . which I must now use to solve this problem and, thereby, get back to my beloved Lea in 2150. So I couldn't turn my two captives over to the police, but I couldn't turn them loose to continue on their murderous path, either. Could I, I wondered, rehabilitate them?

While I had succeeded in using my Macro powers to heal them and to safely bring them to the apartment, would I now be able to heal their twisted micro minds? I knew that I could control their minds and force them to do only what I commanded, but this would certainly not be rehabilitation, not with me acting as the prison warden of their minds. Somehow I must help them see the long-term painful and unfulfilling consequences of their micro existence. As I searched my mind for a way of performing this miracle I loaded a tray with bowls, spoons, a carton of milk, and some granola. I picked up the tray and started off to their apartment.

When I entered the room they were still in their hypnotically induced sleep. I quickly awakened them and got them into the kitchen, where we all sat at the kitchen table. At first they eyed me with fear, but this slowly gave way to puzzled bewilderment as I told them that they were my guests and that I had healed their bodies and was about to start trying to heal their minds. I told them that if we succeeded they would be free to live satisfying new lives without fear of the police. If we failed, and I emphasized "we," to begin developing the idea of a joint venture in which they would have at least equal responsibility, then I could promise nothing but a future filled with misery and unhappiness.

Griff, the tall one, scratched his head and began pulling on his mustache. "Listen, man," he said finally, "I don't understand what's happening. How did you get us to come here with you? And how come you haven't called the cops?"

I wasn't sure how to answer these two questions, so I took my time before saying, "I hypnotized you into coming here, and the reason I didn't turn you over to the police is sort of complicated. You see, I know that you raped and murdered those two co-eds, and if I just wanted you punished I'd let the police have you. But I'm going to gamble on being able to show you a different type of life which will prove so attractive that you won't want to hurt anybody ever again."

"Hey, man," Judd exclaimed, "are you some sort of religious nut? You gonna save us from our sins?"

"No," I assured him, shaking my head, "I'm just going to tell you some things and if what I say doesn't make sense to you, then I'll turn you loose and you can do whatever you wish."

They looked at me suspiciously, then Griff said, "What's stopping us from walking out right now?"

I told him. "That door to the hall is red hot. If you try to open it you'll get burned. You'll find the same is true of the windows."

I could see they didn't consciously believe me. As they both got up, Griff said, "You're plumb crazy, man. There's nothing wrong with that door. I think maybe we should be doctoring you."

Judd reached the door first and started to open it, but as soon as his hand touched the doorknob he let out a scream and jerked backwards.

"Yeowww!" Judd wailed as he frantically waved his hand in the air trying to cool it. "God damn it. That crazy bastard's right. Look at my hand!"

He held his reddened hand out for Griff to examine. Griff apparently accepted the reality of Judd's pain, for

224

he turned to me and said sarcastically, "Okay, man, how the hell did ya manage that little trick?"

"I hypnotized you into believing the door was red hot," I explained. "There was nothing you could do about it because I was working with your subconscious mind, not your conscious one. As long as your subconscious mind holds my suggestion, you won't be able to get out that door."

Judd, still holding his hand, glared at me and said, "Well, if it's all in my mind, then how come I've got these God damned blisters on my hand?"

"Because your body can only do what your mind directs it to do," I answered. "Your mind believes your hand is burned so it directs your nerves to signal pain and your gland system to produce blisters."

"Okay, man," Griff nodded, "we'll buy the science lecture, but how about you knocking off this messin' around with our minds. You were lucky this morning. You don't think you can take us both at the same time, do you? We'd bust you right in half."

"I made a mistake this morning," I admitted, "and I'm paying for it. But I'm not going to fight you again."

"You mean you're just going to stand there and let us tear you up?" Judd sneered. "I can just see that. Sure you are. Noooo, sir. You fight like a madman. You did this morning, and you'll do it again right now first time we lift a fist."

"No, I won't," I responded, "I don't have to. From now on if either one of you tries to harm anyone you'll only succeed in doing it to yourself."

They looked at me skeptically, so I said, "If you haven't learned to believe me, you can try and see for yourself. I'm warning you, though, that you'll only hurt yourself."

"Bash him one, Griff," Judd urged. "Call his bluff."

"So he can get hurt like you did?" I asked.

Griff approached me warily and with obvious uncertainty. Finally he sidled up to within striking distance and began giving me what he clearly hoped was a frightening stare. I remained standing and smiled at him.

225

"Remember," I said, "you've been warned that any harm you try to do to anyone else will only happen to you."

"Okay," Griff said, "I believe you, man. I wouldn't think of hurting you."

With these words he pretended to turn away but when he was half turned he suddenly let go with a twisting uppercut to my jaw. It had tremendous force as Griff soon discovered, for his fist missed my chin and like a boomerang, came crashing back into his own jaw, knocking him off balance so that he fell heavily to the floor.

"What the hell?" Judd exclaimed, "you didn't even move and Griff knocked himself down. What the hell's happening?"

"I told you, but you refused to believe me. How badly do you have to hurt yourselves before you start believing me?"

Griff had climbed to his feet and gingerly touched his sore jaw. He came at me fiercely and stopped just short of my body. A combination of rage and puzzled amazement filled his eyes. Drawing up his fist, he hesitated, then sticking out his index finger poked at my chest. The pokes of course landed on his own befuddled self.

He eyed me thoughtfully. I had a feeling that he was getting ready to give some genuine consideration to what I had to say.

"You've seen that if you think something is true it has real consequences," I said. "Well, I'm trying to show you that the way we think causes everything that happens to us. If we think negatively it has negative results for us, and if we think positively it has positive results for us."

"Crap!" Judd exclaimed." Now we get a sermon on the power of positive thinking. Right?"

"No," I said, "I'm going to give you a demonstration. From now on, every angry thought that you have, about anything and for any reason, will cause a violent headache. It will last only as long as your angry thoughts."

"OOOWWEE! Jesus Christ, man!" Judd cried as he clutched his forehead.

"What's wrong? Griff asked.

"That son of a bitch is sticking daggers into my head," Judd shouted. "Ooooh—it's killing me! Stop it! Stop it!"

"You are the only one who can stop it, Judd," I explained. "When you stop thinking angry thoughts at me the pain will stop."

"Do as he says, Judd," Griff advised. "That bastard's got a hex on us. I guess you better do as he says."

The pain seemed to have reached the point where Judd could think only of it, and the angry thoughts were crowded out of his mind by thoughts of how to get rid of the pain. His face which had been distorted by the pain now gradually relaxed and he gave a sigh of relief as he wiped his forehead with his shirt sleeve.

"There," I said, "all you had to do was stop your angry thoughts and the headache stopped, too. Now I'm going to leave you so you can think about what I've said, and if you still have doubts about the truth of my statements you can test them out. Any questions before I leave?"

"Yeah, man," Griff said. "How long you plannin' on keepin' us here?"

"You've got enough cereal and milk to last you till tomorrow morning. I'll be back then," I answered.

"You're keepin' us here just like the pigs keep people in jail!" Griff protested then spit at me.

A split second later he was wiping his face with one hand while the other held his throbbing forehead. He howled, "I didn't mean it . . . I'm sorry—damn it, I said I'm sorry!"

"You don't have to convince me," I responded. "Just convince yourself that you aren't angry and your headache will go away. Well, see you tomorrow. Here's wishing you loving, happy thoughts."

With those words I left them and walked down to Karl and Neda's apartment. By this time it was mid-afternoon and I was just in time to be invited to a late luncheon which Neda had just prepared. Since I hadn't eaten anything yet, I let Karl and Neda do most of the talking while I concentrated on reducing my hunger pangs. Then I told them about my experiences so far that day.

As I had expected, Karl favored turning my captives over to the police. He wasn't at all happy about having two rapists in the same building with his new wife. Scooting his chair closer to hers, Karl put his arm around her protectively. Neda, however, supported my arguments for trying to rehabilitate them.

"After all, Karl," she kept repeating, "look what Jon did for me. If he can make a silk purse out of an ugly sow's ear like I was, why couldn't he work a miracle with those hoodlums?"

"Oh, yeah," Karl replied. "Well, I've learned something about Jon's Macro philosophy and I know, and Jon will agree, that you can't help anyone who doesn't want to be helped. The person has to actively cooperate. He couldn't have helped you if you hadn't had sufficient desire and belief."

"That's true," I agreed. "Neda had to desire and believe in the possibility of the changes that took place in her in order for them to become permanent."

"See there," Karl said, waving his spoon in the air, "you're licked before you get started with those hoodlums, because they sure don't desire to suddenly become model citizens . . . much less believe it's possible."

"You're right about that, Karl," I conceded. "As of now they certainly lack the necessary desire and belief, but by tomorrow they're going to think twice before they doubt the truth of anything I say. And tomorrow I'm going to start teaching them Macro philosophy."

"That's ridiculous," Karl argued. "Why they're the lowest type of micro scum on the face of this earth, and you've said over and over that the Macro perspective doesn't make sense to micro man. In fact, from a micro view, a concept such as 'all is one', is simply not true. Why waste your time, Jon? Why not just turn them over to the police? You don't want to mess around with people like that. They're sicker than hell and they're damned dangerous, too. They don't deserve . . . "

"Are you about to say that those young men don't deserve help?" I interrupted. "If so, I warn you to be careful how you judge them. Remember the warning words that Rana quoted and consider your judgment carefully before you condemn yourself, too, as being unworthy of rehabilitation."

Karl opened his mouth to reply, but Neda quickly put her finger gently to his lips. "Please, Karl," she asked, "think about what Jon said. After all, he has been cut off from 2150 for thinking just such condemning thoughts. That's about as much tragedy as we need for one day."

Neda had certain natural persuasive advantages that I had never had with Karl, so I wasn't surprised to see him nod his head and yield the point to her.

"By the way, Karl," I said, "would you mind if Neda typed up my journal? By the end of this week I'm hoping our new house guests will be ready to consider what I've written there. If they can believe it, then maybe they'll want to start learning how to live a Macro life."

Neda wanted to start on it right away, but by the time our discussion ended, the day was gone and evening had arrived. When I left them I was convinced that Neda, far more than I, had gotten Karl to accept comfortably the major tenets of the Macro society and Macro philosophy. I retired early that evening knowing that I wouldn't be awakening in 2150, but planning an early start with Griff and Judd.

The next three days were some of the most frustrating I've ever experienced. It seems that my two captives had headaches most of the time, which made them angry, which gave them headaches, which made them angry, which gave them more headaches, and so on. In their frustrated rage they tried to attack me a number of times and, of course, ended up just hurting themselves. They even burned their hands on the door a couple more times.

At first I was astonished at the amount of pain they were willing to put up with rather than learn the simple lessons I had given them. Finally, I realized that a lifetime habit of running away from responsibility for one's own life situation was not quickly overcome. Both Griff and Judd were experts at repressing or forgetting unpleasant details, so they kept forgetting that their own anger produced headaches, that the door was burning hot, and that if they tried to hit me they would only hit themselves instead.

Of course, if they hadn't been so angry at their inability to escape they would have learned much faster. But, as Rana had once explained, all anger is self-anger caused by calling something bad and then feeling inadequate to change the "bad" or "undesirable" situation. She had continued saying that since micro man usually refuses to accept responsibility for his unpleasant experiences, he unconsciously projects the blame onto others. Then he feels justified in projecting his self-anger and self-hate upon others, too. Since these denial-of-reality techniques work temporarily, and micro man forgets they are only temporary, this type of behavior continues to become an even stronger habit until it is extremely difficult to change.

This pernicious "it's not my fault" cycle was what I was seeing in Griff and Judd.

Looking at my own life, I could see this pattern repeated over and over again. I not only had my present life to examine but a number of past lives, too, which all bore out the same lesson: All my problems were self-caused due to my refusal to accept this Macro truth: All learning is based on remembering (accepting) the learning value of one's own mistakes.

Once more the ancient truth: He who forgets his past is doomed to repeat it.

Karl had warned me at the end of the first day that I had better be able to live by the same conditions I forced on my captives. I had assured him that I was perfectly willing to experience a headache any time I gave in to the micro habit of anger. I had felt confident that from my larger perspective it would be impossible for me to get angry. What I didn't realize was that all dissatisfaction produces some anger. In other words, to the extent that I saw anything as being more bad than good I felt anger, and by the second day I was experiencing headaches of my own.

I had realized that from the Macro perspective everything is both bad and good, ugly and beautiful, failure and success. But I hadn't realized how inadequate I was to actually practice seeing both sides of the coin, or the balanced Macro view. I, who had devised what I thought was a brilliant scheme for motivating my captives to learn how to think more positively, was now caught in my own device. By the end of the third day we were running neck and neck for who had the biggest headache—Griff, Judd, or me. I was willing to bet that I won by a head (ache!).

Fortunately, things got better on the fourth day. This was caused by a number of things, but an important factor was Neda. When Neda saw how miserable I was on the third evening she begged Karl and me to let her visit Griff and Judd, taking with her the typed pages of this journal. Both Karl and I opposed this but Neda insisted that anything they did to harm her would reflect right back to themselves instead, so she couldn't get hurt.

I argued that it was a chance I was just not willing to take. Unfortunately, arguing with Neda only made my headache worse, which made me think that maybe she was right. So I gave in—with the stipulation that I act as her guard.

While Karl held out longer, I could see that Neda's lovely persuasiveness was too much for him. She visited my captives with me as her guardian.

I had to ask Neda to open the door to their apartment for I was living my own sentence so completely that the door knob now burned my hands, too.

Neda proved so thoroughly charming that Griff and Judd were soon over their headaches. She managed to prolong her stay by beginning to read my journal to us. I was sure that neither of them was ready to accept this journal as anything more than a ridiculous fantasy. But with Neda reading it and interrupting herself to make comments and to clarify or answer their questions, both Griff and Judd were soon so deeply involved in my journal experiences that they didn't want Neda to stop reading.

I suggested it was getting late, but it was only after Neda promised to come back the following day and finish reading the journal that they were willing to accept her departure.

The next day Neda spent almost six hours with Griff and Judd and still didn't finish reading this journal because they asked her so many questions about herself and about the changes that had taken place in her. I was surprised at how little skepticism they showed, although Neda got me to demonstrate some of the Macro powers for them. They were most impressed by my PK levitations in which I floated some sofa pillows around the room, and they remembered that I had healed the injuries I had inflicted on them. I had also healed their burned hands, at Neda's suggestion, and from then on we had no more problems with the door. They didn't approach it, and it didn't burn me any more.

By the end of the fourth day I was convinced that Neda was a tremendous help to me in getting through to Griff and Judd. I was still amazed at the great personality change in Neda. She was confident, outgoing, patient, kind, and most surprising of all, full of humor, joy, and laughter. When I asked about these psychological changes, she responded, "I'm the living, breathing proof to myself that your Macro philosophy of the future can overcome any problem."

"But knowing about Griff and Judd, aren't you afraid of them?" I asked.

Neda laughed. "As long as I can remember my past I can't imagine being too upset by anything in the future."

"Wait a minute," I interrupted. "How about being raped and murdered?"

She shook her head playfully, saying, "I'm sorry if my lack of fear worries you and Karl, but I'm not being fool-hardy. I just believe in your Macro philosophy, which says that this is a perfectly just universe and we can experience only what we have chosen to experience. Everyone will eventually learn the truth that all is one. So in the long run, the future can only get better, more aware, and more loving. Nothing can happen to me except what I have chosen to grow from. So what is there to fear?"

"I still don't understand how you could have learned to practice this Macro view so quickly," I replied, shaking my head.

"Didn't you tell me that all human problems are caused by resisting and fighting the inevitable changes in our lives?" she reminded.

"Yes," I answered. "However, I—"

"Then try to understand," she interrupted, "that I've had so many changes taking place in my life that I've learned to enjoy it."

"What if you're in an accident," I postulated, "and you lose that newly acquired physical beauty—could you accept that change?"

"Yes," she answered, "I think I could, because now I know what it is—a vehicle; why I have it—we created it through your/our belief in a philosophy of oneness; and why I won't have it if it's taken from me—because I caused and chose it!

"I fully believe, Jon, that as long as I want this body I'll have it."

"That takes care of the beliefs, and it sounds like you have the desire too," I observed. "With those two you can have anything you want as long as you don't cancel it with a conflicting desire or belief."

"I used to have a strong desire to be beautiful and happy," she said, "but I didn't believe it was possible. This made me want to stay away from others so they wouldn't see how homely I was. My desire to avoid rejection, by not becoming involved, was so great that it cancelled out my desire to be beautiful and happy."

"It sounds so complicated when we put it into words

233

that I don't see how we're ever going to explain it to Griff and Judd," I sighed.

Neda teased me saying, "That's because you lack sufficient belief, Jon. But I believe it's possible and I desire to accomplish it, so I will succeed."

I laughed, "You've beaten me at my own game, Neda. I'm going to watch your technique for the next few days. You're probably the answer to my cry for help during those frustrating first three days. 'Ask and you shall receive,' Hmm. Well I asked and here you are, Neda, so I'd better get out of the way and let you do your thing."

I had given myself a week to begin seeing some sign of greater awareness in my captives, and I really hadn't expected any dramatic changes. However, by Sunday, just one week after I had captured them, Griff and Judd behaved so differently that at times I had difficulty believing they were the same men who had attacked three girls and raped and killed two of them. Neda had made the big difference. She had gotten them to listen to her and accept her, then she had persuaded them to accept me.

I don't mean that Griff and Judd were ready to live at a Macro level by any means, because you learn by doing and even a week as intensive and challenging as the one they had just finished didn't give them enough practice to balance the years that went before. However, they had made a beginning at an entirely new way of thinking and it was already showing surprising results. Griff had at first been very depressed at learning about reincarnation and how our soul selects lessons to balance our learning experiences.

"What hope for the future have we got? If what you're telling us is true we'll probably be born girls next time and get raped and murdered," he reluctantly observed.

When I explained that this was only true if they refused to evolve to a more Macro perspective where *karma*, as popularly defined, didn't apply.

"You mean," Judd asked, "there's a way of escaping that damn *karma* thing?"

"Well," I answered, "the law of *karma* is only a prob-

234

lem to micro man because he had more hate or negative thoughts and actions than positive loving ones. At the Macro level people live by the law of love, which does not include penance. Its basis is joyous acceptance of whatever is, as perfectly chosen by each soul for its own development."

They kept asking questions about the law of love until Neda said, "If you can lovingly accept everything that happens to you, then nothing bad or unpleasant will be a part of your future."

"How in the world does a person learn to do that?" Griff asked.

"By wanting to learn it," Neda replied, "and by believing that you can learn it."

Griff kept asking questions, and Neda and I kept trying to answer them until Griff surprised us by saying that he'd like a notebook and a pen so he could start writing down some of these ideas. Once he started writing, he stayed up most of the night creating his own journal about Macro philosophy and how it might be used to rebuild his own life.

During the last couple of days of that week we had almost no headaches. Griff and Judd were both demonstrating greater awareness. Still Karl questioned their sincerity.

"After all," he cautioned, "they know that all they have to do is pretend to listen to everything you say, then promise to live the kind of life you expect of them, and you'll let them go."

"But they really mean it," Neda assured him.

"How do you know?" said Karl. "Don't forget, these guys are probably expert liars and wouldn't know the truth if it hit them on the head."

"Oh, Karl, you wouldn't be so skeptical if you'd spent all the hours with them that Jon and I have. Besides, we can always be sure of their progress by having Jon look at their auras."

"Is that true, Jon?"

"Well," I replied, "I haven't looked at their auras

since I first saw them because they were so depressing, but I'll give it a try tomorrow. Telepathically I see that they're coming along amazingly well. However, if their auras show that they're lying, I'll keep them here."

"But if they pass your aura test with pretty colors, you'll let them go tomorrow?"

"Exactly. Of course, I'll invite them to come back for more Personal Evolution tutoring at least several times a week for a while—"

"Well, I'll be . . ." I said, amazed at my new realization. "I'm a P.E. tutor! Can you believe that, Karl? And Neda—she is, too! It's amazing—simply amazing!"

On Sunday both Neda and Karl spent most of the day talking with Griff and Judd while I devoted my energies to observing their auras. By the middle of the afternoon I had watched them as they answered seemingly endless questions put to them by Karl. They had become angry occasionally, but only briefly, though I felt that Karl had pushed them pretty hard at times.

Still their auras looked much cleaner and sharper than they had been only seven days earlier. At last I asked them the biggest question of all.

"Would you like to stay here another week?"

There was a long silence while they looked at each other, then back at Neda, Karl, and myself. Finally, Judd cleared his throat and said, "I've learned an awful lot this past week; I guess I'd like to stick around a while longer if it's all right."

Then we all looked at Griff, who was staring intently at the floor. I saw Karl start to say something, but he caught Neda's eye and changed his mind. We all waited. Then Griff raised his head and, looking intently into my eyes said, "I want to leave. I've got it written down in my journal that you learn by practicing—by doing—and out there is where I'll find out how much I've really learned this past week. I can't find that out up here four floors above the rest of the world."

First Neda kissed Griff and then Judd while I watched Karl's neck, but he didn't say anything. Then I said, "I promised you both that once you had listened to what I had to say you could leave, and I'm not going to start lying to you now. I hope that you'll come back, Griff, to talk with Neda and me several times a week for a while, but that's up to you."

Hearing this invitation and being assured that it applied also to him, Judd decided that he would go with Griff, but they both wanted to come back and talk with us some more, soon and often. On that note I removed the hypnotic blocks, which had turned their anger into headaches and the doorknob into fire, and we bade them goodbye.

I accompanied Ned and Karl down to their apartment, where we spent the rest of the day until late evening discussing and digesting the past week's experience lessons and contemplating possible futures.

Going to sleep that night I decided that I agreed with what Neda had said earlier about the week: It was the most important learning experience of my life because I took the biggest risks, made the biggest mistakes, and attained some important successes.

I then employed the 2150 custom of closing the day with praise for having taken the risks necessary to grow that day and reaffirmation of my "lifestyle" plan for growth in the future.

CHAPTER 14:

The Challenge

I awakened in the huge bed of our Alpha room to find that it was morning. Carol and the rest of our Alpha were looking down at me.

"Welcome back, Jon," Carol said with a hug.

Then everyone was congratulating me. Lea and Rana, along with other nines and tens, had been able to follow my week's activities in 1976. They observed that I had at last demonstrated love, leadership, and wisdom (the three Macro virtues) along with some Macro powers, so that my aura was now an emission of fresh lemony-orange with tones of pink, purples, greens, blues, and white. I had achieved second-level Macro awareness.

Later that morning, while I was in my lakeside room at the C.I. center, I asked C.I. to provide me with more information about the levels of awareness. Since this was a general question, I soon discovered that I was receiving a lot more data than I could use or understand. However, by interrupting C.I. and asking specific questions I was able to gain some of the following information.

(1) While it was recognized from the beginning of the Macro society (back in the 1970s) that there were ten general levels of Macro awareness, it was not until the year 2025 that anyone demonstrated more than level three. The levels eight, nine, and ten were not achieved until after the year 2100—a rather recent development.

(2) Because of the relatively low levels of awareness in the early years of the Macro society, there had been some regressions in awareness level. This had almost always been associated with the misuse of Macro powers or leadership power. Some of these people had been on Micro Island, where they grabbed power and became the ruling elite. However, in the past 30 years no one above level two had regressed.

(3) One could attain a high degree of Macro power and still not demonstrate level-two awareness since awareness level was determined by the degree of personal evolution or Macro awareness, not by the extent of one's Macro power.

(4) The greatest challenge to the first seven levels of awareness existed on Micro Island and, thus, my best chance of developing level-three awareness quickly was to visit there. However, C.I. pointed out that on Micro Island I also ran a good chance of losing my second-level awareness and regressing to level one.

Figuring that the sooner I got there the better, I began asking all the questions I could think of concerning Micro Island. Some of the most important information involved the dangers I would be facing.

(1) Any visitor from the Macro society was liable to be killed unless protected by Macro powers. The greatest heroes of Micro Island were those who either killed the Macro visitors or persuaded them to give up membership in the Macro society to live permanently on Micro Island.

(2) The current leaders of Micro Island were all former members of the Macro society who had some degree of Macro powers and used these powers to gain

239

personal fame and fortune. This allowed them to lord it over others on the Island. These leader had been seduced by their desire for power with its fame and adulation. In other words, pride was the last and greatest obstacle to the soul's evolution toward greater awareness.

(3)   To attain level-three awareness I would have to demonstrate a personal evolution level which would overcome this last and greatest micro trait—pride. To do this I would have to voluntarily relinquish the protection of the Macro society and all its high level members including Lea and Rana.

I questioned C.I. extensively on this last bit of information and was finally given the analogy that if I wanted to demonstrate swimming proficiency I wouldn't wear a life jacket. From this I concluded that if I let anyone else help me overcome pride I would not be demonstrating level-three awareness.

The thought of being attacked by the inhabitants of Micro Island didn't seem so frightening since my experience with Griff and Judd. However, if I was attacked by someone who had developed Macro powers as great as or greater than my own that would be something else.

That evening I talked over this last possibility with Carol and Rana and received some very disturbing news. It seemed that the leaders of Micro Island were expecting me.

"How could they be expecting me?" I asked Rana. "I've never visited Micro Island."

"You've been told," she answered, "that the leaders of Micro Island are former members of the Macro society, some of whom have highly developed Macro powers. With telepathy, clairvoyance, and precognition they have learned a great deal about you."

"And," Carol added, "they are determined to either kill you or persuade you to give up the Macro way of life."

"But why should they be especially interested in me?" I asked.

"Because," Rana answered, "they know you are a twin soul of Lea, who, with the help of all other nines and

240

tens, has managed our first time-space translation. They would like to destroy our project by killing you or, even better, by getting you to denounce the Macro society and join them on Micro Island."

"That's ridiculous," I said. "They must know that if I joined them I couldn't attain level-three awareness and would lose my chance for permanent time translation."

Rana gave me a long appraising look before she answered. Finally she said, "There is another way of staying here permanently. Since Lea and the rest of us have established the time translation, as long as you are in 2150 time they could complete the translation if you would cooperate with them."

"But . . . but . . . that's impossible!" I exclaimed. "C.I. told me that no one above level seven has ever defected to Micro Island. They wouldn't have the Macro power."

I was shocked to see both Rana and Carol shaking their heads in disagreement with my statement. Then Rana said, "There are over 1,000 former Macro society members on Micro Island with varying degrees of Macro power. When they form a mind net in which all of them link their minds together, they could exert enough psychic power to complete, with your help, the time-space translation. However, while you would be a permanent member of 2150 it would have been accomplished without the help of your twin soul and before you reached the psychic balance of level-three personal evolution.

"My God!" I exclaimed. "Then they can offer 2150 without my having to attain level three!"

Rana nodded, "And they are planning to offer you not only permanent translation to 2150 but also adoption into their ruling elite, making you the third most powerful person on Micro Island."

"Yes," Carol added, "you would rank just below their President, Elgon, and their Vice President, Sela. Elgon was the only level seven in the Macro society who ever regressed levels. It made him so angry that he chose to leave the Macro society some eighty years ago and make himself president of Micro Island. Ten years later he managed to persuade his former Alpha mate, Sela, who had been a level six, to join him as his Vce President."

"But how is it," I asked, "that they can permanently complete my time translation when the combined efforts of every level nine and ten here and in the nearby planets are unable to do the same?"

"Oh, they could do it all right," Carol answered calmly, "but they chose not to until you demonstrate level-three awareness."

"Now wait a minute," I said. "Do I understand correctly that the Macro society has the power to keep me here permanently right now but won't do it because they don't like my level of awareness?"

"Precisely," Rana answered. "But not because we're snobbish over levels of awareness, as you are presently suspecting."

"Well, then, what is the reason you won't let me become a permanent member unless I attain level-three awareness?" I asked, a bit miffed.

"We believe," Rana said, "that if we completed the time translation before you had attained the psychic balance of at least level three you would not be able to withstand the micro pressures and would quickly regress to level one and eventually choose to live permanently on Micro Island."

"Are you sure?" I asked.

"No," Rana answered candidly, "and we are not sure that, even at level three, you won't regress and eventually choose to leave the Macro society, but we all agreed that we'll take that gamble."

"I learned from C.I." Carol added, "that almost a third of the level tens advised not completing the time translation until you had reached level seven. That was before they learned that Lea could only hold you here for three months without completing the translation."

I felt cold and clammy with a combination of understanding and frustration. "What was the minimum level of awareness that you all had agreed on before you learned of the time limitation?"

"Level five," Carol replied.

For a moment I just stared at the two of them while I let this chilling information register completely in my mind. "So you're telling me that even with level-three awareness the odds are against my continuing to expand my awareness in 2150."

"That's true, Jon," Rana replied. "Many feel your future success in the Macro society is very doubtful, due to the fact that you weren't born and raised in this age. Many feel that three months of your time is not enough to overcome the pull of your micro past. But we have voted and agreed to give you the chance if your personal evolution reaches level three."

Now it was my turn to give Rana a long appraising stare. Finally I said, "With your level-ten wisdom and your precognitive powers, what do you see in my future?"

She smiled and answered, "Things about the future can only be known as probabilities, or as possibilities, as they are always subject to change by the altering state of one's desire and belief. It would be unwise to predict your future at this point. I will be happy to help you explore alternative possibilities, though."

I shook my head saying, "I still don't understand why anyone would think that I would give up my twin soul Lea, Carol, my Alpha, you, and the whole Macro society to permanently join a micro society. After all, I've lived in a micro society for twenty-seven years back in 1976 and I know first-hand how miserably neurotic and selfish it is."

"The advantage of a micro society," Rana answered, "is that you can indulge your selfish desires and be acclaimed as a patriot, a statesman, or a hero in some field of endeavor."

Carol took my hand. Then looking at me with great intensity she said, "But I believe in you, Jon. I know that you'll overcome the micro self."

"And I, too, believe in you," Rana added. "It was my statement of belief in you before the Council of Tens

243

that persuaded them to accept a level-three demonstration."

Then I was startled to telepathically hear Lea saying, "And I believe in you—always and forever."

Carol and Rana smiled at me and I knew that they too had picked up Lea's message. Rana said, "Certainly the three of us who know you best ought to be able to provide you with enough belief to overcome your micro doubts."

I replied, "As long as I provide the necessary desire, the thought of losing contact with the three of you certainly provides me with the motivation I need."

"Very well," Carol said. "Now the only question that remains is when should we leave for Micro Island?"

"Tomorrow," I answered.

Rana stretched out her hand to me and said, "I strongly suggest that you wait one more week in which you can continue developing your Macro powers. I feel you will need all you can develop."

"You get that precognitively?" I asked.

"No," she laughed. "I get it logically!"

"All right," I agreed. "We'll wait one more week and I'll do all I can to develop my Macro powers, but that only gives me a little over two weeks to either attain level three or say farewell to 2150."

For the next week I played endless rounds of PK tennis with Carol, Neal, and Jean.

We played some more 2150 chess, too, and an extremely helpful new learning-game called Merge.

The object of this new game was to become one with the object, animal, person, or action; to feel what it feels the way it feels it; to sense what it senses; move as it moves; to know what it knows; to merge with it and be it for a while.

What an awakening experience, and what fun! The hardest part was always giving up my selfhood.

Through hard practice and taking the necessary risks I eventually learned that I never really had a selfhood in the first place, except from a micro view.

I learned that you can't lose what you never really had in the first place, namely, yourself. Since your separateness is only an illusion created by choice, it is there whenever you think you want or need it. It can't possibly be lost or taken away from you.

People are fascinating to merge with, but also the most difficult, the most educational, and the most painful.

Objects are the most dangerous for adults. While children find life so exciting that they jump from adventure to adventure, adults sometimes weary of the challenges and risks of life. If, in this weary state, they merge with, say a huge oak or a lovely big stable rock, it is sometimes extremely difficult to want to come back out. And, since desire precedes action, one must *want* to be a person more than he wants to be an oak before he can come out of an oak back to being fully a person.

Back in 1976 I visited hospitals to practice healing. I used not only PK, but also clairvoyance, telepathy, the beginnings of precognition, and my newly developed ability to merge. As I walked up and down hospital corridors if I "future saw" the possibility of death coming quickly for a patient, I would try to remove this possibility. Interestingly, in attempting this I discovered the truth of free choice.

One afternoon I persuaded (with considerable telepathic effort) the head nurse and two interns that I should be allowed access to the intensive care unit, where I found Bruno. He was a small man of 45 years who was recovering from a heart attack of that morning. According to the intern who examined him he was coming along just fine. But as I examined him clairvoyantly his aura was extremely weak and I "future saw" him riding in a hearse while lying in a casket. Since both these symbols represented death I felt that I had better go to work on Bruno immediately. The moment I made contact I got quite a surprise.

Bruno had been lying quietly sleeping while I clairvoyantly examined him, but now as I reached out and touched his mind I heard him say, "Hello, Azar. It's been a long time since our paths have crossed."

Azar is the name I had in an Atlantean incarnation almost 50,000 years ago. I had been a temple priest in charge of healing. Now that I had been addressed by that ancient name I felt strongly that the mind I was now contacting had once occupied a body which I helped heal during that Atlantean incarnation. I said, "It seems that I remember you from a period in Atlantis which we shared, but how did you remember me so easily?"

With the conscious Bruno still sleeping I heard his subconscious mind saying, "If I were awake I would have no conscious memory of you. However, with my conscious mind asleep I have been free to observe ever since you entered this ward and began using telepathy to hypnotically persuade the intern to let you accompany him. I watched as you clairvoyantly examined some of the patients, and I remembered that your mind had once been clothed in a body called Azar and had healed me."

"I wasn't aware that I was being observed," I said.

"I know," Bruno answered. "Your conscious mind is still extremely limited compared to your Macro potential."

"But," I asked, puzzled, "how do you know about the Macro potential?"

"Because, dear and old friend, another cell of my soul is presently experiencing a life in 2150, which you so often visit. Yet another is deeply involved in establishing the separate culture on Micro Island. It needs to experience power and practice using it properly. By 2085 it will be dead, though," he went on.

"Wait a minute!" I stopped him. "You're here in 1976. You haven't made it to 2000 yet, much less beyond."

"No, Azar. It's you who have not yet gone beyond. I guess you've not yet truly incorporated the concept of simultaneous time into your growth pattern.

"Incidentally, I picked up from your mind your plan of attempting to prevent my evolation, which I am not going to let you do. I appreciated your help last time, but this time I don't want it."

246

"You mean that you don't want to live any more, and are choosing to die?"

"That's right," he answered. "And you'll find quite a few other minds in this hospital who are ready to give up their bodies."

"But why?" I asked. "You've only lived a relatively short time. You must have a family who will miss you."

Telepathically I heard him laugh and say, "When I incarnated, 45 years ago, I promised myself that I would accomplish my purpose as quickly as possible and then evolate. I've already stayed longer than I had planned."

"May I ask what your purpose was?" I inquired.

"I wanted to balance my vibrations. First I chose to be born to a woman who, in my twenty-first-century life, I will probably marry and abandon. In this life as her son I treated her kindly and have taken care of her for the last twenty years since her husband died. Six months ago she followed him."

"How can you balance negative vibrations you won't even create till fifty years in the future?" I wondered if his mind was deteriorating too.

"You will find, Azar, that the past, present, and future are all micro terms—illusions which do not exist from a Macro view. All time is simultaneous.

"Getting on with my answer to your first question, I was a jealous, possessive wife and made my husband's life a living hell. Now for twenty-five years I have been married to a woman who has done the same for me. My two children are grown and married and I leave my wife financially well off, so now I can evolate, having completed my chosen learning experience."

"But now that you've accomplished your purpose," I said, "why don't you stay around awhile and enjoy life?"

Again the sound of his laughter echoed through my mind and he said, "I go to a far better place than this planet Earth will ever be! I invite you to visit me when you perfect your astral traveling enough that you can visit some of the non-physical dimensions. 'Bye for now!"

247

Bruno's body convulsed; his lids snapped sharply open. Only the after-death tremors lingered. He had evolated. My whole being felt an instant of icy hollowness as I saw, staring up at me from his lifeless face, Nancy's liquid brown eyes.

Later in 2150 Rana explained that every human mind chooses when it wants to die. This choice, she explained, is not usually made on the conscious level, but rather on the subconscious or soul level.

During the rest of the week I discovered that Bruno had been correct when he predicted that many other minds would refuse my offer to help heal their bodies. I was surprised at how many minds insisted on the value of suffering.

I remember a middle-aged woman who was seriously afflicted with arthritis. When I offered my help her subconscious mind replied, "Please don't remove my pain, for it is the motivation that will eventually force my micro self to give up its narrow selfish life habits which have psychologically crippled others and which are now crippling me. If you remove the pain I will have to start my lesson over, and I'd rather grow now."

I realized that this woman had never consciously permitted herself to be aware of these thoughts. If she could have heard her subconscious mind talking to me, she would have denied that this was her own greater self talking. When I asked her if she couldn't learn in some less painful way she replied, "I have not yet learned to accept responsibility for the harm I've done to others, so I keep taking the same old life lessons over and over. Eventually the pain will force me to break this "it's not my fault" cycle. Then I can admit my failure, forgive it, learn from it, and overcome it. It's been a long battle, but victory will come."

When I asked Rana about having to forgive yourself she explained forgiveness as acceptance. She said that when you forgive yourself you positively accept your mistakes and, thus, can learn to succeed and grow from them. However, negative acceptance, resignation, leaves

248

one burdened with guilt until it becomes necessary to escape by inducing amnesia. It is then impossible not to make the same mistake over and over again.

She was talking about the law of love which transcends the law of *karma*. Only by completely responding to ourselves with loving acceptance can we look at all the aspects of the self, which includes not only the micro self, but also the Macro self. And we can only see in others what we see in ourselves (even if only in potential) and we can only love (accept) others to the extent that we love (accept) ourselves.

It wasn't until I had examined every person in our university hospital that I accepted Rana's statement that "all illness and injury is self-inflicted."

I discovered that I could heal no one unless I could first persuade them to forgive themselves. Yet, I did find quite a few patients who were ready to forgive themselves. All of these healed in record time, causing considerable consternation among hospital personnel.

Human consternation, I have found, is always the result of a myth being threatened.

Since I had brought my journal up to date, Karl and Neda were becoming increasingly concerned about my forthcoming visit to Micro Island. Karl kept quoting passages that strengthened his warnings about the dangers involved, and I kept quoting passages that strengthened my resolve to go. Neda insisted that I would succeed and that there was no reason to worry about me. Finally it was obvious even to Neda that her constant assurances that I would succeed were an unfailing indication that she feared the opposite.

Fortunately, Griff and Judd visited us regularly and kept her occupied. Both were sincerely trying to live a new style of life. They had quit their motorcycle gang and had taken jobs, Judd at an auto repair shop and Griff with a construction company. They were deeply interested in my further experiences in 2150.

At last the week ended and early one morning Carol and I said goodbye to our Alpha, our Beta, and most of our Gamma and began our run to the building at the end of the lake. As we passed each Gamma I saw more people than I had ever seen before in 2150, for almost everyone had turned out to send both vocal and telepathic messages of support to us.

As we approached the large administration building we could see the rest of our Delta gathered around our transair. I was moved by the tremendous outpouring of loving acceptance that many Macro beings could produce. As we made our way to the vehicle I saw standing beside it Rana, Eli, and my beloved Lea.

I ran to embrace Lea. We stood in complete silence with no one in the crowd making a sound as we fitted our minds into a union that only twin souls can ever attain. To me she was the most exquisitely lovely, completely satisfying woman who had ever lived. Overcome by my feelings and with tears on my face I kissed her gently. Then taking my face in her hands, she kissed me. It was the most enlightening kiss my soul had known since incarnating in matter.

Then Lea turned, touched Carol's face, and disappeared into the crowd. I shook hands with Hugo, our Delta, and Eli, our Ktar. I remembered seeing him when I met my Alpha members, then in his astral body as he visited his Kton, but I still had not spent further time with him, as I had longed to do. I was convinced that I had never beheld such a handsome and wise-looking man before. He took my hands, then embraced me firmly. He looked deep into my eyes for a long time and said, "You never asked, so, at Rana's request, no one ever told you, but the woman who has been your P.E. tutor is also our Mutar. She is, thus, a member of the Council of Three."

I must have looked strange, for I know my breath was gone as I remembered C.I. telling me that the Council of Three—which consisted of the three Mutars (leaders of 100 million) was composed of two men and one woman whose decisions were binding on all members of the Macro society.

I was stunned to learn that my very own tutor, Rana,

was that one woman. No wonder her advocacy of level-three entrance for me had been accepted. I looked at her with awe and a new sense of restraint.

She came over to me and took my hand saying, "Now you know why I hoped you would not learn of my other duties. We who have grown up in the Macro society do not feel awe or a sense of distance between us and our leaders. But I know that you were trained differently."

I found it difficult to say anything, but managed, rather lamely, "Will you still be my tutor when I get back from Micro Island?"

She said with a smile, "I will be your tutor as long as you both desire it and believe it possible."

Carol and I walked into our transair and set the sealing doors in motion.

Eli stepped out from the crowd. In my mind his rich full voice rang as though through a great hall.

"Thank you for your admiration, Jon. Know that it is returned.

"You should also know that during your 20th century a soul made a brief sojourn—just 30 years—for the solitary purpose of bearing a child.

"Having many other duties to tend to, she stayed just long enough to see her young son securely entrusted to the loving care of a soul you now call Karl Johnson."

The doors met and melded together and as we took off I could hear Eli answering my unspoken question.

"For what strength it may give you, my beloved son, . . . I am your mother."

CHAPTER 15:

Micro Island

Three hours later we had traveled some 3700 miles and were approaching the northeastern shore of Micro Island. This large semi-tropical Pacific island had risen out of the ocean during the cataclysmic earth changes of the late 20th century. It was about half the size of 1976's Australia. The Macro society maintained a well-protected base on this eastern coast from which it carried on most of its contacts with the island's interior. Carol had explained that this base, where we were planning to land, was completely protected by an invisible force field which had effectively resisted all attempts to breach it. Now as we came in sight of this Macro society enclave I was startled to see it surrounded on its landward side by thousands of people.

"What an enormous number of people," I exclaimed. "Do the Micro Islanders usually gather in such numbers outside the Macro society base?"

"Not that I've heard of," Carol replied. "In fact, Micro Island has a law against coming within ten miles of our base. They used to patrol this zone with policemen and dogs."

"Well," I said, "either they repealed the law or there are an awful lot of lawbreakers down there."

The force field was momentarily removed and we descended into a clearing beside a Gamma building which was surrounded by about 1,000 acres of beautifully landscaped gardens and parkland with large swimming pools and recreation areas. As our transair touched down I saw a very tall man leave the building and run toward us. By the time we were on the ground he had reached us, and Carol introduced me to Orion, the Gammar of this base. She had talked with him during the past week via C.I. video, so now they seemed like old friends.

"Why the crowd?" I asked.

Orion answered, "It seems that President Elgon Ten has proclaimed an island holiday in honor of your visit. He and his Vice President, Sela Nine, are out there now waiting to greet you. I'm sorry there's no one else from the Macro society here, but all the rest of our Gamma is off in the interior using this holiday as an opportunity to tutor."

"What happened to the law against coming within ten miles of this base?" Carol asked.

"In honor of this occasion," Orion explained, "Elgon rescinded it for today."

"Why did they have a law like that in the first place?" I inquired.

"That's easy to answer," Orion replied. "Elgon and his assistants are afraid of our influence on their people. They don't want to lose anyone to the Macro society, so any islander who is caught talking with a member of the Macro society is punished severely."

"Are you that successful in getting recruits for the Macro society from here?" I asked.

He answered, "We might be if they didn't have that

law. Even with it we find about a hundred people each year who are ready to go to the mainland."

Looking at the crowd packed outside the invisible force field I was surprised at the number of very small children who were permitted to gather among such a crowd without the supervision of their parents.

"Where are the parents of all those little ones, and why aren't they here looking after them?" I asked Orion.

"They're there, Jon, right along with the children," he answered. "You're just not used to seeing such large families. Here on Micro Island birth control is strictly forbidden. It's not unusual to see families with fifteen to twenty-five children. The more children a couple has, the greater their prestige."

"But why don't these people limit the size of their family to just the number of children that they can adequately clothe and care for? Just look at some of them," I remarked.

"Yes, I know," he replied. "They're the victims of their religions which denounce birth control as a mortal sin. The fact is, however, that Elgon would change that if he thought it would serve his purpose. Of course, it won't, for his purpose, publicly stated, is to outbreed the Macro society so he can justly claim the mainland as his territory."

"Don't the women get tired of being pregnant all the time?" Carol asked.

"Yes indeed, they do," Orion answered. "In fact one of our biggest problems with Elgon and his assistants is that they interfere with our distribution of birth control tablets to those who ask for them. You see, both Elgon and his assistants have highly developed telepathic and clairvoyant powers so if a man or woman even desires birth control tablets in their presence they are aware of it and the individual is punished the same as if he had talked to a Macro society member. You probably know that our birth control tablets render the person infertile for anywhere from one to five years, depending on which tablet is taken."

"In a culture like this it would be a blessing to be physically unable to bear children," Carol observed.

"Not really, Carol," he explained. "You see, any woman who is unable to bear children is used as a prostitute and forbidden to marry. That really brands her, for marriage is highly revered here. The only cause accepted for divorce is a woman's inability to bear children."

"I guess if a woman wants a divorce she just takes a pill!" I commented. "But if talking to a Macro society member and taking birth control tablets are both against the law, how do people manage to get the tablets?"

"They know we are telepaths," Orion answered, "so all they have to do is pass us on the street thinking the request and we'll teleport the tablet of her choice to her when no one is watching. The problem is that one of Elgon's thousand assistants sometimes intercepts the signal. Then the person is immediately dragged away to the nearest public penalty square where . . . but then, I needn't tell you of their atrocities. You'll see them soon enough."

My attention went back to the crowd outside the barrier and I remembered that their president, Elgon, and their vice president, Sela, were waiting outside for us. I asked, "Do you think it would be dangerous for Carol and me to go out and meet their president?"

"Not immediately," he replied. "They plan to give you a royal reception, show you what they believe are the virtues of Micro Island existence, and then try to persuade you to allow them to help you complete your time translation."

"Then," I said, "I suppose they feel I'll be so grateful that I'll want to stay here forever among them, right?"

Orion looked at me very carefully for a moment before he said, "They are very clever and will use every trick they can think of to get you to allow them to complete your time translation. You see, they believe that if this happens before you are level three it will mean that you will regress in awareness and be unable to live happily in the Macro society."

"Okay," I said, "then it only becomes dangerous for us when they see that I've successfully resisted their persuasion to let them complete my time translation. We'll plan to return here just before that happens."

I suddenly realized that Orion did not believe that would be possible and was vainly trying to hide his doubts concerning my success with the Micro Islanders. I found myself beginning to share some of his doubts, but I tried to put on a brave smile as I said, "Well, maybe it won't turn out as badly as you think, Orion. But in any event, I must take the risk and grow from the results, whatever they may be. So if you'll be kind enough to open your force field we'll go out and meet President Elgon and the crowd."

He slowly nodded his assent, then walked with us to the beginning of the force field, where he stopped and turned to us. "Be sure to use the number as their last name. It's very important to them as it represents the level of awareness they profess to have evolved to."

Looking deeply into Carol's eyes he lifted her hands to his lips and kissed them. I was somewhat surprised when he turned and gave me the same warmly affectionate farewell.

He then raised the force field and allowed us to step outside the protected area. Once we had done this, both Carol and I could clairvoyantly see the force field return and knew that we now stood unprotected, except by our own minds, before what looked like the entire population of Micro Island.

As we stood uncertainly examining the vast throng of humanity that stood before us, a great cheering began and out of the center of the crowd came two of the most dazzling individuals that I had ever seen outside of a rock concert. As they came closer I could see a powerfully built man at least six and a half feet in height and with a massively handsome face as hard as though it had been chipped out of granite. He was dressed in white robes embroidered with blue, yellow, and green stones and thousands of what looked like sequins that sparkled in

256

the noonday sun. This, I thought, must be the president of Micro Island, Elgon "Ten," formerly level seven in the Macro society some 80 years ago.

He had regressed in awareness level, then added "Ten" to his name and declared himself level ten. He had stopped wearing the aura-reflecting tunic at the same time.

My attention turned to the woman at Elgon's side who I knew must be Sela "Nine," the regressed level six who had been Elgon's Alpha mate. Since I knew she had left the Macro society 70 years ago, I realized that she must now be well over a hundred years old, yet she didn't look a day over twenty-five. Her beauty was the lush sexually stimulating glitter of a film star.

She was so powerfully alluring that I felt my whole body tingling in response to the sight of her. Her costume was a stunning and lascivious creation that bared unnaturally large, firm breasts whose uptilted nipples were touched with a glistening red substance. While the upper part of her gown was little more than an open halter, covered with ermine-like fur sprinkled with green emeralds, the skirt was flowing red velvet slit to the waist on both sides to reveal the most voluptuously exciting legs I had ever seen.

Suddenly Carol's soft laughter echoed through my mind as I heard her thinking to me, "I hope you haven't forgotten about Lea and me already!"

With more effort than I thought it would take, I shifted my gaze from Sela to Carol and washed my mind in her fresh, clear loveliness. At last I managed a wry smile. "Thanks for pulling me out before I drowned."

"I was almost overwhelmed by lust for Elgon," Carol admitted. "Then I realized there must be hundreds of his telepathic assistants in this crowd trying to tele-hypnotize us into believing that we can't live without the sexual pleasure of those two."

"So that's why——" I began when Carol interrupted me with the warning, "Prepare your mind to be attacked and remember your last Macro contact."

I had just enough time to begin the process of Macro

257

contact recall when I felt the delicious contact of Sela's body pressed against mine and the incredibly exciting sensation of her wet tongue touching my lips, then slipping inside my mouth.

Dimly I heard Carol's voice saying, "Please let me go, Elgon. Your overly sexual greetings are not part of our customs, as you well know."

From somewhere deep within my mind I summoned the strength to push Sela gently but firmly away from me. She smiled a mocking smile, and I noticed that there were dangerous lights dancing hypnotically in her glorious eyes. They were darker than the darkest night of hell.

It was not until then that I noticed her magnificent mane of glistening mahogany hair that fell to her waist in rich graceful waves.

"Welcome to Micro Island," Elgon said in a deep resonant voice that I immediately recognized as being powerfully hypnotic. "I am Elgon Ten, President of Micro Island."

"Thank you," I managed to respond in a relatively calm voice. "But if you don't want us to turn around immediately to seek sanctuary behind the force field, you'll have to end the hypnotic barrage."

Elgon locked his eyes with mine and I felt suddenly as if I were teetering on the edge of a dangerous precipice. It took all of my deepest mind strength to overcome the lethal desire to fall into the abyss below. I wrenched my gaze away from his eyes and heard him laughing in a great booming voice. As I turned to Carol he said, "Have no fear, Jon Ten. You have just demonstrated tenth-level awareness by resisting not only the mind of Sela Nine and myself but also of the thousand telepathically linked minds who were sending their hypnotic suggestions at you. You have succeeded beyond anything we imagined, and I promise you we will make no more futile attempts to control your mind. You are Jon Ten and truly as great as I."

"Master," Sela cried out, and knelt before me, "let us show you our island and truly answer all your ques-

258

tions so the misconceptions that C.I. has implanted in your mind will be balanced at last by the truth."

I turned back to Elgon and said, "All right, show us your island."

Sela was back on her feet and shaking her head, "The invitation to visit our island extends only to you, Jon Ten."

"I'm sorry, but I must insist on taking Carol with me wherever I go," I said, deliberately addressing this remark to Elgon and ignoring Sela.

Elgon shrugged his powerful shoulders and said, "Our admiration for you, Jon Ten, is so great that we will bow to your wishes."

Saying this, he made a signal to the crowd, which immediately parted, allowing us passage to where a large open-topped transair stood. Carol and I followed Elgon and Sela into the rear portion of this conveyance that appeared to have two drivers up front separated from the six-swivel-seated passenger compartment by a glass-like partition. We all took seats except Elgon, who remained standing to accept the cheers of the wildly shouting crowd as our vehicle moved slowly past.

When we had left the crowd behind, the transair rose to about 300 feet off the ground and proceeded at a very slow pace, possibly 50 miles an hour, toward the interior of the island. Elgon, after a last wave at the distant crowd, seated himself facing us and began telling us about Micro Island. I'll summarize its main features.

Micro Island had a population of a little over three million and was divided into five states, each of which had its own language, religion, and color. When Elgon assumed the presidency of the island, by virtue of his superior Macro powers, he established firm territorial boundaries for the five states.

The island was roughly circular in shape and Elgon had divided it into five pie-shaped triangles which allowed the states to have a common center, a circle which covered an area of approximately 75 square miles, belonging to Elgon as supreme leader. When I asked him

259

why he permitted all the divisions into separate states, religions, races, and languages he responded by saying, "The history of the world has proven that man evolves fastest when he is divided so that conflict and competition can encourage growth."

For a moment I thought he was being facetious, but then I saw the fanatical gleam in his eye and realized that he was dead serious.

"Oh, I know," he continued, "that the Macro society has brainwashed you into accepting pious ideas of unity and love, but those are illusions at the micro level which we inhabit. If God had wished Macro unity to exist at the micro levels, he would have arranged it that way. On this planet we live on the micro level where conflict and competition are universal laws. Macro man who denies these laws has no place here and will eventually be forced into some other dimension."

"According to the Macro philosophers," I replied, "it is micro man who has been forced into other dimensions, as this planet has been upgraded from a micro one to a Macro one."

"Those are lies," he said, "perpetuated by decadent Macro beings trying to destroy the vitality and strength of micro man. But let me show you the exciting, interesting lives our people live and you can compare their existence with the decadent life of the Macro society."

Elgon must have sent a telepathic message to the driver, for we suddenly swooped close to the ground so that Elgon could point out the many people working in the fields and some nearby factories. Either in the factories, fields, or service jobs Elgon bragged that micro man worked eight hours a day six days a week, which kept him free from the lazy existence of the Macro society.

I questioned him about the people working in the fields and factories on a day which he himself had proclaimed a national holiday. He responded by saying that only in this area were people working so we could inspect their work if we wanted to. I declined.

As we came very close to the workers in the fields I was surprised to notice the intense yellow color of their skin as I remembered that the crowds outside the Macro society base had been white. When I asked Elgon about this, he explained that due to the sinful mixing of the races the original colors were no longer pure so they used artificial dyes to provide the five basic skin colors: black, brown, red, yellow, and white. Their five states were named for these colors.

Our transair landed near a small town that reminded me of a rural community back in the middle 1900s. Elgon opened the door for us and said, "We want you to go talk to the people of this village or any village you wish. We won't go with you, so you'll know that people aren't lying to you just to please us."

While I had my doubts about how free the people would be to talk with us, we quickly accepted this offer and were soon knocking on one of the first doors on the village outskirts. An elderly woman who looked to be about seventy opened the door. She said she had seen our approach on TV and was proud to be the first we visited. She invited us into a small, sparsely furnished living room and when we were seated on the hard metal chairs, invited me to ask any questions I wished.

"Tell me about your life," I said.

She smiled broadly, revealing ugly twisted teeth, as she said, "We live honest, decent, God-fearing lives. Our men and women get married and stay married and have lots of children and live in a home by themselves, not in some huge evil hotel like they do on the mainland."

"Why do you dye your skin yellow?" I asked.

"Because," she explained, "my ancestors had yellow skin until the Macro society polluted us with interracial marriage. Now we must dye our skins to remember our glorious racial heritage. You'll find our yellow state with its yellow religion and yellow language is the nicest state on our island."

"Wait a minute," I said. "You're speaking the universal language of the Macro society, not the yellow language."

261

"We learn the president's language in our schools and on television," she replied proudly, "but we speak only the yellow language in our homes and in our state activities."

"But why do you want two languages?" I asked.

"People," she replied," can't be proud and hold their heads up if they have abandoned the language of their ancestors. Our yellow language makes our yellow people in our yellow state with our yellow religion the most unique people in all the world."

"Tell me about your yellow religion," I requested.

She gave me another snaggle-toothed smile and said, "According to our yellow religion, when God created man he used five colors to distinguish the five different kinds of people. The yellow people God created last and best, and ever since, the yellow race has been God's chosen race to show all the other races the God-like way to live."

Up to now Carol had been deliberately allowing me to ask the questions, but now she said, "I recognize that you honestly believe what you are saying, and I feel that you have an intense dislike for us."

"Only for you of the Macro society, not for this man," she said, looking scornfully at Carol. "He has come from the great age of micro man when the yellow race had a greater population than any other race. Elgon Ten, our president, says that he hopes you of the Macro society have not yet corrupted Jon beyond saving. It is our responsibility to show him the truth."

Leaving Carol with a look of disgust she turned to me and smiled maternally as she continued, "We remain true to the ancient virtues of religion, race, language, and the micro family with its decent and respectable moral standards."

Now she pointed at Carol with a gnarled finger and said, "There stands the whore of ancient Babylon living only for licentious pleasure—godless, childless, parentless, and doomed never to know the holy decency of marriage and the rearing of her own children. She and all her kind are an abomination to this earth. Soon God will destroy these wicked blasphemers."

"Thank you for talking with us," I said, "but we'd better leave now. Your president is outside and we wouldn't want to keep him waiting."

She walked us to the door wishing happiness and truth for me and ignoring Carol. We returned to the transair and I asked to visit another state. We were soon in the air. A transparent top had been raised over the car so that we could travel at a very high rate of speed. On our journey to the next state it was Sela's turn to regale us with the marvels of Micro Island.

She began by pointing out to me that every individual had the right to have children and that women were faithful to their husbands.

"Tell me, Sela Nine," I said, "are you faithful to Elgon Ten?"

She laughed and then said, "I am not married, because the Macro society destroyed my ability to have children."

"According to C.I., Sela Nine, you chose permanent sterilization, and you could still choose otherwise," Carol inserted. "C.I. also said that women who can't or won't bear children are treated as prostitutes here on Micro Island."

Sela gave Carol a look of revulsion and then turned back to me with a smile and said, "The Macro society developed the greatest store of lies in all history and then built a machine called C.I. to disseminate them."

"Then you don't have prostitutes?" I asked.

"Of course we have prostitutes," she replied. "Micro man has always needed sexual variety. It's the oldest profession women have ever known. We are true to the ancient micro customs which permit man to have anything he's willing to pay for. Of course, like many other pleasures, it's illegal to patronize a prostitute."

"What do you mean, 'like other pleasures'?" I asked.

"We have laws against many pleasures so that our people will appreciate them and work hard to earn enough money to afford them," Sela answered.

"You mean you encourage crime by passing laws that you know will be broken?" I asked incredulously.

"Of course," she replied. "Hasn't it always been so? It's one of our best sources of revenue. Besides, look at the history of the world. Crime is an essential ingredient in micro life. It makes life exciting and interesting. After all, you can't have conflict and competition if you don't have the right kind of laws."

"You seem to mean that you and Elgon Ten have organized crime so that it benefits you and your followers," I commented.

"That's right, Jon Ten. That's how it's always been," she answered with a shrug of her shoulders that set her lush bare breasts to jiggling in a way I struggled to ignore. "But it benefits everyone because our organized crime provides everyone who is willing to pay for it the most delicious pleasure of all—rebellion and revolt—which is what breaking a law is all about. Micro man has always thrived on it."

"It's hard for me to believe that the two of you could have grown up in the Macro society, attained high levels of Macro awareness, and then given it all up for this," I remarked.

"But, Jon Ten," Sela cried out, "we didn't give up our awareness. We developed it further. I am now level nine; Elgon is ten. You don't understand. What we left behind was only boredom. Here there is the delicious excitement of forbidden fruits being fought over and taken by the strong and courageous. I tell you, Jon Ten, without pride and conflict life is so deadly dull that it's not worth living."

"You must have forgotten," I said, "that I came from the world of 1976 where conflict and competition were polluting and destroying this planet."

"We haven't forgotten," she replied, "that as long as competition and conflict were allowed free reign there was no great danger of pollution or overpopulation because the strong survived and the weak perished or lived lives of minimum consumption and pollution."

264

"But," I said, "aren't all your assistants with Macro powers called controllers, and aren't you limiting and controlling conflict and competition for your own interests?"

"Of course we are," she replied candidly, "because we are the strong, and the strong always control if they aren't shackled by a mythology of love, equality, and unity."

"You must recognize that no social organization, including your micro society, can survive without cooperation," I stated.

"Yes," she agreed, "we cooperate so that we can better enjoy the fruits of conflict and competition."

Our conversation was interrupted at this point by our landing near a small town in the red state. Carol and I got out and this time walked all the way through this community of generally small unattractive houses. There were, however, a few larger homes, so we selected one of the largest and most ostentatious in the community. Before we knocked on the door Carol commented on the very few people we had seen in the streets, which were almost deserted. Before I could knock on the door it was opened by a short middle-aged man with a large well-fed stomach and bright red skin. He welcomed us into a large and lavishly appointed living room saying that everyone was watching our progress on the TV, interspersed with the gladiator games from the capital city of Elgonia.

"Well," I said as we sat down in luxuriously comfortable form-hugging chairs, "I suppose that accounts for the absence of people outside. But tell us about the gladiator games you mentioned."

His face lit up and he grinned broadly, revealing a beautiful set of obviously false teeth. "They're great!" he said. "Our state gladiators represent us in the games. This gives us a chance to demonstrate our superiority."

"You mean red gladiators fight gladiators of other colors?" I asked.

"Yes," he replied, "but we have many types of competition besides the individual sword fights, fist fights, or wrestling that gladiators performed in the past. We have team conflicts that include football, baseball, and basketball as well as larger conflicts such as capture the flag."

"Well," I said, "I remember playing a game by that name when I was a boy. How does your version go?"

"When we practice it locally," he explained, "we use fewer gladiators, but when it involves interstate competition the standard team size is 100 men who play on a standard size C.F. field of 1,000 square yards. The object of the conflict is to capture the other state's flag. We use both sword teams and bare-handed teams."

"You mean that you actually kill each other in these contests?" I asked.

"Of course," he replied, "but since the gladiators can wear armor in the sword contests, not very many are killed—only ten or twelve a week—but they're still the most exciting contests we have."

"How often," Carol asked, "do you watch these games?"

"Since we work six days a week, and must attend church on Sunday morning, that leaves our evenings and Sunday afternoons for watching the games," he replied.

"My God!" I exclaimed. "Don't you get tired of watching that much fighting?"

He laughed, then said, "There's one thing that we red men never get tired of, and that's fighting!"

"But isn't that sort of brutality against your religion?" I inquired.

"The red religion holds that God created four races of men and was disappointed," he explained. "Then he created the red race to fight for the glory of God. We are the chosen race to lead all other races by our dedication to courage and our loyalty to our race and to God."

"Sounds strangely familiar," Carol commented quietly to me.

"Scoff if you like, decadent woman," he replied angrily,

266

"but our women are proud to bear us warriors, and they are decently married to one man."

Sensing that it might be wise to change the subject, I asked, "As a representative of the chosen red race how do you manage to accept a leader like Elgon, whose skin is certainly not red?"

"It's true that his redness doesn't show," he explained, "but the soul of our president is red. He wears his skin white in sympathy for the weakness of the white race."

"Then how do you know his soul is red?" I asked.

"Because when we asked him, he replied that he would never deny it," was his response.

That Elgon was a sly one, I thought to myself. Then I decided to ask one more question before leaving. "Tell me," I said, "what do you do that allows you to live in such a large home and in such luxury?"

"I was hoping that you would ask," he said, grinning proudly. "You see, on Micro Island courage, hard work, and a good head for business are rewarded. When I was young I was the most famous gladiator on the island, and I earned a great deal of money which I invested in land and various business ventures. Today I own half the houses in our village and most of the acreage surrounding it."

"Aren't you afraid," Carol asked as she glanced at the valuable articles in the room, "that you might be robbed of some of your wealth?"

He laughed rather scornfully and said, "We believe in the value of personal property, so we have law and order. Every tenth person on our island is a police official and we take great pride in our ability as crime fighters. I myself was appointed personally by President Elgon Ten as one of the ten top law officers in our Red State."

Carol couldn't help but insert, "Micro Island is the only place in the world where police are needed, because it's the only place in the world where crime exists. If you didn't place so much importance on personal properties, you wouldn't need to waste all that manpower on policing your people."

The fat red face of our host grew even redder as he glowered at her saying, "Great personal wealth has always gone to the strong, courageous, and clever people who are willing to take risks and live exciting and rewarding lives."

Now he sneered openly at Carol as he said, "Your Macro society has destroyed all sense of decency or pride in its members by encouraging every vice imaginable and by denying all the virtues—courage, loyalty to one's race, accumulation of personal wealth."

Getting to his feet and waddling furiously about the room he shouted, "Never in the history of our world has such evil, wicked, godlessness been permitted to flourish. But God is not mocked forever! You and all your godless, cowardly breed will soon perish from the face of this earth!"

I figured we'd better leave before our host worked himself into some sort of apoplectic stroke. I thanked him for his time and we hastily took our leave, and arrived back at the transair feeling rather depressed at what our host had revealed to us. There was no doubt in our minds that he fervently believed the things he had told us. No one had forced us to choose his home to visit.

Once we were airborne again, Elgon began questioning me about my impressions so far. When I told him quite honestly that I had been depressed by what I had seen, he seemed genuinely sad and shook his great head of long, curly black hair back and forth a number of times before he said, "I'm sorry to hear that the Macro society has already so poisoned your mind against us that you can't see how proud and happy our people are, living free and decent lives."

"Elgon Ten," I asked, "do you really think that everyone—even the poor and unhealthy—is happy here on Micro Island?"

Elgon replied in an extremely sincere and persuasive manner saying, "What you don't understand, Jon Ten, is that the most important thing for man is not wealth,

268

or health, or even fame, but personal pride—the feeling that he is better than the others."

He paused now to let this sink into my mind before continuing, "We here on Micro Island have provided man with many opportunities for personal pride; his own family, his own race, his own religion, his own language, his own property, and his own state. All of these the Macro society has denied man and, by so doing, reduced the life of its members to a state of such monumental boredom that they don't care whether they live or die. They come to Micro Island and break our laws so they can have at least the satisfaction of dying in an exciting way even if they can't live that way."

Now it was my turn to shake my head. "I'm sorry, but I just can't see it that way, Elgon."

"I don't ask you to believe what I say," he responded. "Just believe what your eyes and ears tell you. Talk to more of our people. Talk to the poor ones. Talk to what you call the losers in our system. Why, I tell you, the most miserable cowardly loser on our island has more self-pride and joy in living than any person you'll ever meet in the Macro society. But don't take my word for it, see and hear for yourself."

I agreed to do as Elgon suggested and talk with some more people, so he dropped us off beside a village in the Brown State. Here Carol and I talked with a mother and father of 18 children. The mother was only 36. She had married at 12 and had her first child at 14 followed by the birth of one child each year thereafter—18 of them lived.

This family was very poor. Their house was small and they slept seven to a bed. However they were very proud of their family and the fact that the five eldest sons were in training to be gladiators. The whole family worked as tenant farmers, which did not supply them with enough money to survive, so the two eldest daughters had been working as prostitutes for the past several years to supplement the family income. The whole family was very proud of these two girls.

Their health, by Macro society standards, was atrocious. The mother with two babies at her breasts looked a pale and sickly 50, yet she had told me proudly that she was 14 years younger than that. The father at 39 looked younger than the mother, though most of his teeth were rotten stumps and his body looked bloated with unhealthy fat. In contrast, most of the swarming children looked very skinny, but with complexions just as pallid as their parents'.

When we arrived at their home, they were all happily watching the gladiators fighting on TV, which I learned every family purchased even if it had money for nothing else. They were pathetically proud of their dyed-brown skin, their brown religion, and their brown language, their brown state, which had the bravest and strongest gladiators in the world—according to them.

Once again we got the bit about God creating four races and being disappointed, so he created the brown race to show all the others how to live loyal, courageous, and God-fearing lives. They believed it, and were pathetically happy that they had had the great good fortune to be born as God's chosen people.

Instead of being scornful of Carol, this family were genuinely sorry for her great misfortune at having been born into the Macro society. They honestly pitied this beautiful and healthy young girl.

When I asked them if they weren't unhappy with their poverty, the father said, "We pity the rich, for they no longer have the glorious hope of obtaining riches. We have the exciting incentive of gaining wealth, and soon when our sons enter the games the money will begin rolling in. You see, we have every reason to be happy with our lives."

Carol and I left on that note feeling again depressed but no longer surprised that Elgon would want us to visit as many people as possible. It was becoming obvious that he was showing off the results of the most successful propaganda machine ever created.

Later as we were flying to the Black State I asked

270

Elgon if he had any idea what the average life-span was on Micro Island.

"Yes," he replied. "Men live on the average of about 53 years and women about 52. Of course, you think that's terrible, but, again, let me remind you, Jon Ten, that it is not how long you live, or how much comfort and security you have that really counts. No, in the long run, it's how much pride you can take in your life and how much excitement you've had along the way."

"I don't deny," I said, "that you've been successful at persuading your people into believing what you are saying. My wonder is that even a hundred a year leave your island."

"Those are the older ones," Elgon explained, "who haven't had the advantages of all the improvements that Sela Nine, I, and our thousand controllers have instituted in the past 30 years. I spent the first 40 years here just getting things organized, but now our micro society is more exciting and interesting for everyone."

"You mean it's taken you 70 years to set up an almost perfect propaganda machine that persuades everyone to think as you want them to think," I observed.

Elgon merely smiled his imperious smile and suggested that I visit with more of his people. This we did, but the next two families, one black and one white, gave us the same old story. They were proud of their skin color, their religion, their language, their family, and their glorious state. Naturally they were happy to be God's chosen people and they were out to produce as many of their race as possible. The black family had 18 children, while the white family, due to multiple births, was the record-holder with 53 children.

The incredibly prolific white mother mentioned the growing problem with outlaws who refused to accept the wisdom of Elgon Ten and entertained the blasphemous ideas of the Macro society. She said it was the other states that had the biggest problem with this (naturally).

I began to suspect that Elgon had landed us close to "safe" communities in which he knew the inhabitants were brainwashed. I was happy to hear that people who were seeking out the ideas of the Macro society were a big problem.

I did, however, learn some interesting things from the black family. Since the father was a lawyer he explained that next to being a gladiator, being a lawyer was the most prestigious and best-paying job on Micro Island. This, he said, was because of the masses of conflicting laws. He admitted that there were so many laws covering so many life areas that everyone broke at least two or three laws every day. Of course, if one had a clever lawyer there was no problem. However, since each state had different laws, it was extremely dangerous to travel in another state. Lawyers couldn't practice in any other state, and you were sure to break some of the other state's laws. Then your different skin color would put you at a tremendous disadvantage.

I was fascinated to hear this lawyer defend their legal system in which the rich could hire lawyers to give them virtual immunity from the law, while the poor were constantly suffering from lack of legal representation. As he spoke I realized that their legal system was not much different from that of 1976, where the poor were a hundred times more likely to go to jail than the rich and were the only ones ever to suffer from capital punishment.

He explained that since the rich were obviously more valuable to the state than the poor, it was only natural that they would be able to buy greater justice. However, he carefully pointed out that the law had no favorites— it was strictly a matter of hiring a good attorney and, thus, staying in good with the government. I realized that the micro government of 2150 would applaud the actions of my government back in 1976 which fought inflation by creating unemployment among the poor and allowed a third of its people to live in poverty while it spent billions to support corrupt governments thousands of miles from its shores. But, then, like attracts like, and

272

corrupt governments have always tended to support other corrupt governments.

After having visited all five states, Elgon said we were ready to visit the capital city in the center of the island where all the states came together. During our flight there I asked Elgon about the island's school system. He replied that for almost 90 percent of the children formal education started at five and ended at twelve. Full-time work in the fields, factories, and stores began at this age along with the universal obligation to marry and start having children. It was possible to continue formal education in the gladiatorial, law, or medical schools if sufficient tests were passed. Since these schools were open at night, young people who passed the tests could work during the day and study at night. The wealthy had no problems, for they could hire teachers to guarantee successful passing of all the tests except those of the gladiators.

When I asked about the state and local governments I discovered that only lawyers could hold government positions—sometimes as many as four or five of them at a time. As for Elgon's national island government, all 10,000 positions were appointed by Elgon or Sela and the most important of these—over 1,000—positions were filled with ex-members of the Macro society. I commented on this, saying, "You obviously value the Macro society environment in that it produced your best and most trusted leaders. Doesn't this contradict what you are saying about Micro Island? After all, if life was so good here it ought to produce your best leaders."

Elgon laughed at this and said, "As long as the Macro society develops individuals with Macro powers who later get so bored and fed up with life there that they want to join me here, then I won't have to worry about setting up tutoring systems here to develop those powers."

"But obviously you don't get people with highly developed Macro powers or you wouldn't consider me at the tenth level when I am really only at the second level," I observed.

Elgon merely changed the subject by pointing ahead to his capital city of Elgonia.

"Take a look at it," he said, "and realize it's the only large city in the world, because the Macro society refuses to allow its members the joys of city living."

I looked down and saw a very small city compared with 1976 standards, for it had only 30,000 inhabitants, and a quarter of these worked for Elgon's government. Over 100,000 people worked in Elgonia, but since the presidential territory, of approximately ten miles in diameter, was stateless, most workers preferred to live in their states and commute. There were many government buildings in the center of the city surrounding the magnificent presidential palace that looked somewhat like the Taj Mahal of India.

Elgon Ten was obviously very proud of his capital city and talked at some length on the importance of his strong central government. He rattled off a long list of governmental agencies such as an agency of agriculture, commerce, labor, games, law, education, and intelligence, to name a few. I was particularly interested in the fact that Elgon had nine different intelligence agencies for gathering information about his people. When I questioned him about their functions, however, he replied that intelligence agencies functioned best when their operations were completely secret and, therefore, he couldn't talk about them, even to me. Then he surprised me by saying, "However, Jon Ten, as soon as you join our government I'll make you a Vice President and tell you all about our intelligence operations."

"Thank you, Elgon Ten," I said, declining his invitation, "but I plan to remain in the Macro society."

He laughed a big booming laugh and said, "You still think that someone who grew up in the micro society of the 20th century can live happily in the Macro society. Believe me, Jon Ten, if I who spent my first 50 years in the Macro society couldn't stand it, you won't be able to, either!"

"It was your pride and desire for personal power that

274

made you dislike the Macro society," Carol said to Elgon. "Jon doesn't want personal power, so your offer of high position in your government doesn't interest him."

Elgon's face tightened its granite hardness, and I became aware of a heightened redness in his aura. However, he replied calmly that Carol was too young to understand the delights of micro existence.

Our transair landed in the beautiful courtyard of the presidential palace, where Elgon insisted on giving us a personally guided tour of his glittering domain.

As we walked through his gardens my enjoyment of their beauty was marred by my memory of the faces of the dozens of poorly fed children we had seen during the day. Finally I interrupted Elgon to ask how the people managed to produce such huge families. He explained that people could buy fertility pills that would insure multiple births. Large families were not only a source of great pride and a religious and state duty, but also an economic advantage, since children of twelve or over could earn money by becoming gladiators or prostitutes.

An hour later I had seen enough of the lavishly appointed rooms, hallways, and courtyards filled with rare and precious possessions that Elgon and Sela doted on. Elgon recognized my growing restlessness and escorted us to a sumptuous suite of rooms which he said I could occupy as long as I wished. Then he and Sela left us alone with a reminder that they would see us at dinner.

Once we were alone I threw myself onto the giant canopied bed and said, "I'm tired of Micro Island already, and I'm especially tired of Elgon *Ten* and Sela *Nine*. Let's take a quick nap so I can get through the evening."

Carol didn't reply immediately and I saw that she was standing pensively chewing on her lower lip. For the first time I saw the sparkling pink in her aura give way to the red of anxiety. I reached out to establish mind contact and discovered her mental struggle with some sort of doubt that she kept trying to hide from me.

"Please, Carol," I pleaded, "tell me what's bothering

275

you. I've never known you to try to hide your thoughts from me."

She shook her head slowly and finally, with a sigh of resignation, said, "It's going to start sooner than Rana thought." Then she looked away from me.

"Ok, Carol, don't keep me in suspense," I implored. "What's going to happen sooner than Rana thought?"

"I'm not sure," she answered, taking my hand. "Rana thought they would wait two or three days before putting heavy pressure on you. But I have a strong premonition that something unpleasant is going to happen very soon."

I knew that Carol's precognitive power was much more sensitive than mine, so I said, "Are you sure you don't have any idea what this unpleasantness is going to be?"

Carol looked at me for a long moment, then with a soft cry she buried her face in my shoulder. A moment later we were devouring each other with kisses. Soon our desire for greater oneness was more than we could resist and slipping out of our tunics we began the joyous love play that only two closely attuned souls can ever know. Suddenly with clairaudient awareness I could hear the beat of our soul notes mounting in intensity as our bodies and minds sought ever closer oneness till we attained the ecstasy of Macro immersion.

Later as we swam lazily about in the mammoth sunken pool of our bathroom I remembered that Carol had never answered my last question about her premonition. I decided that if she didn't want to tell me I wouldn't press her. Immediately upon making this decision I received her telepathic note of thanks.

Back in our bedroom we discovered that our aura-reflecting tunics had been replaced by a beautiful golden tunic covered with flashing jewels for Carol and a gleaming white fabric one for me.

Carol seemed to have recovered her usual sunny disposition and, having quickly donned her new tunic, was complaining about its extraordinary weight when five male servants, representing each of the five races of the micro states, came to escort us to dinner.

The dining room in Elgon's palace was large enough to easily accommodate two standard-sized football fields placed side by side, and it was almost completely filled with men and women in stunningly handsome uniforms and beautifully lavish gowns.

We were escorted to a raised platform at one end of this room where Elgon and Sela were sitting at a small table facing the other much longer tables in this vast dining room. It had been filled with the sounds of many voices when we entered, but was now becoming quiet.

By the time Elgon and Sela had seated Carol and me between them the great room was gripped in funeral-like silence and somehow my mind felt like it was in a giant vise that was slowly, inexorably being squeezed tighter and tighter. I became aware of Elgon making a speech of welcome in my honor, but my head felt like bands of steel were crushing it. I realized dimly that Carol, too, was suffering this mind pressure. The rest of the evening was a blur of interminable dishes of strange foods being served along with different beverages, most of which I rarely sampled. I was aware of Elgon and Sela talking to me and that I obviously gave appropriate responses, for they seemed very pleased, but I have no memory of what anyone said. The last thing I remember of that evening was following our five servant escorts back to our room, where Carol and I immediately lay down on the bed without even removing our clothes.

I found myself back in 1976 groping for the night light, which revealed that it was three o'clock in the morning. I was not able to banish the dark fear in my mind. Why was I so frightened, I wondered. Nothing had happened to either Carol or me which could account for my strange feeling of anxiety and dread.

I shook my head in an attempt to clear it and remembered the feeling of great pressure on my head during the dinner with Elgon. I wondered what had caused that excruciating sensation that had effectively blotted out most of my awareness during the dinner. As I pondered this question I felt the answer beginning to rise to conscious-

277

ness from some great depth in my mind. I waited until a picture of the dining room began to form in my mind. This picture was filled with hundreds of faces which were empty except for a single eye brightly staring at me from many foreheads. It was the symbol of the telepathic mind net which Elgon had focused on me again.

But why did I still feel a crushing sense of anxiety and fear? Then I felt almost overwhelmed by a driving need to return to 2150 and discover if Carol was all right. Of course, the harder I tried to put myself asleep the more wide awake I became, until I realized that I must calm myself by balancing my mind with acceptance of what is as perfect. Failing that, I attempted Macro contact recall. A few minutes later, having succeeded in this attempt, I slipped gently into sleep and awakened back in 2150 to find myself lying alone, still dressed, in the great canopied bed.

I was on my feet instantly, running through the five huge rooms of our suite calling Carol's name, but there was no answer. I decided to find Elgon and demand an explanation. As I plunged into the hallway I came face to face with at least 30 ex-members of the Macro society who were easily recognizable by their great size. I asked them to tell me where I could find Elgon Ten but they made no reply—only stared intently into my eyes. Then again I felt the great vise exert almost blinding pressure on my skull. I quickly staggered back into my room, desperately closing the door between me and those penetrating eyes.

The pressure on my mind was still increasing, and I found it difficult to maintain consciousness. I staggered back to the bed, falling full length upon it. Suddenly I realized that my mind had become disconnected from my body and realized what it must be like to suffer total paralysis. I became aware of others in the room and that I was being undressed. Then I felt myself being carried into the bathroom and hurled into the deep end of the huge sunken pool. I sank quickly below the surface and began to see how long I could hold my breath while at

278

the same time struggling to overcome my strange paralysis.

I'm not sure how long I continued this futile struggle, but eventually I began to realize that I would have to use my PK powers to float my body to the surface with my face above the water. Once I began concentrating on this effort I discovered that my paralysis was quickly leaving me. My head broke the surface of the water.

Whether Elgon's telepathic mind net had released me I did not know, but now my paralysis was completely gone. I swam easily about, taking deep breaths of precious air into my lungs.

When I returned to the bedroom I found Sela lying naked on top of the bed. She was obviously amused at my startled expression, for she laughed, then said, "Don't look so surprised, Jon Ten. Elgon Ten and I have decided that if you are going to learn to appreciate the unique virtues of Micro Island you should be permitted to sample its greatest pleasure—me."

As she said this last word she arched her lush naked body so that her huge firm breasts were thrust invitingly straight at me. She rolled the tip of her pink tongue over her full red lips leaving them glistening in quivering wetness. Then she began to slowly undulate her pelvis and breathe in short panting breaths.

Suddenly my mind was again gripped in the crushing vice of the thousand-mind telepathic net which Elgon directed. I quickly lost control of my body and watched horrified as it took on a life of its own and walked over to the bed, climbed into Sela's arms and began caressing her body. At that moment my body returned to my control and I became fully aware of the awesome sensuous power of the velvety voluptuous body which now clung to me in a fervid passionate embrace.

For a long moment I burned with lust that seemed to consume all other desires. I felt myself sinking into a bottomless sea of dark red waves.

If I had never experienced Macro immersion and if I had not now remembered the infinite perfection of the embrace of my twin soul, Lea, I am sure that Sela would

279

have won. From then on, I would have followed her about as a dog follows a bitch in heat. But as I teetered on the brink of that sea of lust my mind filled to overflowing with the picture of my beloved Lea.

I thrust a maniacally screaming Sela away from me and left the bed, walked across the room, and seated myself in one of the high-backed ornate chairs.

Lea and I had won the first battle.

For a few moments Sela flung herself about on the bed and gave vent to screaming, howling rage. Then suddenly the storm passed and she was sitting up smiling at me saying, "Next time, Jon Ten, it will be my turn to win, and you can be sure there will be a next time."

I shook my head. "No, Sela," I said. "Elgon's telepathic mind net with its thousand minds may take over my body and force it to touch you, but know, Sela, that my mind will never choose to wallow in temporal micro pleasures, which are all you have to offer."

For a moment her eyes burned with dark lights, then she looked away and said, "I am Sela *Nine*. You seem to have forgotten your manners. Have you also forgotten your Alpha mate Carol Three?"

"No, I haven't," I said. "But are you willing to tell me what you and Elgon 'Ten' have done with her?"

Telepathically, I had picked up from Sela's mind only that Carol had been drugged and was being held somewhere in the palace. I was not about to admit that I knew even this. Before Sela answered me, the door opened and Elgon entered the room accompanied by three female servants who went immediately to Sela and began helping her into a jewel-encrusted tunic. I was still naked and asked that my own tunic be returned to me. Elgon merely smiled and said, "Only micro man feels uncomfortable when he is naked. Had you already forgotten?"

I ignored this and asked when I could see Carol.

"That," Elgon replied, "depends on how soon you will allow us to help you complete your time translation."

280

"Why is it so important to you to complete my translation?" I asked.

Elgon laughed and said, "I'm sure you must know that as the first person to transcend time and occupy a mentally created human physical body you are very famous.

"We know that the Macro society has denied you permanent time translation unless you attain third-level awareness, which is impossible in the time available. The people of Micro Island will be pleased to save a fellow micro being."

"And you will be happy to thwart the Macro society," I replied.

"Of course," he answered. "But now we will leave you to think over how soon you want us to help you become a permanent resident of Micro Island."

"That will be never," I answered.

Again he laughed and said, "I wouldn't be too sure of that, Jon Ten. I have a precognitive hunch that you'll change your mind before the next two weeks are over."

He turned and walked to the door accompanied by Sela and her three servants. As he walked out of the room he called back to me over his shoulder saying, "You might watch the video screen in your room, Jon Ten. It will help you pass the time."

With these words the door closed behind him and I noticed that the six-foot-square video screen on the wall opposite the bed had been activated. On it I saw a picture of Carol lying on the floor of a barren room.

I was across the room with a bound examining the video picture more closely. Carol was dressed as she had been at the dinner the previous evening. She was obviously unconscious, but with her hands folded across her chest and with the absence of color in the black-and-white picture she gave the appearance of being dead. At first there had been no sound associated with this picture, but now the audio came on with Elgon's voice saying, "Your friend, Carol Three, is in a drug-induced catatonic trance. She will remain in this state until you choose to cooperate with us or until she dies."

The audio portion ended with this message, but the picture remained as a constant reminder of Elgon's threat.

For the rest of the day I wandered about in my suite of five rooms trying to think of some way to rescue Carol and get back to the Macro society.

I tried to make mind contact with Carol's sub-conscious mind, but Elgon's telepathic mind net always stopped me as they did when I twice attempted to go into the outside hallway. I didn't feel desperate, however, because I was convinced that if I asked for help from the Macro society their superior Macro powers would free us both from Elgon's control.

By late evening I was beginning to feel depressed by the sight of Carol's unconscious body on the video screen. I had taken two food tablets during the day so I wasn't hungry, but nevertheless, I had a hollow sinking feeling inside of me that seemed like a premonition of death. But whose death—Carol's or mine, or both?

Finally, I decided to go to sleep so I could return to 1976 and talk my situation over with Karl—my guardian—and Neda. I went to sleep but I didn't awaken in 1976. I had a dream.

In this dream I was lying in the barren room beside Carol's body. I seemed to be paralyzed because no matter how hard I tried I couldn't move any part of my body. At last, exhausted from my efforts, I lay back and stared at the face of Lea, which had appeared floating above me. I telepathically asked for her help, but she shook her head saying, "Think carefully, Jon, before you ask for help. I must remind you that if we help you, it will be impossible for you to attain third-level awareness soon enough for us to complete your time translation."

"All right," I said, "but then help Carol. Take her back to the mainland."

Again Lea shook her head. "I can't do that unless she

282

requests it, and so far she has asked to remain with you even if it means her death."

Then I found myself suddenly awake back in 1976 shouting, "Don't let her die, Lea! Don't let her die!"

CHAPTER 16:

Karma

I had dressed, eaten breakfast, and done a lot of floor-pacing and it was still only 6:45, but I decided to call Karl anyway. He usually woke up at about 7 a.m., but today he answered on the first ring. He had been awake for almost an hour struggling with a feeling that he ought to call me.

Five minutes later I was sitting with Karl and Neda at their kitchen table sharing Karl's carrot juice.

I told them about Eli's revelation.

"I've always told you to pay more attention to what I say!" Karl laughed. Then, looking thoughtful, he added, "Do you suppose there could be something to that, Jon?"

"My dearest and truest friend, there was never any doubt!" I said as I threw my arm across his shoulders. A lump arose in my throat and my eyes burned briefly with the poignancy of restrained love that aches to be expressed.

I told them about my difficulties in 2150. When I finished with Lea's telepathic dream communication, Karl got up from the table and said, "That Macro society of yours will be guiltier than Elgon if they let Carol die when they could easily save her."

"But Karl, they don't look at death the way you do," Neda said. "Besides, from the Macro view there is no problem, since it's a perfectly just universe and no one can experience anything that he hasn't chosen."

"What about the population explosion that Elgon is planning? My God, with 30 to 50 kids in every family it won't be long before they take over the world by sheer numbers!"

"Yes," I replied, "I've thought of that, too, but I know that the Macro society won't interfere with the free will of anyone."

"But they force people to stay on Micro Island," Karl objected.

"That's not true, Karl," Neda responded.

"How the hell do you know!" Karl exploded.

"Because Jon told me," Neda answered as she got up and gave Karl a smile and a hug which melted his irritation.

"She's right," I said. "C.I. told me that although the Macro society originally gathered up all the micro survivors after the disastrous earth changes and plagues and put them on Micro Island, it was not done to punish them, but to help them."

"How's that?" Karl asked.

"Well, they planned to use Micro Island as sort of a grade school where they could show everyone the concepts of Macro philosophy," I explained. "Elgon and Sela were among the early resource people there on the island. It was the misuse of their powers, which they used to control their students, that caused their regression to lower levels of awareness.

"Elgon insisted that there was one way and only one way to attain Macro awareness, and that way was *his* way. He stopped being a modest resource person and became an arrogant teacher declaring himself as the one and only authority on Macro awareness.

"He then gathered about him such souls as he could influence through coercion, intimidation, hypnosis, or just plain fast talk, and started his own little 'family.' His aim was to clean up the Macro society by giving them firm rules to live by, a police force to help them stay within these rules, and a great charismatic leader—himself —to look to for wisdom and guidance.

"As long as his students did as he said, he 'loved' them dearly and praised them as his 'family.' If they did not do as he said, he told them they were inferior, excluded them from his 'family,' and directed his remaining followers to do likewise. One could get back into Elgon's family only by acknowledging his omnicience."

"Then why do all those people stay on Micro Island if the Macro society doesn't keep them there?" Karl questioned.

"Elgon's propaganda has most of them believing they have the best of all possible worlds. Those who are discontent are not permitted to leave. Elgon knows that if they are exposed to a more Macro way of life they will lose their fear of him and he will lose his power."

"But, Jon, if you and the Macro society know this, why don't you capture Elgon and his thousand controllers and put them on another island where they can't control the lives of other people?"

Neda answered, "Because that would be controlling the lives of Elgon and his followers, which would, in the long run, just keep the problem alive."

"How do you figure that?" he asked.

"It would be just like healing someone who had not yet learned all they wanted to learn from being sick. He'd have to start the lesson all over again. If those souls didn't want to grow from a micro experience they would not have chosen to be born into Elgon's rule," I explained. "If we end the experience for them they'll just have to design another experience to learn that lesson from. No, if it's to end, they must end it themselves."

"Then there's no hope!" Karl exclaimed. "You've just got to let everyone crap on you and take it with a smile. I'll be damned if I'll buy that humble pie nonsense."

"You're right, Karl," Neda said. "You'll be damned, by your own negativity. That's what hell and damnation are all about. They are the micro refusal to accept the consequences of our own actions."

"Now, wait a minute, Jon," Karl injected. "Didn't you once tell me that the Macro society doesn't believe in eternal hell or damnation?"

"That's right," I answered. "But remember, our subconscious mind contains the memory of all our past thoughts and actions. To the extent that we try to avoid applying what we learned from the lessons offered by our past experiences, we are unconsciously driven to repeat them. In other words, we attract to us exactly those experiences which we, within our own minds, condemn."

"I was fascinated," Neda added, "to learn that we can only hate or dislike that which is in our selves, and we can only love or like that which is in our selves."

"That's a lot of crap," Karl said shaking his head. "Why, I can hate a rapist and murderer and not have that inside me."

I shook my head, "According to the Macro philosophers, to the pure in heart all is pure. So, if you find yourself hating or condemning anything, you not only have performed the same act in the past, but by actively condemning this action you'll soon find yourself performing it again—possibly in this very life, though sometimes in another."

"I just don't believe that," Karl replied stubbornly.

"I can understand why you wouldn't believe it," I responded. "It's only been since I've been able to recall more and more of my past lives that I've been able to see the truth in it."

Neda reminded us that it was time for Karl to go off to teach his morning class, so I said I would see them later and went back to my apartment. There I wrote in this journal, bringing it up to date.

I spent the rest of the day trying to figure out some way to reach Carol and get her away from Micro Island. By evening I still hadn't thought of any successful way to save Carol without giving in to Elgon's wishes that I become a permanent resident of Micro Island.

That evening I had dinner with Karl and Neda and I explained to them that I felt that Elgon's thousand followers with their telepathic mind net were just too much for me to overcome.

"In other words," Karl said, "no matter what you might try to do they could stop you by overpowering your mind."

"And the reason you're having this experience is because when you were a priest in ancient Atlantis and had Macro powers you frustrated others by controlling their minds. Right?" Neda asked.

"That's right," I agreed. "But being able to remember the classes I failed doesn't mean I like taking them over."

"Well," Karl said, "then the solution to saving Carol is rather simple. All you have to do is cooperate with Elgon."

"You mean," Neda added, "all he has to do is sell his soul to Elgon."

"No, that's not true," Karl protested, "because once he has let Elgon and his gang complete the time translation he will have freed Carol and become a permanent resident in 2150. Then he has the rest of his life to escape from Micro Island with or without the help of the Macro society."

"You forgot one thing, Karl," Neda reminded him. "The wisest people of the Macro society said that if the time translation came before he had attained level-three awareness he would soon regress and lose his Macro awareness."

"But not necessarily my Macro powers," I added, "which would really cause me trouble because Macro powers without Macro awareness are always used for micro purposes."

"Oh, hell!" Karl complained. "The more the two of you talk, the more hopeless it becomes."

"Is it really as hopeless as it looks, Jon?" Neda asked.

I shook my head, "I can't see any way out. It looks like the perfect double bind—I'm damned if I do, and I'm damned if I don't."

"But, Jon," Neda said, "certainly the Macro society wouldn't have allowed you to walk into an impossible situation. After all, Rana said she believed in you. That must mean that she knew your future wasn't hopeless."

"She also believed that the greater the failure, the greater the success—another thing that doesn't make sense from the micro viewpoint," I reminded Neda.

"Wait a minute," Karl inserted, "if you could just attain level-three awareness in the next two weeks the Macro society would know it and then they would complete translation, right?"

"I thought of that," I said, "but going from level two to level three is like going from first grade to ninth grade, according to C.I., and no one has ever done it in just a month."

"Well," Karl replied, "then you can be the first! After all, they've never had a time translation before, either."

"No, Karl," I replied, "that's just too simple a solution. In all my experiences in 2150 there has never—not even in a single case—been an easy solution. Every time I tried to find one I ended up embarrassed by my own ignorance. I've always had to use my head—I've always had to stretch to my limits. This is no exception.

"I can't just up and make level three with a snap of my fingers without giving up some of my micro ways of thinking. And there's the key, Karl, giving up my micro ways of thinking. If I could just see the situation from a Macro perspective the solution would probably jump out at me.

"I don't know, Karl. I'll go back upstairs and sleep on it. Maybe when I wake up in 2150 I'll think of something."

When I got to the door I came out of my daze and

turned to say, "Hey . . . thanks. Thanks to you both. See you tomorrow." I closed the evening and did just what I said I was going to do.

When I woke up in 2150, however, I didn't think of anything new.

For the rest of the week I kept making futile attempts to contact Carol and to break out of my suite of rooms in 2150, while back in 1976 I spent my time pacing the floor or discussing this maddening puzzle with Karl and Neda. But in spite of all the hours of thinking and talking, no solution came to me. Then one evening Neda asked me if Elgon's telepathic mind network blocked out all my Macro powers. I responded affirmatively, and that was that.

Later the same evening while I was trying not to go to sleep, so I could postpone waking up in my 2150 prison, I remembered Neda's question and began to review the seven Macro powers. I considered clairvoyance, telepathy, and precognition. Of these the first one worked, but was no help. The second one was blocked, and the third one I had never developed much but doubted whether knowing the future would be of much help to me with this problem. Considering the next three, retrocognition, PK (psychokinesis), and telekinesis, I again drew a blank, for the first one worked but was no help, while the second and third were blocked. This left only the seventh, which was astral projection. Was that, too, blocked? I didn't know because, since it didn't seem very practical, I had never consciously tried it.

For a prisoner, though, surely astral projection, in which one leaves the physical body and its limitations and moves about in an astral body with no physical limitations, could have definite advantages. I could visit Carol, the Macro society, and Lea. I had wanted to talk with these people, and astral projection was the only way left to do it. Or was it? Could I learn to use it, and even if I could, would the telepathic mind net interfere and stop me? I decided that the only way I could answer these questions was to put them to the test, so I immediately began trying to free myself from my physical body. I failed.

After thirty minutes of failure in my attempts to separate my astral body from my physical one I gave up and began trying to remember everything C.I. had told me about this seventh Macro power.

I remembered that my trips into the future had been via my astral body, which was connected to the 1976 physical body by a sort of electrical-energy umbilical cord that had unlimited elasticity. This was the silver cord that mystics throughout the ages had talked about as maintaining the life-giving contact between the astral and the physical bodies. Once this silver cord, made up of very rapid electrical vibrations, is severed, the physical body dies.

When I had first come to 2150 I had been provided with a new physical body and a second silver cord to provide the necessary connection between my astral body and this new physical body. This worked because the Macro society had my twin soul, who shared an identical astral-soul pattern with me. They used this as a model from which to fashion the physical body, the silver cord connection, and to supply the psychic translation for attracting my astral body through time and space.

If this seems not only complex, but incomprehensible, it is—to the micro self. C.I. had given me a far more lengthy and complex explanation but I had decided that I didn't need to know all about this Macro area so I hadn't paid very close attention. Now I desperately wished that I had. Still, however, the two essential ingredients in all learning were desire and belief, and if I had these, then I could learn astral projection. I certainly believed it was possible because I had already experienced it. The problem, therefore, must lie in the area of desire.

I practiced the Macro pause, in which one instantly expands his perspective from micro to more Macro. It became immediately obvious that, as usual, I had been desiring not to fail in accomplishing astral projection, which meant that my mind had been focused on failure rather than success.

Once I was able to see my efforts from a Macro perspective I could remember that all failure is success (leads to success) and, thus, forgive myself so that I could start again without the interfering load of anxiety and guilt. I began by recalling the sensations I had experienced on my first visit to 2150 when I had awakened in my astral body. Then I began gradually imagining and desiring my astral body to stand at the foot of my bed. The desire built until I began imagining the perspective of my bed and physical body from the foot of this bed.

Suddenly with a sort of snap I was standing looking across the bed at my sleeping physical body.

Again I experienced the marvelous sense of freedom from physical limitations and discomforts. And now, even in 1976, I had two healthy and whole legs. C.I. had said that articles of clothing on the astral level were created as thought forms, so I mentally visualized myself clothed in my 2150 aura tunic. Sure enough, it became a reality so that I could experience the sensation of pulling and tugging on it and having it respond just as my tunic would in 2150.

I now began walking about my room as I would with my 2150 physical body only about a foot off the floor. Levitating this astral body didn't take near the amount of PK energy that I had to expend to levitate my 180-pound physical body. As I approached the door I forgot and tried to open it and had the uncanny sensation of watching my hand disappear through the door. I quickly followed it and found myself out in the hallway. Then instead of walking to Karl and Neda's apartment I visualized myself standing in their living room and instantly I was there.

Walking through the bedroom door and over to where Karl was sleeping, I tried to wake him. Of course, he couldn't hear me and my shaking his shoulder didn't work, as my hand went right through him. I looked at Neda sleeping next to him and tried telepathic contact asking her to wake up. In just a few seconds she opened her eyes and looked about. I immediately used PK to turn on the lamp on her night stand. This startled her, but she didn't look frightened. I used PK to pick up the pencil and wrote the word "Jon" on the pad of paper which Neda used to record her dreams.

She started to become alarmed so I began telepathically reassuring her that all was well, impressing on her mind the concept of astral projection. I could tell that I wasn't completely successful because she woke up Karl and said, "I heard Jon calling me and telling me to wake up."

"When?" Karl mumbled sleepily.

"Just now," she replied, "and when I opened my eyes I couldn't see anything at first, but then the lamp turned on."

"You must have turned it on," Karl said. "You were probably dreaming."

"That's what I thought at first, but when I picked up my dream notebook to write down the dream I saw this," Neda responded holding out the tablet for Karl to see.

He looked at the spot where Neda was pointing, saw my name written there in my own handwriting, and was suddenly wide awake and climbing out of bed.

"I'm going up and see if he's all right," he said as he slipped into his robe and slippers, then started out of the room.

I decided that the quickest way to reassure Karl was to go back and get my physical body—which I did—and met Karl halfway up the stairs. I explained about my experiment with astral projection and apologized for waking him up. He insisted that I come back with him and explain it all to Neda. I did, as quickly as possible, so they could get back to sleep and I could get back to 2150 and try using this new Macro power to solve my problem.

Once back in my apartment I had no trouble getting to sleep and was soon lying under the canopy of my bed in Elgon's palace. My one great concern was that the telepathic mind net might stop me before I could escape from my physical body, or once out of it force me back into it. Therefore, I immediately focused my mind on the end of the bed and again slipped out of my physical body. Once I was completely out of the physical body I visualized the journey back to my Alpha and was instantly there standing in the middle of our Alpha room just as I had visualized it.

The emptiness of the room without Carol punctuated the urgency of her plight and I sought out the rest of our Alpha to ask for their suggestions. It was breakfast time and I found them all in the dining room talking about Carol and me. As I entered the room Steve was the first to become aware of me and he directed the attention of the others toward me. Then everyone was aware of my presence except Adam and Nancy, who were having some temporary difficulty tuning me in. I was pleased to find that I had no difficulty hearing them.

I soon learned that the whole Macro society was aware of all that had happened to Carol and me. Unfortunately, they had no suggestions as to how Carol and I could escape from Elgon without help from the superior Macro powers of the Macro society.

I decided to talk to Rana to see if she could offer a solution to my dilemma. But before I left my Alpha members, something very strange happened. Adam and Joyce asked if they could accompany me back to Elgon's palace.

I refused. "If Carol and I can't escape, you'd just be two more prisoners for Elgon."

"We realize that," Joyce said, "but Adam and I would like to be with you during the next few days, Jon. If we can't help you, we'll at least provide companionship."

I was reminded that if I couldn't raise my awareness level and still refused to cooperate with Elgon I would have just a few more days in 2150. I was touched by Adam and Joyce's offer to share my prison even if it meant becoming prisoners themselves. I thanked them, but explained that knowing Elgon had four of us instead of just two would more than double my anxiety, and if

I needed companionship I could now just project my astral body to visit with them.

It was Adam who then said, "Perhaps we can help you another time then, Jon. You see, we owe you a great debt, for you were of great help to us in another life. In that life you know us as Griff and Judd."

To say that I was breathless, speechless, elated, is an understatement, for beautiful vivacious Joyce and tall handsome Adam bore absolutely no physical resemblance to Griff and Judd of 1976. Yet, as I reached out to make contact with their Macro selves, I knew these were indeed the same two souls who 174 years ago had inhabited bodies called Griff and Judd, and I thrilled with the joy of their growth.

I embraced them and thanked them, touched by their concern. I assured them that any debt to me was amply repaid by their willingness to give up their lives to join me in Elgon's palace. Before I left, I made them promise that they would not try to join me on Micro Island. Then I bade farewell to all my Alpha members. As Nancy's eyes caught mine, my blood felt warm inside me and I wondered if she knew—if Bruno had known.

No time to pursue that now, though. I surrounded her with loving thought and went immediately to the tutoring room to meet with Rana.

It was still early morning and I had always met her in the evening. Still I had an overpowering feeling that she would be there waiting for me. I wasn't disappointed, for, as usual, the door opened before I got to it. Upon entering I found Rana calmly sitting back in one of the chairs smiling at me as if we were meeting for one of our regular Personal Evolution sessions.

"I won't ask how you knew I would be coming here at this time in my astral body," I said, "because I'm sure that your power of precognition is working perfectly along with your telepathy which told me that you'd be here."

Rana nodded her agreement. "I also know," she said, "that you are hoping I will have a solution to your problem with Elgon. You'll be pleased to know that I have learned the solution from your own mind."

"My God! Thank you, Rana, thank you," I said with joyous relief. Then urgently, "What is it?"

She shook her head. "I'm going to disappoint you, Jon, by refusing to tell you what I see you doing in the future."

"What?" I asked, shocked by this turn of events. "Are you telling me that you know the solution but you won't tell me what it is? Are you afraid that if you tell me it won't happen?"

"No," she replied. "Whether I tell you or not, there is only one course of action that you will take at this time."

"Then I can't understand why you won't tell me what it is if it can't affect my future actions," I said puzzled and bewildered.

"Because," she answered, "if I tell you, it will affect your future thoughts, and while this won't change your actions with Elgon, it would change your actions later on."

"I don't understand, Rana," I said. "What do you mean?"

"I'm talking about the problem of good and evil," she replied, "which will be your final test for third-level awareness. You'll remember that these concepts, like everything else, depend on the size of your perspective.

"The measure of a mind's evolution is its acceptance of the unacceptable. What may be unacceptable at the micro level is always acceptable at the Macro level."

"Yes," I concurred, "and I remember that everything is perfect from a totally Macro view. But what's that got to do with the solution to my problem?"

She continued her explanation, "I'm saying that the reason you haven't become aware of your only satisfying solution to Elgon's threat is because you've been using a micro view in which it appears unacceptable and even bad or evil."

"Then you're saying that if you told me what it was I would use it, but for the wrong reasons—because you

296

told me and not because I discovered and accepted it myself, right?"

"That's exactly right, Jon," she replied, "and while this would not affect the distant future it would affect your next ten thousand years and lengthen the time before you and Lea will become one again at the physical and astral levels."

"I hate to say this, Rana, but thank you for not telling me," I said reluctantly. "I'll have to go back to Elgon's palace and see how long it takes me to discover this solution which you say is already in my mind—the one course of action that I can take."

As I prepared to leave, Rana cautioned me to be careful not to see Lea before returning to Micro Island. I asked why.

"Because," Rana explained, "as your twin soul she will not, at this time, be able to hide from you the solution you're seeking, and the effect will be the same as if you had gotten the information from me."

I thanked her once again and agreed to follow her advice. Then I returned to Elgon's palace without attempting contact with Lea.

I realized that in spite of the constant video picture of Carol in her empty room I didn't know where that room was. I would have to explore the palace to find it. Then I made my big mistake.

I forgot that Elgon had stationed a number of his telepaths outside my room and when I came walking through the walls out into the hallway they saw me immediately and tried to stop me. I visualized myself in the huge dining room and disappeared from their view, but they had already notified the rest of their mind net of my escape into my astral body.

Finding myself suddenly in the dining hall I began running with literally the speed of thought, from room to room hunting for stairs leading down into the lower levels of the palace, because I felt that's where I would find Carol. By the time I located the right stairs and had descended to the level where I felt Carol was being held, Elgon's telepaths had located me.

Once again I felt the increasing power of the crushing vise on my mind, but this time I sought to deal with it by not resisting. I tried to respond to it with Macro loving acceptance. At the same time I continued my search for Carol. The underground cellars of Elgon's palace seemed a veritable labyrinth of rooms, but at last I passed through the right door and found myself in the right place with Carol lying as if dead at the center of the room. As I started toward her, I heard deep booming laughter as Elgon emerged from the shadows at my side.

Almost instantly the pressure of the vise upon my mind multiplied and I realized that Elgon was now personally directing the Macro powers of his thousand-member mind net with crushing force upon me. I have no doubt that Rana or even Lea could have handled their telepathic onslaught, but my level-two powers were no match for this mind net.

The pressure quickly overwhelmed me. I could no longer accept it. Then as I began to struggle against it the end came very suddenly. I lost consciousness and awoke back in 1976.

My room was dark. It was only 4 a.m.

I quickly decided to go back to sleep and see what had happened to me back to 2150. While it took me some time to calm my mind from the vivid memory of the crushing vise, I at last managed to fall asleep and awakened back in the canopied bed with Sela bending over me.

The moment I opened my eyes she said, "You are a fool, Jon Two."

I smiled at her in Karl's wry cynical way and said, "I see you no longer keep up the pretense that I'm a level ten."

"That's right," she replied. "We've discovered that your Macro powers are very limited. You'll hardly be attaining level three in these next few days.

"But that's not why I was calling you a fool. Don't

you realize that if you leave your body unprotected while you're gone from it on the astral plane someone who knows how—as I do—can sever the silver cord and separate you permanently from your physical body?"

"Yes," I said. "I knew this, but you want me to become a permanent 'live' resident of Micro Island, not a dead one. My propaganda value would be worthless if I was dead."

Sela gave me her sensuous look in which her tongue touched her lips in a kissing motion before she said, "I don't want you dead, Jon. I want you as my lover, and I know that unless you help us complete your time translation that magnificent body of yours will soon die, and your mind will be lost 174 years in the past."

"Sela," I said, "I no longer desire a micro existence."

"But you have no choice," she replied. "You can either live on Micro Island in 2150 in a well-run micro society or you can live in 1976 in a chaotic micro society."

When I didn't reply to this she finally gave a long sigh of resignation and said, "You leave us no other choice but to release Carol to find her own way back to the Macro society. You realize, of course, that since she will not obey our laws she will be put to death."

"That's murder!" I said.

"It's not murder," she replied. "When a person chooses to break laws that she knows will cause her death, that's suicide. Of course, you can always prevent her death by agreeing to become a permanent resident of Micro Island."

"Give me more time," I said. "Let me think about this."

"You've had plenty of time, Jon," she said, "but to show our generosity we'll give you one more day. If by tomorrow morning you have not decided to cooperate with us we will release Carol and you can watch her cause her own death."

After a long silence Sela left and I began pacing about my prison suite trying vainly to discover the solution that Rana said was already in my mind. What was it, I wondered? What would appear the worst possible de-

299

cision I could make? Well, from one view point, it would be defying Elgon and refusing his terms. That would humble my pride because I would not only lose Carol, but also my chance to live in 2150.

Yes, without a doubt the hardest thing for me to do would be to watch Carol being executed by the Micro Islanders—especially knowing that I could have prevented it.

I remembered Rana saying, "But nothing is terrible from the Macro view. Things can only be terrible from the micro perspective, which is too limited to see that we live in a perfectly just and balanced macrocosm in which we experience only what we have chosen."

Then if Carol dies, I thought, she will have chosen it and it will bother me only to the extent that I view her as a possession of mine that I can lose. We can have anything we desire and believe in sufficiently, say the Macro philosophers, and since each soul has free will and absolute Macro power there is no problem.

All right, I agreed, there is no problem from the Macro perspective—but I don't live at that level! Where I live, there are lots of problems, and at the moment the most important one is saving Carol from death and me from losing 2150. This would be resolved successfully if I would just cooperate with Elgon. Then I could dedicate the rest of my life to finding a way to return to the Macro society. But would I?

I was left completely alone for the rest of that long day and evening while I agonized over what I should tell Elgon in the morning. By the time evening came, I was completely exhausted, having come to the conclusion that I would choose life for Carol, and, thus, life for me on Elgon's Micro Island. Sleep finally came, bringing with it a ghastly nightmare.

I dreamed that I was dressed in long black robes sitting as a judge in a vast desert. In front of me as far as I could see there stretched a long line of people whom I must judge. According to the bailiff standing beside me they had all committed some crime requiring the death penalty. As I listened to each person's explanation of his crime, however, it seemed to me that they all pleaded in such a moving and piteous fashion that I waived the death penalty for each and every one of them. They cheered, thanked, praised me because I chose life for all who came before me.

Then the scene changed to another part of the desert and I found myself walking with the bailiff at my side through a gigantic prison yard where all those whom I had saved from death were shackled by a great ball and chain so that they could barely move. Now instead of praising and thanking me they were all cursing me. I was appalled to see that they were all afflicted with some hideous disease that was destroying their bodies by slowly eating the flesh from their bones. Somehow I felt compelled to look at every one of these prisoners whose lives I had saved and who were now such grotesque and horrifying victims of a plague that slowly and painfully ate away their bodies.

I heard one call out to me. Turning to him, I shuddered and awoke in tears of terror, for the prisoner who last cursed me for saving his life was Karl!

I felt sick at my stomach with self-hatred to think that I could do that to Karl even in a dream.

Why would I have such a dream? What could it possibly mean? As I asked this question I remembered the words of Rana, "All pain, misery, and disease are the results of resisting that which is inevitable—that which we ourselves have chosen to grow on."

Then what was the solution? Again I could almost hear Rana saying, "The only way to balance negative actions is with positive actions. Thus, loving acceptance balances all. The only sin anyone ever commits is denial of the perfection of what is."

Then my dream, I decided, must have been created by my higher self to show me the consequences of trying to deny the perfection—the necessity—of what is. Did this mean that I should take the other path and let Carol die?

Had I let Karl die in the past? Is that why he was in my dream?

From some cranny of my mind came two replays; one in which Karl was finishing off a pint bottle of carrot juice, and one in which Carol was getting her usual from the mechanism in the cafeteria—carrot juice.

Then a double exposure—Carol's 1976 "past" life review of herself as a black student fighting pollution, and Karl ranting about industrial pollution.

My mind raced.

But she's a girl—the girl I love, my soul mate, my Alpha mate!

And Karl? He's a man—the man I most love, my best friend, my stepbrother, my roommate!

"Oh, my God!" I thought out loud. "Oh, my ever-loving God!"

I grasped my arms across my chest and rocked back and forth in my pain, conflict, agony, fear, and joy.

When I finally got it all together and accepted the perfection of this new insight, I went downstairs and laid the news on Karl and Neda.

It hit them just about the way it hit me, and we all ended up in tears of joy and amazement at the incredible perfection of the eternal plaid of our lives.

The big question remained. Should I let Carol—Karl?—die?

I spent the rest of the day trying to answer this question and by evening I admitted to Karl and Neda that the thought of watching Carol die when I could have prevented it was just more than I could take. We talked far into the night with Karl arguing that my decision to save Carol and myself was the only sane and decent one, and with Neda arguing that I should ask my higher self for the answer and follow it, no matter how difficult.

I just shook my head, then went back to my apartment. Once in bed I didn't want to go to sleep until I was sure of my decision for Elgon, so I tossed and turned until finally in desperation I remembered Carol's advice

302

whenever I was particularly frustrated: Macro contact recall.

As I focused my mind on my last contact with the Macro self I felt the anxiety and tension begin flowing out of my body. The rhythm and depth of my breathing changed and again the unspeakable union of all opposites led to the ultimate experience of that which is beyond time, space, and words.

I must have fallen asleep because when I opened my eyes I saw both Sela and Elgon bending over me. Then I heard Elgon say, "I'm glad you're finally awake. We're ready for your decision."

Without thinking I replied, "I've decided to learn the lessons I came here to learn and permit Carol to do the same."

"You mean you are willing to watch her die before your very eyes?" Sela said.

When I didn't reply Sela pointed to the video screen. "Are you sure you can live with that decision?"

I looked across the room at the giant video screen. The picture of Carol had changed. Instead of lying on the floor of a barren room she was now spread-eagled against a wall in the courtyard with manacles at her wrists and ankles. Her body was naked and obviously conscious because it seemed to be writhing in pain. A close-up picture of her face revealed that her catatonic trance had been ended, for her eyes were open and staring at something before her. Then the picture changed and I saw what she was looking at—a howling, screaming mob of Micro Islanders who were being restrained by a high steel-like mesh fence.

"If we raise that fence," Elgon said, "that mob will stone her to death for advocating birth control and refusing to bear children. Since she's a foreigner, the penalty for those crimes is death. Are you sure you won't cooperate with us, Jon?"

I shook my head, not trusting myself to speak.

Elgon and Sela observed me intently without speaking and the silence between us grew until suddenly Elgon

303

nodded his head and the audible sound from the video panel increased.

I tried not to look at the screen but my eyes seem to have a life of their own. I stared at the mob which was now pouring through the opened fence, racing to large piles of small, sharp, quartz-like stones that were piled several feet in front of Carol.

For the next half-hour I watched the mob—men, women, and children—throw the small sharp stones at Carol's suffering body. I watched the whole gory process from the first superficial cuts on her beautiful legs, arms, breasts, and face until her whole body was covered with gaping bloody wounds, and finally to the sight of one eye gone and the other hanging by a shred of tissue down her torn and bloody cheek. Since the stones were small, they left her conscious till the very last, her lovely body literally hanging in shreds from her bones.

Even with the memory of my most recent Macro contact fresh in my mind that half-hour was the most excruciatingly painful of my entire life.

Elgon broke the silence. "It's one thing, Jon, to watch another person die like this. It's quite another to experience it yourself."

With these words Elgon summoned a number of his followers who led me out of the palace to the same courtyard wall from which the remains of my beloved Carol were now being removed so that I could take their place. As they hurled me forward my feet were gouged by the sharp white stones now stained red with her blood.

The mob regathered, shouting obscenities and accusations at me as I was thrust against the slaughtering wall, still wet with blood. As they snapped the bloody manacles around my wrists and ankles, my mind became a blur of memories—Lea, and our brief moments together—Rana and the many lessons I should learn . . . did learn? . . . would learn?—Neda and her incredible transformation—Karl, my faithful friend, and the trauma I had brought into his life these past few months—and his parallel self, my beloved Carol whose warm blood separated me from the coarse brick of the wall behind me.

In the distance I saw Elgon and Sela moving toward me through the crowd. Somehow, though they stood only inches from me now, they seemed also to be miles away. Elgon dipped the tips of his fingers into the red pool below me. Then, wiping his fingers across my chest, he asked me contemptuously if I would like to reconsider my decision. I did not speak, for the answer lay bitterly in my eyes.

Turning his back to me, Elgon bent to pick up two of the red-stained stones. He held these up for the crowd to see, then handed one to Sela as he turned and, facing me now, cast the first stone.

I heard, deep in the recesses of my mind, the voice of Rana echoing, "In ancient Judea, Jon, the souls of Carol and yourself incarnated into a fierce and proud family. You grew up to be beautiful to look at but vain and proud. You were quick to condemn and more than once self-righteously joined in the stoning to death of those you condemned."

I knew why it was happening, but my eyes and my mind were still overflowing with hatred for Elgon.

In my mind Rana's voice was saying, "The measure of a mind's evolution is its acceptance of the unacceptable."

I tried the Macro pause. I tried to think myself into a Macro perspective of loving acceptance. I tried to love and accept Elgon and "what is" as perfect. I tried—but to no avail.

Acceptance of the unacceptable—my final test, and I had failed. I could not lovingly accept Elgon.

There are limits to everything—even pain—but with hundreds of jagged stones tearing at my body, the tide of pain soared through me until it seemed I could not bear to live another second.

My eyes could no longer see, but to my mind Lea appeared.

"Remember, Jon, the measure of a mind's evolution is its acceptance of the unacceptable."

With these words ringing in my mind I awakened in 1976.

CHAPTER 17:

Evolation

A month has passed since my death in 2150, and this long separation from the Macro society has been hard to bear. Yet, as I sit here in the warm spring sunshine on the small balcony outside my apartment, I know that I have come to accept this separation, and even the terror and pain of my last hour in that future world.

I no longer condemn or feel any anger toward Elgon, Sela, or anyone else, for I myself chose my experiences.

Anger, like all other violence, is a last desperate attempt by micro beings to deny responsibility for their life situation by blaming it on others. Violence and anger will, therefore, continue until man learns to accept full responsibility for everything that happens within his life. I hope that I have arrived at that point in my soul's evolution.

And now, Karl, as my mother entrusted me to you, I entrust this journal to you, to do with as you see fit.

Soon I shall come down and join you and Neda for one last meal together. At the end of this evening, I'll kiss you both and say that I look forward to seeing you again soon.

Forgive me for writing my farewell instead of speaking it. You are dearer to me than I could ever say.

It's taken me such a long time to learn that all failure is success—all death is birth.

I'm going to evolate tonight.

You see, last night I had another vivid dream, Karl. It was a vision. I've made a rough sketch of it for you and Neda on the next page.

"Thank you" doesn't begin to say enough, Karl.

Remember your dreams. I'll be there. I am with you always.

I love you.

We are one.

'Bye for now,

Jon

Epilogue

Three months have passed since we cremated Jon Lake's body and scattered the ashes in a woods near our boyhood home. I must admit that at first I had great difficulty accepting Jon's suicide. I said that it was a cop-out and not worthy of his Macro philosophy. However, as the weeks have passed, Neda has chipped away at my micro philosophy until today I see Jon's action in a very different light.

Perhaps the most important factor altering my viewpoint was a conversation we had with Jon a few nights before he left us. Jon didn't include it in his journal and I wish he had because it would have reminded me of the Macro society's view of life and death.

Between Neda and myself we have recalled most of the details of that conversation. As we remember, it began one evening when I remarked about a student in our department who had just committed suicide. I said that

309

suicide was a cop-out and Jon had replied with the following.

"You're complaining, Karl, about a conscious act of suicide which may or may not be an attempt to deny one's own responsibility for his present state of being. Aren't you forgetting that all micro existence is unconscious suicide? It may end swiftly as in a lethal accident, or it may be a slow process of micro aging which results in the long-term decay and deterioration of the body until some vital part fails completely. All of this deterioration is the natural result of resisting the responsibility and the consequences of one's own chosen life pattern. This resistance causes all the life stress that Dr. Hans Selye referred to in his book, *The Stress of Life*."

"All right," I said, "I won't argue unconscious suicide or Dr. Selye's stress theory, but the student we're talking about committed conscious suicide since he left a note apologizing to his parents. Now I say that's a coward's way out."

Jon gave me his big grin and said, "According to that French sociologist we studied, Emile Durkheim, there are two types of suicide: anomic and altruistic. The first, anomic, is due to self-other alienation and is an attempt to escape from a life so overwhelming that the person perceives himself as being completely inadequate to cope with it. This is what I call conscious micro suicide. It is always unsatisfactory to the micro self because when the person wakes up in his astral body he finds that he's still stuck with a mind that believes it's not responsible, a mind filled with the kind of unforgiving self-loathing that the micro self experiences when faced with failure."

At this point Neda interrupted asking, "But, Jon, didn't you say that all actions are perfect from the Macro view? How can suicide be perfect?"

"At the Macro level," he answered, "every negative action is balanced by a positive action and, thus, they cancel each other, leaving perfect balance. From the Macro view one can see that every failure is a success

310

in the long run because it leads to the insight necessary for learning. If a soul has to commit micro suicide, once or a thousand times, in order to learn that there is no escape from its own responsibility for its state of being, then that is necessary and perfect for that soul."

"I see," Neda said nodding her head. "Then what is altruistic suicide?"

"A good example of that kind," Jon explained, "was demonstrated when the Titanic sank. Some of the people aboard went down with the ship rather than deprive someone else of a seat in the very limited number of lifeboats. History is filled with examples of altruistic suicide in which people consciously give up their lives so others can live or profit from their example."

"Suicide as an example . . . ," Neda hesitated. "Is that what the members of the Macro society are doing when they permit the Micro Islanders to kill them? Maybe they're trying to show by their example that physical life is not the ultimate goal."

"That's part of it," Jon responded. "The most famous example of this was the suicide of one of the greatest Macro philosophers ever to be incarnated on this planet— Jesus of Nazareth. He permitted himself to be killed to demonstrate that the Macro self is the master of the microphysical self and that it can even recreate or resurrect a body that has been killed. I think he was also demonstrating his belief that physical existence, while necessary for micro man, is only one very limited perspective along the m-M continuum."

"So the evolutionary goal," Neda added, "is to not get stuck forever at the micro-physical level, but to journey onward toward ever greater awareness until each soul returns to full awareness of its macrocosmic origin."

"That's right," Jon said, "and that leads us to a third type of suicide that micro man is not yet aware of— evolutionary suicide. What the Macro society calls evolation."

"I think you've mentioned that before, Jon," I said.

"Yes, you'll remember that when I was in the hospital

trying to save lives I was thwarted by some of the patients whose subconscious minds had decided on death," Jon said. "Remember Bruno who told me that he had incarnated to balance his vibrations. Now that he had accomplished this purpose he was graduating from this life and evolving on to a new dimension. You may recall that our Deltar, Hugo, also planned to consciously terminate his physical existence—to evolate.

"No one dies until he is convinced at the Macro or sub-conscious level that he has learned all he can or all he wants to in that particular life. This applies just as much to the baffling problem of crib deaths as to deaths due to cataclysmic earthquakes or tidal waves."

"Are you saying that the sub-conscious mind knows what will happen in the future and could avoid an accident if it so desired?" Neda asked.

"That's exactly what I'm saying," Jon nodded enthusiastically. "From the Macro point of view there are no accidents."

"But getting back to evolutionary suicide," I said, "isn't that as big a cop-out as anomic suicide? If you've learned your lessons you'd ought to stick around and help those who haven't."

"That's like saying that everyone should stay in first grade forever so they can help teach the lessons there," Jon replied.

"But someone's got to teach them," I protested.

"There has never, in the history of our universe, been a shortage of teachers—only of students willing to learn. As the Macro philosophers have said—when the student is ready, the teacher will appear. Ask and you will receive is another way of stating this Macro truth. It reflects back to prepotent desire and predisposing belief. If you desire something more than learning or if you don't believe that you can learn, or that you deserve to learn, you'll have to wait until your desire and belief are greater before you succeed," Jon explained.

"I still don't see how you could tell the difference

between a cop-out suicide and evolutionary suicide," I said, shaking my head.

"It's a question of motive, Karl," Jon explained.

"Was the motivation for death to escape the past or to embrace the future? A cop-out suicide is escaping his past and/or present—an evolutionary suicide is embracing his future."

"That's a hard one to handle," I complained. "Wouldn't a person tend to lie to himself about his desire to escape life?"

"Sure, that happens a lot," Jon answered. "In each life there are lessons that must be learned, but if you lie to yourself about having learned all there was to learn in first grade, then commit suicide, you wake up right back in first grade. You see, in this planetary schoolroom it's impossible to be a drop-out for very long. You can't run away from your own greater self."

"Micro man views physical life on this planet as the final stage, rather than just a preparation for experiencing the next dimension. With that sort of philosophy he naturally tends to think that suicide would end it all. He becomes the victim of his own micro philosophy."

"Then is suicide a sin or not?" Neda asked.

"It's hard to generalize about suicide, Neda, since all death is either conscious or unconscious suicide," Jon replied thoughtfully. "As for sin, there is only one sin, and that is to deny the perfection of our macrocosmic oneness with all that is, was, or ever will be. But even that is only a sin from the micro view. From the Macro view there can be no sin, for all is purposively and evolutionarily perfect. The key then, is to accept the perfection of what is by responding to everything with loving acceptance, thereby freeing yourself from the bonds of anxiety, fear, and condemnation which bind you to physical existence. Then, and only then, is evolation possible."

"Ok. If I was Macro I'd know who was living by the rule of loving acceptance and who wasn't, and I'd know everyone's motive for ending their life. Then I'd be able

313

to tell if it was suicide, as we popularly think of it, or evolation. The problem is, I'm not Macro!" I protested, "so I still don't know how to tell the difference!"

"Remember that monograph we read back in Cultural Anthropology? The one on that Indian tribe whose old people, when they were ready to die, just said goodbye to everyone, went up on a hill, and died?" Jon asked.

"Yeah. Kind of like your Hugo's plan to . . ." I began.

"That's it exactly, Karl," Jon interrupted. "If you use anything to do the job with, you committed escapist suicide. If you wrapped up the details of your life then just laid down and died, that's evolation."

That's as close as Neda and I could come to a total recall of that evening's conversation.

It was Jon's comments on evolation, combined with our dreams of him, that ultimately modified my view of Jon's death by broadening my perspective.

I still miss Jon terribly. But Neda reminds me that nothing is terrible from a Macro viewpoint, so I know what level I'm at.

However, I can remember Jon saying that our level of awareness is constantly fluctuating, and that in one twenty-four-hour period an average micro person like myself can run the gamut from micro awareness to low level, or even high level, Macro awareness—the latter occurring mostly when we're asleep and dreaming.

I'll end this epilogue with such a dream.

It was the last of a series of dreams I've had about Jon. In most of them we just talked in our usual manner, but this one was different. We know it was symbolic because Jon had told us that 2150 has neither graves nor tombstones since discarded physical bodies are vaporized.

In this dream Neda and I were standing with Jon before the same great tombstone that Jon had sketched in his last note to us:

314

Died
Jon and Carol
8-927   3-927
members of
Delta 927
of
The Macro Society
1976   2150

Re-Born
Jon and Carol
9-927   4-927
members of
Delta 927
of
The Macro Society
2150

Author's Statement

In closing I would like to say that the ultimate purpose of this book—indeed, of all my publications!—is to encourage the development of a unified, harmonious society for the earth's Aquarian Age.

I will leave you with the most hopeful words ever spoken:

"Ask and you shall receive, seek and you shall find, knock and the door will be opened." (Matt. 7:7)

With Macro love—

Joyously!
Thea Alexander

C.I. Data Excerpts

C.I. ON MACRO PHILOSOPHY

Macro philosophy is a system for relating all things from the smallest (micro) to the largest (macro). Its basic tenets are that all things are not only related but macrocosmically one, and that what is is perfect.

Things are only separate and divisible from micro-limited viewpoints.

Macro philosophy envisions a microcosmic-Macro-cosmic continuum (m-M continuum) in which neutrons, protons, and electrons are indivisible parts of ever larger physical bodies such as man. Continuing, we can perceive man as an indivisible part of a third planet called Earth. Again enlarging our perspective, we can perceive this planet as an indivisible part of a solar system which is, in turn, an indivisible part of a galaxy which is an indivisible part of . . . and so on.

Man feels pain and loneliness and experiences sickness and death to the extent that he: 1) feels separate and divided from self/others/universe/God (the Macrocosm). 2) denies the perfection of what is. 3) refuses to accept exclusive responsibility for all that he experiences.

Why does the feeling of separateness cause anxiety? Because anything or anyone that we perceive as separate, foreign, or alien to us is a potential threat—potentially anxiety producing. To the degree that we feel oneness or union with anything or anyone we can feel comfortable, accepting, and loving—the opposite of anxiety.

From a Macro perspective, all human suffering, fear, hate, pain, and disease are the result of lack of faith that all is one—all is love—all is what you might call God—all is perfect.

This doesn't mean that negative thoughts, feelings, and actions don't exist. It points out that they are the products of unbalanced micro thinking.

All the great religions of the world have proclaimed that "As you sow, so shall you reap." Macro philosophy presents this in terms of the consequences of negative and positive thought patterns. If you are afraid that something will happen, it usually does because that's what you've spent your thought energy on.

The wise man in Proverbs 23:7, over 2,000 years ago, stated that "As a man thinketh in his heart, so is he."

Macro philosophy holds that a negative thought produces a negative feeling and a negative experience, while a positive thought produces a positive feeling and a positive experience. No thought is ever forgotten. All our thoughts reside in our subconscious mind (what the ancients called the heart) where each negative thought continues to produce negative feelings until it is balanced or cancelled ($+$ and $-$ $=$ 0) by a positive thought of equal intensity or strength.

Negative thoughts produce anxieties (psychological pain) such as fear, anger, frustration, guilt, depression, sadness, etc. We try to avoid negative feelings by denying their existence. That is, instead of recognizing that we cause our own negative feelings by thinking negative thoughts, we try to avoid our negative feelings by using psychological defense mechanisms such as repression, projection, and rationalization, to name a few.

All defense mechanisms are designed to reduce or eliminate psychological pain by reducing or eliminating our awareness of our uncomfortable feelings. Thus, we reduce our self-awareness to tiny micro perspectives. One very common technique is to shift the responsibility for our discomfort from ourselves to someone else or something else.

MECHANISMS FOR DEFENDING THE MICRO SELF

Acting-out	Reducing the anxiety aroused by forbidden desires by permitting their expression
Compensation	Making up for frustration in one area by overgratification in another or detracting attention from a weakness by emphasing a strength
Denial of Reality	Protecting micro self from an undesirable aspect of reality by denying its existence (ignoring it), often by getting "sick" or over involvement with job or hobby, etc.
Displacement	Discharging feelings (usually hastility) on people or objects less dangerous than those which aroused the feeling
Emotional Insulation	Withdrawing from emotional involvement to protect self from hurt
Fantasy	Gratifying frustrated desires by imagining their achievement
Identification	Increasing feelings of worth by identifying self with illustrious person or organization

Introjection	Adopting values of others to avoid rejection
Isolation	Prohibiting self from feeling the pain caused by hurtful situations, or separating incompatible attitudes into logic-tight compartments
Projection	Attributing one's own unethical desires to others, or putting blame on others for one's own difficulties
Rationalization	Attempting to rationally prove that one's behavior is justifiable and deserving of approval
Reaction Formation	Preventing expression of dangerous (socially unacceptable) desires by over-emphasizing their opposite
Regression	Retreating to earlier level of development which demands less mature behavior and/or lower level of aspiration
Repression	Blocking painful or dangerous thoughts from consciousness
Sublimation	Gratifying frustrated sexual desires by substituting nonsexual activities
Sympathism	Gaining sympathy from others to bolster feelings of self-worth
Undoing or Atonement	Atoning for immoral desires or actions by causing self to suffer

The consequences of reducing psychological pain by using these techniques of self-denial are, from the short term (micro) point of view, successful in reducing psychological pain. In other words, they do work. That's why we use them. However, they are only temporarily successful because they reduce our awareness so much that we can conveniently forget that, from the larger (Macro) per-

320

spective, all our feelings are caused only by our own thoughts—never by anyone else's.

Perhaps the most important consequence of psychological defense mechanisms is the inevitable development of psychological stress which wears and tears the body down until it becomes sick, ages, and eventually dies. Research in this area was first developed in the 1930s under the leadership of Hans Selye, M.D., who summed up his research by stating that if there is no stress or resistance, there can be no disease, pain, or death.

The ultimate consequence of using these techniques of self-denial is greater pain (psychological stress), because they never eliminate the cause (negative thoughts); they just temporarily reduce the result (negative feeling).

A dramatic example would be the case of alcoholics or drug addicts which were so prevalent during the latter half of the 20th century. To reduce psychological pain they knocked out (denied) vast portions of their minds to temporarily gain relief from their feelings of discomfort and were rewarded by pleasure feelings. But the causes were not eliminated, and when the alcohol or drug wore off, the psychological pain was always greater. So long as they refused to accept responsibility for their own discomfort they were doomed to remain addicts until the pain became so great that nothing reduced it. Then, and only then, were they ready to accept responsibility for their own negative thoughts, to ask for help, to learn a larger perspective and grow beyond their pain to a new life philosophy—a more Macro perspective—a new truth.

What is truth? It depends on whose viewpoint you are using. From one point of view, there is nothing either true or false, good or bad, painful or pleasurable, ugly or beautiful, but thinking makes it so. A dramatic example of this is illustrated by the use of hypnosis.

Having an arm or leg slowly cut off is exceedingly painful. Yet some of your 20th-century physicians and dentists used hypnosis to perform every kind of operation. To the extent that, and as long as, the patient was able to accept the deep hypnotic suggestion that no pain existed, he felt no pain. Thus, thousands of cases demonstrated that we can only feel or experience anything to the extent that we believe we can feel or experince it.

From a micro viewpoint, the way you think, and thus feel, is determined by heredity and environment, neither of which you have any control over. Therefore, your scientists said that man had no free will and that all behavior was completely determined by blind chance. And this is true—from a micro viewpoint.

Unfortunately, this micro viewpoint denies that there is a larger perspective. "The world is flat, as any fool can plainly see." And from a limited micro viewpoint, the world *is* flat—or concave if in a valley, or convex if on a hilltop. Thus, the size of your perspective determines what truth is, within that frame of reference.

Most of your scientists denied the existence or practicality of larger perspectives such as the Macro perspective which includes reincarnation, soul, and macrocosmic levels.

It is ironic that psychology, as generally taught in your time, denied the existence of a psyche (mind or soul) and insisted that psychologists could only "know" physical or sensory data. Thus, Macro philosophic concepts were quite unacceptable to scientists with a micro orientation.

The Macro perspective sees man as a great mind unlimited by time and space—sometimes called an immortal soul—which periodically elects to temporarily inhabit various types of vehicles (called bodies) in order to experience and learn greater awareness in its striving toward ever greater perfection (awareness that all is one).

The ultimate purpose of all souls in all of their experiences is to attain this macrocosmic awareness of their oneness with all that is, all that was, and all that ever will be (what some would call "God").

Another way of looking at these levels of awareness could be:

1. The micro self is an individual's body, personality,

and limited conscious mind which believes that this is all there is of an individual.

2. The evolving self, or subconscious mind, knows that it is only one tiny part of a soul.

3. The Macro self or universal mind knows that all is one and, therefore, is aware that the Macro self contains within it a perfect balance of the positive and negative polarity of all dimensions. While there may be a temporary imbalance in individual souls (which causes their lack of Macro awareness), these individual imbalances, when seen from a Macro perspective, are recognized as the natural life rhythms of a perfectly balanced macrocosm.

In other words, there are no problems at the Macro level. Eventually, all souls will attain this perfect level of total awareness. No matter how dark the night, eventually the light of day and the sun must come.

While mystics in all ages have described this ultimate Macro awareness, perhaps the best known and most available reference to this Macro perspective is found in the 17th chapter of the Gospel of John. In this chapter the great Macro philosopher states this Macro purpose or goal of all souls as ". . . that they may be one, as we are one; I in them and thou in me, may they be perfectly one."

It is only from this Macro viewpoint, in which the human soul and subconscious mind perceive its oneness with all minds (super-conscious, universal mind, macrocosm, or God), that the soul cannot be threatened or become fearful of anything, because all is one. Thus, it is only from this Macro viewpoint that the soul can obey the ultimate, or Macro, commandment: "Love one another, as I have loved you." (John 15:12).

Macro philosophy teaches that what is right or wrong for anyone depends on one's frame of reference or perspective. For instance, while it was right for the Christian to eat pork, it was wrong for the Jew or Moslem. While it was wrong to kill others during peacetime, it was right during wartime. This type of right and wrong belongs in the context of social law or custom and is totally determined by the size of one's perspective.

Most people of your time did not recognize that their personal philosophy determined whether they were fat or thin, healthy or unhealthy and most of all, happy or unhappy. If you examine the size (temporal dimension) of your personal philosophy, or perspective, you will recognize that it is the size of your perspective which determines your awareness of the consequences of your choices.

For instance, if hedonistic pleasure is your major goal and your temporal perspective is quite limited, you will be unaware of the long-range consequences of over-indulgence. You will eat too much and become fat and, eventually, sick. You will avoid strenuous physical and mental activity and become physically and mentally flabby and eventually both unhealthy and unhappy.

Since everyone seeks pleasure, it is extremely important that you become aware of the size of your perspective, for short-term pleasure frequently causes long-term pain. If you are really interested in maximizing pleasure you must expand your perspective in order to become aware of the long-range consequences (pleasure-pain) of your personal philosophy and the choices it determines.

Those who are micro-bound can not truly comprehend anything beyond a physical view of man. Concepts such as the subconscious, or soul, or brotherhood of man, are merely abstractions for micro man. In other words, he can not feel related, brotherly, and loving for any extended period of time. He basically feels alienated and separate from himself (his own subconscious) and, thus, must feel alienated and separate from others.

The Emperor Marcus Aurelius said, "To be vexed at anything which happens is a separation of ourselves from nature."

He was presenting the Macro view that all is one and that, from this Macro perspective, there could be no vexation or anger with anything since everything that is is perfect. It is only when man forgets that he is Macro perfect and all-powerful that he feels inadequate, threatened, abused, fearful, frustrated, angry, and sad.

He who forgets his past is doomed to repeat it. To the extent that man can expand his awareness of his past, he is freed from repeating it. If he cannot remember that it made him sick to eat or drink too much in the past, he will repeat these actions and pay the consequences, over and over again, until he can remember. All learning is the process of remembering the past and applying the lessons you learned from it.

If you could remember everything, you would realize your macrocosmic origin. The soul was once consciously united and one with all souls, everything, God. Some souls became bored. They desired to experience an imperfect event, an exciting, fearful, pleasurable, painful, carnal event. To do this the soul elected—chose—to narrow the focus of its consciousness or awareness until it could not remember who it was, where it came from, or where it was going. It was then that it mentally divided itself into cells, each of which pretended it was a whole soul.

In this state of self-induced amnesia and division, the soul could experience pride and exaltation over others because it had forgotten that it was one with all. It had even forgotten its own soul mates (members of a group of souls who regularly incarnate together) and its own twin souls (those "souls" who are cells of the same over-soul and, thus, have identical soul vibrations).

In this state of amnesia the soul could perceive other souls as enemies because it viewed itself as separate from them. Like the mad paranoic who thinks his fingers are trying to strangle him, because he has forgotten that he controls them, the souls forgot they were all-powerful and that, from a Macro view, they made all the decisions and chose all the results.

Since they had forgotten their greater selves' power, they were doomed to live in the unbalanced, imperfect, micro world they created where no one could remember his past and, thus, no one could forsee the future.

No one can see the end of the journey if his vision is limited to a tiny part of the whole journey. No one can make sense of the jigsaw puzzle if he can see only a few of its millions of pieces.

Since all time is simultaneous, the pieces of the puzzle, "past" and "future," are hidden in our own minds. However, only the relatively wise souls have relearned to expand their consciousness, or awareness, in order to remember more of the "past" and "future" and, thus, see more pieces of the cosmic puzzle.

The great problem of humanity is to evolve to a point where you can accept total responsibility for absolutely everything you experience.

This paves the way for the ultimate challenge—joyous acceptance of the absolute perfection of all that is, all that was, and all that ever will be.

You can see, then, that the measure of a mind's evolution is its acceptance of the unacceptable.

C.I. ON THE MACRO SOCIETY

By 2150 the world has been almost completely united by a universal educational system that begins at birth and ends, formally, at the 30th birthday. This monolithic educational system combines the five institutions of society—family, education, religion, business, and government—into one interdependent whole called the Macro society.

The 20th century's prophets of doom for mankind, such as Orwell and Huxley, were, like most others, caught in the limited micro viewpoint of the 20th century. This micro viewpoint saw man as basically an unbalanced animal doomed to destroy himself with his own selfishness and technical skills which develop destructive devices and massive environmental pollution.

The 20th century was dominated by micro thinking, characterized by hedonistic momentary pleasure-seeking.

A typical example was the politician who put his own temporary welfare ahead of long-term welfare of all people, including his own children, when he voted against pollution controls because industry in his district thought it too expensive.

There are many other examples of selfish short-term micro thinking, such as the belief that war was justified and that billions of dollars spent each year on guns and such devices for killing each other was a more noble patriotic duty than removing the cause of human conflict—ignorance. Educational opportunities were unequal and limited by local special (micro) interests which were dedicated to helping a few at the expense of many.

The most basic institution of micro society, the family, traditionally taught each new generation narrow (micro) ethnocentric loyalties and prejudices and perpetuated the social patterns of stratification and segregation. Thus, the micro family fostered human separation by teaching paramount loyalty to a biological family rather than a spiritual one. In so doing, it denied the universal brotherhood of all men.

With this micro philosophy espousing narrow micro loyalties, separation and conflict were inevitable. Finally, with the development of weapons having almost unlimited destructive power, the human race had to choose between either extinction or the development of a larger Macro philosophy with loyalty to the universal brotherhood of all men.

By the end of the 20th century, micro thinking produced environmental pollution, overpopulation, and human conflict to such an extreme that the micro family almost literally destroyed itself. For the human race to survive, the micro family had to give way.

The human survivors of the early 21st century accepted the practical benefits of the Macro philosophy long proposed by such giants as Lao-tzu, Gautama, and Jesus.

This Macro perspective of mankind proclaimed one spiritual—(macrocosmic) father for all—"Call no man

Father" (Matthew 23:9) and one categorical imperative—
"Love one another." (John 15:17)

Since ignorance and denial of these Macro concepts
had been perpetuated by micro social institutions, they
were replaced by one unifying structure called the Macro
society. This universal social system provided and inte-
grated the functions of education, government, religion,
business, and procreation.

The development and existence of the Macro society
depended on its ability to educate all its members with
a Macro philosophy which produced Macro loyalty and
identity. It minimized selfish micro behavior in its members and maximized unselfish (Macro) behavior.

All hostile, angry behavior is viewed by the Macro
society as the product of micro thinking, which is dedicated to protecting the micro self or micro group against
others who are viewed as outsiders.

There are no outsiders from a Macro view.

Of course, the obvious tremendous advantages of the
Macro society are in the use of one language, one culture,
one religion (Macro philosophy), one government, and
one race—the human race.

Micro man didn't give up his micro loyalties to his
family, religion, government, skin color, language, and
culture without a fight. He literally perished in his struggle
to maintain the divisions that kept the human race from
being united and free from fear, hatred, and ignorance.

The age of micro man is almost over, and those humans
still living on this earth will soon all be Macro beings
who are both willing and able to learn and live a larger
loyalty, a larger perspective—a Macro perspective. These
highly evolved beings will devote their major energies
and resources to developing an educational system which
will foster ever greater sensitivity and awareness of
self/other/macrocosm relationships. The goal of this
educational system will always be to produce Macro
loyalty and Macro identity.

Psychologists of the 20th century held that during
the early learning periods basic life personality patterns

were formed. In the micro family, by the end of six years a child had learned self-alienated, paranoid patterns inculcated by the parents and reinforced by the society. People believed that they were the pawns of their early experiences, unaware that they could, at any time, be whatever they wanted to be and believed they could be.

By 2150 children no longer have to enter this world by micro accident and grow up in a society which is unwilling to provide optimum health, nutrition, and educational opportunities for all its children.

Children can now enter the Macro society, which both wants and loves them. Each new member encounters an environment designed to provide optimum freedom to explore and succeed in the uniquely human task of manipulating verbal symbols. Each child experiences unconditional love from other members of his society and, thus, learns to value self/others, to trust self/others, and to enjoy learning. Positive self concepts are developed by constant interaction with adults possessing positive self concepts, and children are taught the responsibility of and the art of creating their own life experiences.

Since the Macro society established universal spiritual brotherhood, its organizational structure is very different from that of the micro family. A central concept of the Macro society is the law of inverse loyalty: the smaller the unit, the less loyalty owed to its members. Thus, in a test of loyalty, God/macrocosm/universal mind will always win—and by "God" I mean all that is, as opposed to some special group or individual.

The importance of this concept of inverse loyalty can be recognized when it is understood that the Macro society is composed of units, the smallest of which is 10, expanding in multiples of 10 (10, 100, 1,000, etc.) until the largest unit includes all humanity who are working toward the Macro level of awareness.

This is the total Macro society and represents the final culmination of man's long struggle to attain "peace and good will to all men." This universal spiritual brotherhood is impossible for micro man to practice because from his limited perspective he is unable to truly perceive his relationship to self/others/macrocosm/God.

The following chart illustrates the complete organizational structure of the Macro society.

ULTIMATE
MACRO SOCIETY
ORGANIZATIONAL CHART

Unit	Composition	Population	Leader
ALPHA	10 Individuals	10	Alphar
BETA	10 Alphas	100	Betar
GAMMA	10 Betas	1,000	Gammar
DELTA	10 Gammas	10,000	Deltar
ATON	10 Deltas	100,000	Atar
ZTON	10 Atons	1,000,000	Ztar
KTON	10 Ztons	10,000,000	Ktar
MUTON	10 Ktons	100,000,000	Mutar
MAXON	10 Mutons	1,000,000,000	Maxar
MACRO SOCIETY	All Maxons	All Mankind	All Maxars

The basic unit of the Macro society is called the Alpha. It is composed of 10 individuals (5 males and 5 females), one of whom serves as the Alphar, or leader of the group. This leader is elected on a yearly basis by all members of the group and is authorized to resolve all internal disputes in order to maximize group harmony and cooperation.

The Alpha members share a common living area ninety yards square which is divided into seven rooms. Six rooms are thirty feet square and the seventh is thirty by ninety and is their common room. Five of the six rooms are shared by Alpha mates, always a male and a female, while the sixth room is kitchen and dining area.

Since all units in the Macro society are multiples of 10, the next unit, called the Beta, is composed of 10 Alphas and consists of 100 members, 50 male and 50 female. These members also elect, annually, a leader, the

330

Betar, to perform the same functions for this larger unit as the Alphar for the smaller unit. In case of a tie election, the leader of the next larger unit casts the tie-breaking vote.

The Beta occupies one whole floor, one hundred and fifty yards square, which contains the ten Alphas.

The next units in order of size are called the Gamma (10 Beta units or 1,000 persons), the Delta (10 Gamma units or 10,000 persons), and the Aton (10 Delta units or 100,000 persons). The leader of the Gamma, called the Gammar, is also elected annually. The leaders of the next two larger units, the Deltar and the Atar, are elected every three years in order to provide them with greater experience in these more responsible positions.

Each Gamma is housed in a building which is one hundred fifty yards square and twelve stories high: ten for the Betas, one for maintenance, and one divided into an auditorium, meeting rooms, and recreation area.

The Delta, which is composed of ten Gamma buildings, is arranged around a man-made lake which is five miles long by two miles wide with an average depth of thirty feet. The ten Gamma buildings are spaced one mile apart on each side of the lake. At one end of the lake is a building devoted to administration and maintenance, while the central information computer and research center are housed in a building at the other end of the lake. All twelve buildings in the Delta are one hundred fifty yards square and have twelve floors. These buildings and the lake are at the center of a hundred-square-mile area of land divided into cultivated park and farmland called a Delta section.

The leaders of the next larger units, the Ztar, Ktar, Mutar, and Maxar, are elected every six years by the leaders of the next smaller units. For example, all Ktars, who are leaders of 10,000,000, are elected by 10 Atars and must have had experience in the positions of Atar and Ztar. The Maxar, as leader of 1,000,000,000 in a Maxon, must have served at least 21 years in the lesser positions of Atar, Ztar, Ktar, and Mutar, and he or she must have been selected four times by his peers as the wisest among them; 2150's Macro society population of 300 million has no Maxars.

When the Macro society was in its early stages the work life of its members was designed to permit and encourage personal evolution. To insure that work periods would not become micro unpleasant or be used as an escape from other self-development tasks, all workers worked only six hours per day and only five days per week. A one-week vacation was taken every three months by everyone fifteen years old or older.

Here in the middle of the 22nd century, the early work rules are no longer necessary, since high-level Macro beings do not divide their lives into work and recreation. They realize that human creativity and productivity are best served by accepting the will of their higher selves. The results of this acceptance can now be seen in the Macro society which has produced the most creative and productive period in the history of this planet.

Since effective personal evolution is the paramount goal of the Macro society, all persons take whatever time they wish to work toward this goal after their formal education has been completed.

Formal education begins at birth and ends at the age of thirty, though informal learning is highly valued at all ages. These first thirty years are divided into ten triads of three years each. The first triad begins at birth and ends at the third birthday. The second triad begins on the third birthday and ends on the sixth birthday. Thus, the end of one triad is always the beginning of the next one. This reinforces the concept that the end of any experience is always the beginning of another.

EDUCATIONAL TRIADS

Triads	Age	Experiences
1st	0-3	While all educational triads provide ex-
2nd	3-6	periences for love, exploration, and social interaction, the first two triads receive

special attention from ten elder brothers and sisters from the group 21 years of age or older.

3rd	6-9	Beginning in the 3rd triad, students elect
4th	9-12	their own Alphar. 3rd through 6th triad
5th	12-15	Alphas have only one elder brother and sister from the 15-to-30 age group.
6th	15-18	Beginning in the 6th triad, students elect their own Betar and begin vocational training.
7th	18-21	7th through 10th triad Alphas have one
8th	21-24	elder brother and sister from the 30-and-
9th	24-27	over age group, the wisest in the Macro society.
10th	27-30	

This triad system facilitates concentration on the developmental tasks occurring in the first thirty years (covered by the ten triads). It is especially designed to permit the older children within each triad to teach the younger ones. The older students improve their learning of lessons by demonstrating these lessons to the younger students. This also inculcates a strong sense of responsibility for self/others.

The first three years of life are very important in human development, since they contain the greatest number of critical learning periods. If the appropriate development task is not learned during its critical learning period, it will be more difficult to learn the task at a later time. For this reason only persons who have demonstrated outstanding patience, love, and wisdom qualify to work with the first triad children. Each newborn child is placed in an Alpha devoted to 1st triad children and is assigned five older brothers and five older sisters. These older persons will be most carefully selected from the 8th, 9th and 10th triads (twenty-one to thirty) and from older age groups. One of the problems of micro parents has been the fatigue and frustration brought on by many hours and days of constant interaction with their children. To eliminate this problem, each older brother or sister, like other workers in the Macro society, spends an average of four hours daily on the job. They will rotate this time in order to equally experience both waking and sleeping periods in the child's life.

The second three years of life, from three to six years, is another very important learning period. Again, only those five older brothers and five older sisters who have demonstrated outstanding patience, love, and wisdom will be assigned to each child of this second triad. Older brothers and sisters always work with the triad level they are personally best equipped to work with. The minimum age limit for these second triad candidates is 21. Those who are gifted with exceptional ability in working with these younger children will have an opportunity to practice and demonstrate this ability. Those who have demonstrated outstanding patience, love, and wisdom with the second triad children will go on to work with the first triad, if they prove effective there.

In the third and fourth triad each pair of Alpha mates is assigned an older brother and sister who are also Alpha mates. These older brothers and sisters will be assigned from the sixth through tenth triads.

Members of the third through sixth triads are also assigned Personal Evolution tutors who have specialized in tutoring children from these triads. Because of constant interaction and acceptance, there is no generation gap. All students experience at least five hours of P. E. tutoring per week. This time is devoted to learning to understand self/others/the macrocosm and your relationship to them. Learning to responsibly create your life experiences, accept them as chosen by you and you only; learning to identify the lessons within each experience then applying them to your daily life; learning to take the risks necessary to grow; and learning to accept everything as absolutely perfect for its time and place are some of the areas of concentration during Personal Evolution tutoring.

The seventh through tenth triad students (age eighteen to thirty) are also assigned P. E. tutors. These are selected from the wisest and most mature persons in the whole Macro society with a minimum age of thirty. These students also experience at least five hours of tutoring per week.

A typical day for triads three through five is:

7–9 a.m.	Macro contemplation and meditation; statement (or affirmation) of one's life-style plan for growing; and breakfast with one's Alpha.
9–10 a.m.	Study life areas with C.I.
12–12 noon	Macro Development: groups of ten students discuss with master tutors life areas they studied with C.I.
12 noon–1 p.m.	Lunch and relaxation with Alpha unit.
1–2 p.m.	Work with C.I.
2–5 p.m.	Recreation-learning.
5–7 p.m.	Macro dance, swim, dinner.
7–9 p.m.	Personal Evolution tutoring and activities; Macro contemplation and meditation; and restatement of one's own lifestyle plan for growing. (The Macro pause is used regularly throughout the day as needed to expand one's immediate perspective.)

Triads six through ten have a similar daily schedule; however, at least three hours per day are scheduled for practicing vocational activities. These activities are in the areas of tutoring, agriculture, and other applied arts and sciences. In addition, these older students are provided more time for solitary contemplation and meditation—often in the park areas outside.

335

Beginning in the third triad (ages 6–9) students elect their own Alphar. A student Beta unit is composed of ten Alphas including triads one through ten (ages 0–30). However, the student Betar is elected only by students in the last six triads (ages 12–30).

Since the proportion of the population under thirty is maintained at ten percent of the total population, every Delta unit in the Macro society contains one student Gamma unit and nine adult Gamma units. By the year 2100 computers and servo-mechanisms performed all the monotonous and heavy labor tasks that contributed to making man's work life so boring throughout recorded history.

It is recognized that there is a time for people to be together and a time for each individual to be alone. Time for solitary contemplation and meditation is provided every day, and each individual has a study and meditation room in which to be alone. In addition to this indoor solitude, the large wooded parks surrounding the living units provide very beautiful walks where one can be alone with nature. Here in 2150 no one who lives in the Macro society fears being alone.

However, no one sleeps alone, either, for each Alpha provides five bedrooms where a male and female always sleep together. In the Macro society sex is not used as a defense or escape mechanism, for there are no hidden, dark, and fearful areas in Macro minds. It is recognized that each person needs a mate to grow with, to check out their perception of reality with, to love and be loved intimately by, and to accelerate evolution. The vow of one Alpha mate to the other is, ". . . to live with, to help, and to honor, as long as is best for our evolution." The goal of the Macro society is always balanced harmonious union.

The oppressive clinging and neurotic dependency of the traditional micro family is now just a historical curiosity and nightmare. Macro man is free to dedicate his life to attaining conscious awareness of the unity of all things. He is able to love all things, both great and small.

336

For the first time in the history of formal education, learning is always rewarding, practical, and free from intimidation or coercion. No dreary, pointless memorization of facts for regurgitation on competitive examinations. Only practical performance demonstrates degrees of competence or skill in any area of learning. All students are, with the aid of resource persons, tutors, and the learning machine called C.I., free to develop to their own capacity the verbal and numerical skills along with their own special aptitudes or gifts.

With the evolution of Macro awareness, the last great fear of micro man—death—has been vanquished, for Macro man has expanded his awareness to the point where he can remember some of his other lives. Thus, the theory of reincarnation (spiritual evolution of the soul through experiencing many *human* lives) and personal responsibility (what you sow you must reap) is no longer theory, but living conscious truth—which it always was for those who had a Macro perspective.

Since ever-expanding awareness is the goal of the Macro society, the greatest cultural rewards are given to those who demonstrate outstanding wisdom and love for others. The 20th century valued its athletes and entertainers far more than its wise and kindly people, and they reaped chaos. The 22nd-century Macro society does not forget this lesson.

In 2150

Level Composition of Macro Society

127	Level tens
3,306	Level nines
39,710	Level eights
3,000,000	Level sevens
30,000,000	Level sixes
97,000,000	Level fives
78,000,000	Level fours

	62,000,000	Level threes
	20,000,000	Level twos
	10,000,000	Level ones

Macro Society Population Distribution

Unit Name	Population per Unit	Number of Such Units
Alpha	10	30,000,000
Beta	100	3,000,000
Gamma	1,000	300,000
Delta	10,000	30,000
Aton	100,000	3,000
Zton	1,000,000	300
Kton	10,000,000	30
Muton	100,000,000	3
Macro Society	300,000,000	1

C. I. on Micro Man

For ages micro man, with his extremely limited awareness of himself, has been demonstrating the truth of the saying that he who forgets his past is doomed to repeat it. He has forgotten that he is part of an immortal soul created out of the substance of the macrocosm/universal mind/God and in the image or pattern of this universal mind. He has forgotten that in addition to his physical body he has a soul body (astral body) of a much higher vibration which is, therefore, invisible to his physical eyes just as x-rays are invisible. He has forgotten that he periodically chooses to incarnate his soul, mind, and body in a dense matter body which he can see with micro vision, and, thus, believes to be his only body.

Human souls over eons of time narrowed and limited their awareness from macrocosmic to microscopic. By practicing ever more limited perspectives, they lost their powers of greater awareness much the same as fish living in the lightless depths of the ocean lost their ability to see. Why did this happen? It happened because the souls desired to experience self-centered micro worlds.

Since micro man can not remember his past, and, thus, his own responsibility for choosing his state of existence, he has been doomed to live many lives filled with fear, anger, conflict, and brutish pain and pleasure. He has been dominated by the ever-present fear of death, which he desperately tries to deny and repress through all manner of activities designed to provide momentary forgetfulness. Alcohol, drugs, war, and even work, games, and sex have been used to help micro man forget his lonely, alienated existence that will soon be ended "forever" by death. He has even invented mythical gods, heavens, and hells to help him deny his feelings of fear and inadequacy.

Fortunately, there have always been a few beings who have had greater awareness and, thus, could remember more than others. These beings have, too often, been viciously persecuted, jailed, burned, and crucified. However, they have pointed the way to the only real hope of liberation from a micro perspective. Over many ages their cumulative effect has become ever greater.

Micro man has grown weary of micro experiences and is trying to return to his original state of macrocosmic awareness. When each incarnated soul can, at last, remember his oneness with all that is, all that was, and all that ever will be, he will no longer be able to blame others for his own misfortunes. Suffering micro man has long proclaimed his lack of responsibility by wailing that he never asked to be born. When man has expanded his awareness to the point where he can remember his own Macro past, he will know that he alone created it through his own choosing. He will then realize that he alone is responsible for all his experiences.

With this macrocosmic awareness man will know that he must inevitably reap what he sows, and all conflict between individuals, races, and nations will be eliminated.

C. I. on Akashic Records

Akashic records is an ancient concept that refers to the macrocosm's memory of its self.

From a Macro perspective all is one infinite mind and all experiences are recorded forever in that mind. Thus, when you attain total Macro awareness you will know and experience all that has happened or will ever happen.

The akashic records refer to that dimension of the mind where, if your level of awareness permits, you can experience any event that has ever happened. For those with less than tenth-level awareness their own personal akashic record is more like a series of video tapes which present only pictures and sounds of past events.

Every soul has this akashic record of all its experiences since its creation which was the beginning of its devolution from total Macro awareness. Thus, when you examine that portion of your soul or Macro mind in which your memories are stored you are consulting your own personal akashic records. You can relive any past event that your soul has experienced to the extent that you can remember (contact) your akashic records.

Level tens usually use the universal akashic records where a total Macro perspective is available. However, a soul's ability to contact these universal akashic records is limited by his level of awareness.

C.I. on Dreams

For the student of Macro philosophy the quickest and easiest access to the Macro levels of awareness is through dreams. No matter how limited micro man's awareness is while he is awake, during sleep the subconscious or soul mind takes over. It uses dreams to provide solutions to problems to expand your experience, to relax and refresh the body by resolving mental stress, to digest today, and to prepare you for tomorrow.

When man learns to remember and interpret his dreams from a Macro view, he has access to a level of wisdom that provides the solutions to all problems.

If a man refuses to accept responsibility for his own life situation, his dreams cannot help him—and neither can anything else except more of his self-inflicted misery.

C. I. on Expanding Human Awareness

There are three popularly employed emental techniques for expanding human awareness:

1. The Macro pause (the mini-meditation).
2. The Macro immersion.
3. The Macro contact.

(1) The sub-Macro pause was historically the first breakthrough to conscious control of Macro awareness. Once the macro self or universal mind had been redis-covered by the ancients, they began to practice developing the necessary desire and belief which would allow the practice of mind-shifting. By mind-shifting we mean the conscious shifting of mind focus from the micro level of physical body and mind (limited by time and space) to the Macro level of macrocosmic oneness, unlimited by time and space.

When the Macro society was developed, everyone began the regular practice of mind-shifting called the Macro pause. The secret of success with the Macro pause has always been practice, beginning as early in life as possible. However, this does not mean that older people cannot learn to use the Macro pause if they will only develop the following state of mind:

a. Acceptance of a Macro philosophy of life.
b. Necessary desire and belief.
c. Joyous acceptance of the absolute perfection of self/others and the situation at hand.

Once the first two requirements have been achieved, the third one can be employed to achieve the Macro pause whenever one's micro perspective is creating, or failing to solve, a problem.

It is this third requirement that frees the mind from its micro view and permits expansion to the broader Macro perspective. When this is achieved, it's impossible to see anything as terrible.

The best way for a beginner to deal with fear, anger, and frustration, is by using the Macro pause.

(2) After the Macro pause was developed and used by all Macro society members, Macro immersion was discovered. Only from the Macro perspective can the frequency of soul vibrations be recognized. While simultaneous twin soul incarnations have always been very rare, simultaneous incarnations of soul mates, who possess very similar (but not identical) soul vibrations are far more frequent. In the Macro society, which has always attracted souls with Macro potential, the number of soul mates that any soul shared an incarnation with reached eleven in every ten thousand. This, along with the help of C.I.'s audible soul note reproduction, removed the final barriers to Macro immersion.

The essentials for Macro immersion are:
a. Acceptance of the Macro philosophy of life.
b. Necessary desire and belief.
c. Joyous acceptance of the absolute perfection of self/others and the situation at hand (Let go, and let's grow!).
d. Similarity of soul notes (vibrations).
e. Either physical or telepathic perception of your soul notes and that of your partner.

Macro immersion is the union of soul mates with high soul note similarity. This permits union of the physical

342

body and mind as well as the astral body and soul mind, thus freeing sexuality from all micro restrictions.

An enduring sense of fulfillment and well-being are important fruits of Macro immersion.

Macro immersion allowed the Macro society to completely free itself from the micro defensive uses of sex. Once Macro immersion had been attained, no other type of sexual experience was satisfying.

(3) Macro contact was the final step in the expansion of human awareness. It permitted Macro man to attain a more enduring consciousness of the macrocosmic oneness of all. While it is possible for the initiate to attain Macro contact without first experiencing the Macro pause or Macro immersion, this can only occur with the telepathic help of a soul mate who has already experienced Macro contact. Due to problems with desire and belief this kind of help is only effective with the initial Macro contact. However, the usual essentials for Macro contact are:

a. Acceptance of Macro philosophy.
b. Necessary desire and belief.
c. Joyous acceptance of the absolute perfection of self/others and the situation at hand (Let go, and let's grow!).
d. Joyous acceptance of all positive and negative aspects of the universe—self/others/God/macrocosm.
e. Macro contact stimuli (visual and/or audible) may be necessary for the beginner.

Until 2100 only a few members of the Macro society had ever attained anything more than the most fleeting Macro contact lasting no more than a few seconds. In the past 50 years, however, the true Macro contact, which typically lasts an hour or more, was developed by a majority of the Macro society members. This accounts for the swift increase in evolution since 2100 and the beginnings of level ten.

The major problem with the Macro contact is that after one or two successive contacts one's desire is often greatly diminished due to the peaceful state of complete joyous acceptance created by Macro contact. This problem only exists at the lower Macro levels, though.

THE m-M CONTINUUM

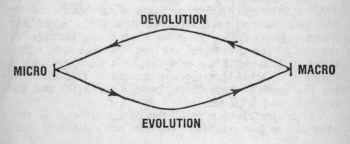

DEVOLUTION

MICRO ⊢ ⊣ MACRO

EVOLUTION

MACRO LEARNING CURVE

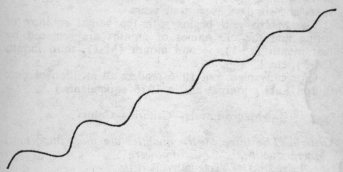

This curve covers any time period- 1 hour, 1 day, 1 week, 1 month, 1 year, 1 decade, 1 lifetime, many lifetimes, 1 cosmic day and night, etc.

C.I. on Metric Time

Metric time	Metric equivalent	1976 time equivalent
M - year	10 M - months	1 year
M - month	10 M - weeks(.1 M-year)	36 days
M - week	10 M - days(.01 M-year)	3.6 days
M - day	10 M - hours(.001 M-year)	8.64 hours
M -hour	100 M - minutes(.1 M-day)	51.84 minutes
M - minute	100 M - seconds(.001 M-day)	31.104 seconds
M - second	.0001 M - day	.3104 seconds

At the end of the metric year (M - year) of 10 metric months (M - months), which is equivalent to 360 days of 1976 time, there is a vacation of five days every three years and six days every four years.

The Macro year begins with the vernal equinox of spring and the old names of months are replaced by first month (M-1), second month (M-2), third month (M-3), etc.

(For convenience of 1976 readers all mention of time in Jon Lake's journal are in 1976 equivalents.)

Macro Levels—Criteria—Colors

Criteria (The three Macro qualities are most important)

Macro qualities	Macro powers
Love	Telepathy
Wisdom	Clairvoyance
Leadership	Precognition
	Retrocognition
	Psychokinesis (PK)
	Telekinesis
	Astral Projection

346

Colors

Level	Color
Level ten	White
Level nine	Aquamarine
Level eight	Blue
Level seven	Green
Level six	Yellow
Level five	Lavender
Level four	Purple
Level three	Pink
Level two	Orange
Level one (lowest)	Gray

Jon's Alpha

Name	Level	Height	Hair Color	Characteristic
Jon	One	6' 3"	Blond	
Carol	Three	6' 3"	Brunette	Jon's Alpha mate
Alan	Six (Alphar)	6' 5"	Blond	Vital, intelligent
Bonnie	Four	6' 2"	Blond	Dimples, smile
Adam	Two	6' 7"	Brown	Sympathetic
Nancy	Two	6' 3"	Brunette	Liquid brown eyes
David	Five	6' 5"	Brunette	Smiling Hercules
Diane	Five	6' 1"	Blond	Small, curvaceous
Steve	Three	6' 9"	Blond	Kind, patient face
Joyce	Four	6' 3"	Auburn	Vivacious

ALPHA AND BETA FLOOR PLANS

ALPHA FLOOR PLAN

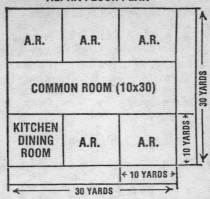

KEY A.R.: ALPHA ROOM   INHABITANTS: 10 PEOPLE (5 COUPLES)

BETA FLOOR PLAN

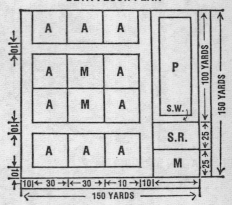

KEY

A: ALPHA   SR: STORAGE ROOM   P: POOL
M: MISCELLANEOUS   SW: SWIMMING AREA   INHABITANTS: 100 PEOPLE

TYPICAL DELTA LIVING CENTER

DELTA 927
POPULATION 10,000

LEARNING CENTER

LAKE

5 Miles Long
2 Miles Wide
30' Avg. Depth

ADMINISTRATION BUILDING

KEY

Gamma (Pop: 1000)

MAP OF MICRO ISLAND

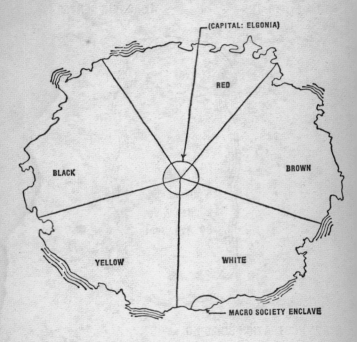

For information on other books and booklets by Thea Alexander send stamped, self-addressed envelope to:

THE MACRO SOCIETY
Box 26880
Tempe, Arizona 85257